my mother's
chamomile

my mother's chamomile

SUSIE FINKBEINER

This is a work of fiction. All characters and events portrayed in this novel are either fictitious or used fictitiously.

MY MOTHER'S CHAMOMILE

WhiteFire Publishing
13607 Bedford Rd NE
Cumberland, MD 21502

ISBN: 978-1-939023-37-7 (digital)
           978-1-939023-36-0 (print)

In memory of my friend Patt Krauss.
She never told me how to give mercy, she showed me.
Her life was a sprinkling of comfort over others.
To know her was to experience a bit of Christ's love.

Just a few blinks, Patt, and I'll see you again.

After she died

it would be years before I realized it.

The dusty aroma that clung to her
scarves, neckline,
her memory,
wasn't a perfume from the old country
at all
but the breeze
from the back porch
dirt from the garden
crushed up chamomile
steeped with honey.

Don't be afraid to break up the fragile parts, she told me
once, cupping the hay-colored flowerheads in her left palm
grinding gently with her right fingertips.
That's what gives the best flavor.

She didn't believe in magic.
It was miracles
chamomile
God

in that order.

By Elizabeth Sands Wise

"God strengthens and comfort spills. Morning comes."
~ Jeff Manion

"Praise be to the God and Father of our Lord Jesus Christ,
the Father of compassion and the God of all comfort,
who comforts us in all our troubles, so that we can comfort
those in any trouble with the comfort we ourselves receive from
God."
~ II Corinthians 1:3-4

Prologue

1967

Olga

Curly, carrot red hair bobbed up and down among the green and purple, yellow and pink of the garden. Such a small bundle of a girl and every inch bounding with energy. That little thing moved from the moment I said, "Good morning" to the time I scolded, "No more getting out of that bed" at night.

Next to the garden stood a big, brown brick building. Out the open windows, funeral music poured. Quivering tones of the electric organ melted together to form a hymn so full of sorrow, I tried to keep its fingers from working their way into my heart.

Inside the brown brick building, out of my sight, mourning people held down wooden folding chairs. They'd wrap their hands around damp hankies and tissues. When their eyes flicked over to the casket at the very front of the room, a hurt would jab in that place between their lungs. They'd breathe in quick and sharp when the big old rock collected in their throats. No matter how hard they swallowed, the grief wouldn't go down. That casket cradled the empty body of a person they loved. The mourning filled the space between the walls. No doubt their cries reached all the way through the vents and floorboards and into the apartment my family called home.

It didn't even take one peek through the window to know what happened in that building. Married to the mortician, I'd seen my share of funerals. More than I would have liked, if I was to be honest.

On funeral days like that one, I had two choices. Either stay inside,

9

cooped up in our apartment and contain my full-of-life four-year-old, listening to the weeping downstairs. Or stand in the sunshine, letting my girl skip and wander and sing to the song of the birds. An easy choice, as far as I was concerned.

That spring, I'd planted my first garden. All I'd put in it were flowers. Every kind that caught my fancy. I never cared too much for growing vegetables. Not after all the years I spent on Uncle Alfred and Aunt Gertie's farm. No endless rows of soybeans for me. I preferred the dotting of color from a flower garden. And nothing so dainty an exploring child couldn't tromp through.

My Gretchen loved nothing more than that garden. We'd put in a tire swing hanging on a thick branch of our old oak tree. And my husband Clive had built her a nice sandbox with a wide umbrella for shade. Still, even with all those choices, she wanted to be in with the flowers.

My eyes moved from here to there as she darted all about, up one path and down the next. When she made her way to the very center, she stopped. Turning her head one way and the other, she lifted her little hands, palms down with arms held straight as yard sticks. Like wings. For just a moment, I worried that she intended to fly away from me. A silly thought, I knew it. Most just-for-a-moment worries of mine turned out to be nothing but silly. Still, I couldn't keep them banished.

Oh, how I fretted over losing her. I'd never had such strong terror in all my life. I'd seen too many tiny caskets in my time living above the funeral home. I prayed, begging to be spared that loss. I didn't know of a parent who hadn't prayed that same thing.

Death never made sense at all. No reason. No rhyme. Willy nilly.

Blinking away the fear, I let my eyes focus back on her. My child. The only one I got to have. The only baby my body didn't reject. I fought off the mourning of those little, nameless ones. In those days, we didn't talk about miscarriages. We didn't allow the sadness. It just sat in our hearts as secret shame.

"Be thankful for the one we got," my husband, Clive, would say, rubbing calloused thumbs against my cheeks, pushing away round tears. "If God wants us to have more, He'll give them to us."

I swatted the thoughts and the doubts, shooing them like a sweat-bee. Trying to be thankful for the one I got, I kept my eyes on the carrot red, curly headed girl.

Her tiny fingertips skimmed the tops of tall flowers. Spinning, she hung her head back, the hair brushing the spot between her shoulders. The faster she went round and round, the tighter she held her eyes shut. Fair skinned face covered with ginger colored freckles. Big old baby-toothed smile from ear to ear.

She stopped her spinning. Wobbling, she stood, the world tipping her from side to side. Her giggle was enough to keep me glad my whole life through. Big green eyes looked up at me, crossing each other and blinking hard.

"You get yourself dizzy, Gretchie?" The lavender plant tickled against my ankles as I stepped around it toward my daughter. "You sure were spinning fast."

When she nodded, those red sausage curls bounced and bumped against her chubby cheeks. Those cheeks begged to be kissed. Never did a day go by without me covering her soft face with smooches a plenty. I had no idea how long she'd abide me loving on her like that. I determined to give all the kisses I could for as long as she'd allow them. Bending down, I smushed my lips into the chub. Putting her hands on either side of my face, she planted a big kiss right on my lips.

"Oh, thank you, sugar plum."

I didn't wipe that wet kiss off. I let it dry all of its own in the warm air. That way, I could feel it a little longer. I believed that kisses from my girl were strong evidence of God's love for me.

"Mama, can you tell me about the flowers?" How her voice squeaked brought joy into my heart. "Please, Mama."

"I like how you asked so nice." My fingers smoothed the flyaway strands of her hair.

"What's the pink one?"

"Well, honey, that's the tea rose." I picked the bloom and held it to her nose. "Go on. Give it a whiff. It smells good, doesn't it?"

She sucked in through her nose so hard the petals stuck to her nostrils. Her giggle again. Oh, the Lord sure knew what He was doing when He designed a little girl's laugh.

"Did it tickle?" Folding my skirt up under me, I sat on the ground in the middle of a path.

She nodded and rubbed her nose. I pulled her onto my lap, letting her sniff in the aroma of that rose until she'd finished with it. We sat in the garden, letting the sun cover us. Every once in a while, we'd look at each other and smile. So seldom did she sit still like that, I cherished the moments with her nestled in my arms.

She turned sideways. Reaching up one of those hands of hers, she touched my hair. "Your hair is orange."

"Just like yours," I said.

"I'm going to be big like you when I'm a mama." She twisted a strand of my hair around her pointer finger.

"Yes, you are."

"When am I going to have babies?"

"I don't know." My arms forming a circle around her little body felt like the most right thing in all the world. "Probably not for a good long time."

"Am I going to be pretty like you?"

"You sure are pretty now, Gretchie." Heat from the sun radiated off her hair as I kissed the top of her head and pulled her tighter to me. "But you know that pretty isn't what matters, don't you?"

"I know, Mama." She rested against me, her head under my chin. "My heart is made of gold."

"A golden heart, yes," I said. "That's what matters."

"Mama, tell me about the fairy flower." She yawned, drowsy from the sunshine. "Please."

Out of the corner of my eye, a lanky chamomile flower danced in the wind. It grew up wild among the other flowers. Tall, green, spindly legs under heads of yellow and white.

"A long time ago, many years before you were even thought of, there was a little girl," I began.

"Was she like me?" She sat up, turning to look into my face.

"A bit like you." I stopped to make a sad face. "But, unlike you, she was a very sad little girl."

Gretchen imitated my expression. Her lips turned down and her eyes went soft. "Why was she sad, Mama?"

"Well, honey, because she lost her mother."

"Did she try to find her?" Even though she knew the story, she followed the ritual of the telling.

"No. See, her mama got real sick and went to be with Jesus." My fingers brushed through her soft hair, pushing some of it behind her ears.

"She died?" Gretchen's little face covered with a frown.

I nodded. "Sometimes that happens. Isn't it just awful?"

That golden heart of hers showed in the tears which gathered in the corners of her eyes. As many times as I told her the story, she never got dull to it. The telling always broke her precious heart.

"Then what happened?" Her eyes grew large. "Something good happened, didn't it?"

"Not yet," I whispered before going on. "Well, the girl was very lonely. You see, she had to leave her home and go live with her aunt and uncle and all her boy cousins."

"What about her daddy?"

"Oh, he wasn't ready to care for her all by himself. He didn't even know how to make piggy tails in her hair. He couldn't raise her right." A bird darted, a flash of red, over our heads. We both paused in our story to watch it pass.

"Go on, Mama."

"Well, her aunt and uncle had a farm. She had an awful hard time getting to sleep. See, she'd lived in the city all her life. A farm has all kinds of different smells and sounds. And it got real dark at night."

"Did she get scared?"

"Oh, did she ever." My fingers twisted the chamomile, snapping it loose and letting it fall into my palm. "But she remembered her mother making tea that helped her sleep. She used flowers to make it."

"Like that one?" She took the chamomile from me.

"Just like that one." I found a few other flowers, picking them and adding them to my hand. "The girl found some of them in her aunt's garden. Can you tell me the colors?"

"Purple, pink, and green." She pointed to each one.

"Very good, honey. You're doing real good with your colors."

She sat up straight and grinned, proud as could be.

"Now," I continued. "This one here, the one with the white petals and the yellow middle, that one's chamomile."

"The fairy flower," she said, her voice a whisper full of awe.

"That's right. And its friends lavender and tea rose and mint." I folded her hand over the flowers. "The girl gathered a little of each of them."

"Did she make some tea?" Sly smile crinkled into the corners of her eyes.

"Pretty soon, you're going to tell this story better than me." I winked at her. "The girl did make some tea from the flowers. A smooth, magic tea. Just a tiny bit sweet. The tea helped her rest."

"Did it make her happy?" She touched the flowers, poking at them with her fingertips.

"No, honey. Tea can't make anybody happy. Even if it is made from fairy flowers. Not a tea in the whole wide world has that kind of magic." A ringlet of her hair fluttered in the breeze. "But it did help her feel a little peaceful. And quiet."

"What happened next?" Chubby cheeks rose, making room for a wide smile. "She got happy again?"

"She sure did get happy." I stood, putting my hands under her arms and lifting her up. "But not because of the tea. She got a bundle of joy out of life."

"How?" She nuzzled her face into my neck.

"God let her be loved." Pushing my nose into her hair, I breathed her in. She smelled like sunshine itself. "Are you hungry, Gretchen?"

She nodded. "May I please have a peanut butter and banana sandwich?"

"Oh, those sweet manners. I'd love to make you a sandwich." I carried her to the house. "Now, Daddy's not done yet. They should be through real soon, though."

"Will Daddy come upstairs for lunch?"

"Not right away. They have to go over to the cemetery first." I pulled the door open to the back way into our apartment. "Remember, we must be hushed until they all leave, okay?"

She nodded her little head again.

I carried her, climbing the stairs, thankful for the way in and out that didn't take us through the mourners. I hated the thought of my little girl, so full of life, seeing something so empty of it. Not that young, at least.

14

"Mama," she whispered, her mouth so close to my ear, I felt her moist breath. "What's the little girl's name? The girl who drank the fairy tea?"

"Hush, honey." I pushed her head against my shoulder as I took the last few steps.

"But who is she?"

"How about I get your crayons out?" I asked. "You can color a picture of the flowers while I make your sandwich. I bet Daddy would love to see it when he's done with work."

"Okay," she said against my cheek.

Her little hand dangled over the back of my shoulder, clinging to the chamomile as tight as her fingers could.

Chapter One

Present Day
EVELYN

The widow sat in front of the casket. Her wide backside filled the seat of a metal folding chair, overflowing it by an inch or so. I wished we could have found something more comfortable for her. Something with a little more padding. She didn't seem to mind so much, though. Her big, corn-fed sons sat on either side of her, both with an arm around her shoulders.

Sunshine blazed on the mourners. They pulled at tight collars and wiped trickles of sweat from foreheads and napes of necks. A glaring gleam reflected off the shiny, gray casket that hung, suspended by thick straps, over an open hole in the ground. Flowers draped across the closed lid, wilting in the heat. Red, white, and blue carnations with an American flag ribbon running through the blooms.

My brother Cal and I ushered the people under the canopy, hoping to keep them out of the sun. Silently, they followed our direction, uncomfortable in the tight space. Thick, humid August air hung from the sky, unmoving.

We stepped back, behind everyone. Out of the way, trying to blend into the silence of the cemetery. Granddad's rules. We weren't to be the focus of the funeral. That was fine by me.

All of my twenty-eight years, I'd known that what our family did made us different. Strange. The funeral business had set us apart from the rest of the town. The loneliness of it had always bothered me more than it did my younger brother. Cal, though, wasn't as concerned with what people thought.

"Cue Old Buster," Cal whispered out the side of his mouth.

Old Buster, or Reverend Barton Thaddeus, as we called him to his face, was one of two preachers in our tiny town of Middle Main, Michigan. The other preacher didn't do funerals. As far as I could tell, he didn't do much of anything. So, we got stuck listening to Old Buster a couple times a week. Much to our annoyance, he was family. Our grandmother's cousin, he brought a fair share of frustration to us. But, really, most of the time, we just stayed away from him.

The way Old Buster stood in front of the casket, his nose pointed up and his barrel chest puffed out, he certainly didn't seem like a preacher about to make himself humble to share in the grief of a family.

Thick Bible in the crook of his elbow, Old Buster flipped through the pages. Finding his spot, his eyes rested on the notes he'd used for years. The same funeral sermon every single time. Before he spoke, he wiped his upper lip with a tissue he kept folded in the palm of his hand.

"Psalm Twenty-Three," Cal whispered.

Shoving the tissue into his jacket pocket, Old Buster opened his mouth. He read, not taking his eyes off the Bible, as if he had never seen the Psalm before.

Finished with the reading, he closed the Bible, holding it to his chest. "Isn't that passage a comfort to our world-weary hearts?" he asked the people who shifted under the canopy.

If he'd really paid any attention to them, he might have realized that the comfort they most needed was a tall glass of ice water in an air-conditioned room.

Old Buster invited everyone to pray. They bowed their heads as he went on and on. Calling down peace and comfort from God. Praying that anyone who hadn't found salvation would seek Jesus in that day of great sorrow. I feared that if he didn't cut it off soon, we'd have to do another funeral from all the heat-exhaustion-induced deaths that were sure to occur.

When he finally said, "Amen," we all sighed in relief. He got himself seated again in one of the chairs of the family row.

A tall soldier in dress uniform approached the widow. With straight, controlled motions, he kneeled in front of her. She white haired and wrinkled, he young and muscled. Lips moving, he shared words of thanks for her husband's service to his country. Their eyes locked, and she touched his arm before accepting the flag he offered. Her hands fell to her lap under the weight of the folded canvas.

Old men lined up to the right-hand side of the casket. The veterans of our town. They wore ancient uniforms that either hung too big on their withering shoulders or too tight across thickened bellies. Still, they stood, and, one at a time, the men pushed red poppies made of paper into the spray of carnations. One at a time, bent backs straightened, bodies shaking from the effort, and hands raised to salute the casket.

The last veteran stood by the widow, his head hanging heavy. He gathered his hands together at his waist and prayed. His words gentle, he only used a few. Enough to matter, though. And enough to dismiss the bereaved. They made their way to cars parked along the curved path cutting through the lush green of the cemetery.

A lunch of deli slices and fruit filled Jell-O salads awaited them in the basement of the First Christian Church on Main Street.

Cal and I waited until the last car pulled away. After the groundskeeper came to lower the casket, we left the cemetery to return to the Big House.

That was our name for the family business. The Eliot-Russell Family Funeral Home. The only funeral home in town.

"We have to grab lunch on the way back," I said, getting into the passenger's seat of the hearse. "I'm starving."

"I don't mind stopping." Cal started up the engine.

"I have an arrangement meeting in about two hours." I sighed. "This summer has been insane."

"So, speaking of Old Buster—"

"We weren't talking about him," I interrupted.

"We are now." Cal buckled his seat belt. "Anyway, I heard he hired a youth minister."

"There are only three kids in the youth group."

"I also heard that he's grooming the guy as his replacement."

18

Looking in the rearview mirror, he smoothed his light brown hair. Always the vain one, my brother.

"Is Old Buster retiring?" I asked. "It's about time."

"Well, that's what I heard." He steered the hearse slowly through the winding cemetery road. "Deirdre is never wrong."

"Seriously, Cal? That's where you get your information?" I rolled my eyes. "She's nothing but an old busybody. You can't believe a word that comes out of her mouth."

"I don't know, Ev. She says that of all the goodies in her bakery, the chocolate cake doughnuts are the best. And she's right about that." He shrugged. "The woman never lies about her doughnuts. I have no reason to doubt anything else she says."

"That makes no sense."

"It doesn't have to." He flashed his smug grin at me. "Hey, so I hear you had a little date the other day." He smirked. I hated it when he smirked. Especially when the smirk was accompanied by the sparkle of mischief in his blue eyes. That smirk and sparkle may have charmed plenty of girls. As for me, it only made me want to smack him right across the face. But no fighting in the hearse. Granddad's rules.

"Where'd you hear that?" I asked, digging through my purse.

"Well, Ev, you shouldn't ask questions you already know the answer to." He glanced at me.

"How did Deirdre know?"

"I told you, the woman knows everything." He pulled around a tractor chugging down the road. The farmer put up a hand, waving at us. "Although, she admitted that she didn't know the guy. She was trying to figure out his name. I guess that kind of blows a hole in the 'she knows everything' argument."

"Really. It was nothing serious."

"His name is Nothing Serious?" Cal laughed at his own joke.

"No laughing in the hearse," I said. "Granddad's rule."

"Right. Thanks for that reminder. The cows we just passed would be so offended to see me laughing." He turned left onto another paved road. "So, what was the guy like? Was he cool?"

"I guess. I mean, he was nice." I pulled the wallet from my purse. "But he'll probably run far away when he finds out I work with dead

19

people for a living."

"He doesn't know yet?"

"It never came up."

"How did it not occur to you to tell him?"

"It just didn't." Unzipping my wallet, I dug out a couple dollars. "The date was going so well, I didn't want to wreck it."

Cal cleared his throat. "If a guy is so easily scared off, he's not worth keeping."

"Wow," I said, a tad surprised. "That was really wise."

"Yeah. Take it from a guy who is absurdly easy to scare off."

"Some of the girls you've dated, you should have been terrified."

He pulled the hearse into the only fast food place in town. It also happened to be attached to our only gas station.

"What do you want?" Cal pulled into a parking spot.

"Burger and fries."

He took my money and got out of the hearse. He walked, hands in his pockets, toward the restaurant. A few college-aged girls stood outside their car, watching him walk by. If he noticed them, he didn't let on.

My cell phone vibrated from somewhere inside my purse. Pushing all the junk to one side, I found the phone with glowing screen at the bottom of my bag.

"Hi, Granddad," I said, answering it.

"Hi, Evelyn." Granddad's voice crooned in my ear. "How'd the committal go?"

"Fine. No problems."

"And Old Buster?"

"Same as always. Long winded and sweaty."

"I don't doubt that for a minute." He laughed on the other end of the line. "Now, don't forget you got an appointment this afternoon."

"Yup. We'll be there in a few minutes." I switched the phone to my other ear. "Hey, do you want us to pick up a burger for you?"

"No, honey. Thanks, though. Gran made me a sandwich already. She'd be sore if I ate a second lunch, as much as I'd like to."

"We don't have to tell her."

"You know I can't keep a secret from her." He chuckled. "See you in a minute. Love you, darling."

"I love you, too." I hung up the phone.

A mini van parked in the spot next to me. A teen boy climbed out, pressing his body against the side of the van. The way he peered into the hearse, I knew he wanted to see if a casket rode in the back.

When the boy locked eyes with me, he sprinted toward the restaurant, almost plowing into Cal. My brother made his way to the hearse, a smile on his face and shaking his head.

"Did you see that kid?" he asked after opening the door and handing me a paper bag full of food.

"Yup."

"He was so freaked out." He snorted, pulling the gear shift to reverse. "Extra ketchup and pickles."

"Thanks." I pulled the burger from the bag. "You're a life saver."

"If I was, I'd be out of work." He drove out of the parking lot. "You'd better wait to eat that. You know. It freaks people out to see us eating in the hearse."

Shoving the sandwich back into the bag, I stifled a laugh.

Just as we turned down the road to the Big House, Cal glanced at me.

"I hope this guy is good to you." He looked back at the road. "Whoever he is."

"Me, too."

I was tired of being alone.

Chapter Two

OLGA

Old wood moaned as I tugged open the dresser drawer. A stack of bleached white undershirts in one hand and a basket full of matched, black socks in the other, I had an easy job putting my husband's clothes away. Sorting Clive's laundry never took much doing.

Over fifty-two years of marriage and his loads hadn't varied in all that time. Unless I considered the size of his dress shirts. The man loved his food, that was for sure. And I enjoyed feeding him.

I nudged the drawers closed with my hip and picked up the empty plastic laundry basket. When I turned, I caught a glimpse of myself in the full-length mirror. As long as that old thing had been there, it still got me all bothered when I saw my reflection in it. Especially because I'd gone up in size right alongside my husband.

"Yes, darling, you are beautiful." Clive stood behind me. "You don't need to look in that old thing to know it."

I turned sideways, dropping the basket on the end of my bed. My backside stuck out a whole lot farther than it had even the year before. At least my stomach balanced it out. I tried to stand up straight as a rail. Tried to suck in my tummy. It took far too much work. Old age had tiptoed up on me. That sneaky cuss.

"How'd I get old so fast?" I stepped closer to look at the wrinkles on my forehead.

"Same way I did." His hands warmed my shoulders. "One day at a time."

From behind me, he wrapped his arms around my waist. Even as strong as he was, his arms had gotten soft. They felt just as safe, though, as the first time he held me.

"I never saw a lovelier woman," he whispered in my ear. "More gorgeous than when you were just a young thing walking down that old country road."

He kissed my cheek. I turned, letting him plant one on my lips. I had to get all the smooches I could. I never could be sure how many more I was good for.

"You got a busy afternoon?" My fingers moved to straighten his collar.

"We sure do. Cal and I got a visitation to get ready for tonight." Clive let me push the tie up against his clean-shaven neck. "Funeral tomorrow and who knows what next week brings."

"Only the Lord, I suppose." I followed him into the living room. "You won't be around for supper, will you?"

"No, honey." He swung his suit jacket off the back of a dinette chair. "I'll just grab myself a sandwich later on."

"I got plenty of cold cuts in the fridge. And a little of the leftover chicken you liked."

"Sounds good."

"I think I'll call Rosetta and see if she wants to get a bite with me."

"That's a good idea. You'll bring me home a piece of pie, won't you?" He eased his arms into the jacket. "Maybe a little slice of coconut cream?"

"I sure will."

"You have a good afternoon, Olga." He winked at me.

Oh, that wink of his still made a puddle out of me.

"I sure do love you, Clive." I wished he could stick around with me all day long. The older we got, the more I wanted to be around him.

"You know I love you back, Olga."

I puckered my lips so he'd give me another kiss. Just as sweet as ever. Sometimes I thought they'd grown even sweeter.

He turned and clomped his way down the stairs. The door at the foot of the steps closed with a familiar click.

Every blessed inch of that house was familiar. The creaky floor and sticky door. I'd lived there so long, I knew where everything went and never had to stumble around in the dark. The chairs in the living room hadn't moved in over thirty years, except when I vacuumed real good. Once I had things the way I liked them, I wasn't inclined to rearrange them.

Except for that darn mirror. I moved that blasted thing from one end of the apartment to the other. I'd put it in just about every room at some point. It always ended up back in my bedroom, right next to the dresser. I hated that old thing, reflection or not.

That mirror had been a wedding gift from Aunt Gertie. She'd said that every bride should have a mirror just like it. She'd gotten it from her mother. Poor Aunt Gertie didn't have a daughter to pass the thing down to. Not for lack of trying, though. She'd got herself a whole pack of boys from all her efforts. Irish twins, we called them. Six boys with only a year between them. That woman always had a babe at her breast, one on the potty seat, and another on the way. She just kept on trying for that girl.

The only one she got was me. The price she paid for a girl in the house was the death of her older sister. My mother. She held that cost against me, it felt. Oh, she'd always taken care of my needs. Put a plate of food in front of me and a frock in my closet. But she never came to treat me like a daughter. More like a nanny for her boys or a maid in her kitchen. That ended up being just fine by me. I never asked for a replacement mother anyhow.

I kept the mirror because I felt beholden to it. Besides my mother's cookbook and one remaining cousin, it held the only link to my family. I treasured the cookbook. But as for Old Buster and the mirror, I could have been happy without either of them taking up space.

Just thinking about it made my memory try to shove its way into ruining my day. I would have none of it, though. I pushed aside Aunt Gertie and all the memories she lugged around with her.

"Goodness me," I said to myself. "You're too old now to be worried about all that nonsense."

I needed to get out of that apartment and away from Aunt Gertie's mirror.

My shoes squeaked against the linoleum on my kitchen floor as I made my way to the back door. Heading down the stairs, I gripped the railing real tight. Each step down got me closer to the outdoors. It didn't matter to me how high the red of the thermometer rose, I craved the summertime air. It only lasted just so long in Michigan. I needed to breathe in as much of it as I could suck into my lungs.

My first gulp of air didn't disappoint. The sweet smell of a newly cut lawn floated my way. I guessed it was as pleasing to the Lord as it was to me. Letting the door swing closed, I leaned against the side of the building, the brick prickling into my skin through my blouse. Turning my face upward, I closed my eyes, letting the sunshine warm me all the way through.

A bird in one of the trees close by sang like his life depended on it. Just trilling and chirping away. The notes hit my ears, delighting me to no end. That aria filled my heart with gladness. I knew the Author of Creation had written that song Himself.

Leaves on the tallest trees clapped, letting the wind toss them together, swaying to and fro. I sure did go out with joy, led forth in peace. Only, out in farm country where I lived, we didn't have any mountains to burst forth into song. Just fields of corn and soybeans. But I believed that God could make that work, too.

The rumbling of a car covered over the birds and breeze and leaves. Creaking of old hinges followed by a sharp slamming sent the songbirds to flight. I opened my eyes to watch them flit away.

In the parking lot, a young woman leaned against a car, puffing on a cigarette. She took long draws off it, pulling the fumes deep into her lungs. As soon she finished off the first, she tossed it to the cement and lit up another.

Another woman sat in the car, waiting. She didn't pay attention to the smoking woman. Just sat, looking out the window into nothing I could see.

I stayed put against the building, watching the two of them and trying not to be caught spying. I hoped they'd go inside soon so I could get out into the garden.

Gretchen kneeled next to me by a row of fresh blooms. She

worked in the soil, pulling on weeds and tossing them to the side. Her hands could be tender to the good plants and tough on the bad. Her discernment rarely faltered in the garden.

"Honey, can you hand me the clippers, please?" I held on to a bunch of chamomile. "I didn't see all these yesterday. Must have grown up overnight."

"Oh, great." She passed the clippers my way. "You mind if I take those to dry?"

"Not at all. Just so long as you make a small batch of tea for me." After I made my cut of the stems, I handed them over to her. "Seems we got more chamomile this year. Must be your sunlamp did the trick."

"I wasn't sure it would work." She inspected the bunch. "Cal's good at remembering to water the garden, too."

"He's a good boy."

"Isn't he?" Soil streaked the thighs of her jeans from wiping her hands clean. Standing, she tried to brush it off. "How about we go over to my house and get a glass of iced tea? I think we got most of the weeds."

She held my hand and pulled me up onto my feet. The effort of getting off the ground throbbed in my old joints. As soon as I got standing up all the way, I noticed a sour look on her face. Her hand pressed against her stomach.

"Are you okay?"

"I think so." She lowered her hand. "I must have eaten something that my tummy isn't so happy about."

"Well, maybe we'll just have to take the rest of the day nice and slow."

She exhaled into a smile and pushed the sweat off her brow with the back of one hand.

"Honey, are you sure you're all right?" I patted her on the shoulder. "You want some antacids?"

"No, I'm fine, Mom." She forced another smile.

She held on to my arm, steadying me as we made our way to her house, just a two-minute walk from the garden. At least that was how long it took my feet to carry me there on a good, clear day.

Clive had that house built for Gretchen and the kids years before.

Goodness, but Charlotte was only a little slip of a thing then. They'd had it rough for a long while. I'd watch over the kids while Gretchen worked in the funeral home with Clive. We liked having her close by so much, even after the difficult days passed. We wanted her to stay put. And she did.

"I tell you what," I said, my footsteps working to keep up with Gretchen's. "It sure was good of Donald to put in this sidewalk."

"He's sweet, isn't he?"

Married almost a full year, and at her age, she still got flushed in the face when she talked about Donald. I couldn't think of a single flower he'd brought home for her. He turned out to be the kind to replace a roof or re-grout the tub rather than send a dozen roses. He showed his affection by doing. Not giving. I wondered if Gretchen understood his way of loving her.

She'd gotten roses aplenty from her first husband, the kids' father. Turned out, though, that he bought flowers in bulk. And he was a little too free and easy with who he gave them to.

And not too bright to get them from the florist that delivered funeral sprays every other day of the week.

Practical gifts of roofs and tubs and sidewalks beat a cheating husband any day of the week.

Just as soon as we walked in the front door of Gretchen's house, the cold from the air conditioner chilled my skin.

"Mom, do you mind if I sit down for a few minutes?" Gretchen asked. One of her hands lay heavy on her forehead under the red bangs. "I feel awful."

"Don't you worry about a thing, honey. I can get the tea." I found two tall glasses in the cupboard and filled them with ice and tea. "Maybe you just sat out in the sun too long."

"It was bothering me last night, too." She took the glass, holding it against her cheek. "Don't worry, Mom."

Asking me not to worry was like asking a dog not to bark. No amount of effort could turn that instinct off.

"Is Charlotte home?" The old rocking chair creaked after I lowered my behind into it. "You know, I don't think I've seen her more than a handful of times all summer."

"You and me both." Gretchen rolled her eyes. "She's out with a couple of friends. I guess Deirdre just got a new espresso machine at the bakery. Char's been spending all her time there."

"Our social butterfly."

"I wish she'd spend a little time looking for a job. Her student loan bills will start in a couple months."

"I'm sure your dad could come up with something for her."

"It's a nice thought." She pushed her lips together and shook her head. "But that job just isn't for her."

"I understand." I took a sip of tea. "It's a tough life."

"She's so sensitive. Dad knows that." Gretchen swept her bangs to one side. "She's a lot like her grandmother."

"Oh, she sure is, poor girl," I said. "I couldn't do the work down there for long."

Gretchen winced. A tight clenching right between her eyes. Her gasping breath made me grip the arm rests of my chair. I just about jumped up out of the rocker. Curling both shoulders, she put her hand on her stomach like before.

"Gretchen?" I pushed my backside to the edge of the chair. So far forward, so fast, I thought for sure that old thing would fall over on top of me. "What is it?"

She let the air back out of her before taking in more.

"Oh." She sighed, almost a groan. "That's not a good feeling."

"What can I do?" I darn near panicked, seeing her in that pain. "Should I call a doctor?"

"No, Mom. I'm fine." The smile she forced formed around clenched teeth. "I think I've just got a bad gas bubble stuck in my gut."

"What in heaven's name did you eat?" Sliding back in my seat, I sighed.

"Don brought home tacos last night." The hair around her face stuck on skin moistened by sweat even in the air-conditioned room. "I'm not eating those again."

"You think you got food poisoning?"

She exhaled, her body easing into the back of the couch.

"Whatever it is, I hope it goes through me soon," she said. "I don't want to miss the last of summer."

She reached for her tea. A twinge of something still bunched up in that place between her eyes.

A flash of memory quickened my already thumping heart. My mother, all curled up into herself on a bed. Pain set into her eyes. Lips pulled over teeth grinding together. And me, standing beside her, powerless to do a single thing to help.

Surging worry pushed the oxygen right out of my lungs.

Chapter Three

Evelyn

My afternoon appointment sat in straight-backed chairs, stiff and uncomfortable. I looked at both of them, Granddad's desk between us. Mother and daughter stared back at me, dry eyed. I double checked the file in front of me. Wanda and her daughter Jamie, there to arrange the funeral of Wanda's late husband, Stanley.

"We went to school together." Jamie's long, spiky, hot-pink-nailed finger jabbed in the air toward me. "You were a couple years behind me, weren't you?"

I nodded, surprised that anyone from high school had even noticed me, let alone remembered me ten years later.

"We didn't hang out, did we?" She flipped her bleached blond hair. "I mean, we weren't friends or nothing. Just went to school together."

Jamie had been a cheerleader, I remembered that much. And she'd been real popular, too. Mostly with the guys. That popularity didn't afford her the best reputation. She was the kind of girl my mom had warned me not to become.

"Let's stay on task." Wanda flicked her eyes toward the clock on the wall. "Who else should we name in the obituary?"

"We already listed everybody." Jamie picked at her pinky nail, chipping off a little bit of the paint. "We got you and me and the boys. There's nobody else."

"What about Art?"

"Who?" Jamie wrinkled her nose and scowled. "Art?"

"Your uncle Art." Wanda straightened her neck and sighed.

"I know who he is." Jamie inspected her thumbnail before chewing it. "What about him?"

"Shouldn't we put his name in the obituary?" Wanda shrugged one shoulder. Then she looked at me. "We should. Right? We should put his brother's name in the obituary? It's only proper."

"Ma'am," I said, pen in hand. "It can say just about whatever you want."

"But don't you think it would be courteous to put his brother's name in?"

"What would your husband have wanted?"

"He would have wanted Uncle Art to die first." Jamie crossed her way-too-skinny legs. "Dad hated him and you know it, Ma."

"That's a terrible thing to say, Jamie." Wanda shook her head.

Jamie and I looked right into each other's eyes. She couldn't have been much past thirty, but her eyes seemed older. Dull with dark, purple bags of exhaustion.

"We aren't putting Art's name on anything." She lifted an overly plucked eyebrow. "I don't care what my mom says."

Wanda turned her head and glared at her daughter for a full minute. I counted the ticks of the clock. A full sixty seconds. And I didn't see her blink once. Jamie just kept gnawing her thumbnail and staring at the flip calendar on the desk. After the sixtieth tick, Wanda turned back to me.

"I guess that's it for the obituary, then," she said. "What's next?"

"Well, we need to discuss what you'd like to do with his remains." I reached to one side of the desk for a brochure. "Do you know if he had a preference?"

"His what? Remains?" Jamie didn't break her gaze on the calendar or take the nail from between her teeth.

"His remains," Wanda repeated my words. "What's left of his body, right?"

"Yes." I pushed the brochure across the desk. "This explains your options."

"He never said anything to me about it. What do you think, Jamie?" Wanda turned her head back to the wide-eyed, far too intense glare at her daughter. "Should we get him a coffin? A nice wood one? A headstone?"

Jamie shrugged. "Or we could just do the thing with the ashes."

"Ashes? What would we do with the ashes?" She kept her eyes fixed on Jamie. I didn't count that time, but it had to have been at least a few minutes. "Do you want them for the mantel?"

"Gross. I don't want them in my house." Jamie shrugged again. "We could scatter them somewhere. Like, outside."

"Can we do that?" Wanda glanced at me out the corner of her eyes. "Is that okay to do?"

"If that's what you'd like." I nodded. "Would you still want to have a memorial service?"

"Well, we could do something small. Just for the family." Wanda blinked hard. Her eyebrows twitched up and down. I didn't think she had any idea that she did that. "Stanley didn't have a whole lot of friends."

"He was shy," Jamie added.

Wanda turned toward her again. That time, though, with a softer expression. As if the two had an understanding. "He was shy, yes. Very shy. He mostly kept to himself. Even with the two of us."

For the first time since they walked into the office, Jamie looked at her mother. Right in the eyes. She pinched her lips together.

"He was kind of hard to be around," she said. "But he was always good to my boys."

"He loved his grandsons." Wanda let a small smile curve on her face. "He'd brag about them wherever we went. He'd pull out his wallet and show off their pictures. He wasn't so shy when he talked about them."

"I didn't know that." Jamie let a tear roll from her eye.

Wanda reached across the arms of their chairs. Jamie raised her hand to hold her mother's. Widowed mother and fatherless daughter sat, hand in hand. I never would have expected that by the way they started the appointment, sneering at each other.

"Would you like a minister with you as you scatter his ashes?" I let my eyes turn back to the paper in front of me.

"I don't know," Wanda whispered. "He wasn't really a church-going kind of person. None of us are. It isn't that we don't believe. We just never got ourselves out of bed on Sunday mornings."

"Except when Dad wanted to go fishing," Jamie said.

The two women shared a laugh.

"He loved to fish." Wanda nodded.

"Why don't we just tell stories about him? He'd like that more than a sermon."

"I think he'd be glad you thought of that." Wanda leaned over and kissed Jamie's cheek.

Jamie tilted her head away from her mother, as if unfamiliar with the touch. I wondered if she felt like wiping the kiss off. Instead, she looked at me.

"Are we done?" She uncrossed her legs and stretched as she got out of her seat.

"Yes." The desk chair rolled out behind me as I stood. "Please let me know if there's anything else I can do for you. You have my number, right?"

"I do," Wanda answered. "Thank you."

The two women walked all the way out of my office and to their car, still holding hands. It didn't seem natural for them, the way their arms stiffened at the elbows and how their hands didn't swing. But, I thought, they both must have needed the comfort of it. As awkward as it must have been. They had to hold on to someone.

In a strange, untouchable way, watching them made me lonely.

Heavy footsteps thudded on the floor behind me. Turning, I saw Granddad's smile.

"Death has a way of drawing people together," he said. "Either that or pushing them completely away from each other. Like a magnet."

Granddad put hands on hips and smiled down at me, making me almost forget the loneliness.

"What did they decide on?" Granddad asked.

"Cremation. They want to do a small family service to scatter the ashes."

"I'll have Cal take a trip out to the crematorium first of the week." Granddad patted my back. "You done real good, as usual. I'm proud of you."

He turned toward the office, his wide shoulders nearly touching either side of the door frame.

Watching him, I thought about what he'd said. That death had a way of acting like a magnet. Up to that point in my life, all death did was send everyone scattering away from me, leaving only my family. Some days that didn't offer a whole lot of consolation.

Chapter Four

Olga

I left Gretchen on the couch so she could get a little shut-eye. The poor thing curled up on that couch, no energy to get to her bed. I knew she'd be snoozing by the time I got off the porch.

Praying away the image of my mother, writhing in her bed, I asked the Almighty if I might have something to make me smile. To make that worry pack up and take a hike.

The sidewalk path took me under branches that joined together, making a tunnel of green. Cool shade on my head felt good, but I longed to warm myself in the sunshine. The hollow tapping of a woodpecker caught my attention as I went on my way. Seemed no matter what tree I studied, I couldn't catch a peek at him.

I did see, though, a car pulling into the driveway. Out of the corner of my eye, I spied a bird flying away. Must have been my woodpecker. I figured I couldn't be too upset. I had books and books full of bird pictures I could look at any day. But my youngest grandchild had grown up so quick. Soon, she'd be off into the world, and I'd miss her terribly. My Charlotte was worth far more than a forest teeming with woodpeckers.

She got out of her car and waved when she saw me. Oh, how I envied the way she ran toward me without the fear of falling.

"Gran," she called. "Hi."

"Am I ever glad to see you." I reached my arms to her. When she got to me, I pulled her close and ran my hands over her smooth hair. Carrot red like her mama's. Only she took a straight iron to the curl. If I'd had my druthers, I'd have seen her hair wavy every day of the week.

"I have good news." She pulled away from me and clenched her teeth together in a wide smile. Not even the sun could outshine the gladness on her face.

"Well, what is it, honey?"

"I was just at the bakery. I talked to Deirdre about some of the pastry classes I took last year at college."

"How about that?"

"I guess she's been looking for someone to help her out."

"Isn't that something." I grabbed her hand.

Her eyes, green as the grass in spring, widened with optimism. I, on the other hand, worried to my toes about her working in that bakery. Deirdre could be a hard woman. I never had gotten along with her so well. I wasn't the only one in town who had gotten into a spat or two with her. But, as sensitive as she was, the Lord also made Charlotte one determined girl. Brimming full of spunk. She never took garbage from nobody, no how.

My mind told my heart she'd be okay. My heart pretended to believe it.

"Seriously, this will be so good on my resume. Especially if I ever want to make a real career out of baking." She bubbled over in excitement. I loved that half-moon smile on her face.

"I didn't know that was what you wanted to do for a job."

"Ever since the first time we made cookies together."

Now, if that girl didn't know how to make my heart swell. I about lost a few tears over those sweet words of hers.

"Well, how about you and me go over and get some practice?" I patted her hand. "I was thinking I'd go bake a batch of something yummy for Granddad. Maybe you could teach me a trick or two from your classes."

"I don't know anything you didn't already teach me." The way her eyes sparkled reminded me so much of Gretchen's. And her smile, too. Warm and toothy. With a little crinkle across the nose. She looked so much like her mother, it almost hurt.

We walked side by side up to my house, stopping for half a second to watch a fat bumble bee dipping and diving among the flowers. Then up the steps and into the kitchen.

"Have you eaten lunch yet?" I asked. "I still make a mean peanut butter and jelly."

"I'm good. Thanks." She dropped her cloth purse onto one of the chairs in the living room.

"I guess you're too grown for a good old PB and J." I washed my hands under cool water from the tap.

"Do you have any pop?" She pulled open the refrigerator.

"I got a couple cans right there on the bottom shelf, honey. Help yourself." I pointed, even though she didn't look at me. "You want a glass?"

"No thanks." The can cracked and fizzed when she opened it.

"What do you think we should whip up?" I made my way to the shelf where my cookbooks lived. The one I pulled out felt heavy in my hands. Weighty with all the family recipes I'd cooked and baked my whole life.

"How about cookie bars?" Standing together at the counter, she put her cheek on my shoulder. "The ones with chocolate chips."

"Good choice."

The pages of that cookbook crinkled as I turned them. Bits of dried up sugar stiffened the paper. Flour dust had settled over the handwritten recipes.

"I thought you had all these memorized." She lifted her head.

"When you get old like me, relying on memory is dangerous." I reached up and held her face in the palm of my hand. She leaned right into it.

"You aren't that old, Gran." She smiled real gentle and then turned toward the book and touched the yellowed paper. "I can type these up for you. We could print them on special paper."

"Aren't you a sweetheart." I brushed a hand over the pages. The history of times in the kitchen making birthday cakes and Christmas pies gritted under my skin. Cookies baked to soothe a broken heart. Yeast rolls to thicken hungry bellies. I read those stories, my heritage, in the old handwriting of the recipes. "You know, I like looking at all those chicken scratches. Some of them are my mother's. This book reminds me so much of her. And, boy, could that woman work her way around a kitchen."

I pulled my glass mixing bowl from the cupboard. One that my Clive had got for me years ago at an antique shop. Charlotte took it from my hands. My poor shoulders felt grateful for the help.

"I was only eight years old when my mother died, you know." My hands on the countertop, I rested against it a spell, still trying to blink away the picture of her face grimaced in pain. "I watched them lower her casket into the grave. Of course, back then, they had the family stay and watch it go all the way down into the hole. I even had to toss in a handful of dirt."

"Really?" Charlotte lowered the bowl to the counter so carefully, it didn't make a sound.

"Awful thing to make a child do." A chill sent a shudder down my spine. The way the clump of dirt had bumped and spread across the top of the wood casket, the sound of it, played in my mind. Then the shovelfuls of earth piling on top. Just too much.

Charlotte pushed a tear out from under her eye. "I can't imagine."

"I didn't mean to upset you."

"It's okay, Gran."

"My aunt Gertie kept all my mama's recipes for me. Gave them to me a couple years before she passed. I put them all in this book here." I patted it. "Maybe one of these days I can hand it down to you."

"I couldn't take it from you."

"Well, you'd have to do all the cooking and baking for me and Granddad. Doesn't seem too shabby a deal, as far as I'm concerned."

Charlotte smiled as she tried to pull open the utensil drawer. It stuck, warped after years of use and humid days like that one. I reached over and bumped it with the palm of my hand, the way I'd done for ten or so years. She laughed when the drawer opened without a protest. She grabbed the beaters and rubber spatula and measuring spoons.

"You need these spoons? Or can you still eyeball it?" That wink of hers got a little bubble of delight out of me.

I pointed at the hollow of my hand. "Best tool in the kitchen right there, honey."

"I'd never get the right amount."

"I guess I don't know exactly if I do get it right. I just put in what I think looks good." I winked back at her. "But it always seems to work out okay. I haven't blown the place up yet from a batch of cookies."

We cracked the eggs and dumped the sugar into the bowl. The smell of melted butter warmed the room. A puff of flour hung in the air. The two of us kept our mouths quiet, letting the sounds of mixing fill our ears. Baking with Charlotte healed a long-wounded place of my heart. I thanked God for the mercy of her standing next to me in the kitchen.

Charlotte dumped the chocolate chips into the batter, sneaking one. "I had to make sure it was good," she said with her sideways smile.

"Spoken like a true baker." My grin felt like it took over my whole face. "Now, honey, go on and grab that rubber spatula, please. You hold the bowl and I'll scrape out the batter."

The dough dropped into the pan. I pushed it around, making it even. I let Charlotte have the honor of lowering the whole shebang into the oven.

"How about we go sit a spell and wait on those to bake." The dinette looked like a nice easy spot for me. "Remind me, how long does that recipe say it needs to bake?"

"Thirty-five minutes." She traced the words with her fingertips. "But somebody wrote, 'thirty-one to keep them gooey.'"

"Well, how do you like them, sweetie?" I pulled a chair away from the table.

"Gooey." The light coming through the window over the sink caught the green of her eyes just right, making them look like jewels.

"Thirty-one minutes it is, then." I put my backside into the chair. "I wrote that note years ago. I've always liked them a tad on the soft side."

Charlotte picked up her can of pop from the counter and joined me at the table.

"Gran, do you think Granddad will be sad that I got a different job?" she asked. "I don't want him to be upset that I'm not working with him downstairs."

"Honey, do you even know how hard it is to upset that man?" I rested my elbows on the table. "He won't be anything but proud of you."

She leaned into the back of the chair.

"Now, you've had yourself one humdinger of a summer, haven't you?" I slapped the table. "I want to hear all about it. I've hardly seen you for more than ten minutes at a time. So, spill the beans."

We sat and chatted it up a good long time. She told me about trips here and there. A few dates that didn't pan out. Friends that came to visit from the city. Most of it I already knew. More secondhand from Gretchen than anything. Still, I didn't mind hearing it straight from the horse's mouth. She told it better. And didn't leave out the things she hadn't wanted her mother to know.

She'd experienced more in that one summer than I had in a full year at her age. Maybe even two years. Of course, by her age, I had a wedding to plan. My, how things had changed.

When the timer buzzed, she got out of her chair and pulled those goodies from the oven, resting them on a rack to cool just a smidgen.

And as we snuck a square each, I had to force myself to trust that Gretchen would be okay. I told myself that it was just a stomach bug.

But I'd never seen a bug cause that kind of pain.

Chapter Five

EVELYN

Granddad kept every room in the Big House as cold as it would get. Especially the prep room, where we embalmed and dressed the bodies in our care. Even on the hottest day, I needed a sweater in that room.

Goosebumps raised on my arms as I walked between the embalming table and the wall. I couldn't help but think how disappointed the boy at the restaurant would have been to see the room. Just like any other. Sterile and organized. More like an operating room than anything. No cobwebs in the corners or body parts tucked away in a shadowy room.

Of all we did as funeral directors, the work done in that room held the fascination or fear of most of the town. It kept them from inviting us to dinner or out for coffee. As a kid, I never got to go to sleepovers. The other children were too afraid of me.

The blinds gathered, folding up to the top of the window, as I pulled the cord, letting in a little light. My doctor had told me to get more sunshine. That it would help with the depression. I figured it couldn't hurt. As well lit as we kept the prep room, it couldn't beat the warmth of natural light.

I made my way to the casket that stood against the far wall. A simple wooden one with cream colored lining. I flipped on a light near it to illuminate the face of the woman who lay within. A file with a name had been placed on the counter. Loretta Allen. We'd buried her husband less than a year before.

"Poor family," I whispered, opening the folder.

I looked at the picture clipped to the folder. Pulling it loose, I held it close to my face. It had to have been thirty years old.

"How am I supposed to make you look like this?" I asked the woman in the casket.

The photo was one of the square, faded orange ones from the nineteen-seventies. The woman in front of me had to have been at least twenty pounds lighter than the younger version of herself in the picture. And her hair was pure white and thinning instead of dark brown and thick.

My drawer pulled open, jostling the tubes of foundation and cakes of eye shadow. Every color imaginable. I set brushes and foam applicators on the counter next to the curling iron and hair spray.

With Mrs. Allen, I'd have to do my best at guessing on the colors. Especially with the strange, peachy tint the photo gave her skin.

Glancing out the window, I saw my mom walking toward the Big House. She was hard to miss. Her shocking red hair, still so bright I suspected she dyed it. She never would have admitted it. But I just knew she'd touched it up. At least a little. Hair dye or not, she was a beautiful woman. Not stick skinny, but I thought she looked better for the curves, anyway.

I lost sight of her when she went around the other side of the building. No doubt she'd come to see Gran. The two of them could hardly go half a day without seeing each other.

I went back to figuring out colors for Mrs. Allen. After a minute, the prep room door swung open.

"Hey, Ev." My mom stood in the doorway. "I hope I'm not interrupting anything."

"Nope." I turned toward her. "Come on in."

"Busy day, huh?" With her fingers, she pushed the hair off her forehead.

"Yeah." Arms crossed over my chest, I leaned a hip into the counter. "I'm not sure how we're keeping up on everything. Cal must be working really late."

"That boy has always been a hard worker."

"Well, he's going to get burned out."

"I don't know about that." She yawned, covering her mouth. "Goodness. Sorry about that."

Standing across the room from her, I tried to remember the last time she'd been in the prep room. Dressing the body had been her job for years. Until she married Don, at least. He told her she didn't have to work anymore. So, she retired. I should be so lucky.

"So, what brings you over here?" I asked, turning back to the file and the picture.

"Oh, I saw the blinds up and figured you were down here. I thought I'd see how you are."

"Doing fine. Just busy." Turning my head toward her, I noticed the creases on the side of her face. "Did you just get up from a nap? Since when do you nap?"

"I'm not feeling so well today." She yawned again and patted a hand on her chest. "I'm worn out."

"What's going on?"

"Just my stomach. It's bothering me."

"You look pale."

"I'm fine." The charm on her necklace scraped across the chain. Back and forth.

"I know you're retired and everything, but do you mind giving me a hand here?" The photo between my thumb and pointer finger, I held it next to Mrs. Allen's face in the casket.

"Sure." Her arm bumped up against mine when she stepped to the casket. "Is that Loretta?"

"Yeah. But all I have is a really old picture."

"Well, I'm out of practice." Her sigh carried a low tone in it. "But I guess I'd say, just go with a medium shade of foundation. Something with a little olive to it."

"So earthy tones?" I asked.

"I'd think so." She touched my shoulder.

"Have you called the doctor about your stomach? It might be food poisoning. You should get it checked out." I squeezed a dot of foundation on a sponge wedge.

"If it isn't better tomorrow, I'll go in." She watched me smooth the foundation on Mrs. Allen's cheek. "That's a good color. You'll need to use a nice rich color for the blush, too."

She rummaged through the makeup drawer for a few more shades, handing them to me.

"Now, Gretchie, what are you doing down here?" Gran's voice sang into the room before I heard her footsteps. The corners of her eyes wrinkled with the grin she wore on her face. A dusting of flour whitened the front of her shirt.

"Hi, Gran," I said.

She put an arm around Mom's waist and gave her a little squeeze.

"How'd that nap do you?" Reaching up, she used the inside of her wrist to feel my mom's forehead. "Feeling better?"

"A little."

"That's good."

"Do you mind if I take you up on the antacids?"

"Sure, honey. They're upstairs on my side of the medicine cabinet."

Gran and I watched my mom walk from the room.

"I tell you, that mama of yours is bound to give me an ulcer from worry. We won't have enough antacids to go around." Gran shook her head, then reached her arm around me. "Hi, Evelyn. How's it going with Mrs. Allen?"

"Do we have a more up-to-date picture of her in a file somewhere?" I grabbed the picture again. "This one isn't all that helpful."

She took the picture, shifting her glasses so she could see through the bifocals. Still, she had to squint her eyes.

"Oh, my. Is this ever an old picture. I bet this is from when Loretta and John prearranged years ago." She handed it back to me. "You remember John. He passed last year. That's him in the picture with her."

"They were cute together."

I gave the picture another look. Mrs. Allen faced the camera, her smile wide. I figured she was in the middle of a laugh. Her husband's arms wrapped all the way around her thick waist as he kissed the top of her head. His eyes closed, the corners of his mouth turned up.

Using my finger to blend the foundation on Mrs. Allen's jaw, I wished I could make her look more like the mid-laugh, joy-filled woman in the picture. I'd do the best I could with the makeup. But that woman was gone.

"Oh, how those two loved each other. Deep as the ocean," Gran said. "They couldn't get enough of one another."

"How long were they married?"

"You know, their wedding was right around the same time as Granddad and mine." She reached across me, grabbing the comb from the countertop. Her hands moved swiftly through Mrs. Allen's hair. "Of course, they were a bit older than us. Granddad and me got married real young."

"Gran, how did you and Granddad get together?" I asked, watching her flick the comb through the brittle hair, giving it a little lift.

"Oh, that old history?" She smacked her lips. "Honey, you've heard that story more times than I can count."

"Please, Gran," I begged. "At least tell me how you knew he was the right one for you."

She stopped moving her hands. I felt her gaze. "Now, Evelyn, is this about the date you just went on? Cal told me all about it."

"I think Cal's as big a gossip as Deirdre."

"Well, I agree with you on that." Her fingers went back to work. "Now, you know I love your Granddad to bits and pieces."

"Everybody knows that," I said.

"I didn't know right off when he first started coming around. The last thing I thought about was being married to him." She shook her head. "Back then, I looked for about any reason to get out of Aunt Gertie's kitchen and away from all those boys. And she wanted me to get married off so she didn't have to feed me anymore."

"She must have been a delightful woman."

"Well, she didn't have things easy. But that's beside the point. I liked getting away from the house, even if it was just to take a little stroll with Granddad."

"Where would you go?" Using a brush, I dusted a light brown shadow across Mrs. Allen's eyelids.

"In those days, honey, there wasn't much of any place to go. And I certainly didn't want to get myself into trouble." Her voice dropped in volume. "You know what I mean by that, don't you?"

"I think so," I answered, laughing.

"Good. I wouldn't want to be the one to explain all that business to you. Especially since we're going to need to get you married off sooner than later." Gran giggled. "Oh, when I was a girl, we didn't know anything about that kind of thing until we were married. Sometimes not even then. Some brides got an unwelcome surprise on their wedding night, I tell you. That caused all kinds of trouble."

"You don't have to worry about me." The eye shadow brush clunked back into the drawer. "I know all about that stuff. Not from personal experience or anything."

"I'd hope not." She raised her eyebrows.

"Anyway." Flushed, my cheeks burned. "Go on."

"So, I told Granddad that if he wanted to make time with me, he'd have to walk me over to Marshall's for a chocolate Coke. Of course, it was Marshall Senior who owned it back in those days. Young Marshall slung burgers before he inherited the place." She swatted her hand in the air. "That detail doesn't matter so much. What does matter is that Granddad came around twice a week. Sometimes more. I never had intentions of falling in love with him, though. I just liked getting that chocolate Coke. A girl like me wasn't so accustomed to such luxuries."

"What happened then?" I painted an earthy tone on Mrs. Allen's lips.

"One day, good gravy, it must have been after walking together for a whole summer, he told me that he loved me. He wanted to go steady. It was right at the gate leading up to Aunt Gertie's front door." She sighed. "I could tell he wanted to plant a kiss on me."

"How could you tell?"

"Haven't you ever been kissed before?" Gran nudged me with her elbow and grinned. "Anyway, he tilted his head a tiny bit and gave me this dreamy look with his big, blue eyes. I thanked him for being so good to me. Then I told him not to kiss me or ever come around again."

"Poor Granddad."

"Well, some fellas don't get the point unless you're a shrew," Gran said. "And I guess that man was one of them. He came back the next day and asked me to go get a chocolate Coke with him. And every day after that."

"So, when did you feel like you loved him?"

"I don't really remember, honey." She smoothed Mrs. Allen's hair.

46

"But I do remember when I made that decision. It's a very different thing, Evelyn. Feeling in love and deciding to be."

"What do you mean?"

"You know, for all the talk we hear about romance and all the feelings that go along with it, we just don't understand it so well, do we?" Her forehead scrunched up. "There are too many movies filling our minds with what romance can't really be."

"You're going to have to explain that one."

"Well, so many young ladies these days think that romance is meeting the eyes of a handsome man and just knowing, right in that second, that he's the only man God created just for her. And that man just happens to be Mr. Somebody Perfect. That romance is the feeling she gets in the place between her stomach and her heart." She swatted her hand out in front of her face. "Hogwash, I say. Romance is as much of a feeling as a dog is a cat."

"Then what is it?" I dropped the lipstick into the drawer.

"Romance is waking up next to the same old mug, year after year, morning after another, and realizing you'd pick him all over again. Hairy back, bald head, and all."

A laugh came up and out of me. "Goodness, Gran."

"I mean it." Gran wrapped her fingers around the top part of my arm. "I knew Granddad was right for me when I stopped caring that there might be other choices."

Her gray-green eyes sparkled.

"And, honey, let me tell you, I had a whole lot of choices. But none of them mattered one bit. Not after I decided to love Granddad."

"I can't wait to find a man like Granddad."

I didn't add, though, that I hoped he wasn't a funeral director.

"One thing you've got to remember. No man is perfect. Not even Granddad." She rubbed my arm. "And you need to remember that you can't change a man. It doesn't happen. He might change. God might bring that about. But you can't be the one to force him."

"I know, Gran."

"You just make sure you're praying about it. God will make it all happen for you."

"That sounds so easy." It took all my effort not to let my voice break.

"But it's true."

"Let's just say, then, that God needs to hurry up. I'm not getting any younger."

She used a knuckle to push up her glasses. "From where I stand, you still look like a spring chicken."

"Thanks, Gran." I put the makeup back in the drawer and unplugged the curling iron we hadn't used. "I'm just hoping that I don't end up alone."

She wrapped her arms around me. "I know, sweetie."

After she left, I checked my phone. Still no calls from Will. Our date had been nearly a week before. It felt a whole lot like being brushed off.

I wondered if it was my job that repulsed people magnetically. I feared it was just me they didn't want to be around.

Chapter Six

Olga

Dinnertime memories from Aunt Gertie's house made me cringe. Her table filled up fast with those six boys come meal time. We had to keep all three leaves in so there'd be enough room. Still, pointy elbows jabbed into ribs and clumsy hands knocked over glasses of milk.

I'd had to learn to gobble up my food, quick as I could. If I didn't, one of the boys would snatch it right off my plate. Half the time, though, I got plain disgusted by the munching teeth and the belching.

Even as much as I disliked those barbaric meals, in my older years, I couldn't take eating all by myself with only my thoughts to keep me company. And I never did abide taking a meal in front of the television.

Nights when Clive had to work through supper, I said an extra thank You prayer for Rosetta's friendship. We'd met after her husband passed. Clive had buried him. She needed a family to draw her in, and I needed a good friend. Closer than sisters we'd become over the years. She with her brown skin and black hair. Me pale as buttermilk and with hair to match. But sisters, just the same.

Now we two sat at our usual table at Marshall's Diner, right by the front window. We sipped our coffee, tummies full of dinner. The waitress brought over two slices of pie, all golden of crust and red of berry. With, of course, fluffy dollops of whipped cream.

"Here we made it all the way through our supper and I forgot to tell you about something." Rosetta shook her head.

"What's that, Rosie?" My fork pushed through the crust of my strawberry pie.

"Well," Rosetta started. "You remember that old couple that lived down the hall from me?"

"For heaven's sake." I giggled. "Aren't they all old in that place? They don't let young people live in an old folk's home, do they?"

"No, honey. I mean the really old couple. The Watertons." She put her fork across her plate. "They just moved over to the nursing home. I guess they needed a little more help."

"That's too bad."

"Well, that's not what I wanted to tell you, really."

I knew she was up to something by the way one of her eyebrows curved.

"Now, don't you look at me like that, Rosie," I said. "What are you thinking?"

"I don't mind telling you."

The waitress carried the coffeepot over to refresh our cups. Decaf, of course. I would have been up into the next week if I'd had any leaded that time of night. She also dropped off our bill. Her nail polish caught my eye. Green as a frog with a little sparkle to it. She smiled when she caught me eyeing them.

"It's my favorite color," she said before walking away.

"Such a sweet girl." Rosetta blew the steam off her fresh coffee. "Anyway. That apartment down the hall is empty now. I hear they're planning to put in new carpet and paint all the walls. They might even put in a new tub."

"Is that so?"

"Well, I think it would be good for you and Clive."

"You do?" I wiped at my mouth with a napkin. "I don't know, Rosetta. Clive hasn't talked about retiring in months."

Even then, when Clive mentioned it, he said how he dreaded the thought of retirement. That he didn't want to stop being useful.

"How old is he, Olga? Seventy-four?"

"Seventy-six. But he'd be thrilled to know you guessed younger."

"Doesn't he know he's an old man? He can't keep going on like that for too much longer." She took a long sip from her mug. "That's a hard job. And I'm not just saying so to get you to be my neighbor."

The bell over the diner door rang. Bev took slow, shuffling steps right over to our table. Once she got to us, she folded her skinny, tanned arms across her stomach. If somebody had asked me, I would have said that no eighty-something-year-old should have a stomach so flat as Bev's.

She scowled at us, squishing her face. I wondered that she could move her face around with all the thick makeup caked on.

Bev lived on the second floor at the retirement home. When I thought about it, I couldn't remember how she and I got to be friends. As sweet as Rosetta was, Bev matched it with sour.

"You girls didn't want to wait on me?" she groaned.

Bev never said a blessed thing. She groaned it. Or moaned it. Every now and again, she'd grump it.

"Well, Beverly, you told me you wanted to eat at the home." Rosetta put on her very sweetest smile. "You never like to miss out on clam chowder night."

"You didn't even wait for me to come have a piece of pie." Bev rolled her eyes under lids that only lifted up halfway. She slid into the booth next to Rosetta.

"I was just telling Olga about our plan for her to move in."

"For goodness sake, Rosetta. Wasn't my idea. I don't care if they move in or not." She yawned. "I think they should do whatever the heck they want to."

"Now, what are you talking about?" Rosetta leaned her upper half away from Bev, glaring at her. She pressed her full lips together. "Just yesterday you said it would be nice to have Olga around to play cards with."

"How am I supposed to remember what I said yesterday? Maybe I didn't say that at all. Maybe you need your hearing checked." Bev blinked at me. "Besides, you'd have to keep an eye on your husband. What's his face."

"Clive," I said.

"What kind of name is that? Did his parents name him after an herb or something?" She shook her head. "Anyway, you'll want to keep that man under lock and key. Stupid name or not. And that's all

I've got to say."

"Oh, Beverly." Rosetta tsk-tsked her lips. "Don't you get going on that again."

"On what?" I hated to admit it, but I liked getting the buzz as much as anybody else.

"Don't you encourage her, Olga." Rosie clucked her tongue. "Beverly just wants to gossip."

"It ain't gossip if it's true." Bev glanced out the window.

"It most certainly is."

"Well, that's what the Bible says." Bev grumbled it this time. "Anyway, you'll need to watch out for Sophia. That Sophia is a husband stealer."

"You don't know that," Rosetta said. "You stop spreading trash around. You're better than that."

"Don't you tell me what I'm better than." Bev let her head bob up and down. "All I'm saying is what I heard. That old coot Bill hasn't slept in his own bed for weeks. Or was it Albert? I can't remember. Old men all look the same to me."

"Beverly," Rosetta scolded.

"That Sophia's been tempting them with cake. That's how she's getting them into her apartment."

"Now, how do you know she's been doing that?"

"The housekeeper told me she hasn't had to make Bill's bed in a long time."

"Maybe he's making it himself," I offered.

"You see, this is why nobody's calling you Nancy Drew," Bev mumbled. "No man's going to make his own bed. Everybody knows that. Besides, there's a whole lot of monkeying around in that place."

"Why's that?" I raised my last forkful of pie into my mouth.

"Old folks just got nothing to lose."

At Bev's words, Rosetta nearly doubled over laughing. She smacked her hand on the table. "Oh, Beverly, Beverly," she squealed between fits of giggles.

"I don't see what's so funny." Bev crossed her arms again. "The last thing I want to do is be with a stinky old man in my clean bed."

"I never have been able to understand all the goings on between elderly people," Rosetta said, her giggles all worked their way out.

"After my Hamilton passed, I didn't even want to think about another man. Still don't. It took us so many years to really fall in love all the way. I don't have enough time left on this earth to get started up with another man."

"Well, isn't that nice for you." Bev checked her watch. "Not everybody got a good one the first time around like you did, you know. You just got lucky."

Rosetta hummed, her voice buzzing between her lips. "The way I see it is, I was blessed by the Lord with my Hamilton. With Him by my side, I don't have any use for luck."

"Right. Right." Bev's eyes rolled, slow and lazy, from one side to the other.

The three of us got up from the table, slower than turtles. Creaking and groaning joints and all.

"Oh, I sat too long." Rosetta sighed. "I'm going to need my arthritis cream."

"Maybe Bill can help you put it on." Bev actually let a smirk crack on her face.

"You're a bad girl, Beverly." Rosetta shook her head.

We paid for our meals and stepped outside. Round and orange, the sun hung in the middle of the sky, still warming the air.

"I've got a really good life." My voice felt thin coming out.

My life wasn't just good. Blessed, more like it. But, in that moment of thanksgiving, I remembered that twinge of pain between Gretchen's eyes. I remembered how worried I got over every cough and sniffle. Imagined life turning on us. Destroying our joy. Taking our daughter. It took all my will to shake that dreadful fear.

"Amen, hallelujah." Rosetta put her hand on my shoulder, pulling me back to her and the sunset and the praise I felt a moment before. "And you're part of my really good life, my friend."

Bev cleared her throat.

"You, too, my dear Beverly." Rosetta reached out and pulled Bev near.

The three of us decided to stretched out our sore legs and walk on over to the park to watch the sun dip all the way down the horizon. And maybe get a little ice cream, too. After all, we old folks had nothing much to lose.

All the way home, I thought about the goodness of life. How happy being married to Clive had made me. Being a mama to Gretchen and a grandma to the kids only added sweetness to my joy. Everything so good. So wonderful.

I couldn't help but worry that it'd all fall apart soon enough. Nothing could ever stay that good for long.

Nothing ever did.

Chapter Seven

EVELYN

The family arrived all at once for Mrs. Allen's viewing. Three sons and two daughters, their spouses, and a handful of grandkids stood in the lobby of the Big House. They didn't talk to one another, but kept hands in pockets or crossed over chests. Their eyes avoided the front of the chapel. Instead, they let them rest on the carpet or the walls. They stood so close together, their elbows touched.

"Would you like to see her?" Cal asked. "Whenever you're all ready."

"I think we need to get in there." One of the sons nodded, turning toward the chapel. I wondered if he was the oldest. He had the most gray around the edges of his hair.

A few of them linked arms. A couple others held hands. The family walked together, as a unit, to view Mrs. Allen.

When they got to the casket, they took turns getting up close, looking at her face, touching her hands.

"She looks good." One of the daughters, the one who'd done most of the arranging, touched Mrs. Allen's fingers. "So peaceful."

Sacred silence shared between them, they paid respect with gentle mourning. Every few minutes, one sought a hug. Another offered a tissue. No words needed. They knew from the way an eyebrow lowered or a chin quivered. The family spoke the language of grief well. They'd become fluent.

Warm air rushed into the lobby when the outside door opened. Cal moved to stand in the entrance to the chapel, blocking the new arrivals until the family had gotten their time alone with her body. After a moment, one of the sons nodded to my brother.

"We're ready," he said.

Cal and I stood against the wall, watching half the town gather in the chapel. Their voices buzzed and their bodies heated the building. Granddad would have to turn up the air conditioner.

"Hey," Cal said. "When are you going to tell me about your date?"

"Not anytime soon." I made my voice quiet.

"Come on, Ev. All Deirdre could tell me was that the guy had dreadlocks and those big disc things in his ears."

"Seriously, you have got to stop getting your information from that woman."

"But when I listen to her long enough, she slips an extra doughnut into my bag." Cal flicked his eyebrows up and down.

"You're using her."

"Anyway, I was thinking of taking her out for dinner."

"Gross, Cal." My gag reflex triggered. "Deirdre's old."

"Wait. No. Not like that." He cringed. "I mean so we can figure out who Mr. Dreadlocks is."

"You're kidding me, right?" I shook my head. "He has black hair. No piercings or tattoos."

"That you know of."

A woman walked across the lobby. "Bathroom?" she mouthed.

I pointed down the hallway.

"Deirdre didn't tell me the dreadlocks thing, by the way," Cal whispered. "I made it up. But you took the bait."

"Wow. You are so very clever."

Cal straightened, nodding as a man walked in from outside, the thick odor of cigarette smoke trailing in behind him.

"So, where did he take you?" he continued. "What did you do?"

The woman came out of the bathroom, waving me over to her.

"You're out of toilet paper," she huffed.

When I got back to Cal after stocking the rest rooms with paper products, he smiled at me.

"I've got an idea. You want to hear it?"

"I really don't like the sound of that."

"Do you have his phone number?"

"You aren't going to call him, Cal." I leaned against the wall.

"No. That would be ridiculous." He snorted. "I'd never do something so immature."

"Then what are you going to do with his number?"

"Nothing. You are." Cal crossed his arms. "You need to call him."

One of Mrs. Allen's sons walked into the lobby. The one with the silver along his hairline. He wiped at his eyes with the back of his hand. Stepping into the office, I grabbed the box of tissues off the desk, holding it out to him.

"Thanks," he said, taking two from the box. "This is a lot harder than I expected."

"I'm so sorry." I used my calm, soothing voice. "Can I get you something?"

"I'll be all right." He nodded at me before turning back to the chapel.

Standing by Cal, I realized how really pathetic my life had become. Friday nights spent at the funeral home with my younger brother who was dispensing dating advice.

"So, are you going to call him?" Cal asked.

"Eventually." I snuck a look at my brother. "Maybe."

I couldn't decide which was worse. Loneliness or the risk of rejection.

Mrs. Allen's viewing had run long into the evening. Well past the nine o'clock ending time. Granddad wouldn't charge them more. He never did. Fortunately, we didn't have to set up the chapel for the service the next day. That would be over at the church.

Granddad walked us to the porch of the Big House. Pulsing dots of fireflies flitted in front of us. Cal reached out, cupping both hands to catch one. The little bug crawled across his skin, glowing every few seconds. Raising its wings, it lifted off Cal's palm, hovering near, still lighting up.

"As much as I'd love to sit here and watch you catch lightning bugs all night, I'm beat," Granddad said. "And I think all three of us could use a good night of sleep."

"Sounds good to me." Cal stepped to the edge of the porch, teetering off the side.

"I feel awful making you kids work on a Saturday." Granddad shoved his hands into the pockets of his pants. "Wish I could give you both a bonus. We've had nothing but busy weekends all year, it seems."

"It's not a problem, Granddad." The warmth of the evening forced a drowsy yawn from my mouth.

"I love you both. You know that." His heavy arm rested across my shoulders. "Tomorrow, I expect a lot less chitchatting between the two of you. Don't think I didn't notice."

"Sorry about that." Cal tipped himself off the porch to the sidewalk.

"Don't be sorry, just be better at keeping your traps shut."

Granddad stepped back into the funeral home and closed the door behind him. The lock clicked into place before the lights switched off.

Cal caught a few more fireflies while we walked to our cars.

"Man, I wish I had a jar," he mumbled. "Remember how we used to fill a whole jar full of these?"

"You wanted to make a lantern."

"It never worked." Jumping, he missed one. It glowed just out of his reach.

"You're going home, right?" I asked.

"I thought I'd stop over at the church. Make sure everything's ready for tomorrow." He took his eyes off the bug.

"If you keep working so much, you're never going to meet anybody." I pulled my car door open.

"Yeah. But who needs friends when I have my big sister?" Winking, he pulled the keys from his pocket. "Drive safe, Ev."

"Don't work too late."

Pulling out onto the dirt road, I flipped through the radio stations, looking for something other than country music. A tall order out in the sticks where I lived.

As soon as I felt the smooth, paved road under my tires, I accelerated. I could have driven that road blindfolded. Every day, I navigated the bumps and curves and potholes of the roads to and from the Big House. My eyes lost focus for just a second, but I knew that road stretched out straight in front of me. On a clear night like that one, I wouldn't have any problems.

My phone buzzed from inside my purse, jiggling the coins in my wallet. I reached for the whole thing, pulling it by the straps to the passenger's seat. Feeling around, I pushed my wallet to one side and a book to the other. Finding the phone, I grabbed it, taking my eyes from the road for a moment. The screen glowed. I looked back at the road.

That was when the first deer darted across my path. Instinct took over. All the times Granddad repeated, "Don't veer for a deer" worked for me that night, and I didn't swerve. I just gripped the wheel tighter and stepped my foot on the brakes. Tires squealed. I barely missed the animal.

Then the second one leapt out in front of me before my car came to a complete stop.

My whole body tensed, jolting with the hard thud at the front of the car. Gasping, I looked at my hands. Knuckles already white, I tried to open my fingers and let go of the steering wheel. Numb and shaking wildly, somehow, I was able to put the car into park.

"Don't freak out," I said to myself. "Don't panic."

Forcing myself to look out the windshield, I hoped to find that the animal had somehow gotten away. Run off into the woods or something. But she hadn't. She lay in the middle of the road, a few yards in front of my bumper.

When she moved, I jumped in my seat. Her long legs jerked, the hooves clicking against the pavement. She arched her neck every so often.

Forcing myself to breathe slowly and calm down, I stuffed my emotions deep. Years of working in the funeral home helped with that. Bending down, I grabbed my phone from the floor where it had fallen. It buzzed again. Cal's name flashed on the screen.

"Hey." I kept my voice steady.

"Ev, I want you to be careful, okay. The deer are hopping tonight," he said. "I've seen at least five already."

My eyes fixed on the writhing doe in the road. Blood trickled from her mouth.

"Are you there, Ev?"

"I hit one."

"You did? A deer?" He paused. "Are you all right?"

"Yeah." Swallowing, I kept my eyes on the doe. "She's still alive."

"You want me to come?" he asked. "I can be there in five minutes. I haven't gotten to the church yet."

"I'm on Crane Street."

"Be right there. Just stay in your car, okay? Seriously. Don't get out. And put your hazards on."

Waiting, stuck in the car, ended up being more difficult than I'd thought. No matter how I tried, I couldn't pull my eyes from the animal. Putting my hand on the water bottle in the cup holder, I tried to figure out how to hold her head and give her a few drops of relief. At a loss, I let go of the bottle.

If she'd already been dead, I would have been able to handle it. I wouldn't have struggled to know what to do. As it was, with her moving in pain, I felt guilty. Helpless.

Cal's headlights illuminated the deer even more. She'd already lost a lot of blood. One of her legs angled unnaturally. The slamming of his car door aggravated her more and she kicked from where she lay in the road. I imagined she wanted to get on her feet to run away.

My brother got to the passenger's side of my car as fast as he could.

"You really got her," he said.

"I know." My best efforts to keep myself flat and calm took all my energy. I didn't want Cal to know how upset I was. "Do you think insurance will cover the damage?"

A pang shot up through my chest. I'd betrayed her. Belittled her suffering by asking about insurance.

"You should be covered." The screen on Cal's phone glowed. "I sent a text to Randy. He'll be here in a few minutes."

Randy Shoop, the deputy sheriff of Middle Main, had grown up with us. He'd been the captain of the football team and, more than likely, dated most of the girls at our high school. Not me, though. Not that it bothered me. Not at all.

"Why did you have to call him?" I asked.

"He's got a gun."

"But why not a veterinarian or animal control?"

"Ev, they wouldn't be able to do anything for her."

We waited for Randy to come. We didn't say anything. If I talked, I'd lose it. I kept moving, though. Knowing that the animal lay, suffering, made me restless. She deserved more, and I could do nothing for her.

"Good old Randy." Cal turned in his seat when the red and blue lights of the squad car blazed across the soy bean fields on both sides of us. "I bet he's super excited to have something to tell Deirdre in the morning."

When the squad car pulled up next to us, Cal got out. "You stay in here, okay?" He held the door open. "You might want to close your eyes."

He shut the door. Pushed it closed so it wouldn't slam.

The headlights of my car shining on them, Randy and Cal shook hands. They turned their heads toward the deer. The sounds of their low voices mumbled through my window. I couldn't hear what they said.

I pushed my door open and got out onto the pavement. Randy unholstered his handgun and switched off the safety. He held it up. The hammer clicked when he pulled it down. He looked down the barrel, aiming at the doe.

"Don't," I said, stepping beside him. "Just wait a second, Randy."

He lowered the gun. "I have to."

"There's nothing else we can do? We can't help her at all?"

The deer lifted her head toward us. She'd stopped flailing. A huffing grunting sound pushed out of her nose and mouth.

"She's suffering, Ev."

I'd known Randy since kindergarten. In all those years, I'd never heard him use a gentle voice. Always rough and full of bravado. He'd been known as a macho guy. After all, he was the first kid in our class to grow a mustache.

That night, though, he used a softer voice.

"I've got to put her out of her misery," he said. "As soon as I can. It's cruel to make her wait."

Stepping backward, I covered my ears and waited for him to shoot.

He raised the gun again, and the deer lowered her head to the pavement. Her long lashes flicked down, covering her large eyes. She huffed once more, heavy air out of her lungs. Her last moment.

I felt the gunshot before I realized I'd heard it. Gasping, I tried to regain the breath the concussion had sucked out of me.

"Okay, Ev?" Cal's words sounded as though they traveled through water.

I didn't answer him.

"What are we going to do with her now?" So still. So quiet. I hated to stir the night air with my voice. "We have to do something."

"We'll put it on the shoulder." Randy holstered his handgun. "I'll call somebody to come pick it up first thing in the morning."

He made his way to the deer. His hands under her, the head moved, loose and free. The mess under her turned my stomach. Somehow it was different than what I saw every day.

"Cal, buddy, you mind giving me a little hand over here?" Randy tugged on the doe.

The two of them hefted the body, leaving her on the gravel shoulder of the road. Exposed and vulnerable. It bothered me that she'd be out in the open overnight.

"I'll call a wrecker for your vehicle, Evelyn," Randy said. "I don't know that you'd be able to drive very far with that punctured radiator."

Green oozed from under my car. It crept close to the red that had bled out from under the doe. So much mess.

"Old Jay Bunker's boy can come get it. He'll like the business. Unless you wanted me to call somebody else?" Randy rubbed his soiled hands against each other. He lowered his head to look into my eyes. I nodded. "I bet Cal can get you home. I'll just wait here for the wrecker."

Cal held the door open for me. Red stained his white shirt. It streaked all the way across his chest and arms. He'd wiped his hands in the grass, but still, the blood dried on his skin.

"I hate leaving her like that," I said before getting into the car.

"Me too." He turned over the ignition. "But there wasn't anything else we could do."

"It doesn't make me hate it any less."

"I know, Ev." He closed the door.

Cal kept his eyes open extra wide all the way to my apartment. He drove slowly. More for my sake than anything.

Chapter Eight

OLGA

Most mornings, I beat the sun getting up. That lazy bum had nothing on me. Before it got itself up in the sky, I'd already read my Bible, had a cup of coffee, and made breakfast for my Clive.

That habit started years before. If I hadn't gotten up and scrambled a couple dozen eggs and toasted a few loaves of bread before Aunt Gertie's boys got up, they'd tear the kitchen apart looking for food. A pack of feral bobcats, that's what they were. And I'd have been the one to miss school, putting everything back together. Even with more than fifty years between me and that farm, I still got antsy if I slept past sunrise.

That morning, a Saturday, with a cup of coffee close at hand, I spent a quiet moment or two at my dinette. Done with my reading for the day, I closed my Bible, pushing it across the tabletop. I prayed with my eyes open. I didn't figure God minded too much. If I let my eyes shut for too long, I'd start snoozing. Not that God would have been angry about that, either.

Most of my younger years, I took to my knees when I prayed. Aunt Gertie would have called that "storming the gates of heaven." I never understood what she meant by that. It seemed a little too forceful for me. I preferred to, with prayer and petition, make my request known to God.

That morning, in the dim of my kitchen, my request was for

Gretchen. As it had been so many mornings from the time I felt her in my belly. The way she hurt, though, the day before had made me more than a little uneasy. It made my mama's heart throb with anxiety. When Jesus told us not to worry, He talked about food and clothes. He didn't give us much idea about how not to worry about our children.

I said what I needed to. Asked God for health and protection and joy. Maybe even a little peace thrown in, too, for good measure. My prayers never lasted long. No babbling like the pagans for me. I didn't think God cared for big, curvy words that I didn't know the meaning of. He wanted my heart. I tried my very hardest to let Him have it.

After I said, "in Jesus's name, Amen," I got myself another cup of coffee. Oh, how the Father of Lights spoiled His children with such pleasures. Even if it was only decaf. I still praised Him for the gift in my mug.

"Morning, darling," Clive said, walking from our bedroom.

"You're up early." I tried to hide the little jump of surprise I'd done when I heard his voice. "I haven't even got your breakfast made yet."

"I don't have time for much more than a piece of toast and cup of joe." He kissed the top of my head. "We've got Mrs. Allen's funeral this morning. I need to get to the church."

"Let me get that toast for you, then." I busied my hands, dropping slices of bread into the toaster. "You want me to put a little cinnamon and sugar on that?"

"You know how to love me, don't you?" He cocked one side of his mouth into a smile that charmed me right down to my toes. "How about tonight I take you out for a date? Maybe dinner some place that doesn't have a buffet."

"Oh, Clive."

"Unless you have other plans."

"That would be a real treat." Giddy bubbles swelled in my heart. "You sure are good to me."

"That's a promise I made fifty-two years ago." His lips warmed my forehead with sweet comfort. "Besides, I like having you to show off. You're good on my old eyes."

The browned bread popped up from the toaster. Buttered and sugared and put on a paper plate, I got him his breakfast.

"Thank you." He gave my cheek a kiss before making his way down the stairs.

I tagged one more thing on to the prayer. A rejoicing in the Lord for the good man He'd given me.

Worth more than a billion cups of coffee.

The first-in-the-morning sun started its trip up the sky. Something about that wee time of the day called me into creation. Inhaling the brand new morning air, letting it fill me with sweet aromas of grass and flowers and what had to have been mercy from God Himself. Another day and another breath sure seemed that way to me.

"You're good to us," I said right out loud into the air. Not one person around to hear it. Just Him.

Sometimes those simple prayers, the ones said while getting my shoes wet with dew, got caught up in my throat. Those prayers made me a better woman.

I walked all the way around the garden once. Checking on the flowers, wishing them a happy day. When I reached the far side of the plot, I saw Gretchen sitting on her porch swing. I watched her for a minute or two. She pushed a bit of her red hair behind one ear. The squeak of her swing echoed off the trees.

I got found out. She saw me and waved.

"Come on over, Mom," she half yelled.

I didn't make her ask twice.

"Good morning, honey," I said, making my way to her porch. "You feeling better today?"

"A little." She moved over a bit to make room for me next to her. "Isn't it a beautiful morning?"

"I was just about to say the same thing." Climbing the steps, I was thankful for the railing Donald had put in a few months before. "You hungry?"

"I'm fine, Mom." She breathed in deep. "I just want to enjoy this for a few minutes."

"Sounds like a nice idea." Sitting so close to her and relishing a little bit of beauty made my heart beat with thanksgiving.

We sat on the porch swing for goodness knew how long. Quieting our mouths so we could hear the chirp of birds and chatter of squirrels. Every so often, a little wisp of breeze tickled our faces. The clouds, so full and round, made shapes across the blue of sky.

After a while, Gretchen touched my knee. "I could use a cup of tea," she said. "I have some raspberry, if you'd like to try it."

"That sounds good." Really, though, I could have sat on that porch swing another couple hours with her.

We sat on the couch, mugs of steaming tea in our hands. Oh, did the raspberry delight my tastebuds. Nothing spoke summertime into my soul like the taste of berries.

"Char starts her new job with Deirdre next week," Gretchen said. "She's excited, isn't she?"

"I think she is. It's a good opportunity." Her eyes glimmered at me from over the top of her mug. "She'll need to go in strong. I don't want Deirdre to stomp all over her."

"Oh, I think Charlotte'll be just fine."

"You're right." Gretchen's contented smile made little wrinkles right above her cheekbones. I never would have thought wrinkles could be so lovely.

Motion out the big picture window caught my eye. I looked through the glass to see Rosetta and Bev making their way up the porch steps. I pointed and Gretchen watched, too.

Rosetta carried a baking dish. No doubt, something rich and full of butter and soft for us to share. My stomach rumbled, reminding me that I'd skipped breakfast.

"Knock, knock," Rosetta called in through the screen door.

"Oh, for goodness sake," Bev grumbled. "They already seen us coming. Just go in."

"Beverly, where are your manners?" Rosetta's voice scolded. "You can't walk into someone's home without knocking first."

"You stormed into my apartment the other day." Bev's voice rumbled.

"Well, you didn't come to dinner. I thought you were dead."

"I wasn't dead, for Pete's sake."

"I know that now, don't I?" Rosetta giggled.

Gretchen and I shared a smile. My best friends sure made me laugh.

"Come on in," Gretchen called, standing.

"I told you," Bev said.

They walked in, the warmth of cinnamon wafting in with them.

"How nice of you both to stop over." Gretchen wrapped her arms around Bev and then Rosie. "You just made my morning."

"Rosetta made coffee cake." Bev crossed her arms. "I've had to smell it all the way over here."

"It's only a five-minute drive." Rosetta lowered the baking dish onto Gretchen's table. "And I'm the one who had to smell it baking."

"Well, I'm sure it's delicious." Gretchen went into the kitchen for plates and forks. "Should I brew some coffee?"

"What's a coffee cake without coffee?" Bev asked.

"A sad coffee cake, I guess." Gretchen handed the dishes to me before setting up the coffee maker. "Mom, can you do me a favor and grab the creamer out of the fridge door?"

After all the fuss over making coffee and setting the table, the four of us sat down.

"How about we ask a blessing?" Rosetta asked, putting her hands on the table.

"How's about we skip it." Bev picked up her fork. "You don't think God can bless this mess without us asking Him every couple of hours? I'd be downright irritated if people kept coming to me, asking me to do things for them all the time. I'd set a once a day limit, if I were Him."

"Well, Beverly, we can all be glad that you are not." Rosie folded her hands. "But I'm still going to give Him some thanks. You don't have to if you don't want to."

"Nothing like sending me packing on a guilt trip."

Rosetta clenched her eyes. "Thank You, Jesus." She opened them again. "That work for you?"

Bev humphed as she sunk her fork into the coffee cake on her plate.

"This is good, Rosie," I said around a mouthful. "You sure know how to bake, honey. You'll have to get me the recipe, if you don't mind."

"I'd love to." Rosetta nodded.

Footsteps thudded from upstairs. I watched the stairs to see Donald coming down to the main floor. He must not have heard the bickering and chuckling. I knew because he only had on his boxer shorts. Other than that, he was just the way the Lord knit him together.

"Gretchen," I whispered, pointing my head in Donald's direction.

She slapped a hand over her mouth, silent laughter shaking her body and giggle tears filling her eyes. She watched him walk right past us and into the kitchen. Bev's eyes grew even bulgier in her head than usual and Rosetta blushed, covering her face.

"Who is that?" Bev hollered.

Donald jumped, holding an empty mug in one hand. Good thing he hadn't filled it with hot coffee yet. He would have singed his bare belly.

"Gretchen?" He didn't turn around. "I didn't realize we had guests."

"Who is the naked man in your kitchen?" Bev yelled, picking up her fork and shoving more coffee cake in her mouth. She didn't take her eyes off Donald for a second.

"He's not naked," I said. "He's got his knickers on."

"Don't you think I'd know a naked man when I'm looking right at him?"

I couldn't see Donald's face, but I was darn sure his cheeks were red. Seemed when that man got embarrassed, he blushed all over.

Gretchen slipped over to the living room and snatched a nice, long afghan from the couch. She wrapped it around Donald's waist like a sarong.

"Sorry, babe," he said. "I smelled the coffee and came down as I was."

"Oh, you provided a good bit of entertainment for our little breakfast party." She gave his thick, bare arm a tiny kiss.

"Would you like a piece of coffee cake?" Rosetta offered, eyes still covered. "Forgive me for not serving it. My hands are busy with more pressing work."

"Let me get back upstairs first." My son-in-law held on to that blanket like it kept him connected to the world and rushed up the stairs. Quicker than a jackrabbit.

Gretchen returned to her seat, hand on her stomach. She breathed out, making her mouth a circle.

"What's wrong, Gretchie?" I asked. "Is it the stomach again?"

"Laughing hurts." She shook her head. "This bug just isn't letting go."

"Did you make an appointment?"

"First thing, Monday." Her breath wheezed going in. "I'll probably be past it by then."

"I sure hope so."

That old pest called worry buzzed around in my head and in my heart. My intuition screamed. Just enough to make me batty.

Chapter Nine

Evelyn

Cal picked me up the morning after the deer accident. Fortunately, I'd gotten the crying to stop early enough in the night so my eyes didn't swell too much. And good makeup covered over the rest. I didn't want my brother to know how hard I'd cried over an animal.

"I saw your car at the body shop," he said when I got into the passenger's side. "It's really bad."

"Is it totaled?" I buckled my belt.

"Probably not. But it's messy."

"Gross."

"So, speaking of deer guts, are you hungry?" He snickered, pulling away from my apartment building.

"That was bad, Cal. But I guess I could eat."

"Let's stop for doughnuts." I hated the way he twitched his eyebrows at me.

"No way. The bakery's always packed on Saturdays." The clock on his dashboard had to have been at least an hour behind. I checked my phone. "It's not worth it. We'd be late. We'll be cutting it close as it is."

"I can't believe you would speak such heresy. Of course it's worth it."

"Then you go in this time."

"See, here's the thing. I don't have any money."

"So, really, you just want me to buy you a doughnut. Right?"

"Or two." He stopped at the intersection. "At least two."

"How are you not a thousand pounds?" The fabric of my black jacket stretched to cover my tummy. "Fine. I'll get the doughnuts. But if Deirdre starts in on her talking, I'm walking right out."

"Just make sure you get the doughnuts first."

Not only the owner of the bakery, Deirdre Sanchez also held the long undisputed title of Town Busybody. A stealthy, vicious one, at that. She possessed the ability to take something as small as a disagreement between friends and work to manipulate it into a full-on family feud. More than a few relationships busted up because of her. With a reputation like hers, I wondered how anybody could believe a single word that spewed from her mouth.

Somehow, she got the whole town hooked on her cakes and cookies. She'd lull them with sugar before filling their heads with all the nasty gossip she could come up with.

"Don't worry, Ev," Cal said. "She'll be way too busy to talk to you."

He pulled up to the curb, happy to actually find a parking spot. The bakery, positioned between the police station and the beauty salon, ended up being the perfect place for Deirdre's snooping ways. We used to joke that she had peepholes on either side to get all the news. As an adult, I didn't think it was too far from the truth.

"You're coming in with me, at least, aren't you?" Pushing my door open, I put my foot on the pavement.

"Well, see, I have to go into the Beauty Hut for a few minutes." He rolled his head on the back of the seat. "I'm out of hair gel."

"I thought you didn't have money."

"Just enough for some product. For my hair."

"You are something else." I narrowed my eyes, glaring at him.

"So, I'd like a couple jelly-filled doughnuts." Checking himself in the rearview mirror, he straightened his tie. "Not lemon, though. That tastes like disinfectant."

"How do you know what disinfectant tastes like?" Then, on second thought. "Never mind. I don't want to know."

Cal had been right. People packed into the bakery. Every seat had an occupant, shoving doughnuts or cinnamon rolls into their mouths. I saw them through the blue gingham curtained windows.

When I opened the door, I couldn't even hear the buzzer overhead. The pastry eating crowd muffled all sound with their munching.

Even with the crowd, even with the noise, I'd been spotted as soon as I stepped inside.

"Don't move, Evelyn," Deirdre called over the chaos. "I got to get me a hug."

Before I could consider a getaway, Deirdre had her doughy arms wrapped around me. That was when I knew. Cal's stupid doughnuts wouldn't be in my hands until the gossip monster's appetite had been quenched. She wanted a scoop of something juicy. She had absolutely no other reason to hug me.

"How are you doing?" Head tilting to the right, eyebrows raised in fake concern, she looked into my eyes. "How's the family holding up?"

One of her tricks. Pretending to know some deep, unspoken hurt in order to draw out something she could pass around town.

"We're good." I took a step away from her. "Cal just wanted some doughnuts."

"Oh, is he here?" She glanced around the room.

"No. He had to pick up something from the Beauty Hut."

"I see." Her arms crossed, bunching up her apron that matched the curtains. "He's still trying to get a date with Grace."

"Who's Grace?" I bit on the bait. Doggone it.

"He hasn't talked to you about Grace? Goodness, he's in here most every day telling me how it's going with her." She sunk the barbs in deep. "Grace is the new girl over at the Beauty Hut. And Cal is just beside himself over her."

"Well, I'm sure he's mentioned her. We've been busy." Unhooking myself from her line, I tried to act disinterested. "So, I'm just going to get the doughnuts real quick."

"Oh, Cal and his food. He sure can pack it away, can't he?" She shook her head but didn't budge from her spot. "I always make sure to have a couple extra raspberry on hand. You know, his favorite. Or maybe you didn't know that about him either."

"No. I knew that one." Keeping my face blank, I tried to ignore her lure.

"How he stays so thin, I'll never know. Do you think he could have gotten a tapeworm or something? From one of the bodies?"

"No. That couldn't happen," I answered. But, secretly, I wondered.

She pulled me toward the bakery case at the back of the dining room. Her clammy hand on my elbow, the moisture seeped through my sleeve. As we walked, she put her mouth close to my ear. Her breath hit me with the smell of sage and garlic.

"You know, I'm worried to death about something right now, Evelyn." She stopped us right at the counter. "I've been wanting to talk to you about it for a couple days now."

"Today might not be good." I pulled money from my wallet. "How much are the doughnuts?"

"Are you in a hurry?" She crossed her arms again.

"Yes. A little."

"Mrs. Allen's funeral today? You've got time." When she cleared her throat, she pursed her lips together. "I made a cake for the luncheon, you know."

Keeping her arms crossed and her lips smushed together, she made her way around to the opposite side of the counter. Leaning forward, her round elbows rested on the glass top of the display case.

"You know we're getting a new pastor over at First Church." She squinted, lifting one eyebrow. "He's going to work under Old Buster."

"I heard about that already." I tapped my fingernail against the counter. "How about I add a glazed doughnut to Cal's jelly-filled."

"He's single." She nodded, smiling with all her corn colored teeth.

"That's nice." I looked over her shoulder at the doughnuts. "And a chocolate cake one."

"He's probably divorced, you know." She licked her lips and nodded. "That's what I heard, at least. Why Old Buster would put up with that is beyond me."

"Well, I don't know anything about that. Add a couple powdered ones, too." I pointed at the case. "I don't know that it's any of my business, you know. The new minister's marital status."

"Really? You don't?"

"No. It's not like I know him."

Straightening, she thrust a hand onto her hip. "Really. I could have sworn you went on a date with the man."

"Deirdre, I have no idea what you're talking about."

"I even seen you with him." Turning, she used a small piece of waxed paper to pick out the doughnuts and place them in a box. "I hope you don't mind, I gotta use this cake box. I'm out of the paper ones."

"I don't care what they're in." I fidgeted with my wallet. "Listen, if you're talking about Will, I have no idea what he does."

"I'm telling you," she said, her back still to me. "He's a pastor."

"Okay, fine."

"Are you telling me that you didn't know that?" Deirdre snapped the clear, plastic top onto the box.

"We didn't talk about our jobs."

"So, he didn't know what you do?" She lifted a hand to touch her lips.

"It didn't come up in conversation."

"Oops." Her lips curled down in a fake frown. "Sorry."

"You told him. Didn't you." A flash of anger burned inside my chest. "Of course you did. You can't keep anything to yourself."

"I thought he knew. I swear I did." Her eyes twinkled. She loved the drama. "And I guess I thought it was common knowledge. I mean, everybody knows what you do."

"How much for the doughnuts?"

"Five dollars, thirty-four cents." She took the cash from me. "What? Are you afraid your job is going to scare him off?"

"Keep the change." When I pulled the box across the counter toward myself, the lid popped open. I held it closed with my hands.

"You know, if he can't handle your job, maybe I saved you a lot of time." She dropped my bill into the cash register. "And some heartache, too. All that death all the time. You've got to understand how hard that is for some people."

Then she smirked all the way from her lips to her eyes.

"What?" I could tell she had something else on her mind.

"Some people are just meant to be alone, Evelyn."

"Really, Deirdre, you need to mind your own business."

She handed me the receipt. "I'm not trying to make anything my business. I'm just worried about you."

"Yup. Thanks so much. But you can stop talking about me to other people." I turned fast, the doughnut box in my hand, the lid shifting again.

"You sure you don't want your change?" she called after me.

I turned my head. "No."

Before looking back in the direction I was going, I fell into a table I would have sworn hadn't been there minutes before. My box landed right on top of some kid's doughnut, sending powdered sugar puffing into the air. He screamed and gave me a dirty look. In my effort to pick up the doughnuts, freeing his flattened pastry, the top of my box tumbled off and, somehow, I fell right into the contents. Glaze and sugar and raspberry jelly smeared across my white shirt.

The kid stopped with his dirty look and started in with the most enraging laugh I'd ever heard.

Leaving the box, what remained of it, at least, I rushed out the door. That time, I did hear the buzzer when the door opened. The buzzer and the kid's laugh were the only sounds in the whole bakery.

Walking down the sidewalk, or more like stomping, I just about rammed into Cal as he stepped out of The Beauty Hut, his arms loaded with hair products.

"You stink," I barked at him.

"No, I smell like hair spray," he answered, looking at my shirt. "Are you wearing my doughnuts?"

The way his mouth fell open, I knew he had a laugh about to erupt.

"Don't you dare." I stuck my finger in his face. "I will hurt you."

"It might be worth it." Pushing the button on his key, he popped the trunk of his car. "Did you start a food fight in there or something?"

"We will never talk about this again."

"Can we talk about it now, though?" He leaned an elbow on his car. "Just for a second?"

"No." I slammed his trunk before walking around to my side and getting in. "I need to change my clothes."

"What are you talking about?" Cal asked, sliding into his seat. "You look great. Absolutely delicious, one might say."

"As if I didn't feel like enough of a freak in this town." I rolled my eyes. "I've got to move far away from here."

"Oh, come on. You aren't going to move."

When I didn't say anything, he turned toward me. "Ev, you aren't moving. Right?"

"Well, sometimes I think it would be a good idea."

"Why? Because Deirdre upset you?" He pulled away from the curb. "That's no reason to abandon your family."

"I mean, how would she feel if I denigrated her profession to the entire town?"

"Whoa, too many big words."

"What if I ripped on her job to everybody?"

"The woman supplies the town with baked goods, Ev." Cal pushed his finger into a smear of jelly that had made its way to my shoulder. "Nobody's going to believe a cross word about that."

"Where would they be without us, Cal?" I swatted his hand. "We do for them what they could never do for themselves. They'd be completely lost without us, you know. And they all think we're creepy weirdos."

"I wonder if they also think we're weird creeps?" He cleared his throat. "You didn't happen to grab the doughnuts after you pulverized them?"

"I'm not going back."

"Come on, Ev."

"No way. I'm never going back there."

"Really? Not even for the guy who drove the getaway after you murdered the deer?"

"Seriously, Cal. That's not okay." I turned on the radio, waiting for an entire song to play before I let my shoulders slump. "I'm so sick of being an outsider."

"Rebel, really."

"Cal, I'm serious."

"Okay. You want me to be serious." He straightened up in his seat and pushed up his tie. "People have a hard time being around us. We know that. We've known that since we were kids. And it's because we remind them of something they'd rather not have to think about every few minutes. We remind them that, one of these days, they will die. That someone they love will die. They see us and remember that they don't have the slightest bit of control over when or who or how. They don't like having mortality shoved in their faces."

"But they need us," I mumbled. "They should be a little more accepting of us."

"Ev, this job is all about comforting them. It's not about being popular. We don't need them to understand us. They aren't going to. But we need to be there in the worst of their lives anyway." He pulled down the sun visor. "When they need us, they're desperate. And we're the only ones who can help them. So, we go and do it."

He pulled into a parking spot right outside my apartment.

"Hey, Ev," he said, stopping me right before I got out. "Don't let her get to you."

"I know." I pushed a strand of hair behind my ears.

"Seriously. Besides that bakery, gossip is all she has." He scratched his chin. "I don't think she'd know what to do with herself if all the drama magically disappeared."

"I know. It still bothers me, though." I clenched my jaw. "I hate it when people talk about me."

"They wouldn't bother talking if you weren't so great."

"Thanks."

My brother clearly didn't understand the mind of women, but I decided to take his kind words anyway.

"Are you really thinking about leaving?" he asked.

"I don't know." I looked at my shoes. Powdered sugar speckled the black leather. "Probably not. Everyone I have is here."

"It would be nice to have a little break from death." His mouth made a half smile. "We need a puppy."

I hadn't wanted to laugh at him. Or at anything, for that matter. But I couldn't help myself.

"Hey, can I ask you a question?" I was surprised by how my emotions surged. The idea that Deirdre knew something about my brother that I didn't upset me more than I would have thought. "Why did you really want to go into The Beauty Hut?"

"Her name is Grace." He sighed. "And she's awesome."

"Did you ask her out?"

"Yeah." He smiled. "She shot me down in the nicest possible way."

"Sorry about that."

"No problem." He scratched a spot on his neck right under the stiff, white collar. "I'm just going to show up tomorrow with some flowers."

My brother was becoming more like Granddad all the time.

It made me lonely to think that only a handful of men like them existed. I worried that I'd never find one of them for me.

Chapter Ten

Olga

I didn't get too many chances to wear a nice dress. In fact, I only had a couple to choose from that weren't sensible or black. For a date with Clive, I thought my red one best. Too fancy for everyday and far too sassy for Sunday morning, let alone a funeral. I had that dress reserved for special occasions. I even put a bright shade on my lips for added ritz.

Old age had settled in and took up housekeeping, but that didn't mean I couldn't get dolled up for my love.

When Clive got his peepers on me, his jaw hung low before his mouth pulled back up in a smile. I didn't mind that one bit. To play it up, I took a twirl, letting the red fabric fan out around my legs.

"My, my," he said, gliding his way toward me. His hands on my hips, he led me in a swaying back and forth dance. "If we didn't already have reservations, I'd say we should stay in for the night."

"I suppose I'd better wear this dress more often." I smoothed his collar. "Just so long as it gets me out of cooking dinner."

"If you wore it every day, my dear, I'd hire a cook." He checked his watch. "Oh. I could stay like this with you all night. But we'd better scoot. We've got just enough time to get there."

He took my hand in his and led me to the stairs. I knew that hand as well as my own. Knew the calloused spots on his palm and the way his thumb rubbed the tender inside of my wrist. But I still got a shiver of delight from our skin touching.

He escorted me all the way to our car and opened the door for me. "My love," he said.

"You still haven't told me where you're taking me."

"Someplace nice." His kiss on my lips warmed me all the way through. "You'll find out soon enough."

Sitting in my seat with the belt strapping me in, I watched Clive trot around the front of the car. I hadn't seen him so bouncy in years.

"You're downright giddy, Clive," I said once he got into his seat.

"Honey, the way you look, I can hardly help myself."

The little bit of youth left over in my heart jumped up and down to hear my husband say such things.

We rode along, the warmth of the day softening as the evening sun inched down. We drove past houses and fields we'd known our whole lives. Still, in that familiar place, the beauty hadn't grown plain to me. Instead, I carried all those sights and smells in my soul as gifts from the Almighty. Precious and interwoven into my very being.

Clive reached over and patted my hand. His flesh on my flesh. Our flesh together that so long ago had become one.

One flesh, riding with the sun glowing and the smell of someone burning brush. Not needing to make a single sound, but knowing when to meet eyes for the smallest and sweetest of moments. One flesh, letting the windows stay rolled down because his scalp was bare and my hair didn't mind the whipping wind.

Romance meant riding in our old, reliable, never-once-broke-down Buick along a fresh grated country road. Realizing that, even after fifty-two years of marriage, we still worked together at figuring out what being in love meant.

Clive parked the Buick. Oh, but did that man pick my very favorite place a few towns over? He certainly had. The kind of restaurant made out of an old railway car. I wouldn't even have to look at the menu. My mouth started watering for the salmon as soon as we pulled in.

Once we got ourselves inside and seated at a table, I locked eyes with Clive. Those baby blues of his made my heart pitter pat. I hardly even noticed the way he fumbled with his cloth napkin and took extra sips of water. But from those little cues, I figured he had something on his mind. He acted just the way he had the night he asked me to be his bride.

"Honey," I said. "What is the matter?"

He stilled his fidgeting. Then the man smiled so big, I saw the gold crowns on his back teeth.

"Well, Olga, I wanted to talk to you about something." He waited once the waitress came to get our orders. When she stepped away, he looked back at me, nervous as all get-out. "You know we're getting older."

"I noticed."

"Seems like life hasn't worked out the way we thought it would." He took a sip from his water glass. "In fact, nothing turned out the way we planned it."

"I'd venture to say it all ended up far better than we'd expected."

"I'd have to agree with you on that." He reached into his jacket pocket. "Remember how we wanted to see parts of the world so far away, we'd have to ride an airplane to get there?"

"Oh, that silly dream." Sighing, I tilted my head to the side. "Such young dreamers."

"I never thought that it was so silly."

"What are you getting at, Clive?"

"I'm thinking it's about time for me to retire."

"Truly?" My heartbeat thudded in my ears.

"Now, I don't know when. But I know it's getting harder for me to do the work these days."

My fingertips reached up to hold the scream of excitement that about burst out from my lips. Even a seventy-two-year-old woman had the giddies bubble inside sometimes.

"I guess I wanted to ask you a few questions. First, are you ready for me to be around all the time, taking up space?"

"It's the best thing I can imagine," I answered.

"Good." He pushed himself up from his seat and walked around to my seat. Getting down on one knee, he turned his eyes to my face. "Next, I'd like to know if you would be ever so kind enough to join me next year in Hawaii for the honeymoon you never got?"

In his hand lay a white, fuzzy box. A gold ring with a milky, flat stone caught my eye. My poor heart skipped at least two beats, and I thought I'd never be able to catch my breath.

"Of course," I whispered. "Yes."

He pulled the ring from its box and slipped it right onto my finger. "That's mother of pearl. Charlotte helped me order it from a little place in Hawaii. Maybe we can even find the shop when we're there. Get you a pair of earrings to match it."

The ring fit just right.

"It's so pretty."

"You make it even prettier." He winked at me. "Now, I got to figure out if I can get up off this floor. Last time I was on one knee I didn't seem to have such a problem."

Using the table, he pushed himself up. Thank goodness it held sturdy and Clive didn't get himself stuck on that floor. But, really, I wasn't paying him all that much mind. The mother of pearl ring had my attention.

"Well, honey." He settled into his chair. "What do you think?"

I sipped on my peppermint iced tea. "Retirement is a big word, Clive. A big, heavy word."

"Don't I know it." He blew out a puff of relief. "I've been carrying it around all by myself for the last few weeks."

"Why did you wait so long to tell me?"

"I had the darnedest time getting a reservation. And every time I had one on the books, I'd get a call for a funeral."

And if that didn't put into one sentence our entire marriage, I wouldn't know what did.

We turned our words to dreams of Hawaii. Waterfalls and luaus. Fresh blue water and flowers of every color in my imagination and beyond. We talked of putting our little tootsies in the ocean and drinking straight out of a coconut. Even seeing a palm tree would seem a miracle.

Our food arrived, steaming and smelling like a piece of paradise come all the way to our corner of Michigan. The way it tasted proved that, indeed, it had.

"Where will we live?" The question popped up, so suddenly to my mind, I let it tumble from my lips.

"What do you mean, honey?" Clive sawed a knife into his steak. "You want to try a bite of this?"

"I'll trade you for a taste of salmon." So tender, the pink fish flaked apart when I touched it. "I mean, after you retire. Will we move?"

"I haven't gotten that far in my planning." He pushed a generous portion of beef off his fork and onto my plate. "Do you think we should?"

"I don't know that we could stay in our apartment and have you keep your handsome paws out of the business." My fork scraped under a mound of rice. "I'd have a hard time being away from Gretchen, though."

A wave of anxiety rippled through my heart. What would we do about her? It wouldn't feel right to move even a mile away from her.

"We never meant to live in that apartment so long, did we?" A piece of garnish fell off his plate as he worked at his steak. "I wanted more for you. And for Gretchen."

"Oh, Clive. You know all I've ever wanted was to be a family alongside you. And God blessed that." The wet roll of a tear inched down my cheek. "I never cared where we spent our life. Just so long as we got to do it together. And the apartment worked just right."

His eyes got good and watery.

"Honey," I said. "You've made a good life for us."

Returning to fill our iced teas, the waitress asked if we didn't think we'd like to save room for dessert.

Of course we would.

She left us to finish our last bites of supper before bringing out plates of fancy torte cakes with hoity-toity names. My mouth didn't much care what they were called. I just enjoyed the rich sweetness of chocolate and cream.

We finished up. Clive paid the bill. Together, we walked out into the cooled off evening. We got into the Buick for a bit of a drive.

My thumb rubbed against the smooth shell of my new ring. After so long, one conversation over steak and salmon had changed a whole lot of my life. Retirement. Moving. Having more of Clive to myself. Most of my life had stayed the same for years. Even down to the way I arranged the furniture. The very idea of change flipped my stomach upside-down.

But, glancing over at Clive, I remembered the sweet wealth of all that would stay the same.

Chapter Eleven

EVELYN

Two churches shared an intersection in our little town. Really, it was the only intersection we had. Blinking yellow light and all.

Middle Main Bible Church and First Christian Church of Middle Main stood across from each other on a narrow, two lane road. Ironically, First Church came second. More accurately, it split from the Bible Church with a defection led by none other than Old Buster. According to Gran, it all caused quite the stir back in the nineteen-sixties. And all before Deirdre's reign as village gossip.

I wondered how news spread back in those days.

My family attended First Church. More out of obligation than anything. But I usually skipped out. The last thing I needed was to hear Old Buster's voice even more than I already did.

But that Sunday I showed up, Charlotte alongside me. I had to see for myself whether or not Will had been hired. And find out if he was really divorced.

Besides, I wanted to see him again.

Apparently the rest of Middle Main wanted to catch an eye-full of him, too. Char and I couldn't find an empty pew when we arrived.

Shoulder to shoulder, people filled the sanctuary. No doubt they felt thankful for the air conditioning that had been installed the year before.

"Great," I whispered to her. "No seats."

We'd have to stand in the narthex, looking in through the glass wall and listening to the service through an old speaker hanging from the ceiling.

"Sorry," she whispered back. "I tried to hurry."

"It's all right."

Really, I'd just wanted to get a seat where I could see Will. Maybe be seen by him. I'd even worn a skirt. And shaved my legs. Just in case I got the chance to talk to him.

One of the ushers frowned at us. I stuffed down the desire to frown back.

"Your hair looks fine, Char." I turned from the grumpy man. "Stop touching it."

The service began. The congregation stood for the praise time. A middle-aged man wearing socks and sandals stood on the stage, guitar slung across his torso. His voice shook into the microphone with overdone vibrato as he sang tired, repetitive, fluffy songs. Old Buster took great pride in what he called the "contemporary worship" at First Church.

Standing next to me, Char sang along, her voice bouncing back to us from the glass wall. Such a clear tone, she didn't need to show off. I, on the other hand, chose to mouth the words for a very specific reason.

"You all go ahead and have a seat for a minute," the guitar man said after finishing the last song. "Zeke Filler has our communion meditation."

Sitting, the congregation turned their eyes to the man who moved with solemnity to the stage. His hair had been slicked to one side and his face held the expression of a man delivering a eulogy. He wore what could only be described as a leisure suit. The burnt orange polyester made the royal blue ascot really stand out.

"I'm so impressed," I whispered to Charlotte. "How does something like that survive after forty years?"

"Polyester is the cockroach of fabric," Charlotte answered. She had to turn around to laugh.

Guitar man spread his arms, offering a hug to old Zeke. He looked guitar man up and down before turning his back to him and taking the microphone in his hand.

He spoke about the dangers of consuming communion in an unworthy manner. That to do so would make one guilty of the blood of Christ. From the severe look in his eyes, I figured he meant it. Making fun of a man's ancient suit qualified as unworthy, I guessed. The frowning usher didn't bring the communion trays to us anyway.

Next, the wicker baskets passed around from pew to pew, collecting cash and checks. A woman made her way to the microphone. She wore a bright yellow dress and red shoes. Grabbing the microphone, she nodded at the guy in the sound booth.

"God is good all the time," she said over the music, her voice smooth and sticky sweet. "All the time, God is good."

As if watching something ascend into the air, she moved her gaze to the ceiling. Opening her mouth, she pulled in a deep breath that seemed to fill her up down to her toes.

And then she sang.

When I was a kid, Gran had talked about how God didn't choose to grace everyone with beautiful singing voices. She said that, when those people sang, it truly was a noise with joy tossed in. And that, to God, it was a beautiful sound.

The woman on the stage sure did make a noise. Though I wasn't sure she'd remembered to include the joy. She clung to the microphone so tightly, I wondered how it didn't short out. As the song went on, the noise from her vocal cords turned shrill and loud. Flaring nostrils grew wider and wider as she approached the end note. Eyebrows raised up so far into her forehead, they almost became bangs. At the high note, she got a strangle hold on the microphone. Mouth opened wide and lips pulled up, she screamed a fierce war cry I was sure had gotten half the dogs in town barking.

Before the accompaniment had a chance to stop, she'd clipped the microphone back onto the stand and rushed off the stage to her seat in the front row, keeping her gaze down.

Old Buster stood from his seat behind the pulpit. I hadn't noticed before how stooped over he'd gotten. And how tired his face looked. I almost felt sorry for him. Taking his place center stage, he lifted a hand in greeting. Smoothing the lapels of his suit jacket, the American flag pin he wore caught a glint of light. He moved his hands up to his head, patting down the combed over hair.

"Good morning," he boomed.

A few from the front seats echoed him. Old Buster grimaced.

"Oh, come on." Wagging a fat finger at the congregation, he scolded them. "You can do better than that. I said, 'good morning.'"

Five or six other voices echoed him that time. He turned down his mouth and closed his eyes before lifting his lips into a smile.

"I guess that's better than nothing. We'll have to keep working on that." Surveying the congregation, he lifted his greeting hand again. "Looks like we're full up this morning. I'm so glad you came. And feeling really blessed that we got to share in that special music. Wasn't it just beautiful? Like listening to the angels sing."

I wondered what kind of angels he meant. The ones who sang to the shepherds on the night of Christ's birth or the ones in the book of Revelation with eagle heads and swords of judgment.

"How about, before I get rolling on this sermon, you all get up, turn around, and say hello to somebody you don't know."

"Seriously. Does he not realize how small this town is?" I turned to Char. "We practically know each other's shoe size."

"Except for the new minister." She pointed to the front of the sanctuary.

Outstretched hands all around him, Will tried to shake as many as he could. Moving from person to person, he nodded and smiled. I could hardly see him beyond all the people. Every few seconds I caught a glimpse of his dark, wavy hair. Or a glint off his glasses. Once I even saw the dimples in his cheeks. I hadn't intended to be so eager to see him.

"Poor guy," I whispered, lifting up on my tiptoes to see over the crowd. My heart pounded despite my efforts to keep it calm.

"He looks nice." Char nudged me, almost knocking me off balance. "You should go ask him out."

"Are you kidding me? Just go up there right now and ask him out?" I rolled my eyes. "You're crazy."

"I dare you."

"I'm not doing that, Char."

"I know for a fact that Deirdre made up that thing about him being divorced."

"How do you know?"

"Because it came out of her mouth. Of course she made it up."
Grinning, she nudged me again. "If you don't go talk to him by the
end of the day, I'm going to give him your phone number."

"You'd be wasting your time," I whispered. "He already has it."

"What?" She leaned in closer to me. "Are you for real?"

I shrugged my shoulders.

"All right," Old Buster returned to his center stage spot. "Enough
of this chitchat. Let's get going on this service."

Reluctantly, the congregation returned to their seats, getting
ready for an hour-long sermon.

Will turned before sitting, looking at the faces. It seemed like he
was searching for someone. I let myself think it was me.

"Now, some of you already met this fine young man down here in
the front row. Keep on your feet, William."

Will shrugged, embarrassed, and scratched his scalp.

"That young man is William Todd. He's going to be ministering
to our youth. I'm so pleased he's here." Old Buster said a few more
words.

I didn't hear them, though. Because Will and I met eyes and he
smiled. At me. And then the air didn't come into my lungs without
effort. He raised his hand in a small wave before sitting down. A few
heads from the congregation swiveled in my direction.

Thank goodness my phone buzzed with a text message from Cal.
Otherwise, I might have stood there all day, numb and with a shaky
kind of feeling in my head.

"I've got to go," I whispered to Charlotte. "Nursing home removal.
Sorry."

"He looked at you, Ev," Char said.

"I know." I gave her a smile. "Can you get a ride home?"

She nodded.

For the first time in years, I didn't feel so much like the odd duck
in Middle Main. I didn't feel so lonely. The way Will smiled made me
want to stick around.

Chapter Twelve

OLGA

Most days, after I got the lunch dishes done up and drying in the strainer, I'd make my way into my old sitting chair to catch a quick nap. It did my aging body good. But I hadn't caught my nap in days. What with getting my hair done for my date, church on Sunday, a few busy days at the funeral home, I didn't get half a chance. By Wednesday, my comfy chair called to me.

Sitting down felt good, the chair cradling my back just right. And the way I could lift my legs up, taking the pressure off my tired ankles, oh, it did me good. The minute I drifted off, though, I heard footsteps traveling up my back stairs.

"Hi, Gran." Charlotte's singer voice rang clear into my home.

"Oh, come on in, honey." It took all my will to pull the lids up off my eyes and all the muscle I had to push my feet down and sit up straight.

"Did I wake you?" Craning her neck, she looked past the lamp on my side table to peek at me. "I can come back another time."

"No, sweetheart. You come on." I had to make a couple tries at getting up to standing. But I got on my feet after all. "Didn't you have to work today?"

"We were slow. Deirdre let me go a little early."

"You like that job, don't you?" I made my way to the kitchen. "Before you answer that, would you like a little iced tea? Or a can of pop?"

"I can get it, Gran." She stepped toward me. "Yeah. The job is going really well. I like it."

"I'm glad to hear it." I pointed at the fridge. "Help yourself to whatever's in there, honey."

"Deirdre's been nice to me so far."

Grabbing a couple of glasses from the strainer, I set them on the dinette. "You know I'm proud of you, don't you? Deirdre can be a tough cookie. No pun intended."

Jostling bottles of ketchup and mustard and jars of pickles clinked when Charlotte tugged open the refrigerator door. She pulled out the pitcher of tea.

"Well, I'm there to work. I try to ignore all the drama." She put the pitcher on the counter and reached into the freezer for ice. "She makes up most of it anyway."

"I bet she does. Maybe she should have been a writer, the way she creates stories."

"Some of the things she comes up with are pretty terrible." The tea rushed over the ice cubes, making them crackle. "Mom says it's a good dose of the real world."

"Your mama's right."

"Well, she didn't hear the girls from the dorm. I think they were worse."

Taking my glass, I walked back to my comfortable chair. "Come on over and sit with me."

Charlotte chose to sit right in a puddle of sun that flowed in through my picture window. Gleaming off her red hair, it formed a halo that circled the back of her head. She sunk right into the couch.

"I still feel badly." She worked her lips into a quick frown.

"About what, sweetie?"

"Not working in the funeral home." Slumping her shoulders, she sighed from deep down. "It's not for me. You know?"

Ever since that no-account father of hers took off, Charlotte had spent a lot of time worried about everybody else. She'd only started kindergarten when he'd gone. She'd wanted everybody to be okay. Especially her mama. That part of her hadn't grown out as she got older.

She had the nice girl part down pat. Good thing she could also

91

bare those teeth of hers when she had to. Along with the sensitivity, she had a fierce sense of loyalty.

"Charlotte, I don't think you should feel bad at all." I put my glass of tea on a coaster next to me.

"Whenever I've thought about doing that job, even just in the office, I get stressed out. I couldn't hear all the sad stories every day." Squeezing her eyes shut, a few tears gathered on her eyelashes. "I'm not strong like Cal and Ev."

"No, you aren't," I said. "But, honey, you're strong in a different way."

"I don't know, Gran. I'm too sensitive." Her green eyes glimmered more for the tears that watered them. "I feel everything too deeply. I'm weak."

"Sensitivity has nothing to do with being weak, Charlotte. You hear me?"

Below us, slow, soothing music played. A recording of some piano playing old hymns. Funeral music. Listening to those tones made my memory decide to go for a little jog.

"Back a real long time ago, I played the organ for church." I relaxed into my chair. "I'd sit behind it and move my feet over the pedals and my fingers over the keys, making music. Oh, I've loved music far longer than I've loved Granddad."

That got a little grin out of her. It made me glad.

"I could sing, but never joined the choir. Guess it scared me too much. I preferred to hide behind a giant instrument. It made me feel I was a whole world away when I played. My aunt Gertie, of course, thought it an awful waste of time. She didn't care a lick for music or art or reading. To be honest, I don't know if the woman ever learned how to read more than a recipe. That's how it was for some women in those days." The back of my head rubbed against the doily I'd laid on the chair years before. The old lacy thing fell to the floor. I certainly didn't have the energy to pick it back up. "Anyway, the preacher at the time, he had his wife give me lessons on the organ. I never had such joy as when I put notes together to play a song. It felt like power and grace and praying all at once."

"Why don't you play anymore?"

"Well, for one, take a gander at these fingers." I spread my hands on my legs. "Crooked as a drunk farmer's rows. I wouldn't be able to move these things on the keys if I wanted to."

"That's not it." She shook her head. "You wouldn't let something like that stop you."

"You know me so well, don't you?" I sighed. "Well. Let me tell you. After Granddad opened the funeral home, I'd play for the services. These days they use a recording. But, back then, I had an old electric organ. The first couple funerals bothered me a bit. Mostly because I knew everybody in town for all my life. I had to learn to keep my eyes fixed on the sheet music and not listen to the crying. Good night, the sound of crying has always gotten to me."

Muffled voices added to the gentle music from downstairs. Sounded like a good sized crowd had gathered.

"One day, we had to do a funeral for a little one. A baby. He'd just died in the middle of the night. Nobody knew what happened. He just never woke up in the morning. The mother found him." Something caught in my throat, making me cough. I sipped a little of my tea before going on. "The parents wanted to see the wee thing before the funeral. Then Granddad would close the casket before everybody else showed up. Back in those days, people didn't view the young ones. They didn't think it was appropriate. It's a hard thing to see. That's why they didn't want to look."

Charlotte's big eyes filled up with tears, and she let them tumble down her cheeks. How had she grown so mature as not to be ashamed and wipe them off or try to hide them? I wondered when I'd become so grown-up, even as an old lady.

"I was pregnant with your mama. It was still early on, but far enough that she liked to make her presence known. I kept my hands on my belly, feeling your mama moving, just like butterflies. And the other mother, she walked to the casket, hands touching her stomach, too. I imagined she remembered the fluttery bumps she had not too long before." I let my eyes shut for a moment before opening them again. I saw the way that baby looked. I'd dressed him just that morning. Such a doll. That's how I'd gotten through it. Made myself pretend he was a doll I was dressing up.

That memory stabbed at me.

"She caressed her baby's face. All over. I was afraid she'd pick him up, as if he was just in a crib, finishing up a nap. The father, though, he stood back with his arms crossed, working so hard at being strong. I can't imagine it wasn't eating him up completely. But completely."

Closing my eyes, that time, I let them stay shut longer. I saw the woman standing at the tiny box. A wooden one. No lining. No hinged top. It had been the one that would cost them the least. They couldn't afford much of anything. Clive hadn't charged them full price for a single thing. But we were young and barely making ends meet. Trying to get ready to welcome Gretchen into the world. For how little we charged them, though, we had to eat beans and rice for a full month to make up for it.

That mother, she stood over that casket, touching her baby. Touching her stomach. The sobs coming out of her settled right into the pit of me. She leaned in close to his small face, talking to him. Her quiet voice sounded like swishing air to me. I never did know what she said to the boy. Wasn't for me to know anyhow. Just for her and the baby. And God, I supposed.

Mousy hair hung in her face as she nodded at Clive, not connecting with his eyes. He stepped forward and lowered the top onto the casket. That husband of hers didn't loosen his crossed arms. Didn't so much as give his wife a tender look. He stood like a statue and watched as she melted from the smoldering grief.

Voices filled the lobby as the people came into the funeral home. They didn't stop at the doors of the chapel. We didn't have anybody extra to stand at the doors, keeping them out. They just walked right in and saw her falling to pieces. I got myself to the organ and played the notes on my sheet music, letting the strains pull out long and mournful, the way my soul felt them.

Then she screamed. The mother. I'd never heard anything like that scream before. It didn't sound like it could have come out of a human. It terrified me. I played louder and louder, trying to drown out her grief. Because I couldn't take it anymore. Because it reminded me of what could happen. That my baby could die, too.

After Gretchen came along and we brought her home, I'd wake from the nightmares drenched in sweat. Nightmares of my girl, dressed like a doll and in a cheap, wood box. I'd have to get into Gretchen's room and feel the warmth of her skin before I could calm down.

"Gran?" Charlotte's voice broke through my memory. "What happened next?"

"Oh, honey, I'm sorry." I snapped my eyes open. "I got swept away, didn't I? Well, it was too much for me to take, that funeral was. I couldn't do any more of them. Guess you got your sensitivity from me."

The music from downstairs fizzled out. So did the buzzing murmur of talking. Old Buster's voice almost shook me out of my chair. That man rattled me so.

"What's it like being his cousin?" Charlotte asked.

Now, I didn't mean to roll my eyes. They just did it all on their own.

"That good, huh?" She laughed. Oh, but it sounded like a song.

"How about we bake a pie?" I wanted to move on from the memory. Not wanting it to haunt me for the rest of the day, but knowing it most certainly would. "Now, I don't know how Deirdre puts together her crusts, but they tend to be a little on the dry side. You ought to know how to make a proper crust. My mother's recipe will be perfect."

As we mixed and rolled and formed the dough, I told her stories about Old Buster. What it was like growing up in Aunt Gertie's house with him. How he got that nickname from his tendency to bust people. Especially for busting his little brothers and me.

But, in the back of my mind, all I could hear was the screaming of that mother. And me, pounding away at the keys and stomping on the pedals of the organ, wanting to drown out the possibility of losing my child.

Chapter Thirteen

EVELYN

Charlotte pulled her car up to The Beauty Hut. It was a rare thing for us to have time, just the two of us. I needed a fresh look. I'd grown tired of the bun I wore every day for years. But I didn't trust myself enough to go alone. The last time I did that, I ended up with a black dye job and a haircut I couldn't manage.

"Okay, I think I'll just get a trim." Remembering the hair tragedy gave me cold feet.

"Come on, Ev." Charlotte looked at herself in the mirror attached to her visor.

"I'm a little nervous." I touched the long hair of my ponytail. "What if she scalps me?"

"She won't." Char turned toward me. "If you really hate it, though, we can go somewhere and get it fixed."

"Scalped can't be fixed."

"It's just hair, Ev. It'll grow back." Grabbing her purse, she found lip balm and rubbed it on. "Besides, we've got to get you all prettied up for your next date."

"He hasn't asked me for another date."

"Yet." She offered me the lip balm. "You need some?"

"No thanks."

"I think you should get some color done." She unbuckled her belt. "Oh, Cal asked me to talk him up while we're here."

"The boy needs to learn to take a hint." I touched the top of my brown hair. "She's already turned him down three times."

"Just wait till you meet her, Ev." Char opened her door. "You'll understand."

The last time I'd been inside The Beauty Hut, I was five years old. Martha, the old owner, had given me such a bad haircut, my mom never took me back. That morning, as Char and I made our way along the walk to the salon, I couldn't shake the nerves, fearing that I might leave the place with some kind of unspeakable hair disaster.

Bad hair seemed to be a theme in my life.

Char opened the door for me. I'd expected the smell of thick hairspray and moth balls. Instead, a mixture of lavender and peppermint laced the air. The old dark wood paneled walls had been painted a bright, robin's egg blue. Fresh Gerber daisies in vases sat on counters all around the small room. The only thing that had remained the same was the sign over the door.

A beautiful, blond-headed lady stood behind a chair, blow-drying Deirdre's hair. She looked over her shoulder at us.

"That's her," Charlotte whispered. "That's Grace."

"No wonder Cal won't give up," I said. "He never told me how pretty she is."

"Hi, there," Grace said, loud enough to be heard over the dryer. "Be right with you."

My sister and I sat in the waiting area. Charlotte picked up a magazine from the table and flipped through the pages.

Deirdre's husky voice caught my attention after the lulling hum of the blow-dryer turned off.

"Everybody treating you pretty good so far?" She followed Grace's reflection in the mirror. "Nobody's giving you a hassle, I hope."

"I guess everybody's been nice to me." Grace pulled strands of hair flat against Deirdre's cheeks, checking the length.

"Uh oh. I know what that means," Deirdre said. "Who's giving you grief? You tell your friend Deirdre. It won't go anywhere outside our little chat."

"Yeah right," I whispered to Charlotte.

"You know, as much as I appreciate it, I'm good." Grace grabbed a can of spray from the counter, spritzing Deirdre's hair. "Anyway, when people are nasty to somebody, it's usually because they've got some heavy stuff happening. You know what I mean? I try to remember that."

Deirdre fidgeted in her seat as Grace back-combed the crown of her hair.

"I mean, bad things aren't an excuse to be mean, you know?" She unsnapped the black cloak from Deirdre's neck and patted her shoulder. "But it helps me have a little more compassion for them, when I think of things that way."

"Well, and this town is full of people with issues." Deirdre worked her way out of the chair. "But I'll tell you, if you run into somebody you can't handle, you just come on next door and tell me about it."

"That's nice of you, Deirdre. But I don't want to bug you with my problems." Grace rubbed the side of Deirdre's arm. "I'll tell you what, though, if I've got something really nice to say about someone, I'll make sure you know."

"Cal needs to marry her," Char said from behind her magazine. "Grace, I mean. Not Deirdre."

I couldn't help but smile at my sister. Grace and I hadn't even spoken, and I already liked her. No wonder Cal couldn't get her out of his mind.

"You stop on over to the bakery any time." Deirdre handed Grace money.

"I'd like that. I will tell you that working next door to your bakery has been really nice." Grace held Deirdre's hand for a second. "You've made me feel so welcome. Thank you."

"Sure thing, Grace." Deirdre turned and saw Charlotte. She stopped, looking at her for a moment before talking. "Enjoying your day off?"

"Hi, Deirdre." Char lowered the magazine. "Your hair looks pretty."

Deirdre touched the side of her neck and batted her eyes. "Thanks," she said. Then, noticing me, she straightened her shoulders. "Evelyn."

"Hi," I said.

One of Deirdre's eyes squinted as she looked at me. I'd never looked into her face all that long before to notice that she had a scar over her left eye. I wondered how she'd gotten it. And how, being so wide and long, I'd never noticed it before. She turned her eyes from my face. I hoped she didn't realize I was staring at the scar.

"You stop over next door later." She adjusted her purse strap. "I owe you half a dozen doughnuts."

She walked out of The Beauty Hut and stood on the sidewalk for a moment, gathering the keys from her purse, just before she stepped into the bakery.

"Okay," Grace said, looking at Char and me. "Which of you ladies is first?"

"Go ahead, Ev," Char said.

Grace led me to the chair, still warm from Deirdre's behind.

"My name's Grace." She pulled the rubber band out of my ponytail, letting my hair loose. Working her fingers through it, she tossed it around gently.

"I'm Evelyn."

"Nice to meet you." She walked around the chair to face me, leaning back against the counter. "What are we doing today?"

"I'm not sure, really." Looking at my reflection, I noticed how limp my dull brown hair hung next to my face. It had been so long since it had a little bounce or shape. No wonder I felt invisible most of the time. "I guess anything would be an improvement."

"You've got a lot to work with. Your hair is really healthy."

She squinted and let her head lean to one side. Reaching toward me, she moved a few strands of hair.

"What do you do? For a job?"

"I'm a funeral director." I shrugged.

"That's cool." Her flip-flops slapped against the floor as she walked across the room. "So, I'm guessing we should stay away from the purple hair dye, right?"

"Yeah, that's probably a good idea."

"Maybe something a little lighter for you. Amp up a few of those red tones you already have."

"I have red tones?"

"Yeah." She pulled a couple of bottles from the cupboard. "Then finish up with some layers. How do you feel about a bob? Maybe give you a little swing to really frame that gorgeous smile of yours."

I couldn't remember anyone other than my mom or Gran saying

99

such nice things to me. I found myself at a loss for words.

"So, how'd you become a funeral director?" she asked, mixing the dye in a small dish. "Like, what drew you to that job?"

"Well, it's a family business."

"Wait, so, does that mean you're related to Cal?" She looked up from the dish and stopped stirring. A little pink rose in her cheeks when she said his name.

"Yeah. He's my brother."

"He's a nice guy." She walked back toward me and draped a fresh cape over me. "Now that I think of it, you look a little like him."

"I don't know what to think about that," I said, smiling.

"It's a compliment for sure." She nodded toward the waiting area. "So, Char's your sister, then, right?"

"She is."

"And I met your grandma the other day, too. She's so sweet and cute."

"I know." I pushed myself up a little taller in the chair. "You need to see her with my grandpa to get the full effect of cuteness."

"I'd like that." She put her hands on my shoulders. "You're one blessed girl to have all this family around you. I can't even imagine how nice that is."

"It definitely has its moments."

"Yeah, I'm sure it isn't perfect." She used a brush, spreading the dye on my hair. "But you have to know how fortunate you are."

She moved her gloved fingers through my hair, working the dye into the strands. The whole time I sat in that chair she asked me about my life. Not about the funeral business. I couldn't remember a conversation I'd had that didn't steer in that direction.

It felt as if a divider between me and the rest of the world crumbled a little.

Chapter Fourteen

Olga

My Gretchie ran away from me into the garden. Her tiny body bobbing up and down among the flowers, pulling the chamomile with her in those chubby fists of hers, tearing it from the ground. The field moved in dream waves, all over creation. I couldn't see her half of the time. But when I did, it was only red curls peeping out amongst the pale blooms.

She'd got herself too far from me. I didn't like not being able to reach her. I tried to grab her. My arms wouldn't extend enough. Every moment, she got farther and smaller. She'd started to shrink. Teeny and tiny and itty bitty. But the red hair grew and grew, taking over her. Almost as if it liked to swallow her up.

Turning to me, her wee little face swapped its bright smile for lips in a quivering frown. Shrill and blood chilling, her scream made my heart drop. Her voice sounded like the woman after closing the casket on her baby. But, in my dream, I had no music to cover the sound. Nothing to do but to keep hearing her scream.

And what she screamed was my name.

"Mama!"

"You're too far, honey," I whimpered, my voice holding on tight to the insides of me, not letting itself loose. "Come back this way, Gretchie. You hear me?"

The flowers had wilted, blackened into weeds and thorns. The ground dried up and cracked. Shards of jagged rock grew up from the dead soil.

Then the ground shook, shifting the dirt, carrying her farther and farther off. Her head sunk under the level of dirt every now and again. Emerging from the flood of soil, covered with rock and dirt and sand, she'd reach for me.

"Mama." Her tiny cry barely made any sound over the crashing ground.

My young woman's feet lifted up off hard earth, running to rescue her. Weaving between tall, snapping weeds. Past an old tree as it fell in the midst of the shifting land. Dodging the crashing branches, I stumbled. My hands caught the weight of my fall. A thorn bush sliced my flesh. I fought against the barbs, getting tangled in its snaky stems. Crooked, veiny hands struggled to push my old body up. I looked at my fingers. The nails had turned thick and cracked. My young body had gotten old in the shortest of moments, and I couldn't get myself up. Stuck as if in cement, I could hardly move. The more I struggled, the more I got sucked further into the thorns, watching Gretchen sink deeper and deeper until she disappeared. All that was left of her were those red curls bobbing among the weeds.

"Olga," Clive called after me from somewhere. I couldn't see him. My neck wouldn't allow my head to turn. "Olga."

Even in my dream, I knew that his voice should have shaken me into reality.

"I can't go," I tried to say, holding on to sleep. "I can't leave her."

But my mouth had got set in drying cement.

"Olga, honey." His voice sounded closer. I thought for sure I smelled his aftershave.

"If I go, I'll never get her back." The cement cracked at the corners of my mouth.

Like an earthquake, my limbs shook. Just enough to break me loose. The cement sloughed off me like scales. Standing, I couldn't see a hint of Gretchen. Even the curls had disappeared. The weeds had calmed and the flowers bloomed anew, right before my eyes. Chamomile in bunches all around me glowed from their yellow centers.

I wondered if she'd ever truly been mine at all, my Gretchen. I wondered if she'd existed or if I'd only dreamed her.

"Olga." That time, I felt Clive's warm hand as it touched my forehead, so gentle. "I need you to wake up."

The dream world faded and, thank goodness, I switched back over to the real one. But my eyes had the hardest time opening up.

"You must have had the worst nightmare," he whispered. "Are you all right?"

Lifting my eyelids, I saw the light from the living room, streaming in through the bedroom door. Clive handed me my glasses.

"What time is it?" I pushed them onto my face.

"Half past three."

"And you're dressed?" I had to grab hold of Clive's hand to get me up.

"We got a call." Standing straight, he buttoned his starch-crisped white shirt. "It's a bad one."

"What happened?"

"An accident." He turned, watching himself looping the tie around his neck in Aunt Gertie's mirror. "Kids."

"Jesus, have mercy," I prayed out loud.

The muscles in my shoulders ached when I reached to turn on the lamp on my bedside table. Eyes flinched with the bright light.

"Randy didn't know how many yet," Clive said. "He'd just got to the crash site. Said I ought to come on down there."

"Where was the accident?"

"Bunker's farm. That curve in the road." He pulled on his suit jacket. "Randy said Jay Bunker's all shook up. I'm nervous about what I'm going to see this morning."

"What can I do, honey?"

"Call the kids. Have Cal meet me down at the Bunker farm. I'll need his calm nature down there. And Randy does, too. Have Evelyn come here and get things ready for us." He turned back and looked at me and sighed. "It's going to be a beast of a day."

"I'll do whatever will help, honey." I pulled the soft sheet off my old, pale, purple-lined legs. "You need some coffee?"

"I'm okay. I need to get going." He made sure to give me a good kiss before walking out the door. "Love you, Olga, dear. More than the sunshine."

Cal and Evelyn got up and going just as soon as I got off the phone with them. Those kids didn't wait a second longer than they had to. Clive had taught them well. It did my heart good to see them help without so much as a grumble.

The living room window overlooked the darkness of way-too-early in the morning. A pinpricking of bright stars poked through a sheet of black sky. I'd learned a whole lot during my seven decades of life. One of them was to never overlook a clear night. That, I understood, was part of God's majesty. Another was how fragile life could be. How quick it ended sometimes. That it took so little for a life to snuff out completely.

The courage to take a meager step some days exhausted me. But bravery could bring glory to my Lord. I just had to believe it.

"Make Clive brave, Lord," I prayed. "And spread a little courage on Cal and Evelyn, too. And, while You're at it, I could use a little boost to push me through this day."

The good Lord's first boost got me moving right along. A couple hours later, the morning still dark, I'd got a cup of coffee in me, a pan of muffins cooling on baking racks, and my Bible open in front of me on the dinette.

I hadn't moved that fast in twenty years. Maybe even longer.

"You didn't mess around this morning, did You?" I said to Him in awe. "I sure am grateful. Now, if You'd make sure You're doing that for Clive, too, please."

I got all the way through my Bible reading for the day when the sun finally rose. But, before I could shut the Good Book, the phone rang.

"Eliot-Russell Family Funeral Home," I said into the receiver. "How may I help you?"

"This is… Well, I'm calling because my daughters…" The woman on the other line stumbled over her words. "See, they were in an accident."

"I'm so sorry." I rubbed right under my jawline.

"They told me they'd bring the girls to you. The policeman did. I wanted to come… Later, I guess. My husband and I want to come and…" Her voice paused, but her crying hadn't. "I don't know what to do. Is it okay that I called?"

"Yes. Of course."

"They didn't make it." Her breathing came through heavy from of the other end of the telephone. "I'm their mother."

"I'm so sorry." Pinching the skin of my forehead, I tried to silence the screaming that hung on since my dream. "You come on over whenever you're ready. We'll be here."

"Both my daughters are gone. The police officer told me that you'd have them later," she whispered. "They're my only children. And they're gone. And you'll have them."

Jesus, I thought in prayer. *Have mercy.*

"I'll need to get it arranged. You know. The services."

"Yes. We're here to help you with that."

"Later. I'll come then."

"When you're ready."

"I'll never be ready."

She hung up the phone—it clicked in my ear.

The pages of my Bible made a crisp sound as I flipped to the Psalms. I needed to read of anguish. And, if nothing else, the psalmists knew misery. They waited and watched all night long for a little bit of God's mercy.

Oh, how I'd watched, too. Some nights longer than others.

Without even knowing it, I'd raised my arms up over my head. I'd never been the kind to do such a thing. I'd learned long ago that prayer happened when hands were folded and heads bowed. But there I sat at my dinette, hands lifted in prayer.

"Lift us up," I said, as quiet as could be, my shoulders aching. "This deep is too far down, Lord. That family is stuck in a low down pit. Help them. Do something to help them. Please."

And, clear as a bell, I heard Him. I was just sure of it. Never before in all my life did I hear His voice like that. As if He sat right across the table from me.

"There is mercy with Me," He said. "Hope in Me."

Crying my eyes out, I allowed myself to feel held by His words. "Okay," I said, uneasy about my choice of words, but having none other to say.

Arms lowering and resting on the dinette, I used my crooked fingers to wipe my cheeks dry. Just like that. It felt strange to get up and pour myself another cup of coffee after hearing the voice of God. But, as with all sacred things, they don't put a stop to the act of living. They make the act of living possible.

"Gran?" Evelyn's voice carried up the steps from the funeral home. "I'm on my way up."

"Okay," I answered. The same word I'd said to God. That seemed strange, too. "You been here long?"

"A little over an hour." She made her way to the top of the steps and scanned her eyes around the apartment. "Is someone here?"

"Just me." I grabbed a mug from the cupboard. "Let me get you some coffee, honey."

"Thanks," she said. "I thought I heard you talking to someone."

"Oh, yes. I was just having a few words with Jesus."

"I see." She gave me a thin-lipped, suspicious smile. That girl would have had me locked up in a padded room if I told her that Jesus had talked back to me.

I just gave her my best, sweet old lady grin and handed her the cup of coffee.

"I like how you got your hair done, Evelyn," I said, touching it with my fingers. "It suits you."

"Thanks. Grace did it."

"Oh, isn't she just wonderful?"

"Yeah. She's great." She sipped her coffee. "I stopped by the accident on the way. They've got the whole road closed in front of the Bunker farm."

"Oh, dear," I sighed.

"Two sisters were in the car, Gran. It's not good."

"Their mother called."

"Already?" Evelyn asked. "It's a good thing no one else was in the car. The sisters had just dropped off a friend."

"It's going to be a long few days, isn't it?" I pointed at the cooling rack. "Have a muffin. They're still warm. I got the butter dish right next to them."

"Thank you, Gran." She took one of the muffins.

"You're welcome, Evelyn." Crossing my arms, I looked at my

granddaughter. Such a beauty.

"I've got a ton to do to get ready." A few crumbs fell to her shirt. "Love you."

"I love you back." I handed her a napkin.

"Thanks. And thanks for the coffee." She lifted the mug. "I'm going to need a lot of this today."

I didn't have the heart to tell her that the cup of brown mercy was decaf.

Chapter Fifteen

Evelyn

I worked as quickly as I could to get the Big House ready for Granddad and Cal. The prep room needed the most attention. Moving tables and trays around to make more space. Refilling embalming fluid into the Porti-Boy embalming machine. Getting all the instruments lined up on trays and counters. After I'd finished all that, I couldn't bring myself to just sit in the office, even though I had plenty to do in there. So, I set to work, getting the chapel ready for whatever kind of use it might have.

Hoping for a little sunshine, I pushed the curtains wide open. Doctor's orders. I needed a little lift in my mood. But the sun had hidden behind thick, storm-threatening clouds.

"Just as well." I sighed.

Granddad had always said that storms come. They rage on the good and the bad. Sometimes the rain served to grow things. Other times, to tear them apart. I'd seen more of the destructive storms fall on good people than bad. And, usually, the growing rains made pretty nasty people prosper. It never made sense to me.

The doors clunked open. Out in the lobby, Cal stood, holding two paper cups of coffee.

"Deirdre sent these with me. I figured I might not be able to drink both of them." He lifted up one of the cups. "So I thought you might like one."

"Oh, man. You have no idea how much I need that." I rushed across the room toward him. The cup he handed me warmed my fingers. It tasted as good as it smelled. "That's so good. Thank you. I don't think Gran makes her coffee strong enough."

"She only has decaf up there."

"You're kidding me." I wanted to fall over from the exhaustion.

"I'm for real." Cal sighed. He leaned back against the doorjamb of the chapel. "Okay. So, here's what we know. It seems the driver misjudged the curve out by the farm. She was going too fast, but they don't think drugs or alcohol were a factor. Just teen recklessness. The car didn't make it. Instead, they went head first into the big oak tree."

"Did they die on impact?"

"Yeah. Randy thought so, at least." His adam's apple bobbed up and down. "I really hope so."

"How are the remains?"

"They're in bad shape." He pushed off the wall, standing straight. "We'll have to do closed caskets for both of them."

"I hate this job." As soon as the words came out, a wave of guilt rolled over. "Days like this, at least."

"It's rough. That's for sure." Rubbing a hand over his face, he yawned before turning and walking to the prep room. "I'll be in there if you need me."

All business. My brother had already detached his emotions from the deaths. He and Granddad could do that. Push their horror into a different part of the brain. Suspending the feelings and shutting some kind of steel trap on top. How they did that without becoming hard and angry, I couldn't figure out.

I, on the other hand, had to work double-time to control my emotions on days like that. I grabbed the small, orange bottle from my purse. The pills made a tapping sound as I shook one out.

Hating my weakness, I wished I could be stronger.

<hr />

The parents of Shelly and Josie Rogers sat across the desk from me. The mother's eyes fixed on me, red veins in crooked lines marking the whites. The father kept his face turned down. His hand held so tight to his wife's, I thought it would have hurt her. She didn't notice, though.

Shock had them numb one minute, talking calmly and making decisions without a problem. Then, the next, they remembered where they sat and why. They realized who they didn't have with them. Then the grief choked them.

"I'm so sorry for your loss," I told them. Over and over.

I wondered if they believed me.

Regaining herself, the mother opened her eyes, focusing back on me. "Okay. I'm sorry."

"Please don't be sorry," I said. "Are you okay to continue?"

"Yes. Go on."

"Have you considered what you would like to do with your daughters' remains?" I let the words fall gently from my mouth. Those last two words didn't belong in the same sentence.

"We never thought this would happen." Her voice brimmed with begging. Pleading.

I stayed quiet, unmoving, allowing her a moment of control. She breathed, lifting her whole body with the effort. Little trembles moved from arms to hands as she touched her face.

She looked at her husband, forehead wrinkling. Resting her cheek on his shoulder, she resigned to silent crying.

"We don't want them cremated." The father spoke in a voice so deep I had to strain to hear him. He rubbed the fingers of his free hand against his close-cut beard. "We'd like them buried so we can visit them."

"I can guide you through that."

"Can we have their caskets open?" She blinked her eyes quickly. "It would be a good thing. Right? To see them."

Dread sunk like a rock in my stomach. I regretted drinking the coffee Cal brought me. It stirred in my gut, mixing with the anxiety of what I had to tell them.

"Your daughters both suffered trauma." The words stomped up from my throat. "If you wish for the caskets to be open, we will do everything we can to make them viewable."

"What does that mean?" She jolted up, moving to the edge of her seat. "I can't see them? Is that what you're saying?"

"No." The father shook his head, wrapping his arm around her, anchoring her back to the seat. "You can't, hon. I saw them. You don't need to. I don't want you to carry that with you."

"But you got to see them." Her lower lip folded over, resting on her chin.

"Please believe me," he said. "It's not something to have in your memory."

"We might be able to do a private viewing. Just for you and your family." I tried to make eye contact with the mother, but her pleading eyes reached too deeply into my heart. "We have to go through the embalming process first. And, unfortunately, they may not be viewable."

"How is this happening?" Her words came slowly as if from far away. "This can't be real."

"I wrote up the obituary." Lined, college ruled paper in his hand, the father reached across the desk. The edge of the page still had the bumps from where he tore it from a notebook. "I wanted them to be together. Is that okay? I think they'd have liked that."

"Of course." Unfolding the paper, smoothing it into the folder in front of me, I let my eyes move across the words, written in pen. In several spots, the ink had smudged and dried in wrinkled distortion.

"I'm not much of a writer," he said. "I did the best I could."

"Can we look at the caskets?" The mother moved, agitated, in her seat, still under the weight of her husband's arm. "Do you have any we can look at? Can we pick them out?"

Standing, I pointed for them to walk out of the office. "This way." I led them into the next room.

Two walls of uncovered windows usually gave the room a soft, warm, natural light. That day, though, I had to turn on the overhead lights to make up for the gloom of the storm. Caskets lined the walls. All different colors and materials. A book shelf in one corner held an assortment of urns.

Stepping softly among the caskets, the parents looked about, wide-eyed. She glanced around, her mouth open a bit and fingers fidgeting.

Rain tapped on the windows. From miles away a rumble, deep and heavy, sounded.

"Is there a difference between the metal and the wood?" The

111

mother ran a fingertip along the chestnut casket by the door.

"Mostly, it depends on your preference." I stood to one side, hands clasped in front of me.

We never played salesmen. Never tried to influence a grieving family in order to make a few extra bucks. Our business was more about helping them. Guiding them through the worst moments of their lives. It was never about money for us. Granddad's rules.

"The metal looks nice, I think." She stepped toward the center of the room and directly to a pearly, pink casket. She touched the silky, ivory lining. "This is pretty. But Shelly doesn't like pink. She'd never go for it."

She worked at swallowing, her chin dipping to her neck.

"And whatever Shelly doesn't like, Josie doesn't like either." Fingers still caressed the smooth fabric. "Those girls are best friends. Always together."

Touching the small rose on the inside of the casket lid, she gasped. Once. Twice. Then the sobs erupted, sinking her to the floor. Her husband rushed to her, lowering himself to one knee and putting his face near hers. He held her shoulders with his two large hands.

"I can't remember," she cried, gagging on the grief. "I don't remember their favorite colors. I knew yesterday. I promise. I knew then. But today I can't remember. I thought I'd give Shelly a call to ask. Like when I'm shopping for them. I was going to ask which one she wanted. And which one for Josie. Then I realized they aren't here anymore."

"I know." He pushed his face against hers. "I know."

"And I can't even see them." The words chopped their way out of her. "They're too broken."

He lifted her to her feet. They stood like that together, arms around each other, for a long time. He shook from the effort of holding all that sorrow.

I moved closer to the door, wanting to leave. To give them privacy. That moment had nothing to do with me. I shouldn't have witnessed it. But I heard him speak and I stayed, trying to blend into the room.

"Shelly would have liked the green one over there," he said into her ear, but loud enough for me to hear. "She didn't like pink. You were right about that. Remember, she said it was too easy for a girl to like pink. Do you remember that? She said that when she was in kindergarten. So I think we should get the green one for Shelly. That's the one she'd like best."

"Yes. We let her watch *The Wizard of Oz*." She hiccupped in spurts of air. "The Emerald City was her favorite part. Her eyes got so big with all the green on the screen. She sat right on my lap with her arms around my neck."

"And see the silver one?" He pointed across the room. "With the dark blue lining?"

"Yes," she answered.

"It looks like Josie's prom dress, doesn't it? Silver and blue. Just like that." He pulled the wallet from his back pocket and flipped through the pictures, pointing to one near the back of the album. "See? She'd be so happy about those colors."

She grabbed hold of him, pulling him closer to her. As if she wanted to melt into him. The way his face moved around the agony made me retreat to the lobby. I closed the door behind me, turning the knob so it wouldn't make a noise.

I sat on the steps leading to Gran and Granddad's apartment. I needed to be alone for a few minutes. I knew Gran wouldn't come down that way. And Granddad was too busy to go up. It seemed a good hiding place.

It bothered me that I wasn't crying over the girls. Over the parents. The whole situation. I'd bawled my eyes out over the deer. An animal. But I couldn't find a few drops for a couple of teenage girls. I didn't feel human. More like a machine or robot. And I hated it.

"Hey, Ev," Cal called from the other side of the door. "Where are you?"

I reached out and rapped my knuckles against the door. It opened and Cal peeked in.

"Tough day, huh?" He didn't look right at me. "Are the parents gone?"

"They left about half an hour ago."

"Are you crying?"

"I wish," I answered. "How are you doing?"

"All right." He cleared his throat. "We need you in the prep room. We're done embalming. But we've got a bit of a problem."

I used the railing to get myself up. "I'm exhausted."

"You and me both, Ev."

I followed my brother to the prep room, as much as I wanted to run the other way. Apparently, I couldn't feel grief, but I did feel fear. I didn't want to see the girls. I wondered if Cal felt a bit of that dread, too. His steps slowed the closer we got to the girls.

But I went for the mother with the bloodshot eyes. And the father who knew his daughters' favorite colors. They deserved a little bit of my courage.

Running water splashed against Granddad's hands and forearms as he worked the suds against his skin. He glanced over his shoulder at us.

"We got a conundrum, Evelyn," he said before turning back to the sink.

"We can't show their faces." Cal stepped toward one of the girls, pulling the sheet from her face, just enough for me to understand.

"Some things can never be unseen." Granddad kept up the scrubbing. "They're going to have most of the high school kids in town coming through. They can't see the girls like that. It wouldn't be right."

My eyes took in the damage of the ruined face. As I stood a foot from her remains, I knew that she'd stay in my mind for the rest of my life. No amount of antidepressants or sunshine would cure that.

"We'll have to keep the caskets closed," Cal said. "The other one is just as bad."

"Didn't the car have airbags?" I looked from one damaged spot to another on the girl, trying to think of how I could make her viewable. The mother needed to see them. Even just a little of them.

"Honestly, it didn't matter. Not the way they hit the tree."

I stepped nearer, lifting the sheet to cover her face again. "How are their arms and hands?"

"Some bruising. A few abrasions on their arms." Cal shoved his hands in the pockets of his pants. "Nothing makeup and long sleeves can't cover."

Pushing the sheet up to find her hand, I touched the cold fingers.

The green polish on her fingernails looked like she'd just put it on.

"Their parents need to see them." I closed my eyes. "We can put cloths over their faces."

Chapter Sixteen

Olga

Clive hardly touched his supper. Just pushed the mashed potatoes around on his plate and stared off into nothing. A few of his peas even rolled over the edge and onto the dinette without him noticing.

Days like he had today took more out of him than he ever cared to admit. But, as for me, they liked to make me sick with worry for my husband.

"Darling, I know I told you I might have another year of work in me, but many more days like this and I'll need a casket of my own." He stared into his mug full of black coffee before setting it back down on the table. "Today took a lot of life out of me."

I collected the plates and silverware from the table. We never were the kind to let food go to waste. But that night neither of us felt much like eating. I scraped the food into the trash bin before stacking the dishes up in the sink.

"I'm getting more and more itchy for my retirement and our trip to Hawaii," he said.

My feet ached, and I longed to put them up. Still, I made my way to Clive. Patting his cheek, I noticed how the overhead light caught on my mother of pearl ring. "I'd be content just to have you to myself."

"Of course, when I retire, I'm going to get restless." He rubbed a hand over his lips. "And, living up here, I won't be able to watch the kids do all the work."

I didn't remind him that I'd said nearly the same thing a handful of days before. In our marriage I'd learned, most times, I did better to let him think he came up with ideas right out of his own noggin.

"An apartment's just opened up at the retirement home." With tired fingers, I undid the top button of his shirt. "Rosetta said it's right down the hall from her."

I dipped my head to catch Clive's eyes. His brows pinched together, lips turned down in the corners. "That's one option, I guess."

"We could have a cleaning lady come by once a week to do the dusting and vacuuming. She could even scrub the toilet for me."

"I wonder if you'd find someone else to cook, too." He winked, easing his frown a bit.

"Well, I'd fix supper for us in the evenings, if you'd like." My hands slid across his shoulders, feeling the tension of the day in tight muscles. "But we could have lunch in the dining room with the other old folks. I think I'd like that little break."

"I'd help you a bit, if you'd want me too. I can't cook, but I'm a good potato peeler."

"Honey," I said, "all I want is plenty of time with you. And no phone calls to pull you away."

He took my hand and put it on his cheek. His warm hand held mine in place. The end-of-a-long-day stubble prickled my skin.

"I worry about the kids taking care of everything after I retire." He leaned into my palm. "They'll do a good job. That's for sure. But days like this are too much for anybody."

His jaw moved, opening his mouth. I could tell by the way his forehead wrinkled that he had something to say. He didn't make a peep, though. Just shut his mouth and breathed out his nose.

Creaking, the back door opened.

"I think we got company," I whispered.

"Just me," Gretchen called.

"Hi, sweetheart." Clive kept his eyes on my face.

When Gretchen got herself up to the kitchen, she smiled at Clive and me. "Am I interrupting something?"

"Nah." Clive patted my hand. "We lock the door if there's ever anything that could be interrupted."

"Clive Daniel," I screamed, slapping my hands against my cheeks.

I was sure they'd turned a pink shade of embarrassed.

"You want something to eat, Gretchie?" Clive asked, still chuckling.

"I'm fine, Dad." She sat across from her daddy. "Don just made me eat some soup."

"Isn't your stomach feeling better yet?" I took a step away from Clive.

She didn't answer me. Instead, she knocked a couple crumbs off the table and into the palm of her hand.

"It's been going on for a long time. Too long." Crossing my arms, I watched her dump the crumbs onto a napkin. "Didn't the doctor give you anything for it?"

"Don't worry, Mom." She reached a hand across the table and touched Clive's arm. "How are you holding up, Dad?"

"I'm all right, I suppose." Leaning back in his chair, Clive rubbed his bare scalp with both hands. "What I'm really dreading is catching up with Old Buster in the morning."

"He's doing the funeral?" Gretchen asked.

"That's what I've got to find out." Clive shook his head. "That man is all right at the funerals for elderly folks. As good as I can expect, at least. But I've seen him cross a couple lines when it came to younger people's funerals."

"I think he's just gotten worse the older he gets." Shaking my head, I let the grumbly complaint loose. "He's just full up with judgment for anything that moves in a way he doesn't care for."

"Honey, if he does the funeral, I'll make it clear as crystal that he's to mind his manners." Clive looked at his knuckles. "He gets me all riled up."

"That's only because you're so tired, honey. Why don't you head on in to bed?" I asked. "A good night's sleep will do you a lot of good."

"I don't mind if I do." He scooted his chair away from the table. When he got up, he didn't stand quite as tall as usual. Shoulders rolled over and head hung low, he moved himself around the table to give Gretchen a smooch on the forehead.

"Sleep tight, Dad." She patted his arm.

"I intend to." Clive took a step over to give me a peck. His embrace startled and pleased me. His lips brushed against my earlobe. "I love you."

"Love you, too, Clive."

"If you want to move, I'm all for it, darling." He pulled away from me and on to our bedroom.

Only a minute or two after he left, his snores started up, rumbling through the door.

"What a heavy day for him," I said.

"I can tell." Gretchen wet a washcloth. "How about you?"

"Well, God's been kind to me. He's kept me on my feet." I joined her at the sink and drew hot water over the dishes. The dish soap made a tired sputter when I squeezed it.

"Make sure you get a good night's sleep tonight, Mom." She took to scrubbing at the table. "Do you have enough chamomile tea?"

"I sure do, honey." The water heated my hands, relaxing my fingers, making them feel lazy. Running a dishcloth over a plate, water sloshed up on my shirt. "I hate to complain, but I am tired of handwashing dishes."

"Why don't you have Dad put in a dishwasher?" Gretchen asked. "Over fifty years of washing by hand is plenty."

"More like sixty." I wiped my brow with the back of my wrist, wondering how I got to be old enough to do anything for sixty years. "Seems like I've done dishes every blessed day of my life."

I sprayed water out of the faucet, rinsing a plate I'd washed so many times, the paint had started to wear off. I thought about washing at Aunt Gertie's house. I'd learned most of my housekeeping there, with a faucet that barely trickled out. Oh, how greasy the water'd get from the lard she cooked with. She wouldn't allow me to change the water for fresh, but I had to get those dishes spotless and sparkling. And, heavens, if a dish got chipped, it came out of my hide, no matter who'd dropped it.

"Maybe you'll get a dishwasher for Christmas." Gretchen's voice pulled me from the memory.

"That would be a treat." But really, I hoped to be in an apartment down the hall from Rosetta by then. If only I could pack Gretchen up and move her with me. "Really, I've got no right to whine and moan like this. At least I have dishes and a sink to wash them in."

"I'll finish up." Gretchen took the dishrag from my hand and nudged me with her hip. "You sit down and talk to me."

"You won't hear me argue against that." Using a dish towel, I dried my hands before sitting at the table. My eyes got heavy right away. My head, too.

"I didn't want to tell you this in front of Dad," she said. "I don't want him getting worried right now."

"What is it?" The tired went right out of my eyes and head. Worry took its place.

"My doctor ran some tests." She kept her back turned toward me. Must have made it easier for her to do the telling that way.

"What kind of tests?"

"Well, a couple of blood draws. Then they did a scan and ultrasound."

"You aren't pregnant, are you?"

She looked over her shoulder. "I hope not."

"Then, did the doctor have some kind of idea what's the matter?" I felt my forehead wrinkle in concern.

"She has a few thoughts." She rinsed a handful of silverware. "She wants to discuss the results tomorrow."

"She couldn't talk about it over the telephone?" From what I knew, they only called folks into the office for bad news. My stomach tightened, forcing burning bile up my throat.

"I don't know." She sprayed water into a pot, swishing away the suds.

All the possibilities stabbed in my mind. The thoughts came so fast, they made me all kinds of dizzy.

"Would you like a little company for your appointment?" I tried to cover the panicky shrill in my voice. "Maybe we could get a bite to eat afterward. If you're up to it."

"I'm sure it's nothing big." The way her the words thinned, I doubted she believed them.

"Gretchen, you don't think this is just a bad case of the flu, do you?" Tingling pinpricks of anxiety dotted up and down my arms and limbs. "You think it's more, don't you?"

"I'd like to have you with me." She slid a plate into the strainer. "How about I make you a cup of tea?"

"Would you rather have Donald go?"

"He doesn't know yet." Water gurgled its way down the drain when she pulled the stopper. "He'd just worry."

"He's your husband, Gretchen."

"I know. I'm used to doing this stuff on my own." She turned, leaning back against the counter and wiping her hands dry. "Sometimes I just don't feel like putting another burden on him."

"Are you sure, honey?"

"Yes. Pretty sure." She gave me a smile I knew was meant to make me feel better. It didn't work. "Now. How about that tea?"

She moved about my kitchen like a whirl of wind. In no time, I had a cup of fairy tea steeping right in front of me. She'd even remembered the drizzle of honey I liked.

"Thank you, sweet girl." Pushing my fingers against the smooth mug, the heat was almost more than I could bear.

"I better get home." Her hand on my shoulder felt heavy. "I'll swing over to get you in the morning. Probably right around nine."

She grimaced and touched her side.

"Honey?" I stood, getting breathless myself. The mug of tea tipped over. The doggone thing spilled on my foot. Thank goodness I still had my shoes on.

"Are you okay?" She grabbed the towel from off my counter. Stooping, she sopped up the spill on my foot. "Did it burn you?"

"No." Tears brimmed over, spilling from my eyes. "It's all right."

"How about I get you another cup?" She didn't wait for my answer before setting about to make more.

After she left, I got up and carried the mug of tea with me to the window. I watched her walk past the garden. Dusky evening let off just enough light for me to see her as she stopped to snap off a handful of chamomile, bringing it to her nose and breathing it in.

Hand to my stomach, I felt a longing for her. It thudded in my gut. Of all the babies I'd carried, she was the only one that made it into my arms. Since her first breath, I'd lived my life for her. Keeping her housed and fed and happy.

I couldn't do much about keeping her healthy. Not anymore, at least.

I feared losing her more than anything else.
That old familiar worry.

Chapter Seventeen

Evelyn

Cal and I left the funeral home at the same time. I followed behind him, hoping that his bright tail lights would keep me awake. The last thing I needed was to hit another deer. I'd just gotten my car back from the shop.

The day had seemed to go on forever. By the end of the evening, long after we'd sent Granddad upstairs, Cal and I reached the end of our abilities. And at the last of our emotional strength, too.

A hot shower, soft bed, and dark chocolate sounded pretty good to me. I didn't care in what order they came. The image of the girls' missing faces wouldn't get out of my head. Not that I expected chocolate to do the trick. But any distraction would help.

Right before we reached the curve in the road in front of the Bunker farm, Cal slowed, his break lights blaring red. I realized we'd driven right toward where the accident had happened. I wondered if he'd forgotten that Randy had closed the road. When he turned into the yard of the old farmhouse, I figured we'd have to turn around and detour.

Pulling in behind him, I saw the yard full of cars. Twenty or more lined up, parked right on the grass. Jay Bunker pointed to a spot by his mailbox, nodding to let me know he wanted me to park there.

Cal got out of his car, pulling his jacket back on, regardless of the sticky hot evening. He tightened his tie. Always on duty.

Jay met us at the base of the driveway and put his hand out for Cal to shake.

"How you holding up?" Jay asked, his lip full of chewing tobacco.

"We're fine, thanks," Cal said. "Tough day."

"My wife's real tore up about this." Jay took off his cap and wiped his head with a faded blue bandana. "I didn't let her see them girls or nothing. But she's just beside herself anyhow. Said we should'a cut down that blasted tree years ago."

"You can't let her feel guilty." Cal put his hands on his hips, pushing his jacket open. "It's not her fault."

"Least we could do was let these folks pay vigil tonight." The hat back on his head, he nodded across the street toward the ruined tree. "The wife's been pouring lemonade for them all night. She made probably seven jugs of the stuff."

"That's good of her," Cal said.

"It's what she can do."

Around the accident site, a semi-circle of people had formed. Flickering candlelight glowed on their faces, catching their tears and making them sparkle. Teens huddled together, parents behind them, shifting their feet uncomfortably.

"The crash darn near shook the house." Jay pointed at the tree with his middle finger. "That tree hardly budged an inch. But it made the loudest noise I ever heard. Woke us both up, my wife and me."

Turning from us, he spit on the grass.

"I run out to see what happened." He adjusted the tobacco in his lip with his fingertips. "Could barely tell it was a car at all. I yelled for her to call for help. Then I got into the ditch to see what I could do."

Using the bandana, he scrubbed the back of his neck.

"Never seen nothing like it." Spitting again, he got a small dribble on his boot. "I tried to get the door open to pull them out. Didn't know if the darn thing was going to catch on fire, you know. It steamed so out the hood. But I couldn't get the door open. It wouldn't give way. The glass was all busted out one of the side windows. I reached in and touched one of them girls." He rubbed his hands together, like he tried to wipe them clean. "Her skin was still warm."

He cussed under his breath.

"I hope you don't mind my French," he said, looking at me. "It's just the worst thing I ever seen."

Headlights moved across us as another car pulled in. Jay stepped away to find a parking spot.

Cal and I stepped through damp grass to get to the back of the semi-circle. Someone had set up two crosses at the bottom of the tree. Pinned to the splintered bark, pictures of the girls caught the occasional beam of headlights or flicker of candle. I hadn't even thought about what their faces had looked like before. I'd only seen them after. Looking from photo to photo, I tried to pull those images in to displace what I'd seen on the embalming table.

A few parents held on to their kids. Arms wrapped around from behind, holding their shoulders. I wondered if they begged God to spare them that kind of tragedy.

Death had stepped too close to each of them through Shelly and Josie. They'd think about how they would stop squandering their lives. Make a list of all the adventures they'd have before they died. Think of all the people who needed to hear "I love you" a little more often.

Sadly, though, a week or a month would pass and they'd forget that life was so easily lost. The people who truly valued life were those who paid attention to how close we all stood to death.

I scanned the group, trying to read the language of crying, swollen eyes, and sorrow-weary bodies.

One face stood out.

"Who's that?" Cal asked, seeing the same guy I did.

"That's Will Todd. The new youth minister," I whispered.

"Right. I forgot all about him." Cal raised his eyebrows at me. "Your boyfriend."

"He's not my boyfriend." The last thing I needed was for Cal to start his teasing.

"Uh-huh."

Will noticed us staring at him. When I locked eyes with him for a second, I had to look away. I'd never been so thankful for the dark. It covered my blushing cheeks.

"He's coming over here." Cal elbowed me. "We should step back a little."

Will's sandaled feet crunched across the dirt road. He followed us back, closer to the cars so we wouldn't disturb the vigil.

"Hey," he said to me. "Good to see you."

"Yeah. You, too." I joined my hands in front of me.

Cal cleared his throat, not to be overlooked. "I'm Cal Russell."

"Right." Will took Cal's hand. "I'm Will."

"Good to meet you finally." Cal nodded at me. "My sister's told me a little about you."

"Hopefully, only good things." Crossing his arms, Will shifted his weight to one foot. "So you guys are funeral directors, right?"

"We'll be the last ones to let you down." Cal smirked.

"That's bad." Will shook his head. "Anyway, I'm doing the funeral for the girls. I need to talk to you about how everything's going to work."

"You're doing the service?" Cal asked.

"Barton had a few other things to do." He shrugged. "I think he wasn't completely comfortable with doing it himself."

Cal and I shared a glance and grinned. No one called Old Buster by his first name. We joked that his wife wasn't even allowed to call him that. Everybody called him Reverend Thaddeus to his face and Old Buster as soon as he turned around.

"You should stop over at the funeral home tomorrow and meet our grandfather. He can fill you in on all the details." Cal crossed his arms. "You know where it is, right?"

"Yeah. Barton's driven me all around. I think he's taken me to the bakery about twenty times in the last two weeks."

"The man likes his bagels," Cal said. "I'm glad Barton's taking good care of you."

I caught Will eyeing me. He looked away quickly. "So I'll see you both tomorrow."

"Sure," Cal said. "Ev can show you around. Seeing that you already know each other."

"I'd like that." Will glanced over his shoulder. "It's nice to meet you, Cal. I'd better get back over there."

I watched him rejoin the semi-circle. He stood off to one side, waiting just in case anyone needed him. Old Buster would have demanded everyone's attention. Wanted to deliver a sermon. He would have asked his angel singer or the guitar man to lead the group in repetitive songs to up the emotional buy-in. Then he'd offer an altar call. A time of decision or rededication.

Instead, Will waited on them, not asking a single thing from them.

"I know he's cute." Cal tapped me on the shoulder. "But we'd better get going."

I only had to take a few steps to get to my car. Cal stood next to me.

"He seems like a good guy, by the way," he said.

"I think he's pretty nice." I opened my car door. "But he never called for a second date."

"Did you call him?"

"Well, no."

"You might want to think about that one." He winked at me. "Hey, your hair looks nice. Grace said she was glad to meet you."

"I like her." I sat down in my seat. "And I'm getting used to the hair."

"It sure caught Will's attention." He winked at me again. Him and his winking. "Sleep tight. Sweet dreams."

Cal waited for me to get my car started before he left his spot. Jay Bunker waved his hand at me as I drove away.

That poor man. I doubted he would have sweet dreams for a long while after what he'd seen that day.

Chapter Eighteen

Olga

The mother of the girls had called late into the night. Clive didn't even flinch when the telephone rang. The poor man just kept sawing away at logs, as tuckered out as could be. I, on the other hand, hadn't gotten so much as a wink of sleep. Too much pulled at my mind for me to put two dozes together.

So, when she called, I didn't mind all that much. I got up and pulled on a pair of slacks and a blouse and opened the front door of the funeral home.

"Would you like a little tea?" I asked. "Maybe some coffee?"

Not answering, she followed me into the lobby.

"The chapel is right this way," I said.

"I'm sorry." She stopped behind me. Hands clasped under her chin, as if folded in prayer, she let her eyes close and drew in long breaths.

The sound in her voice, the way it quivered, resembled most every parent I'd ever met who lost a child. It was the worst thing I could imagine. And those parents I knew cried and screamed and suffered the complete terror of it.

"I can't sleep. I keep thinking of them. That if I could see them for a minute…" She cut herself off, wiping a tissue under her nose. "But I don't think I can look at them. I'm just too…"

Taking her hand, I gave it a tiny squeeze.

"But having them here, away from me, is too much." Covering her face with both hands, she let her eyes peek out between her fingers. And the way those eyes filled up with tears nearly broke me in two.

Reaching out my arms, I pulled her into a hug. I figured that's what neighbors would do. And she needed a good neighbor about then. It wasn't really the thing for a funeral director to do, but that didn't matter so much to me.

"I keep thinking they're at a sleepover or something, you know? Like they're at camp for a couple days." Her jolting breath hit against my neck. "But then I realize they're gone. They aren't coming back. Not ever."

"I'm sorry," I whispered. To tell the truth, I knew those words weren't enough. Like giving a stick of chewing gum to a starving man. "I want you to take all the time you need."

Straightening up, she stepped out of my hug, letting me look right into her eyes. That poor woman. So swollen and red around the hazel of irises. I doubted she'd stopped crying for all the hours since she'd heard the news. I knew I wouldn't have.

"You know what I used to say to people? When they lost someone?" For all the wiping of tears, her face still didn't get dried off. "I used to tell people that God needed another angel with Him. That's why He took them."

Not knowing what to say, I nodded.

"Isn't that awful? Today I realized what a terrible thing that is to say." She shook her head. "And I don't want to think about what that would mean about God. Because I think it would make me hate Him so much for it. He knows I need them more than He does."

I understood what she meant. Exactly.

"I wish I'd never said that to anybody." Her lips pulled right down into a frown. "It makes God seem so selfish."

"You must have thought it would comfort them," I said. "You didn't mean any harm by it. You were trying to help."

"I'm having the hardest time understanding why this happened, though. I can't figure it out." She gasped for breath. "Why would God have let this happen?"

As she searched my face, I couldn't find a single answer, either. As much as I wanted to say something wise to carry her through the grief, I couldn't think of a blessed thing.

Aunt Gertie made it a habit to tell me that I must have an answer for the hope I had. But, looking at the suffering mama in front of me, I didn't have a thing to say. I figured it would have been wrong of me to offer it then, even if I did know. Part of wisdom, I thought, was knowing when to keep the answers shut in your trap. And, while I wasn't always so wise, the Holy Spirit took over in my distress.

So, instead of yapping my jaw, quoting Bible verses pulled thin as glass and handing out easy answers, I stood before her, letting the silence work as a salve between us. And without my own shaky voice pulling the attention from her, the loss got a moment to work inside her. As hard as grief hurt, it needed to run the long course through her.

After a minute or two, she dabbed at her sore eyes again.

"Have you seen them?" she asked.

I had and I told her so. As much as I wished I could have said no. Evelyn had needed my help getting the cloths pulled over their broken faces.

"Do they…" She stopped herself. "Are they bad?"

Closing my eyes, the image of the girls lingered. More in my heart than in my head. The only words I could think of to describe was "there's nothing left to see."

But "nothing left to see" means little to a grieving mama.

"Tell me." Reaching to touch me, she stopped short and pulled her hand back. "Please."

"We did the best we could." I swallowed good and hard. "But we weren't able to make their faces viewable."

"So I can't see them?" Weaker than before, her voice whimpered. "Even for a minute?"

"We put handkerchiefs over their faces. Like shrouds."

"Can't I see them?" she asked again.

"Would you like to hold their hands?" Touching the door, I readied myself to push it open. "You could sit with them and hold their hands. As long as you want."

"I never wanted to move out here." She took one step toward the chapel but paused. "My husband said this would be a good place for the girls to grow up."

She let the place between her eyes gather into folds. "They were in elementary school then. He wanted them to be safe. He told me they would be safe here."

After all I'd seen in fifty-two years living above that funeral home, I knew no place was all the way safe. I didn't tell her, though. She'd learned that for herself.

Breathing in and out a couple times, she made eye contact. The way she set her face, like a warrior stepping into battle, told me she was ready.

The chapel lights flickered when I flipped the switch. Two caskets, head-to-head, stood, open at the front of the chapel. We thought the family would have wanted it that way. Evelyn had done a good job covering the bruised and cut up arms with makeup. All the work of dressing the bodies for the parents and no one else. We'd close the caskets for the public viewing. But the parents needed to see them. Otherwise, they might wonder all their lives if their children really had died. They'd know in their minds. But somewhere, deep in their hearts, they'd wonder. And that would add torture to agony.

Eyes turned toward the caskets, she stood next to me, all folded up into herself.

"He picked the right ones," she said. "My husband picked good caskets for the girls, didn't he?"

"He did a fine job."

The way she wrung her hands, I wondered how they didn't get sore.

"Which do I go to first?" She turned toward me. "I can't pick. I don't love one more than the other. But I'm afraid they might not understand if I picked one first."

The floor of the chapel had a few boards that groaned if I stepped on them. I tried to avoid them as I made my way to the caskets. I pulled on those caskets, thankful for the wheels on the bottom of the pedestals. Putting the girls side to side, I left enough room for the mother to stand between them.

"Thank you," she said when I walked back to her. "Will you stay back here? I don't want to be alone."

"I'm not going anywhere, honey."

Those old floorboards moaned along with her as she made her

way to the girls. Somehow, even though she wept, she didn't fall apart. As if she kept herself strong for their benefit. Her final act of courage on their behalf. She stood between them, touching their fingers, smoothing the hair she could see that spread out on the pillows.

I sat in one of the comfy chairs in the back. The warmth of the room and the dim lights made the exhaustion pull at me. I let my eyes close, partly because they weighed about two tons. But, also, I wanted to give the woman privacy. She'd be doing plenty of public mourning later on. She deserved the dignity of grief that flowed between her and God. I would have wanted that if it had been me.

My rump in the chair, though, I had to fight off snoozing. Sleep would lead to snoring and a body unwilling to get back up. So, I tried to remember all the thoughts which had kept me awake earlier in the night. Chief among those thoughts was Gretchen's appointment. I tried to pray it into being something minor.

Only a few minutes later, though, I heard humming. Some lullaby, it sounded like. Opening my eyes, I saw the mother sitting in a folding chair between her girls, holding their hands. She hummed to them. Then the hum grew to singing, her voice shaking. It dipped into a sob every now and again.

The only words I caught were "sleep" and "rest."

I prayed those words for her, too.

She sat between her girls until the sun rose. I kept vigil in the back, sharing in her pain from far off.

Chapter Nineteen

EVELYN

Standing in the center of the Big House lobby, surrounded by floral arrangements, I realized that I'd left my coffee all the way on the other side of the room. I would have to tiptoe around all kinds of extremely expensive sprays and potted plants and wreaths to get to it. Somehow, I'd have to get across the labyrinth of flower without smearing my black pants with various hues of pollen.

"How'd you get yourself in that position?" Granddad asked, walking out of the prep room and right past my mug.

"I have no idea." I pointed at the coffee. "I haven't had enough of that to think straight."

"Good luck getting to it." His eyes smiled as he made his way around to the other side and toward the office.

"Hey, thanks for handing me the coffee, Granddad." I laid the sarcasm on thick. "Seriously. Could we get more flowers in here?"

"It's a hard thing when young people die," Granddad said from the office. "Folks are doing what they can. And, right now, what they can do is send flowers."

Opening the front door, Cal hardly squeezed in past the arrangements. "More flowers," he said in a far too chipper voice.

He held two oversized sprays. Lilies and roses and daisies and carnations exploded from the centers. Had I not been so grumpy that morning, I might have appreciated the handiwork of the florist.

133

Instead, I rolled my eyes.

"We're going to have to add on to the building." Standing in the doorway, surveying the lobby floor he tried to figure out where to lower the sprays. "Or dig out a path."

"I'm working on it," I said, more sharply than I should have.

"I'll take these right into the chapel." He grinned at me. "Don't worry, Ev. We've got plenty of time."

All the things I loved about Granddad annoyed me in Cal. Patience, calm nature, sense of humor. In Granddad, I found them endearing. In Cal, they made me crazy. Especially that early in the morning.

"Calvin," Granddad called from the desk. "You didn't happen to stop over to Deirdre's for doughnuts, did you?"

Cal slumped his shoulders. "Nope. Sorry."

"Maybe I'll call and see if Deirdre'll let Charlotte deliver some." Granddad picked up the phone.

"I can't believe Char's working with that woman." I attempted to pick up a potted plant without spilling soil all over the carpet. "I hope Deirdre doesn't ruin her."

"I don't know what you're talking about, Ev." Cal stepped gingerly over a wreath. "Deirdre's nothing but sunshine and puppy hugs."

"Charlotte's doing just fine, from all I hear." Granddad dialed the phone with the eraser end of a pencil. "She's stronger than any of us realize."

Cal pushed the chapel door open with his backside and held it open for me. I followed behind him, potted plant in my hands. I used my elbow to flip on the light.

"Looks like it was a late night in here," he whispered, lowering the arrangements to the floor. He moved the caskets back in place and folded the chair between them.

It took both of us several trips before we got all the flowers into the chapel. Then we searched all over the Big House for every spare pedestal and table. I opened the curtains, letting in as much natural light as I could. The blooms clumped in the middle of the room, I checked the little paper cards held up by spears stuck in the soil or padding. Family members' arrangements went closer to the caskets. Then the rest, I positioned by color, size, and flower type.

Once I got started, the work went fast. Soon, the chapel brightened up with all the flowers. As bright as a funeral home could look.

"Nice job." Cal walked up behind me, a stack of picture frames in his arms. On top of them, a small paper bag. "The family dropped off a few things."

"Okay," I said. "Photos?"

"Yeah." He lowered them to a chair. Picking up the bag, he handed it to me. "Whatever's in there needs to go with the girls."

"What is it?" I asked.

"Don't know." He turned for the door. "Didn't have time to look. Granddad jammed the printer again. I have to go play Mr. Fix-It."

In the sparse space I had left, I set up easels for the larger picture frames and made room on the tables for the smaller ones. The girls had been beautiful. And, from the way they smiled, I could tell they'd been deeply loved. The photos added what had been missing from the room. Faces for the girls.

Then, I picked up the wrinkled, brown paper bag. Unwrapping it, I reached in and pulled out two tiny, pink Bibles. Names engraved in gold on the front.

"Josie Lynnette" and "Shelly Rose."

I carried the Bibles closer to the window. The sun warmed my hands as I felt the cracked, imitation leather covers. The Bibles hadn't been the kind kept on the shelf as keepsakes. Those Bibles had been the kind toted to church in play purses and read at bedtime.

On the front page of Josie's Bible, her name had been printed with careful, curling letters. Probably right after she studied cursive at school. She'd put a sticker on the inside cover. "I love Sunday school!" the sticker announced. A rainbow hung over a cartoon church with a smiley face sun shining over the steeple.

Clear packing tape held the cover of Shelly's Bible together. JESUS LOVES ME had been written on the first page in choppy, little kid letters. The Es had too many lines drawn up and down. Exactly how Charlotte had done hers when she was small.

Soft, slow steps carried me to the caskets. Josie's on the left. Shelly's on the right. Josie in her silver and blue prom dress, looking like Sleeping Beauty with her face covered. Blond hair swirled on the pillow. Shelly in a dark green dress. One that matched her nail polish.

I tucked the Bible under her fingers.

I noticed a smudge in the green on one fingernail. It looked like she'd touched it before the paint had completely dried, leaving a perfect impression of a fingerprint. Loopy, curving lines in the green.

Something snapped in me, taking me over with grief I couldn't hold back. It wasn't a loud cry. I didn't lose sense or get sick to my stomach. But the tears had come. Sitting in one of the soft chairs along the edge of the room, I let myself release the emotion.

The chapel doors opened. I used the back of my fingers to wipe my face. Will stood in the back of the room, up against the wall. He breathed out his mouth with big sighs. Wherever he turned his eyes, he tried to avoid the caskets. Fidgeting, he eventually settled on putting his hands in his pants pockets.

"Hi," I said, getting out of the chair.

"Hey." He looked at me. Starting to smile, he stopped himself, putting on a more somber expression. Almost a frown. "Is this the… Those are the girls?"

"Yes." I stepped toward him. "You want to get some fresh air?"

"I'd like nothing better," he answered, sighing. "I haven't really been around, um, this kind of thing all that much."

"I understand."

"Nobody told me they'd be right there. You know. I wasn't ready. Usually, I'd be okay." His words stumbled one on top of another.

"Yeah. Let's get that fresh air."

On the porch, he leaned against the railing, letting his head rest back on the wood.

"Are you okay?" I asked.

"I guess I wasn't ready for that." He turned toward me.

"Do you need a glass of water?"

"No. I should have eaten breakfast. That's what I should have done." He shook his head. "I have to hand it to you, you have a tough job."

"It's not usually this bad."

"Still," he said. "It's tough."

"Well, I guess I'm used to it." I felt the back of my neck.

"Right." Turning his head, he looked out over the side yard. "Is that a garden over there?"

"Yes." I took a step closer to him. "Would you like to see it?"

Walking off the porch, we moved onto the soft grass. After all the cut, arranged, stinky flowers inside, the fresh, delicate, living ones comforted me. The air around the garden seemed cleaner, smoother. I couldn't name more than a couple of the flowers, but I did know how beautiful they were.

"It's really pretty out here." He tipped his head back and took in a deep breath. "I've only ever lived in the city. I don't think I've seen so many trees in my whole life."

"We like it." I stood beside him. "You know, my grandparents live right above the funeral home. I grew up in that house over there. I don't know anything else."

Lowering his head, he took in the sight of the field of flowers. "I really have no idea how you do this job."

"You've never seen a decedent before, have you?"

"A what?"

"Sorry." I smiled. "That's funeral speak for a deceased body."

"Got it. My parents didn't let me go to my grandma's funeral when I was little." He pushed the dark hair off his forehead.

"Well, it can be a shock if you're not used to it."

"And massively embarrassing on top of it."

"You're embarrassed?" I asked.

"Well, yeah." He shifted his glasses up his nose. "I wanted you to think I'm cool."

"I do think you're cool." The humidity had already thickened the air. I wiped a trickle of sweat off my forehead.

"If I had your job, I'd break down every single day." He swatted at a fly. "Or pass out. Several times a day."

"I can't imagine the ministry is much easier," I said. "I'm sure you see your share of hard days."

"Yeah. Long hours, lots of complaints about loud music and church budgets." He grinned. "But I get to hold brand new babies and go to about fifty open houses every summer."

"And weddings, too, right?"

"The best part of a wedding is the cake." Turning toward me, he leaned his head to one side. "Listen, Evelyn. I feel terrible about not telling you that I'm a pastor. I should have told you right away."

"Don't worry about it."

"I wasn't trying to lie to you or anything."

"Well, I didn't tell you that I'm a funeral director," I said.

"To be honest, my job tends to scare people off." Crossing his arms, he shrugged. "I figured if I could get a couple dates with you, I'd charm you so much that you wouldn't care about my job."

"You really think your job scares people off more than mine?"

He pushed his lips to one side of his face. "Okay. I can see that."

"So, is that what happened? Did my job spook you?" I asked. "After Deirdre told you?"

"No." He shook his head. "Why?"

"I don't know." It seemed too pathetic to mention that he hadn't called me. Instead, I pushed the hair behind my ears, holding my hand against the side of my neck.

"Evelyn, I've been trying to work up the nerve to call and ask you for a second date." He let his eyes wander over my shoulder. "I'm a ninny. I was sure you'd shoot me down."

"Seriously?"

"Yeah. How pitiful is that?"

"So...are you asking me out now? Because if you are, then I guess I can carve out some time."

"In that case, then, yes, I am asking." He scratched his head. Looking down at his feet, he flinched. "Unless this is a wildly inappropriate thing to be talking about, considering." He nodded at the Big House.

"That's the thing." I smirked. "If you waited for a time when someone wasn't in there, we'd never get together again."

"Good point," he said. The way he smiled at me drew my breath away from me. His was a pure, true smile. With no false charm hidden behind it. "Then maybe on Sunday? After youth group."

"Great. Meet me at Marshall's?" I rocked onto my tiptoes and back down again.

"Unless you want to hang out at youth group. I need a few more volunteers."

I cringed. "See, here's the problem with that. Those kids don't need to see the funeral director who just buried their friends. You know?"

"Right." He squinted at me. "That's a good way to get out of helping."

"I'm good at getting out of volunteering."

"We'll work on that."

"Listen, I have to get back inside," I said. "I've got a ton to do before the viewings today."

"Right." He turned toward the building. "I shouldn't have kept you so long."

"Trust me, you made for a good distraction. That's kind of nice on a day like this."

"I'll be in soon," he said. "And I promise, I'll be ready. I won't freak out again."

"No hurry."

"It's nice out here. I like this garden."

"My grandma and mom have kept it going for years." I kicked at the grass with the toe of my shoe. "Gran planted it when my mom was little. She used it as a kind of escape from the funeral stuff."

"That makes sense."

"You think so?"

"Yeah. A garden is alive."

I smiled at him, glad that he smiled back, before turning to the Big House.

My steps felt lighter.

I'd never understood Gran more than in that moment.

Chapter Twenty

Olga

The waiting room of the doctor's office smelled like someone took a long dip in the aftershave. I suspected the man sitting in the corner with hands folded over his big old belly. That man, bless his heart, had about the worst cough I'd ever heard. It sounded like his chest would crack in half whenever he barked from that deep down.

His coughing made me jump every single time. Not getting any kind of sleep the night before wore on my nerves. To be honest, I couldn't have been happier when the nurse called him in.

"How are you holding up, honey?" I asked Gretchen as soon as we had the waiting room to ourselves.

She looked up from the magazine on her lap. She'd stared at the same full page advertisement for shaving cream for minutes on end.

"What?" Flashing a smile at me, her eyes stayed distracted by the magazine. "Great. I'm not worried."

But the tapping foot and chewing of her lip told me otherwise. This wasn't a clear result we were coming to find out about. The doctor had some bad news to deliver. My mama's intuition knew it. And I knew my daughter knew it, too.

It was all I could do to keep still in that chair, the silence of the waiting room putting me on edge.

"Gretchen?" the nurse called, holding open a door with her backside.

Gretchen stood up straight as could be. Crumpling on the carpet, the magazine had slid off her lap. She looked at it as if she'd never seen such a thing before.

"It's okay, honey," I said, bending down to pick it up.

"You're coming with me," she said. "Right, Mom?"

"Sure." Getting to my feet, I had to use the arm of the chair to steady myself. "If that's what you want."

"Can she come in with me?" Gretchen asked the nurse. "She's my mother."

"Yes." The nurse tapped her clipboard with the end of a pen. "This way, please."

I followed Gretchen, who followed the nurse through the longest hallway in all the world. At least that's how it seemed to me. We passed a closed door, the coughing man barking inside, his aftershave wafting into the air to choke us.

At the end of the hallway, a door stood ajar. Pushing it open with the palm of her hand, the nurse ushered us into the room, pointing at the chairs next to a desk.

"Go on and have a seat," she instructed. "The doctor will be right in."

With dark eyes, the nurse watched my daughter walk past. I knew the look that passed over her face. In my life, I'd seen it a thousand times. I'd given the same look on a few occasions myself. Right then, in that fleeting expression, I knew the news wasn't just bad, it would be tragic. The way the nurse let her eyebrows soften, for only a second, told me everything.

She'd looked at my daughter, my only child, with pity. I'd never known fear like in that moment. Not once in all my years on the earth.

Only one thought occupied my thoughts. My daughter was dying. Why else would we be in that room?

Gretchen sat in one of the rich-looking leather seats in front of the biggest monster of a desk I'd seen. Her shoulders moved up and down a tiny bit with each breath she took.

Lord God, I prayed silently, keeping my eyes on Gretchen. *Please. Please. Help me.*

For the first time, I didn't believe God to be trustworthy with what He'd given me. Job's ancient words mocked me. He gives and He takes away.

Why the taking away? Why would He be so cruel?

I begged for a growth of mercy, but a seed of doubt worked its way into my heart.

"Come sit down, Mom." Gretchen patted the chair next to her. "You're making me nervous."

"Sorry, Gretchie." I took a seat. "Just looking at that desk."

"It's a little much, don't you think?"

I grabbed her hand. Really, though, I wanted to hold her in my arms.

Put the sickness, whatever it is, on me instead, I prayed.

"Did you see the garden?" Gretchen pointed out the window. "Can you imagine having something like that in our yard?"

Out the glass, I saw a courtyard filled with flowers. Proper flowers like irises and lilies. An orchestrated splattering of color. They'd built up tiers lined with wooden beams and rocks with stone paths cutting through the very organized flower beds. A little too perfect for my liking. But nobody asked me.

One bunch of chamomile spiked up next to a row of daffodils. I figured it grew in that place by accident. It didn't rightly fit in with the rest. Probably some bird dropped a seed or a squirrel planted it there. Chamomile wasn't always welcome in gardens like that one.

"Do you see the fairy flower?" I asked Gretchen.

She didn't hear me. Just kept her eyes on that long and wide desk.

Some young kid walked about the flowers. Tromping his oversized shoes without much care for the life around him. He looked at the chamomile plant and kicked at it with the toe of his shoe. Wrapping his hands around it, he strangled it, tugged it, yanked it right out of the ground. He tossed it aside as if it were nothing.

Just like that.

The violence of it turned my stomach.

"I thought we could get a sandwich on the way home," Gretchen said. "My stomach feels better today."

"That would be nice."

"Something quick. I know you're tired."

"Don't worry about me, honey."

The clicking of heels made its way down the hall. A petite woman wearing a long, white jacket walked into the office.

"Sorry to keep you waiting," she said, voice calm and full of business. She closed the door behind her and walked the long distance around the desk. She never took her eyes from the file in her hands. "One moment and I'll be present with you."

She eased back into her chair and right away scribbled a note in the file. With that small woman behind the desk, it seemed even bigger. Like it separated us from her by a mile.

"If I don't write things down right away, I forget them." Finally, she lifted her face to us. "Thank you for being patient."

Gretchen's hand in mine, I couldn't tell if the pumping pulse was hers or mine.

"I'm glad you were able to come in. Especially at such short notice." She turned to me. "Is this your mother?"

"Yes." Gretchen squeezed my hand.

"Nice to meet you." She half stood up to reach her tiny hand across the desk. It took all the stretch in me to get to her. "I'm Doctor Ferris."

Her dry hand in mine, it felt like her skin would soak up all my moisture. "My name is Olga."

"Nice to meet you," she said again before letting me go. "It's good to have family at these meetings."

She pulled a different file across her desk and opened it flat against the wood. Touching her long, dangling earrings, she read, making a gentle tinkling sound. I looked back out the window, hoping to see the chamomile on the ground one last time. But the kid must have taken it with him.

"We ran the tests we'd talked about." Her nose whistled as she inhaled. "After a scan like yours, we wanted to see what we're dealing with."

"Did you find anything?" Gretchen asked.

"As we discussed before, the tumor we found was of substantial size."

Goose pimples rose up on my arms. I turned to Gretchen. Her eyes, big and round, didn't leave the face of the doctor. She hadn't told me about a tumor. Not even on the ride over. It wasn't a small one, either. No wonder she'd been so sick. No wonder she hadn't eaten in weeks.

As much as I wanted to listen to the doctor's words, I couldn't get myself to focus. Her mouth moved, but I didn't understand the sounds she uttered. As if, all the sudden, she spoke a different language. The sound of her voice made a garbled, jumbled din in my ears. The swishing sound of my thudding heart added to the confusion.

"I'm sorry." Doctor Ferris closed the folder in finality and laced her fingers together on top of it. "I'm very sorry."

Silence. All I heard was the whistling of the doctor's nose. If only the thudding and swishing would come back, I might pretend not to know a lick of what was going on.

"Is this curable?" Gretchen asked. "I mean, do we need to do surgery or chemo? I'm up for whatever it's going to take."

The doctor swallowed hard, her chin jutted out and the tendons in her neck flexed. "At this point, any treatment will only serve to extend your life. Even then, we don't know by how much."

"I don't understand."

"Gretchen, your cancer is in the fourth stage. That means it's spreading."

"What's after the fourth stage?" Gretchen asked.

My heartbeat slammed through me.

"Nothing." The doctor's voice chilled the room. "Stage four is the final stage."

Dead, cold, pain-filled silence.

"Chemotherapy might shrink the tumor. But the cancer has spread." Her voice kept going and going. "We'll monitor how fast it goes."

Gretchen hadn't looked away from the doctor's face. "How long do I have?"

"I don't know," she answered. "I can only guess, really. I'd have to say seven to nine months with the treatment. Five to six without. But that's not a guarantee."

Not even a year. Hardly time to breathe. But, in that moment, I didn't care if I never took in oxygen again.

"It's an option to skip the treatment?" Gretchen asked.

"Treatment is always optional."

"But why would anyone decide not to do it?"

"Because the side effects can be hard to live with." Doctor Ferris blinked slowly. "Sometimes extending life only means the patient is sick longer."

"Mom. I'm sorry." Gretchen turned to me. Her eyes brimmed over with fear. "I should have told you. But I thought it was nothing."

I pulled her to me, holding the back of her head, feeling her body rise and fall when she inhaled. I couldn't stop the shaking.

It was both of us, quaking in our seats. Scared beyond our ability to hold still.

But I trusted You with her, I cried out from that deep place.

I pulled her even closer.

Chapter Twenty-One

EVELYN

I slept most of the weekend after the funeral for Josie and Shelly. During the few moments of wakefulness, I watched reruns of old TV shows and ate ice cream. Truth be told, I ate an entire half gallon of mint chocolate chip in two days. I wasn't proud of it. But once I got started, I couldn't make myself stop.

Sunday afternoon, shaky from the sugar and in need of real food, I scavenged through my cupboards. Gran would have called my food supply "Mother Hubbard cupboards." Empty. Except for some tea my mom had sent over the week before and a package of rice noodles. Well, and something far past its expiration date in the back of the fridge. But I didn't even want to think about that fuzzy mess right then.

"Hey, Char," I said into my cell phone while changing out of the sweatpants I'd worn the entire weekend. "What do you have going on tonight?"

"Nothing," she answered. "My social life is pathetic. Thanks for the reminder."

At her age, I worked at the funeral home full time. That meant on call all day, every day. Even Christmas.

I rolled my eyes. The girl had no idea what a pathetic social life even looked like.

"Okay. Let me be your social life tonight, okay?" Buttoning my jeans, I had to suck in my gut more than usual. The ice cream had made my clothes a little snug. "Meet me at Marshall's for dinner."

"Um, Ev, did you forget that you already have plans?"

"I have no idea what you're talking about." Pulling a shirt from the closet, I knocked its hanger onto the floor. I left it there for later.

"Don't you have a date?"

"I do?" My brain caught up with the conversation. "Oh, I do."

"Better get ready."

"How did you know? I didn't tell you."

"Did you forget who my boss is?" She laughed. "Hey, call me as soon as you get home, okay? I want to hear all about it."

Hanging up the phone, I tugged on the material of the shirt, stretching it away from my midsection. I realized that I couldn't place all the blame on the ice cream. The doughnuts and lattes had to have done some damage, too.

Looking in the mirror over my dresser and touching my hair, I realized I hadn't gotten a shower all weekend. With two hours before I had to meet Will, I'd have time. I hoped I'd have a few spare minutes to stop by a store for a shirt that fit.

I slipped into the only empty booth at Marshall's, successfully avoiding eye contact with the other diners. Just to be sure no one talked to me, I pulled a book from my purse, holding it over my face.

"Hey, there," Marshall said, standing to the side of my table. "Rough week, huh?"

Lowering the book, I sighed. I certainly didn't want to talk about work. Especially not Josie and Shelly's funeral. How most of the high school kids showed up, holding on to one another and crying. How Jay Bunker had broken down when he met the parents and apologized for not being able to save them. The mother who couldn't leave her daughters' gravesides for an hour after everyone else had already left. Her husband had stood at their car, waiting. Giving her time.

People in my town always got their noses into things, hoping for a little extra information. "Yup. It was a really rough week." I stared at the menu and tried to discourage any more questions.

"Shelly worked here, you know," he said, his voice real deep.

"I didn't know that."

"She was a good worker. Never gave me an attitude." Marshall scratched along his jawline. "That's rare these days."

"I'm sorry, Marshall."

"Yeah. Me, too. It come as a real shock. I don't even want to imagine what those parents are feeling right now." He put his hands on his hips. "You all doing okay? Must have been hard to see."

"Yup." I smoothed out the paper placemat menu. "I think we're all exhausted. Lots of late nights the past week or so."

"Fair enough." Marshall folded his skinny, hairy arms over his chest. "What you having to drink? Want a shake or something?"

"Diet pop is fine. Thanks." Although I really did want that shake.

"Suit yourself. I think you're skinny enough already." He pointed a long finger at the empty seat opposite me. "You waiting on somebody?"

"Yeah."

"Right on. That's cool." When he smiled, I saw the big gap in his front teeth. "A date?"

"Kind of."

"All right. That's good. I won't tease you too much."

He walked to the counter and drew a diet pop from the machine. When he set it on the table for me, he grinned again.

Moving from table to table, he attended to the other diners. He didn't usually mingle so much or wait on the tables. Typically, he kept to the kitchen. I wondered if he was covering Shelly's shift.

Will slid into the booth opposite me. "Sorry I'm late."

"It's not a big deal," I said.

"How's it going?"

"Okay, I guess." Resting my elbows on the table, I leaned forward. "How was youth group?"

"Oh, I don't know." He slumped in his seat. "Four kids showed up. They sat in a clump in the corner and texted the whole time."

"Kids these days."

"Seriously." He looked around the restaurant. "So this is

148

Marshall's?"

"Yeah. Is this your first time?"

"Barton didn't have very good things to say about the food." Will moved in closer to me. "He said Marshall's a pagan."

"He did?" I shook my head. "That's not true."

"Between you and me, I'm learning to take Barton with a grain of salt."

"That's probably a good idea."

"Oh, I met your sister today."

"At church?"

"Yes." He laughed. "She was nice. But…"

"What?" I closed my eyes, sighing. "What did she do?"

"She tried to give me your phone number."

"Oh my word. You're joking."

"Nope." He laughed again. "She said you were waiting for me to call."

"No way." I didn't know whether to be proud or mortified.

"Now, she works at the bakery, right?"

"Yeah." I sipped my pop. "She's not cut out for the funeral business."

"There are people cut out for that?"

"I think so. I mean, I think Cal and my grandpa were made to be funeral directors."

"Not you?" he asked.

"I'm still trying to figure out what I'm cut out for." With my thumb, I wiped condensation from the glass. "Some days it feels like it's suffocating me."

Resting head on hand, he lowered his eyebrows. He stayed quiet, not opening his mouth. I appreciated the silence.

"I could always get a job at the bakery, I guess."

"Oh, that's a dangerous place." He sat up straight and patted his stomach. "Barton's taken me there for staff meetings a few too many times, as you can see."

I exhaled, grateful he'd let me change the subject.

A glass of water in his hand, Marshall approached our table. He set the glass in front of Will and pulled a straw from his apron. Then he crossed his arms and looked down his nose.

"You the new guy over at First Church?" he asked.

"I am." Will extended his hand to shake Marshall's. "You're Marshall, right? I'm glad to finally meet you."

"Uh-huh." He didn't take Will's hand.

"I've heard a lot of great things about your food." Will lowered his hand back to the table. Somehow, he was able to act like the situation wasn't completely awkward. "Lots of good reviews."

"Sure. I bet you have." Marshall wasn't going to make anything easy for Will. "Listen, this is the only place you're likely to see me."

"Okay."

"Sunday's my busiest day around here. All the people coming for brunch or after church lunch."

"I hope they tip well." Will leaned back. "Especially the ones coming from church."

"They don't," Marshall said. "Maybe that's something you should work on with them over there."

"I'll have to do that."

"Anyway, I can't close down on Sundays just to come to church." Marshall narrowed his eyes at Will, waiting for a response.

"Well, then…" Will hesitated. "I guess I'll have to come in on Sundays. Just to see you."

Marshall's stone-set face cracked into a wide smile. Letting his arms loose, he grabbed hold of Will's hand and pumped it up and down.

"All right, then." His laugh filled the restaurant. "Here I thought you was coming in here to get me to come to church. Instead, I'm getting you to come and eat."

"If your food's good, I'll keep on visiting." He rubbed his belly. "I'm a big eater. I come by this gut honestly."

"I like you, man." Marshall smacked Will on the shoulder. "What do you kids want to eat?"

"I'll take the chopped salad, please," I said.

"You want fried chicken on that."

"Grilled." My stomach growled.

"You better get a side of fries," he insisted.

"No, thanks. Just the salad."

"Now, listen here, Evelyn. Just 'cause this boy's here don't mean you have to eat like a rabbit. He don't care if you get a big juicy burger and have the grease running down your chin. That's right, ain't it?" His hand smacked against Will's shoulder.

Will nodded.

"Evelyn Russell, what are you doing, ordering food in my restaurant if you ain't going to really eat?"

"Marshall, I'm ordering off the menu you made." My fingernails tapped on the tabletop. "Just the salad, please. No dressing."

"You see that?" Marshall said to Will, pointing at me with his pencil. "That right there is a strong-willed woman."

"Best kind." Will smiled.

"Miss Evelyn." Marshall wagged that pencil at me. "You don't blame me when you leave here hungry. Got it? I won't have people around town thinking I let you get away without eating."

"Yes, sir."

"And you, Rev?" Marshall turned to Will. "Don't you dare tell me you want a salad. I'll shut this place down."

"How about I try the special?"

"That's more like it." Marshall jotted a note. "You want the extra gravy. Trust me on that."

Chicken pot pie with a side of french fries. The special at Marshall's for twenty years. So good, it never had to change.

"I'll have that right out to you." Marshall walked back to the kitchen, shaking his head.

"Good job, there," I said. "It's not easy for a preacher to get Marshall to laugh."

"Didn't seem too hard to me."

"Let's just say that Old Buster kind of soured Marshall to church people."

"Old Buster?" Will scrunched his face. "Who's that? Sounds like a guy I need to avoid."

"That's what we all call Barton." I took a long drink from my glass. "I guess back in the day, he was pretty bad. If you got in his way, you got beat up. I'm not kidding. Legend has it he was single-handedly responsible for breaking at least twelve kids' arms one summer."

"No way."

"I'm serious."

"That's insane."

"I know. He's my grandma's cousin. You better believe she has all kinds of stories to tell about him."

Marshall carried two milk shakes to our table. He put them on the placemats in front of us.

"On the house," he said. "And I expect you to drink the whole thing, Evelyn."

I rolled my eyes.

"Thanks, Marshall," Will said. "Hey, you mind me asking how long you've lived around here?"

"All my life."

"Then could you tell me how Old Buster got his name?"

"Man." Marshall swatted his hand in the air and put a sour scowl on his face. "That dude was one bad...well, you know what. One summer, he busted up my brother's arm so bad, he couldn't go fishing for a couple years. Even then, his arm never grew right."

"How about that." Will widened his eyes.

"Yeah, you best watch yourself around that old man." Marshall shoved a hand into his apron pocket. "He's still got a bad temper. I'd hate to see you come in here with a cast."

"Thanks for the warning." Will lifted the glass full of chocolate shake. "And thanks for this. You just made yourself a new best friend."

"Wait till you taste the fries," Marshall said, walking to the kitchen. "They'll make you want to skip church."

Will cringed. "The potential for getting my arm broken is enough to make me want to skip church."

"Don't worry. Old Buster's changed." I sunk a straw into my shake.

"I hope so."

Will and I stood on the sidewalk outside the diner. It had taken us over an hour to eat our meal. It seemed like every other bite, someone came over to chat it up with Will. Of course, few even acknowledged me. I hated how much it hurt my feelings.

But Will had left a generous tip for Marshall who, in turn, insisted that dinner was on him. As we walked out, Marshall had given me a thumbs up.

That made my feelings a little better.

"Hey, how about we go for a drive?" Will pulled the keys from his pocket. "I think it would be nice to get out of town for a few hours."

"Have you been to the lake yet?"

"Which lake?"

"You're kidding me, right? Lake Michigan."

"Nope. Not yet."

"If we leave now, we can make it by sunset."

"Let's go." Grabbing my hand, he led me to his car. "I think we should hang out a whole lot."

"I'd like that."

"I think you're fun."

"Me? Really?" I laughed. "I don't think anyone has ever said that about me."

"That surprises me."

"Just wait until you see me when I'm stressed." Feeling the phone in my pocket shake, I stopped walking. "Shoot. Speaking of stress."

"What's wrong?"

Not letting go of his hand, I lifted the phone to my ear. "It's Cal. I have to take this. I'm sorry."

"Hey, Ev." Cal's voice on the other line sounded lower, gravely. "What are you doing?"

"I'm on a date."

"No way," he groaned. "We just got a call."

"Okay."

"I'm super sick. I've been barfing all day."

"Gross, Cal." I sighed.

"I'd call Granddad—"

"No," I interrupted him. "I'll do the removal."

"You're my favorite."

"I know. Text me the address, okay?"

"Yup."

"Feel better." I touched the screen to hang up.

"You have to go." Will squeezed his hand around mine. "It's okay."

"I'm not happy about it."

"I've got a ton of things to do for this week anyway." He looked down at our hands. "This is nice, though."

"When can I see you again?" I asked, surprised at how natural the question felt.

"How about tomorrow night? Even if it's at two in the morning. I don't care."

"I can make that work." Letting go of his hand, the place where his skin had touched mine chilled in the air.

"I like you, Evelyn."

"You're making me regret my decision to help out my brother."

"Then call me tonight, okay?" Dimples formed at the sides of his mouth when he smiled.

"I will."

Walking away from him and to my car, I got a little giddy. I knew that I'd need to calm myself down between changing my clothes and picking up the hearse. After all, I had to face a family in their worst moment. Right in the middle of one of my best.

Chapter Twenty-Two

OLGA

Papers spread all over our dinette. Clive shuffled through them, sighing and pinching the top of his nose. His pencil moved across scratch paper as he scribbled notes. Working numbers on the calculator, he used the eraser on his pencil to punch in the buttons. All the while, he kept his head bowed a little. I hadn't noticed how many liver spots had popped up on his scalp before.

"What can I get you, Clive?" I asked. He'd barely eaten any supper. "You want me to warm up something for you? I got a good piece of roast from the other night."

"I'm not hungry." His lips curved up, but he didn't look happy. The way the eyelids drooped over his blue eyes told me I was right. "Thanks, though, sugar."

"Honey, you haven't eaten a decent meal in a handful of days. You got me all kinds of worried about you."

"You know, I got plenty of reserves stored up right around my middle. I'm not going to starve any time soon." He took in a deep breath and let it out in one big puff. "You never worry so much about me unless you got something else upsetting you."

"Now, don't you go changing the subject." Turning my back to him, I took in a breath that made my head spin. I hated to keep a secret from him. "I wish you'd eat something."

"Olga, don't worry about me."

155

"Maybe I'll get a good bedtime snack into you, then."

I went about wiping counters I'd already scrubbed. Anything to keep me from thinking about Gretchen. All I wanted to do was tell Clive.

"You are the most beautiful thing I've ever seen," he said.

Still, after all those years with him, words like that made my heart flutter. More than anything else, because I knew he meant it. That night, though, the heartache of Gretchen's news thudded harder, drowning out both the pitter and the patter.

"Oh, I'm all turned upside-down over how to bill these people." Scratching the pencil across the paper, he marked out all kinds of figures. "I just don't feel right draining them. They lost both their kids. I don't know how I can charge them."

Sweat beaded on his forehead. He used a napkin to wipe it off.

"Are you hot, Clive?" I asked. "You want me to turn up the air conditioner?"

"It's a hard thing, losing a child." He shoved the papers into a file and folded it closed. "I don't know what's worse, losing them all at once like that or little by little."

"I don't know."

"I've seen both. It's one thing I can't figure out."

"They're both bad, Clive."

"That's the truth."

The living room window filled up with sunset. The round sun had dropped so fast. Like it had some place to be. Across the street, the corn glowed red.

"Would you look at that," I whispered. "The corn's blushing."

"I'll bet you anything Gretchen's sitting on her porch with a cup of tea right about now," Clive said, turning in his seat to see the sky. "She's always loved the sunset."

"Remember when we took her to the beach for the first time?" I stepped toward the window.

"She was just a little slip of a thing."

"And she thought the sky was on fire." My heart smiled with the memory, warming me all the way through. But, then, the weight of not telling Clive a word about her appointment stomped the smile away, turning me icy all over. "Oh, Clive. I can't keep this anymore."

"It sure is beautiful," Clive said, still looking at the red as it turned deep purple.

"I'm not talking about the sunset, honey." Flip-flopping, my stomach threatened to make me sick. "This isn't something I'm supposed to say a word about. But it's a burden I can't hold anymore."

Scraping across the floor, Clive's chair moved out from under him as he got up. His arms wrapped their way around me. "What is it?" he asked.

And I told him. Gretchen had asked me to keep it quiet until she figured out details. I wanted more than anything to respect her wish, but I just couldn't. Not from the other part of my flesh.

The fear for her had built up, bloating me. But when I told him, the pressure didn't ease. Instead, it filled me even more till I was fit to burst.

"This has always been my worst fear." Clive's words trembled.

Old age had made my memory slippery. As far as I could remember, Gretchen had been about two years old. Not a tiny baby anymore, but not quite a big girl, either. I did remember we had her in a small bed with a rail to keep her from rolling out in the night.

One evening, Clive came upstairs, the words blubbering out of him. I couldn't make out the meaning of a single one of them. I'd got him to sit down in his easy chair with a cold glass of water before he could get out the words to tell me what had happened.

Earlier that day, he'd had to embalm a little boy. Not much older than our Gretchie. The poor little thing had choked on something and passed away in his mama's arms. Fast and terrifying. If I'd let myself think on it too much, I knew I'd lose my mind.

For close to a month after that day, Clive slept on the floor of Gretchen's bedroom. He'd wake in the night, in a cold-sweat-panic, having to check on her to make sure her chest moved as she breathed. He'd cover her, but not let the blanket get up too close to her face. He'd turn her if she'd got rolled over on her stomach. During the day, he'd search the apartment for things she might swallow and get caught in her throat. He insisted I cut her food as small as I could. I'd never seen him scared like that before.

As much as worry had become a part of my mothering, his horror wore on me. His anxiety lorded over me, weighing me down like a yoke. I couldn't carry the burden of it.

Never before and never after had I thought about leaving. But, in those months, I darn near had my bags packed.

"We can't put her in a bubble," I'd said one night, at the end of my patience. "She's a child. We've got to let her play and explore. We can't keep her from everything that might hurt her. This is no life, Clive."

"You didn't see the father's eyes, Olga." Finger shaking, he pointed it in my face. "You didn't see the way he watched that little casket go underground. I won't let that happen to us."

Making my touch tender, I wrapped my fingers around his pointing hand and pulled it down. "We have to let her be a little girl."

"What if something happens?" Still yelling and with his face fierce, tears streamed from his eyes.

I'd used my other hand to cup his cheek, feeling the heat of his skin, even on that chilly day. "We have to trust that God isn't going to let that be. He's got her in His hands."

"What about the little boy?" His voice almost didn't make it to my ears. He quaked so hard, I worried he'd make himself have a heart attack. "I know it's not right, but I keep feeling like God failed him."

"No, Clive."

"Listen, Olga." His voice had turned hard. "I can't help but wonder when He's going to fail us, too."

After I told Clive about Gretchen's cancer, he'd got real tired. We'd made our way into bed. I slept for a little bit before waking. The dark sky outside my window and our apartment silent, I rolled into the warmth of Clive's side, feeling his breath on my face. Moving his arm to circle behind my back, he pulled me in and let my head rest on his chest, his undershirt, soft under my cheek.

"You awake?" he asked.

"Yes." Grief settled, a burning pit in my stomach. "Are we going to be okay?"

"Okay isn't always the best place to be, sweetheart." Soft lips pressed against my head, he kissed me.

I couldn't release words past the tightening in my chest and throat. All I could manage were quiet tears and prayers begging for mercy.

Chapter Twenty-Three

EVELYN

Storm-heavy clouds hung low in the early morning sky. Getting out of my car, I breathed in the sharp, chalky scent of coming rain. Maple leaves turned upside-down, preparing for the downpour. I looked from the leaves to the tree to the house. My mom's house.

Framed by the picture window, she sat curled up on the couch, holding a book close to her face. Her bare toes, pulled up under her, wiggled. She turned a page, lips moving a little as she read.

The smell of coffee welcomed me as I opened the screen door.

"Hey, Ev." She closed her book. "What a nice surprise."

"I was up early." I didn't mention how I'd been on the phone with Will until dawn. "I figured I'd come see you for a few minutes."

"I'm glad you did," she said. "You've been so busy lately. It seems like I haven't seen you in ages."

"It's been pretty crazy at the Big House." I slipped my shoes off and stepped into the kitchen. "Do you need a warm up on your coffee?"

"No, thanks. I'm having tea anyway." She uncurled herself and dropped the book on the coffee table. "I brewed that pot for Charlotte."

"She's working today?" I poured a cup for myself.

"Yup. And she had a really late night." Scrunching up her nose, she pushed her lips together. "I guess some of her friends called to hang out."

"When did she get in?" I asked, stirring creamer into my mug.

"Well after two in the morning." Leaning over, she picked up a piece of paper from the floor. She sat up, holding a spot under her ribs. "I'm trying to remember that she's an adult. My heart doesn't agree, though. It still thinks she's my baby."

"Deirdre isn't going to make life easy for her."

"Especially if she shows up late."

"When does she have to be there?" My first sip of coffee burned my tongue.

"Nine."

I checked the clock. "It's half past eight."

"I know." My mom shrugged, half her mouth tugging up in a smirk.

"Has she gotten up yet?"

"Not that I can tell." Picking up her mug, she took a sip. "And I'm not going to wake her."

As if cued, Charlotte stormed down the steps, pulling her hair into a ponytail.

"I can't believe you didn't get me up," she shrieked. "I'm late. Deirdre's going to fire me. Thanks so much."

"Good morning, sweetie." My mom's voice came out as a song. "I made coffee for you."

"Great. Awesome. I can take it with me to the unemployment office." Charlotte's tone sliced through the air. "Do me a favor and wake me up next time when you know I have to work."

"Set an alarm," I said. "It's not Mom's fault you need to grow up."

"Shut up, Evelyn." Char dumped coffee into a travel mug, spilling a puddle worth on the floor in the process. She let a word slip that I was pretty sure she hadn't intended on our mom hearing. "Sorry."

"Have a nice day, Char," my mom called after her, waving.

Charlotte rushed out the door, letting it slam behind her.

"Well, that was a nice way to start the day." I made my way to the kitchen, grabbing a towel to wipe up the coffee on the floor.

"She'll feel bad about that later."

I nodded, knowing that she was right. Charlotte's conscious never let her alone for too long.

"How about you come sit with me for a little while." She pulled a pillow to her stomach. "Do you have a few minutes?"

I tossed the coffee-soaked towel into the sink. Walking back into the living room, I realized I'd left my mug on the counter. I'd planned on getting another cup. But I didn't want to take the time right then. Her voice sounded thin and sad.

Sitting, I let her take my hand. I hadn't held her hand since right before my father left. After that, she didn't have time anymore. She only had time to keep the four of us on our feet. Single parenting made her carry the world times three.

Growing up all the sudden like that had made childhood seem even lonelier.

"Ev, there's something I need to tell you."

"What's going on?"

"I have cancer."

"Okay." I blinked, letting the word sink in. "What kind?"

Breathing in and out through her mouth, she held her lips in a tight circle. "I'm kind of nervous talking about it."

"Don't be. I'm not upset."

"I don't want you to be scared."

"Don't worry about me right now, Mom," I said. "What kind of cancer is it?"

I hoped she'd say thyroid or an early stage of breast cancer. Something treatable. Something they caught fast enough.

"I have a large tumor on my liver."

My eyes fell on the pillow that covered her stomach. "What stage?"

"Four."

Stage four. The last stage. I'd embalmed so many people who had died after years of battling cancer, only to have it occupy their organs and bones. Even taking over their brain. Stage four rang like a death knell.

"Have you gotten a second opinion?" The calm that held my emotions back surprised me. Years of training, I supposed.

"No." She touched my hair. "I really like how you got your hair done. It's so pretty."

"Thanks." I moved my head away from her fingers. "When do you start treatment?"

"Next week." She pulled the pillow tighter.

"Can they operate? Sometimes they can remove tumors like that." Her hair hit against the sides of her face as she shook her head.

"Did they tell you how long?" A warm, salty tear made its way into my mouth. It surprised me. I'd thought I had my emotions pushed down. "Do you know?"

Letting her elbow rest on the arm of the couch, she held her head up with one hand. "With your hair like that, it really makes your eyes stand out."

"Mom, don't do that right now. No changing the subject."

"Well, I don't have many answers, Evelyn." She rested her head back. "All they could do was guess. And I really want to forget all about having a deadline."

"I'm sorry, Mom."

"I mean, it's terrible to think that my life is on this countdown."

Life was exactly that. A countdown. The time just ticked away louder the closer death got.

"Are you scared?" I asked.

Eyes open, her pupils so small I almost couldn't see them, she looked into my face. "Yes," she answered. "I'm really scared. I just don't know what scares me the most about this whole thing."

I couldn't stand looking at her anymore. A few tears weren't bad, but I didn't want to gush to her. She didn't need that. And I didn't want her to comfort me.

"I should have more faith. Right?" She let go of my hand, holding the pillow even tighter than before. "But I'm dying. And I have so much more I wanted to do. And I'm not going to get the chance."

"Why not?"

"I've got all this treatment I have to go through and appointments to keep. And I'm going to get sick and my hair's going to fall out." She tossed the pillow to the other side of the couch. "I'm sorry, Ev. I was doing so well keeping myself together until I started talking about it."

"Don't be sorry."

"It's stupid that I'm fifty years old and dying."

"I'm sorry." I could have smacked myself. Couldn't I have given a more human response? Not the robotic, funeral director words I said to every person I worked with?

"Thanks." She covered her face with both hands, muffling her voice. "I'll be fine in just a minute or two."

I reached for her, touching her back. "You don't have to be fine, Mom."

Lowering her hands, she put them around my neck, pulling me close.

She didn't let go of me for a long time.

Chapter Twenty-Four

OLGA

Rosetta sat across from me at my dinette. She'd brought me a cheese danish that just about melted in my mouth. Light and creamy comfort from my dear friend.

"Do you think God will have something so sinful in heaven?" I licked a stray bit of icing off my finger.

"Now, Olga," Rosetta said. "Whoever deemed this delicacy as sin? Certainly not the Almighty Creator who made cows for butter and cane for sugar. This is all part of His good and perfect gift to us, don't you think?"

"I suppose I shouldn't argue with that."

"Besides, these are blessed baked goods."

"Is that so?"

"Sure are. Last night, when we talked on the phone, I knew something was wrong." Rosetta folded the napkin in her hands. "This morning, when I got up and out of bed, the Holy Spirit said, 'Rosie, you get over there. And take something yummy.'"

"The Holy Spirit calls you Rosie?"

"He does, indeed. Why not? He knows me in and out." Thick, shapely lips smiled across her face. Such a beauty, that Rosetta. "The baked goods, though, were a streak of genius on His part, don't you think?"

"I wonder if Deirdre doesn't know the high and holy calling of her pastries?"

"Maybe. I don't know. But I do believe Charlotte does." Rosetta sipped from her mug. "She knows what it is to worship in the kitchen."

"She is in love with that job." Pushing my fingertip into a loose crumb, I lifted it to my mouth.

Rosetta took the last sip of coffee and watched me over the brim of her mug. When she put the cup down, she pushed her lips together. "Now, Olga, how are you doing? I mean to get the truth. Don't you tell me 'fine.' I'll know that's not the whole truth."

"You get right to the point, don't you?" Grabbing for her mug, I made to get up. "You want some more coffee?"

"Not yet." Her hand on top of the mug, she prevented me from taking it. "In a few minutes. Thank you."

Folding my napkin, I was sure her eyes stayed on me, smiling. That strong-willed woman would sit in her chair all day until I answered the question. I figured I might as well just give in.

"Rosetta, I don't know how much I can tell you." The pressure on my chest made me breathe real shallow. "I was asked not to tell anybody just yet. And I already broke that promise to tell Clive."

"I'm not here for a tidbit, Olga." Taking her hand off the mug, she reached across the table. Her brown hand on my white one. "I'm here to check up on my friend."

"You're so good to me."

"It's because I love you, honey," she said.

"I'm not doing so good, Rosie." Rubbing the spot between my eyebrows, I tried to stop the headache that had started up. "And that's the truth. I'm having it rough right now. We got some news about Gretchen that's got me all kinds of worried."

Rosetta lifted her hands to touch her cheeks. Those rich brown eyes of hers filled all the way up with tears.

"Oh. My sweet Olga. I am sorry."

"Thank you."

"How can I comfort you?" Rosetta went back to holding my hand, patting it a couple times.

"I don't know."

"You aren't accustomed to receiving comfort, are you?"

"I can't say that I am."

Fifty years Clive and I'd held the hands of our neighbors, soothing them through loss. We'd learned the right words, the soft expressions. We practiced comfort, never having need for it to come our way. Until then. And I didn't know that I could absorb the mercy.

"Olga, I don't know how you expect to keep on dealing out comfort like you do without receiving some yourself."

No words. Just nodding.

"It's like a well, dug deep. If the comfort isn't coming in, it sure can't go back out." The table shifted a little when she leaned on it. "Do you see what I'm saying?"

"I think so."

"You need to learn how to fill up on mercy."

"Gretchen's sick." The words burst out of me. "Real sick. We don't know how long she's got. Not really. But we do know she's probably not going to last another year."

"Oh my soul." Rosetta's mouth turned down at the corners. "My soul is heavy for you, Olga."

"I can't do anything for her, Rosie."

"Oh, honey."

"All her life, I've been the one to fix whatever was wrong. When she fell down or got teased at school, I had a bandage or an encouraging word." The back of my hand knocked a tear from my cheek. "And when she got divorced, we came and got her and the kids. We gave them a place to live. We fixed everything."

Muscles sore from fighting the fear and grief tensed up all at once.

"Now, Olga, I got to ask you a question. And you might not like to answer it. That's all right by me." She lowered her eyes to catch mine. "How are you feeling about God right now?"

Pulling lips in, I set my jaw so hard, it ached. "I never doubted Him before."

"But you're doubting Him now?"

"He isn't doing right by my daughter," I said.

"Don't let that suffocate you, Olga. It will drown the faith right out of you. Don't you let it have that kind of power."

"Rosie, I never thought I'd be so tempted to curse God and die." The tears came faster than I could wipe them away. "But I'm furious. I've never been so angry about anything in all my life."

167

"You can be angry. He's used to that, I imagine." Her voice turned into a smooth, cool balm, relieving a bit of my raw, beat-up heart. "What you can't be is bitter."

"I know."

"I won't sit back on my hands and watch the bitterness eat you up." She clucked her tongue, like she always did when she had a hard truth to tell. "I've been watching what bitterness has done to our Beverly. And I'll tell you what, Olga, it will make all the difference in how you live through this time. Curse God and die will only get you more hardship with no one to carry you through. But you keep your hope in the Lord, even when you don't feel like it, and He'll provide more than what you ask."

My body couldn't take sitting anymore. I felt like jumping out of my skin. Up and to the counter, I hovered myself over the sink and took off my glasses. Running the water, I splashed a little of it on my face. It cooled my hot, sore eyes.

"This is too hard," I cried. "I can't bear it."

"Then don't." Rosetta had got behind me, her arm wrapped around my waist. "Let me be the hands and feet of Jesus to take good care of you. To love on you. You got me, honey. And I got a whole well full of mercy and comfort to spill over you."

The water dripped from my nose, dropping into a cup at the bottom of the sink.

"Let the comfort wash over you. It can rinse away all the anger you got boiling inside."

I prayed for a flood.

Chapter Twenty-Five

EVELYN

I didn't want to leave my mom. Not with all that cancer inside her. With the undefined amount of time I'd still have with her. Especially not after the way she'd clung to me. My whole day could have been full of cleaning and cooking. Taking care of her could be my job. I wouldn't mind a hiatus from the funeral home. Granddad would have understood. I wondered if I could sublease my apartment. Move back into my old room.

"I need to rest." Her words broke my planning. "I'm so exhausted."

"Go lie down in your bed." I sat up straight. "I'll stay down here and take care of things. I'll call Granddad and ask for the day off."

"I really am tired, Ev." She sighed. "You know I wouldn't be able to rest. I'd want to help you."

"You wouldn't even know I'm here."

"I would."

"I can be quiet."

"Evelyn, today I feel well enough to do the dishes and stick a meal in the Crock-Pot. So that's what I'm planning on doing after a nap." She pushed the hair out of her face. "Soon, though, I won't feel up to it. Then, I'll need your help. I'll let you know when that time comes."

"I could just stay. You'll need me."

"Later, Ev." She closed her eyes. "I don't want my kids taking care of me yet."

My phone beeped with a text message. The third from Cal that I'd ignored.

"How about we all have dinner over here tonight. After you're all done with work." Opening her eyes, she looked out the window. "I'll catch up with everybody first."

"What did Don say?" I asked. "You told him, right?"

"Honey, you need to let some things be between Don and me."

"He didn't take it well, did he?"

"Evelyn, it doesn't matter how he took it." She pushed the hair off her forehead. "I'm not having this discussion with you. It isn't fair."

Standing, I grabbed the pillow and handed it to her. I hated how I'd turned the conversation into an argument. Disappointment in myself joined my anxiety for her. "I'm sorry."

"I know it's still hard to get used to, but he's my husband, Ev. Some things are just between husband and wife. Even after only a year."

"Yup." I made my way to the door. "I didn't mean to upset you."

"You didn't."

"Well, I'm sorry anyway." I pushed the shoes onto my feet. "It wasn't right for me to ask."

"He cried, Evelyn," she said. "When I told him, he cried."

Exhaustion pressed against the inside of my head. Not just from the sleepless night. Thinking of Don crying made me want to curl up and sleep the sadness away.

"This isn't going to be easy on any of us." Standing, my mom picked up her mug. "We have to lean on one another, you know."

"Yeah."

"And Don needs to be included, Ev. I know he hasn't been around all that long, but he needs us to act like his family."

Never before had I wanted a dad more than that moment. Letting Don fill that void seemed such a risk. But I didn't have another option.

"Oh, goodness." Resting hands on hips, she closed her eyes. "Here I've spent all this time talking about me and I didn't ask about your date."

"It's okay, Mom. You've got more important things going on."

"But I want to hear about it." She sighed and pointed to her stomach. "This isn't the only thing going on around here, you know."

"It went well," I said. "He's great. I like him a lot."

"I'm so glad, Ev. I want you to be happy."

Happy seemed so out of reach. An hour before, it would have been a much better word to use.

My phone buzzed yet again. I exhaled, my chest tightening.

"Well, you'd better get to work, huh?" She took a step toward me. "Can't let Cal and Granddad do all the fun work."

"I'm hoping that if I get there later, I won't have to embalm anybody." I forced a smile.

"Here's to hoping."

"Hey, Mom," I said. "Please don't be scared."

"I'll try not to."

I walked along the sidewalk toward the Big House. For the first time in years, the urge to pray rushed through me. Like a rustling wind whipping around my chest.

Most people I knew fell into prayer like a conversation with an old friend. Gran never had a problem. I could have sworn that woman had a direct line to God. Not me, though. I'd had to work at it. Struggle for the words. Force myself to thank God for my food and family. I'd have been the first to call my prayer life immature.

I didn't feel qualified to tell Him how to do His job. He had plenty of people doing so without me adding to the noise.

Usually, I stuck to "thanks" or "ugh." Most of the time it worked okay.

That day, though, it seemed He could use a little direction, as gutsy as I felt for the idea.

Years before, Granddad had a thick oak tree cut down. The branches had hung too close to our roof. With every storm, the wood knocked against the house, threatening damage.

The stump had remained. Cal and I had used it for games of King of the Hill. In those days, I usually won.

That morning, however, as I climbed onto the stump, I doubted I could out-muscle anyone.

Knees bent to my chin, I wrapped my arms around, hugging my shins. A rough spot in the wood snagged on a string in the hem of my pants, pulling it loose.

"Of course," I huffed, breaking the string free. "Stupid day."

I had to breathe in and out several times, working myself up to pray.

"I don't know what to say to You about this," I whispered. "I've seen too many people beg You to save someone and You don't do it." A fly or bee buzzed around my head until I swatted it away. "I don't feel like begging."

Waiting, I hoped He'd send me some kind of communication. A sign, perhaps. Something to transcend my doubts and fears. Nothing. Just a breeze through the leaves above my head, carrying with it the smell of a storm.

"You could heal her, but I don't think you will. I guess that's bad of me." I sniffed, wiping my nose. "All I'm going to ask is that You don't let her be in a lot of pain. It wouldn't serve any purpose. And it wouldn't make You look all that good."

My phone beeped again. Another message from my brother, wondering where I was.

"Anyway," I said. "That's all I ask. Make it easy on her. Please."

Unfolding myself, I hopped off the stump and headed down the sidewalk toward the Big House. I'd have to use thread from the prep room to fix my hem before it unraveled.

Granddad sat on the funeral home porch. I'd never seen him out there. He always kept himself too busy. Never allowing himself time to sit unless he was working in the office. Even during slow weeks or months. He kept working.

Stopping on the sidewalk, I watched him for a while, knowing how hard this thing with my mom must have hit him. Every few seconds, he'd drink from his mug.

All my life, he'd been the big, strong one. The base of our family. I believed nothing shook him. That morning, though, he seemed small. Older, even. Folded up on himself.

While You're at it, I added to my silent prayer. *Take it easy on Gran and Granddad, too. They deserve some gentleness.*

I shifted my weight to the left. Under my foot, a twig snapped and Granddad flinched, turning in my direction. He had no smile in his eyes. No spark of anything, really.

My heart broke even more.

"Hey," I said, nearing the porch. "Good morning, Granddad."

He stared at his feet, frowning and tilting his head from one side to the other, making the bones in his neck crackle.

"Looks like a good storm's rolling in," he said.

"We could use it."

"Yup." He cleared his throat. "You just talk to your mama?"

Leaning against the porch rail, I tried to find something to say. Nothing came to mind. At least nothing that wouldn't have reduced me to a sobbing mess. So, I decided to keep myself quiet.

"How are you holding up?" he asked.

I should have known the emotion would surface once I got closer to him and heard his voice. He had that way with me. I turned my face toward the garden.

Avoidance. Redirection. Denial of feeling. My coping skills since childhood to keep a handle on the chaos around me. At least that's what my therapist had called it. Whatever. I only hoped it would work for me again.

"I don't know," I answered.

"That's a good answer, I think. As good as any I can come up with." He sighed. "I can't figure it out, either. Part of me is angry. Suppose that's a normal reaction, huh?"

"I feel like I should start praying a lot harder." I rolled my eyes at the Sunday school answer.

He rubbed his fingers over the top of his head. "I don't feel much like praying at all."

Exhaling, the tight spot in my chest tensed a bit. "I'm scared."

"Me, too." He patted the seat on the bench next to him. I watched his hand move up and down. Thick fingers tapped the old, graying wood. His gold wedding band knocked against a metal fastener.

When I sat down, he put his arm around me and his hand on my shoulder, pulling me close. I lowered my head to rest on him. His shoulder cushioned my head and his heart thumped in my ear. Rich aftershave, spicy and warm smelling, made me tear up. He'd worn that same kind as long as I remembered. If I had to pick one smell that made me feel at home, it was Granddad's aftershave.

"I'm not ready to lose her," I whispered.

"Me either, Evelyn." His voice resonated from within his chest. "I couldn't guess how many times I've seen something exactly like this. Somebody gets sick out of nowhere. And the family is absolutely knocked out by it. That's how I feel this morning. Knocked out."

I could have fallen asleep, held against Granddad's shoulder, hearing the life beating inside him. He'd held me like that after my father walked away from us. He didn't mind me crying on him.

My phone sounded again. Cal's text message read, *Am I the only one working today? Remember me? I'm the sick one!*

"Cal doesn't know yet, does he?" I asked.

"No." He shifted his weight. "But I'm worried about how he'll take it. It's real hard on a man when his mother dies. Real hard."

"And Char." I sat up, leaving a spot on his lapel where the fabric had soaked up my tears. "She's so sensitive."

"I expect she's going to have a rough time of it."

"Mom wants to have a family dinner tonight," I said.

"That's a good idea." He managed half a smile. "I'll order a couple pizzas."

"I'd better get inside." Standing, a thousand white dots rushed across my vision, making me dizzy. I held on to the railing of the porch. "I'll send Cal over to Mom's in a little while."

"Listen," Granddad said, stopping me. "If you don't get the accounts payable done today, it's all right. They'll still be there next week, if need be. We all need to try and take it easy for the next day or two."

I made it through the front doors of the Big House and into the bathroom before I lost it. The water rushed from the faucet as hard as I could turn it. I hoped it would drown out the wailing that heaved out of me.

Reaching into my purse, I dropped the last pill into my hand before putting it on my tongue. I washed it down with a handful of water. It would take half an hour for the medicine to move through my blood stream and into my head. Even then, it still wouldn't have the power to reach the pain.

Chapter Twenty-Six

OLGA

Clive told me to take a nap. He'd never been the kind of man to order me around. But he knew when I needed to take a good rest. And that day I needed it. I'd not gotten a whole lot of sleep for weeks.

When I turned to make my way to the bedroom, he told me about dinner at Gretchen's house that night. He'd not hear about me cooking, though. He'd already ordered the pizzas.

I submitted to my husband and got in a nap. He submitted to me and agreed to let me make a salad. It might not have been what the Apostle Paul had in mind, but that kind of submitting to each other worked out just fine for us for over fifty years.

My nap ended short, though, to the sound of the refrigerator door slamming.

"Clive?"

"Sorry, Olga," he called from the kitchen. "I was getting myself a drink of lemonade."

I about rolled myself out of the bed. My poor body disagreed with my decision to move it out to the living room. It protested with cracking hips and grinding knees.

"I think that nap did me more harm than good," I said, walking up behind Clive.

He stood at the window, overlooking the garden. He didn't answer me. Didn't even turn my way. Just rested hands in his pants pockets. The glass of lemonade sat on a coaster in the center of the coffee table. For the first time in my memory, I hadn't had to remind him to use a coaster.

"What are you looking at, honey?" Lacing my arm through his, I drew close to his side.

He pointed out the window. Gretchen wore leather gloves on her hands and a wide-brimmed hat on her head, standing among the lavender and chamomile. The storm earlier in the day had given the plants a good drink of water. I guessed she was checking for new blooms or weeds.

Turning her head, she saw us looking down at her. Her gloved hand waved back and forth. The smile on her face grew. Just the way she had as a little girl on stage at church, singing in the Sunday school choir. Oh, how her life had been ours. How we'd lived through her.

"Our daughter is the strongest of all of us, I think." Clive's voice trembled. "How did she learn such courage?"

"Now, don't you let her see you crying, Clive." I gripped his arm tighter. "She's happy right now, see? Let her have that."

"Look who's coming," Clive whispered.

Charlotte walked the path from their house, the ponytail on the back of her head swinging from side to side. She darn near skipped to her mama. Twenty-two years old and still spirited like a little girl. Once she reached Gretchen, she said a few words. I wished I could have heard what she'd said. Whatever it was, those two hugged so tight, I could almost feel it.

"I can't watch this." Clive let my arm loose and turned his back to the window. "It'd just break my heart worse."

The floor to the kitchen creaked under his steps. I didn't even think to remind him about his lemonade. He probably wouldn't have wanted it anyway.

I watched Gretchen shake the gloves off, letting them fall to the ground on either side of her. She grabbed both of Charlotte's hands. She nodded as Charlotte talked to her. I bit my fingernail, worried about how she'd tell her youngest child. The baby of our family.

Charlotte's perky smile sunk into a frown and melted into a calm, quiet crying. The girl sat down on the ground. She crossed her legs and put hands over her face.

Gretchen stooped, landing on her knees with so much grace. She pulled Charlotte into a deep, warm embrace. I could about feel that one, too.

All around the two of them, the chamomile tipped back and forth in the wind.

Chapter Twenty-Seven

EVELYN

In every major tragedy, Gran entered what we called "fix-it mode." That basically meant she cleaned and cooked without stopping until either the crisis was averted or she crashed from exhaustion.

When I got to my mom's to help set up for our family dinner, Gran had already cleaned out the refrigerator and washed all the bedding.

She'd banned my mom to the couch, leaving her to watch as we set the table.

"Do you know where she keeps the paper plates?" Gran asked me.

"Why are you whispering?" I held a stack of napkins.

"I don't want her to get up."

I searched the pantry, pushing aside cans of corn and jars of dried tea.

"What are you looking for?" My mom stood from the couch.

"Paper plates."

"Evelyn." Gran swatted me with a dishcloth.

"It would be easier if you'd let me show you where they are." Mom walked into the kitchen, pulled open the cupboard above the stove and pointed. "They're right up there. I'll even let Ev grab them if that'll make you feel better."

Granddad carried a stack of pizza boxes in through the front door. When he met my eyes he raised his messy, gray brows. I grabbed the top few boxes.

"Hi, Dad." My mom reached for one of the boxes.

"I got it, baby girl," he said. "I don't want you getting any of those gut pains tonight."

"Now, those pizzas can go on the table." Gran held a bowl of pasta salad. "We'll be all set in a couple minutes."

"Gretchen, how about you go sit." Granddad nodded at Gran. "Let Mrs. Fix-It take care of things tonight. It'll keep her happy."

Obediently, my mom returned to her designated spot on the couch. Gran had set her up with pillows and an end table covered with tissues and a water bottle. Next, I imagined, she'd be offering ginger ale and beef bouillon. Gran's remedies for just about any ailment.

Struggling with the screen door, Cal walked in, bags of chips filling his arms. He dumped them onto the table next to the pizzas.

"Don's right behind me," he said.

"Oh, good." Mom peeked out the window and waved. "I asked him to pick up some ice cream."

"I'm so hungry." Cal pulled open one of the bags. "Where's Char?"

"Up in her room."

"How's she doing, honey?" Gran asked.

"I don't know." My mom twirled a strand of hair around her finger.

"Who is that out in the yard with Donald?" Gran asked.

Standing on tiptoes, I strained to look out the window over the kitchen sink. Will walked to the porch, carrying a white cake box from Deirdre's. My heart dropped out of my chest.

"Are you blushing, Ev?" Cal winked at me.

"Oh, is that him?" Gran lowered the bowl to the table. "I haven't gotten a chance to meet him yet."

"He was really glad I invited him." Cal smirked at me.

"Are you serious? You couldn't have warned me?" I threw a washcloth into the sink full of soapy water, creating an explosion of suds that splashed all over my shirt.

"I'm happy he could make it." Cal walked over to my mom. "I hope that's okay with you."

"It's fantastic." Mom's smile beamed for him. "I've been dying to meet him."

Everyone stopped moving and looked at her. Gran put both hands on her stomach, as if feeling for something. They moved as she breathed.

"Oh." My mom pulled her hand up, covering her mouth and laughing. "That was a poor choice of words."

Cal joined her in laughing. He put his arm around her shoulder and kissed her cheek. "Such a joker."

Will and I sat on the loveseat. Cal had insisted with winks and knowing smiles. It had turned out to be a good idea, inviting Will over. I wouldn't have admitted it to Cal, though. He'd have gloated for at least a week. But Will diverted a little of the tension while managing to charm my family. Even Don.

The two of them talked all through dinner. All about fishing. Will admitted that he'd never been. Still, Don went on and on. And Will asked all kinds of questions. I didn't hang on to every word of their discussion. I heard enough to know that the two of them could get along. Then again, I'd realized that Will could make friends with just about anybody.

"Donald," Gran broke in. "I think you found yourself a kindred."

"Why's that?" Don turned toward her.

"Well, I've never heard you talk so much." She winked at him. "I guess I should have asked you about fishing a long time ago."

"Oh, I talk plenty." Don put his arm around my mom. "Just ask Gretchen."

"He talks my ear off all the time." My mom giggled. "He says the funniest things in his sleep."

I cringed, not wanting to hear about my mom sharing a bed with Don. But when I watched them, the way Don kissed her cheek, I knew he loved her.

"So are we going to keep avoiding this?" Charlotte slid her untouched pizza on the coffee table.

"Avoid what, buddy?" Cal asked from his seat next to her.

"Mom's cancer." She cleared her throat. "I mean, we might as well just talk about it. We all know she's got it. And we're sitting here talking about fish. Why aren't we talking about what's really going on?"

If the air hadn't been sucked out of me before, Char's words did it just then.

"Charlotte," I whispered. "Maybe we should wait until Mom's ready to talk about it."

"She's right. We should talk about it." Mom rested her hand on Don's knee. "Go ahead, Char."

Will stretched his arm out around my shoulders. Back stiff, I couldn't relax. Strangely, I felt very far away from the discussion. Numb. A lot like how I felt as a funeral director. Detached from the situation. Observing only.

"Well, I guess I don't understand why this is such bad news." Char breathed out her nose. "I mean, I'm upset just like everybody else. But people beat cancer all the time."

"Honey." Mom dragged out the word. "It's not the kind of cancer that can be beat."

Will leaned over and whispered in my ear. "I'm going to sit on the porch for a few minutes."

After he left and the screen door closed behind him, I wished I'd asked him to stay. Without him there, I'd have to really feel the emotions. I couldn't handle that. Sitting on one side of the loveseat, by myself, I felt small and alone.

"What do you mean you can't beat the cancer, Mom?" Charlotte asked, tilting her head and wrinkling her nose.

"It's stage four," Cal muttered.

"I'm going to die from this." My mom got up from her place on the couch and kneeled by Char. "I thought I explained that to you."

My little sister covered her face with both hands and folded in half. She didn't know death like the rest of us did. The inevitability of it hadn't touched her before that day.

"I don't want to think about fighting this. Because I'm going to lose no matter what I do. You know?" My mom kissed Charlotte's head. "I don't want to lose."

Don got up from his seat and kneeled next to my mom, wrapping his arms around her. Somehow, I hadn't noticed that she'd started crying. He whispered in her ear and rubbed her back.

For the first time since I met him, I didn't resent Don.

Chapter Twenty-Eight

Olga

I woke up on Sunday morning to pouring down rain and booming thunder. A flash of light flickered through a gap in my bedroom curtains. I counted before I heard the thunderclap. Ten seconds. For the life of me, I could not remember what that meant.

Clive grunted as I touched his arm, but his eyelids didn't lift. So I got up to make me a cup of coffee. It ended up too bitter and with a bunch of grounds at the bottom of my cup. It only served to sour my already grumpy mood.

"Sorry, Lord." I closed my Bible. "I don't feel like making a joyful noise today. The joy's all used up."

By the way the storm growled, I figured He'd have to settle for that noise a little longer.

Aunt Gertie would never have abided my moping about. She'd have taken her measuring stick to my behind to remind me to do all things without grumbling or protesting. Her way of getting things done proved pretty effective. With me, at least. Just a glance at that ruler pushed the complaint right back down my throat. Those six boys, though, took a whole lot more whooping before they'd mind her. As for me, I swallowed my grumbles. Aunt Gertie had a strong swing on that stick.

That stormy morning, though, a grumbling attitude clouded over my soul. My entire family hurt. Every single one of them. I couldn't come to make myself say "blessed by Your name."

So, breaking my normal morning routine, I skipped my Bible reading. I washed the picture window in my living room. Dusted a couple knickknacks. Even put a load of dirty clothes in the washer. Still, I couldn't cut off the pull to sit at my Bible. I could have sworn it called at me to come read. And if that didn't make me even more sour, nothing would have.

I gave up the fight and sat down. Not because I wanted to. But because my spirit demanded. That time, my weak flesh gave way to the willing spirit.

"You better make this good." I prayed quietly so I wouldn't wake up Clive.

My old fingers flipped through the thin pages to Exodus. The poor Israelites stood at the edge of a riverbed, crying about bitter water. They'd gotten only a couple days into their one-way trip to the Promised Land and found nothing but bad water.

"You got me, Lord."

I remembered learning that story in Sunday school. Flannel graphs of pale-skinned men in brown robes and a wild-haired Moses with his two tablets of commandments in hand. Never mind the bitter water came long before the Ten Commandments.

Oh, the selfish, spoiled Hebrews. Getting everything from God and grumbling anyhow about bitter water. What a stiff-necked people. Those fools.

But as I read of their crying, I couldn't find fault in them. I'd learned those past days what the desert felt like. Dry and hot and life draining. I imagined the wide cracks in the soles of their feet as they shuffled around in that scorching sand. The terror of having nothing to offer their children to eat or drink. Nothing but rancid water.

Outside my house, the rain beat up against the windows.

I supposed I preferred rain to drought.

But even with all the rain, I felt closer to those dry-mouthed Israelite mothers, looking from their withering children to the bitter water. Their starving children and the dusty rocks on the ground. I wondered how many of those children died and got buried under that shifting sand.

They cried out, challenging God. No wonder they thought He

didn't care. He'd taken them from a land of plenty to a land of nothing but shriveled death.

"Why did You bring us out to the desert just to watch us die?" they'd asked at the top of their voices. Parched throats screamed for an answer.

My own head bobbed up and down in agreement with their interrogation.

"Why did You give me a daughter if You were just going to take her away from me?" I believed my heart wore a sneer as I cried out.

"You know Me better than that." The words, so clear, I looked around to see who said them. "Read."

I recognized that voice. I'd heard it only a few weeks earlier. The voice of Jesus.

"Lord, if You keep on letting me hear Your voice, I'm going to end up in the looney bin," I said.

"You know Me better than that," He repeated.

"Do I?" I asked.

"Read."

I huffed a little but obeyed anyhow.

Moses tossed a stick into the water and God made it sweet. The people must have filled every jug and basin they had. I wondered if they drank the whole stream dry.

What I knew about the story that the poor Israelites did not—stomachs bloated with sweet water—was that in the next chapter, they'd be without again. Then the next chapter and for the rest of their lives. They would tromp through the sand, wandering, unable to reach the land of milk and honey.

Even Moses, leading them on the journey through the desert, didn't get into the Promised Land. Even he died in the desert.

"Is it ever coming down." Clive came into the living room in only his shirt and underpants.

I'd fried up a couple of eggs for him and buttered his toast. The smell of breakfast usually did the trick to get him up and at 'em.

He picked up his plate from the counter and kissed the side of my face before taking his seat at the dinette.

"Good morning." I handed him a fork. "You sleep well?"

"Must have. I feel better than I have in weeks."

"I'm glad, honey."

"You going to get dressed for church? Or are you planning on wearing your nightie?" He winked. "Course, I think you look pretty in it. I just don't think Old Buster'd approve."

"Are you thinking about going in your skivvies?"

"It doesn't take me so long to figure out what to wear as it takes you."

The orange juice refreshed me with its crisp aroma as I poured it into a glass for him.

"I don't think I'm going to church this morning." I put the glass to the side of his plate.

"Olga Eliot, I don't think you've ever missed a single Sunday morning service in all the time I've known you." He sat at the table.

"I have." I spooned sugar into the black of my fresh-made coffee. "You just don't remember it."

"Are you feeling sick?" Piercing the yolk of his eggs, he let the yellow ooze onto the plate.

"No. I just don't have it in me this morning."

"Well, honey, I can't force you." He cut a bit off the egg and slid it onto his toast. "But I'm going with or without you. My faith is weak this morning."

"It seems like a whole lot of work for a whole lot of nothing."

"Olga..." Clive lowered his fork. It clinked against his plate and the egg slipped off.

"What, Clive? You tell me that you aren't angry. You tell me you're happy with how God's dealing with this family."

"I am angry." He dropped the bread onto his plate and pushed the whole mess of food away from him. "And I'm tired. I'd rather go and see if I can get a little something out of the singing and preaching than sit here and mope. Even though the moping is what I feel like doing more than anything."

Squeezing dish soap into the sink, I turned on the faucet, letting the warm water rush over the fry pan at the bottom of the sink. I wiped against it with my cloth, working loose the grease and egg.

"I've never been so angry," I said.

"What's that?"

"I'm just plain mad." I turned off the water. "I wasn't this angry when my mother died. Must not have known that I could be back then. It feels like God's sitting on His big hands, watching us squirm."

"I don't know what to say to that, Olga." He closed his eyes. "But I do know I'm struggling. It would do me a lot of good to have your hand to hold during church today. I'm suffering and I need you."

What else could I have done? I dried the suds off my hands, leaving that old fry pan to soak, and went right to my room to put on a dress. Not for me. For my Clive. And my red dress, no less. The one that made his jaw drop.

I sat through Old Buster's miserable preaching and pretended to pray along with the rest of the congregation.

I did pray. Just a different prayer than everybody else.

I prayed for the bitter water to somehow turn sweet.

Chapter Twenty-Nine

EVELYN

I'd never been to a church so big. The stone building nearly scraped the sky and reached both ends of a city block. My mom and I stood at the door, neither of us ready to pull it open. Swooshing air up at us, the cars zoomed past.

"Are you sure we put enough change in the meter?" Mom opened her purse. "I might be able to find a few more quarters."

"Mom, we put five dollars in. That's enough for the rest of the afternoon." I hoped we wouldn't be there more than an hour.

"I'm just not used to all this." She looked around. "It's too busy. Everything's too close together. It makes me nervous."

Two country bumpkins come to the big city. We felt out of place among the fast-walking people and the noise of traffic.

Charlotte had found a cancer support group. Somehow, she'd talked our mom into going. From the way my mom folded into herself, I doubted she felt good about being there.

Standing on the sidewalk, watching the cars whiz past, we stalled for time. Buildings towered over us. Somewhere, horns blared. Lots of them. Then a siren whirred and screamed, echoing off the buildings.

"I could never live in the city," she said. "I'd have a nervous breakdown every day."

"Me too." I breathed in the air, thick with exhaust.

A woman wearing a burgundy scarf on her head rushed by, pulling on the door. She could only get it to open an inch or so. And even that took a lot of effort. A man walking near her stopped, offering to open the door. She huffed at him, but stepped aside to let him help her.

"It must be hard to need help opening doors," my mom whispered. "That's going to be tough for me, too."

"We should go in, Mom." I checked the clock on my phone. "It's time."

The church basement smelled like a combination of singed coffee and mildew. Mom stopped just inside the door next to a table of brochures. A group of ladies chatted and laughed on the other side of the room. In another corner, a few women hugged. The lady with the burgundy scarf sat alone, legs crossed, checking her watch.

"Is it too late to leave?" my mom whispered.

"We're here," I said. "You might as well see how it goes."

We walked together to the circle of metal folding chairs. As we neared, a woman came toward us, almost jumping out in front of my mom.

"Hi." She thrust her hand at us. Every single one of her teeth showed as she smiled. Red lipstick had smudged across the top row of overly white enamel. "You're new, right? I'm Debbie, and I facilitate this group. Welcome."

Looking between my mom and me, Debbie made a little too much eye contact. I directed my eyes to the pink ribbon pinned on her lapel.

"My name is Gretchen." My mom took Debbie's hand. "This is my daughter, Evelyn. She came to support me today."

"Isn't that nice." Debbie touched my mom's shoulder. "Listen, we're about to get going with our gathering. Feel free to grab yourselves a cup of coffee before you find a seat."

She turned to the rest of the group and clapped her hands three times. I wondered if she'd been a school teacher before.

"All right, everyone. Let's find a seat and get started." Her voice resonated in the small room. "We've got a lot to get through today."

My mom clutched her purse and held it against her stomach as she sat in a chair. Her knee hopped up and down.

Touching her leg, I made eye contact. "It's okay, Mom."

"I have no idea how these things work." She blinked fast. "What if they make me talk?"

"You don't have to do anything you don't want to," I whispered. "We can always take off if you feel uncomfortable."

Debbie sat in a chair at the front of the room. Smiling, she met the gaze of everyone in the circle.

"Welcome." She rubbed her palms against her thighs. "I'm so grateful that each one of you is here today. You made the choice of a warrior today. I couldn't be happier to be in battle with every single one of you."

The room stayed quiet. A few swishing whispers from one end of the circle turned my head. I couldn't tell where the sound came from.

"We have a new friend with us today."

Debbie extended her hand and pointed in our direction. I felt the weight of every eye in the room. My mom gave them a thin-lipped smile.

"How about we all go around the circle and introduce ourselves." Debbie breathed deeply. "I'm Debbie. Of course, you already knew that. What you don't know is that I beat breast cancer five years ago."

She turned and raised her brows to the woman next to her.

Everyone in the circle shared their names and a little about their cancer story. It seemed they all had hope to be cured. Not a single one of them had stage four cancer.

I considered grabbing my mom and pulling her out of there. But the way she listened to each of the women, I couldn't do it. She had compassion for them. I saw it in the way her eyes welled up with tears. She, a woman with stage four, terminal cancer, felt for the women who weren't nearly as ill.

With grace and dignity, my mom listened to their stories.

"I'm Stacy." The woman in the burgundy scarf carried a sharp edge in her voice. "I have leukemia. And I'm angry today."

That was all she said.

"Would you like to explore that feeling, Stacy?" Debbie leaned forward.

"Not particularly."

"Okay." Debbie widened her eyes and puffed air out her mouth for the benefit of the other women in the circle. Then she turned to my mom. "I guess it's your turn."

My mom grabbed my hand. Her fingers were so cold, I tried to warm them. The desire to scoop her up and run out of the room came back. That group wouldn't help her. It would only bring her down. She didn't need to be there. The place for her was at home, with us. Or out in the garden with dirt under her fingernails and a rose-scented breeze blowing around her. A cup of chamomile tea warming her hands, soothing her soul. Miles and miles between her and the city of clamor and chaos.

Instead, we sat in those chairs, surrounded by a dozen strangers.

"I'm Gretchen." Her quiet voice quivered. "I just found out that I have liver cancer."

"Thank you for sharing, Gretchen," Debbie said.

"What stage?" Stacy asked.

"Stage four."

Debbie's smile fell. Her eyes darted around the room, no doubt analyzing the mood. No one else moved. The room sank into cavernous quiet. Only the sounds of traffic from outside broke the silence.

"I'm glad you're here." Stacy nodded her head, keeping gentle eye contact with my mom.

"Thank you," my mom whispered.

"Are you doing treatment?" Stacy asked. "Not that it's any of my business."

"It's okay." Mom touched the back of her hair. "I start tomorrow. I've got no idea what to expect. I'm scared."

Stacy crossed her legs and arms at the same time.

"I know I'll probably get really sick and that my hair will fall out." Mom wiped a tear from under her eye. "And I'm okay with that, I guess. But I'm worried that I'm going to have all that treatment and it won't make any difference in the end."

Stacy narrowed her eyes. "Yeah. It's kind of hard to know how it'll go. It's all about how your body reacts. There's never a guarantee that treatment's going to help."

"That makes sense."

"I mean, for me, if my stuff keeps getting worse, I'm just going to quit the treatment and try to enjoy the little bit of life I have left." She touched her scarf. "I guess you have to choose your battles."

"It just seems like a fight I can't win," my mom said, just loud enough to be heard.

"Who says you have to fight it?" Stacy leaned forward, resting elbows on her crossed legs. "I don't. I think it's better to live at peace with yourself. Accept the process and get as much living packed in as you can."

"Well, thanks for sharing, ladies." Debbie cut off the conversation, her smile more of a grimace. "We need to carry on here."

Stacy and my mom kept eye contact for another few seconds.

"Anyway, on a happier note," Debbie continued. "I thought we'd discuss the cancer walk coming up next month."

Debbie went on and on about times and locations and what everyone should bring along. She reminded them to bring water and healthy snacks. At the end of her talk, she folded her hands and put them in her lap.

"Remember, this year we're walking for Shonda." Debbie's face looked more human in that moment than in the whole time we'd been there. I read grief in her eyes. She turned to my mom. "Shonda was part of this group. She lost her battle a month ago."

"I'm very sorry." My mom touched the hollow spot between her collarbones.

"She fought with everything she had." Debbie's face relaxed. "And that's why we decided to walk this year. For her. To remember her, but also to keep the fight going in her place."

"Shonda told me the cancer was the best thing that ever happened to her," Stacy said. "That was the last time I talked to her."

"Why would she say that?" A woman from across the circle scowled. "That's terrible, Stacy. She wouldn't have said that."

"She did, though," Stacy said back.

"Well, she must have been on something." The woman glared at Stacy as she pushed the words out of her mouth. "It's the worst thing I can imagine, having cancer."

Stacy wrapped her arms around her middle. Her bare eyebrows

lowered, and she stared at one of the tiles on the floor. Her lips pressed together.

"She said that she didn't really love life until she got cancer," Stacy mumbled. "It made her realize what was important."

"I don't believe you," the other woman said.

"Now, friends." Debbie snapped her lips up over her teeth, forcing a smile. "Shonda wouldn't have wanted us to argue. She'd want us to remember her and all the great things we did with her. And that's what we're going to do. We're going to remember her and smile."

The way Debbie held her lips, wide and gaping, didn't convince me at all. Apparently, it didn't get to Stacy, either. She kept her arms crossed, holding herself.

"Cancer isn't cute." Stacy's eyes closed. "I'm sick to death of everybody trying to make it cute. Pink ribbons on teddy bears and boxes of cereal. It's not cute, and it isn't fun. And I don't always feel like smiling, you know? Some days I just feel like sleeping all day after I've been barfing my guts out. And, as not cute as that is, it's real."

"Sometimes we all feel a little weak. We let our negative emotions get the best of us," Debbie said with, I thought, a tone of scolding. "We can't push our negativity off on other people, though. It's not fair."

A few of the women in the seats nodded their heads. Stacy did not. Neither did my mom.

Stacy caught up to us after the meeting. She moved faster than I expected her to. The three of us stood on the sidewalk outside the church building.

"Hey." She wheezed, trying to catch her breath. "Don't let that meeting bother you."

"I'm fine," my mom said. "I didn't know what to expect anyway."

"It's just hard for them to hear about people with stage four."

"That's what I wondered." My mom sighed. "I guess I'm their worst nightmare."

"Not you. It isn't you. It's just what's happening to you that scares them." Stacy looked over her shoulder at a group leaving the building.

"See, they're all trying to learn how to live with cancer. Stage four is more about learning how to let go of life."

"Well, and they're dealing with their friend's death." Mom wiped her nose with a tissue. "That's difficult for all of you, I'm sure."

"It has been. Shonda was everybody's best friend. You know? Her death made some of us realize that this isn't some little party we've got going on." Stacy yawned, covering her mouth. "Sorry, I'm worn out."

"It was nice to meet you, Stacy."

"You, too." Stacy held my mom's hand. "Are you coming back next week?"

"I don't think so."

"Well, then. I'm glad I got to meet you." She took in my mom's face with her eyes. "I hope it goes well for you."

Stacy walked away from us, the ends of her scarf flowing behind her.

As soon as I pulled off the highway on the Middle Main exit, my mom rolled down her window, letting fresh air into the car. Her face turned away from me, toward the breeze. I imagined her with eyes closed, breathing in the good country air.

"I need to figure out how to tell Charlotte that I'm not going back."

"You don't have to tell her." I pulled onto the road that led to her house. "We could just pretend we're going to the meeting and get coffee instead."

"That sounds good to me."

We came to a stop in her driveway. Neither of us moved for a minute or two.

"I think I want to go for a walk." She pushed her door open. "It's a beautiful day."

"Would you like a little company?" The thought of her walking away, by herself, made me anxious. I wanted to be with her. To hear her talk to the flowers and watch her smile at the singing birds. "Unless you'd rather be alone."

Turning toward me, she smiled. Her real, full faced, easy smile. "You know, I think I'd like having a little more time with you."

Together, we walked to the garden by the Big House. Her arm held tightly to mine. Not because she stumbled.

I had. And she held me up.

Chapter Thirty

OLGA

It seemed I blinked my eyes and September had come. Even though the air still warmed my skin like summer, the breeze whispered fall. A couple of the trees had a crimson kiss on the edges of their leaves. Soon enough, I told myself, they'd all be ablaze.

God's artwork. I thanked Him. The prayer seemed thin, but, I figured it was better than nothing. And for weeks, I'd given him a whole lot of nothing in my prayers. But I felt Him waiting for me. Like the gentleman He's always been.

I let myself into Gretchen's house. Donald stood right up to the kitchen counter, staring down a loaf of bread like he'd never seen such a thing before. When the screen door creaked behind me, he looked up. The skin around his eyes sagged.

The first three weeks of Gretchen's chemotherapy swirled past us. Drives out to the clinic for treatments. Trying with all our might to keep her comfortable through the shooting pain in her gut. Searching for something she could eat without getting sick. Filling all the spots she occupied. None of us had an idea of all she did until we had to take over.

That girl of mine did more for the people of Middle Main than I ever could have guessed. My three weeks had filled up fast with pushing people in wheelchairs all over the grounds of the nursing home, delivering meals to sick folks, and teaching the toddlers

Sunday school class at the church.

Being Gretchen just about wore me out.

But Don wore the weariness I felt. In his stooped shoulders and the purple half-moons under his eyes.

"Let me make you a sandwich." I nudged him away from the counter. "You want ham or roast beef? Or both?"

"Oh." He looked back at the bread, surprised to see it there. "I don't know. I guess I was thinking of taking something to work for lunch."

"I could wrap it up for you."

"No. I don't want to put you out. I'm not hungry anyway." He rubbed the meat of his hands into his eyes. "Gretchen's still sleeping. The chemo wiped her out."

"I know, Donald."

"If it makes her so sick, why is the doctor still making her go through it?"

"Because it should help a little, I guess. I hope."

"It's too much for her." He looked at the treatment schedule stuck on the fridge with magnets. "I mean, look at this. As soon as she has time off to get better, they've got her coming back in for more."

"I know. She'll get a break soon."

We stood next to each other in that kitchen. Donald leaned back, resting against the counter.

"Sorry about the mess." He nodded at the sink piled high with dirty dishes. "I'll get to it later."

"Don't you worry about that. I can do them up lickety-split."

"Thank you." He checked his watch. "I need to get to work. I hate that I've got to leave right now."

"No. It's fine, Don."

"I have to keep the insurance."

"We all understand that."

"Thank you." His voice thickened so that I thought he'd start crying. He hadn't. I wondered if it wouldn't do him some good. "Can you please make sure Gretchen eats something today? She isn't doing so good with getting food into her."

"I'll do my best."

"Just broth. It might be good on her stomach." The keys clattered against each other as he grabbed them from the counter. "I never thought this would happen to us. Not so soon."

"I know it, honey." I patted his back. "Maybe pick up some flowers on your way home? That might help her heal up a little."

"Yeah. Maybe I'll do that."

He walked out, not saying another word. Got into his car and drove away. How his heart must have been torn in two.

Right away, I set to work on that sink. It took a whole lot more scrubbing than it would've the day before. Oh, how milk could stick to a cereal bowl. By the time I got to the stainless steel bottom of the sink, my hands ached and fingers had turned to prunes. But, soapy cloth in hand, I kept going, making my way through the fridge and all the counters. If I'd stopped, I would have had to deal with my thoughts. I wiped down the windows and got to dusting the bookshelf. My last stop was the bathroom. After I finished swirling the brush around the toilet, I heard somebody in the living room.

Gretchen had got herself to the rocking chair without me even knowing she was awake. There she sat, moving that chair back and forth, real gentle. She'd already picked out a book to read, holding it in her hands. She always had loved a good book. She could sit and read for hours on end. So lost in the story, she'd jump like a jackrabbit if she got startled. I thought I'd warn her that I was in the house.

"Gretchie?" I called, nice and easy. "Honey, I didn't want to scare you."

She turned and looked over her shoulder. "Hi, Mom."

As much as I knew she tried, her voice just didn't have its normal pep lilting through it.

"How are you doing?" I made my way to the living room. "Donald said you were having a bad morning."

"Oh, well, now I know what it feels like to be run over by a tractor." Closing the book, she shut her eyes. "Especially my head."

"Can I get you something for that? Maybe a little tea?"

"I don't know." One of her eyebrows pushed up. "Sorry, Mom. I'm having a hard time thinking. My brain would rather be sleeping."

"Don't worry about it, honey. You just let me know when you're ready for something."

"I think tea might be nice." Two of her fingers pressed into the side of her head. "Maybe the peppermint one? It's in the pantry."

I set to work getting the tea ready. For the first time in years, the electric kettle sat empty and unplugged. I'd have to heat the water the old-fashioned way. That didn't bother me at all. Not until that old copper kettle screamed at me, sputtering water out its spout. I nearly jumped right through the ceiling. Was I ever glad nobody saw me.

As for Gretchen, she'd fallen asleep, her head tipped back on the rocking chair. Sleeping so hard, she hadn't heard the kettle.

Pulling the afghan off the back of the couch, I let it drape over my arm, the soft yarn rubbing on my skin. Gretchen complained of being cold next to all the time. That old throw blanket had been her comfort most days.

When I pulled the book from under her hands, she opened her eyes halfway. The twinkle that sparkled from the corner of her eyes did my heart a lot of good.

"I was just about to put this afghan on you." I held it up to show her. "I thought you might be a little chilly."

"Oh, thank you." She lifted her hands to let me cover up her legs. "I'm cold all the time."

"I know it. I'm sorry, honey." Walking to the kitchen, I tried to think of what else I could do for her. "You still want this tea?"

"Yes. Thanks, Mom." She let her eyelids fall again, real heavy. "I'm not going back to sleep, I promise."

"You can if you want." The ball full of the loose peppermint leaves clicked against the inside of her mug. "I'll help you get to the couch if you think you'd be more comfortable there."

"No. I don't want to sleep the rest of my life away." Pretty green eyes peeked out from under her lids. "Maybe I'll just drink that tea and it'll perk me up."

I carried the hot mug to the living room. Our hands touched when I handed it to Gretchen. Oh, but to have the power to remember all the times I'd held that hand or kissed those cheeks. Every hug or tickle. And the ability to erase the memory of days I fell short as a mama. Just knowing that a day crept up when I wouldn't have her to touch made me long for more contact.

She sipped her tea and made a sour face.

"What's wrong?"

"Everything tastes funny." Her breath huffed out of her with a small groan attached. "Maybe it just needs to cool off a little."

She lifted the mug back to me. That time, our hands didn't touch so I bent over and kissed her forehead before putting the cup on the side table.

"I love you, Mom." Such sweetness.

"Do you need me to do a load of laundry for you?" Looking out the window, I tried to hide the saltwater tears that pooled in my eyes. "I don't mind doing it."

"No, thanks. Charlotte's been really good about that." She pulled the afghan up to cover her stomach. "Why don't you come keep me company? I need that more than anything."

"I don't mind that job in the least."

It seemed every sore spot on my body decided to tense up when I lowered myself into Donald's recliner. They reminded me that old ladies should take the housecleaning a little slower.

"Oh, nothing makes me feel more feeble than when I'm getting down into a chair," I said.

"I'm beginning to understand what you mean." Her laughter sang sweet water into my soul.

Jesus, I prayed, *thank You for her laughter.*

The prayer came without effort. I thanked Him for that, too.

"Did you get to Bible study yesterday?" she asked.

"Only for a minute or two." The truth was, I couldn't sit with those ladies for more than a few minutes without crying my eyes out. I didn't want her to know that, though.

"I wish I could have been there."

"Well, honey, you were certainly missed. The ladies wanted me to tell you that they've been praying for you."

"That's nice," she said.

"Well, except for Bev." A grin forced its way onto my face. "She asked me to tell you that she forgot you were sick. That's why she isn't praying. She keeps forgetting."

"At least she's honest," she chuckled.

"She's something else."

"I wouldn't mind if a few of them came to visit. Can you tell them that, please?"

"Sure thing, Gretchie."

"I'm just lonely sometimes." She tried her tea again, forcing herself to swallow. "Well, at least it feels good on my throat."

"Honey, does it hurt your feelings that nobody's been over?"

"Maybe a little."

"I wonder if they're just wanting to let you rest up a bit," I said. Then I winked. "You want me to ask Old Buster to come on over?"

She rolled her eyes. "Oh, heavens no."

"Now, Gretchen, why ever not?" I teased.

"Did you know that when I was a little girl, I thought he was married to Deirdre?" She giggled, shaking her head and holding her stomach. "Oh my goodness, it hurts to laugh."

"Are you okay?" I leaned forward, touching her knee.

She nodded. "I'd rather laugh than cry, even though it hurts worse."

"I don't mind seeing that smile."

But that smile faded. Not all at once. Just a little at a time. Her lips made a quivering frown.

"I'm afraid, Mom," she whispered. "That's really why I want people to come over. Because I'm afraid."

"What are you afraid of?"

"Of being forgotten." Her lips made a tiny smacking sound as she rubbed them together.

"Nobody's ever going to forget you." Squeezing her knee, I realized how bony it had gotten. "Nobody forgets someone so precious as you."

"I guess I mean that I want them to remember me for being me. I don't want them to think about me and remember this cancer." She breathed in shaky gusts of air. "I don't want everyone to remember me for the way I died."

Words just plain refused to come to my mind. Even if I had found a few to say, I didn't know how they'd help her.

When I thought of my mother, I had a picture in my mind of her with a white sheet pulled up tight and tucked under her armpits. Her wheezing and fighting to catch a breath, tears spilling down the sides of her face and teeth bared. Legs fighting against the taut sheet. It took a little more work to remember other things about her.

You're Almighty, I prayed in my silence. *And I'm low down. Fix the words in my mouth or change the subject real quick.*

The screen door slammed and Gretchen's body tensed up all over. We both turned toward the door. Charlotte stood just inside, eyes wide.

"Sorry." Charlotte cringed. "The wind caught it."

"It's okay, Char." Gretchen grabbed for a tissue out of the box next to her. "I thought you had to work today, though."

"I asked Deirdre if I could come home a little early." Charlotte slouched at the shoulders, making her way to the couch. "I've got a pretty bad headache."

"I'm sorry, sweetie." Gretchen blew her nose into the tissue.

"I made truffles this morning before I left." She lifted a small, white bag. "Deirdre told me to bring some home."

I thanked the Lord for the interruption and the added bonus of chocolates.

Because of His great mercy, He didn't hold my weeks of silence against me. Instead, He held me tight.

Chapter Thirty-One

EVELYN

Pulling into the driveway, I saw a woman standing at the window, looking right at me. She rushed to the porch of her house, waiting for me to get out of my car.

"Thank you so much for making it all the way out here. I made a cake." She watched as I walked up the steps to the porch. "It's nothing special. Just a chocolate layer cake."

"That sounds delicious." I forced a smile. Exhaustion had settled in the place behind my eyes.

"Do people usually eat cake for these things? Or is it morbid? My husband thought it was terribly strange. But I've made a cake for all of Justin's big days. And it seems like this is a pretty big one."

"Well, I think it's fine."

"Good. Good." Her little brown eyes looked all over my face. "Thank you for coming."

"It's no trouble." I stood next to her on the porch. "I'm Evelyn Russell from the funeral home."

"I know who you are. You went to school with Justin." She grabbed my hand. Not to shake it, but to pull me into the house. "I'm Yvonne Eames. Justin's mother. You remember him, don't you?"

"Yes." I followed behind her through the house. "But he was much more popular than I was."

"He's always been well liked, you know." She looked at me over

202

her shoulder. "He's such a nice boy."

She stopped short in the kitchen so fast, I almost ran her over. Still holding my hand, she turned her gaze up at me. Quite a bit shorter than me, she had to tilt her whole head to connect eyes with me.

"Now," she continued to talk, making her voice a little quieter. "We've got Justin all set up in the living room. It's the only place we could fit his hospital bed. He's such a tall boy, we had to rent a special bed for him. You know, he could have had a future in basketball, he's so tall. But he picked up the guitar instead." She threw her free hand in the air. "What could I do? And he almost made it big, you know. I'm sure you saw it in the papers. He could have been something. But he got sick instead. Life is a cruel joke."

Back to walking, she pulled me through the dining room. Pill bottles and medical supplies covered the table.

"Would you look at all that?" She waved her hand at the table. "Hospice took over my house. Completely took over. Not that I'm complaining. I need the help. I couldn't do this without them. They're angels. Just absolute angels."

I smiled. Not that she saw it. Pulling me through her house occupied all her attention.

"There's the bathroom, just in case." She pointed down the hallway. "We've got our shower all set up for Justin. He's got a chair in there. Thank God for that nurse. She gets him undressed and into the tub. He still does all the scrub-a-dub-dubbing, though."

She pulled me into the living room before letting go of my hand. Sunshine poured through the large picture window in the middle of the wall. All the furniture had been pushed to the perimeter of the room to make room for the hospital bed. A sunbeam rested right on Justin's feet. That's what I saw of him first. His long, skinny feet that stuck out from under the sheets.

Justin sat, propped up by pillows. He looked almost exactly the same as I remembered him. Just more facial hair and darker circles under his eyes.

"Justin," Yvonne almost yelled. "The funeral director is here."

"Hey, nothing gets a party started like a funeral director," he said, his voice flat. "Hello." I tried to calm my nerves. Even though he'd been younger than me, he'd still been several social circles above me.

Funny how all that carried into adulthood.

"I think I remember you. Remind me of your name," he said.

"Of course you remember her." Yvonne lowered her eyebrows at him. "This is Evelyn Russell."

"Right." He grinned. "I don't think we ever talked back then. Sorry. I was pretty full of myself."

"It's okay." I shrugged.

"You've got a brother, right? Cal?" He smirked. "That dude was crazy."

"He still is."

"That's good to hear." Justin cleared his throat. "Tell him to come over and visit sometime. I'd like to see him."

"I'll do that."

"Let her sit down, Justin," Yvonne interrupted. "She just got here, and you're already talking her ear off."

I made my way to an empty chair at one side of the bed. Yvonne had been right, it was extra long. I'd have to make a note about his height for when it came time to remove his body.

"Hey, this is my girlfriend." Justin reached over, putting his hand on the knee of a woman sitting next to him.

"I don't know what we'd do without her. Esther has been a Godsend." Yvonne sighed. "Now, Evelyn, are you comfortable?"

"Yes," I said. "Thank you."

"Good. I'll be right back. I need to get the cake."

She left the room, humming as she went.

I didn't quite know what to do or say. I'd never had to prearrange the funeral of someone younger than me. Usually, young people died suddenly. Unexpectedly. Not over a long time from terminal illness.

"So did you go to college to be a funeral director?" Justin asked.

"Yes. Mortician school." I pulled a file from my briefcase.

"Sounds like a wild school." Justin yawned.

"Okay, here comes the cake," Yvonne announced, walking past us, carrying a beautifully decorated cake. "Darrell's got the plates and forks. That's my husband. Justin's dad."

"Mom, why did you make a cake?" Justin pulled the sheet up over his waist.

"Listen, I've made a cake for all your milestones. Birthdays and graduation. I made one when you moved to Nashville and when you came back. Today is not the day for me to break tradition." She put the cake on the hospital issue tray and pulled a small camera from her pocket. "Now, I'm going to need a picture of you with Evelyn."

"Mother, no." Justin rolled his eyes.

"Why not?" She put a hand on her wide hip.

"Arranging a funeral isn't a happy occasion. No pictures with the funeral director." He looked at me. "No offense."

"Don't be rude. She's a friend from high school."

"And is that chocolate cake?" Justin asked. "You know how much I hate chocolate."

"Oh, now you're just being selfish." Yvonne cupped a hand to the side of her mouth. "Darrell. Plates."

"I'm coming," Justin's father yelled from the kitchen. "I got a little sidetracked."

"By what? What's so interesting in that kitchen that you can't get in here with the plates? The forks, too." She looked at me and sighed. "I swear, that man is about to make me lose my mind."

"Yvonne," Darrell called. "Where do you keep the spoons?"

"I want forks," she yelled back. "And they're in the exact same place they've been for the last thirty years."

"The bottom of the sink?"

"Oh, that man." She rushed past me. "You'll need to arrange two funerals today, I think."

Darrell came into the room, carrying a stack of at least ten plates.

"Having fun in here?" he asked, his voice far too loud for the room.

"Of course we aren't having fun." Yvonne walked in behind him. "We're planning Justin's funeral. This isn't the most enjoyable thing in all the world."

"But worthy of cake, apparently." Justin leaned his head back on the bed.

"Do you want me to throw the whole thing in the trash? One more word and I'll do it." Yvonne cut the cake, serving it onto the plates. "Darrell, why did you think we needed all these dishes?"

"You said to get the plates." Darrell stood as close to his wife as he could. "You didn't specify how many."

Yvonne passed out the cake. We held our plates, not eating. She glared at us.

"Why aren't you eating? I didn't poison it, you know."

I opened my folder and put my cake on an end table. "How about we get started planning a few things. You all can eat while we're talking."

"Did you hear that?" Darrell grinned. "Permission to talk with our mouths full."

"Darrell, of all the goofy things." Yvonne shook her head.

"All right, I actually have a few things figured out." Justin handed his untouched cake to Esther. "I'm an organ donor. I don't know what they'll be able to use by the time I'm done with them, but they're welcome to whatever they can salvage."

I jotted a note in my folder.

"And I have a suit all picked out." Justin smirked. "It's awesome. And orange. I got it at a secondhand store."

"Son, I don't know what makes you want to wear that ugly old thing." Yvonne sighed. "It's enough to make me demand a closed casket."

"And I have an idea of what I want my gravestone to say." The rough sound of him clearing his throat gave way to wheezing.

"Justin, you need that breathing mask on," Yvonne said, mouth full of cake. "Stop gabbing for a minute and breathe."

Esther jolted up and pulled some tubes up to Justin's face. She helped him get them hung on his ears and tight across his face. The oxygen machine roared, then lowered into humming as it pushed air into his lungs. He gulped the air.

"He just gets so excited, he forgets to inhale." Yvonne licked the frosting off her fork. "He's always done that. Even when he was healthy. He'll just need a real good nap this afternoon. Do you hear me? A good nap, Justin."

"You talk like he's a little boy," Darrell said. "He's a grown man."

Yvonne flashed her husband a narrow-eyed glare.

"Okay," Justin continued, regaining his breath. "I want my name and birthdate and death date and all that—"

"Beloved son," Yvonne interrupted. "Write that down."

"Then, I want it to have a quote from me." He turned toward

Esther. They shared a smile. "I've had this planned for a long time."

"Is it from one of your songs?" Yvonne turned to me. "He writes wonderful songs."

"I want it to say, 'I wish I would have worked more.'" He barked out a laugh that tuned into a dry cough. Esther stood, her chair thudding against the wall. She rubbed his back and whispered in his ear. He pulled her arm to his chest, making her hold him through the coughing fit.

"You aren't having that on your headstone." Yvonne spoke over his hacking.

"Yes, I am," he said between gasps for breath.

His coughing lasted for several minutes. When it was over, he let go of Esther's arm and relaxed on his bed.

"Anyway," he said, barely above a whisper. "That's what I want on my tombstone."

"Why would you want to do that?" Yvonne put her plate on a table so hard, I worried it would shatter.

"So when someone says, 'Nobody, on their deathbed, ever says they'd worked more,' you can say, 'Well, actually, yes. Somebody did say that.'"

Darrell's laughter filled the room. "I'll pay extra for that."

"You really want to read that every time we visit our son's grave?" Yvonne crossed her arms.

"Yes." Darrell's laughter stopped. "That is exactly what I want to read. I'll think of him and hear his voice. And I'll remember the way he smiled when he just said it."

Yvonne still sat with arms crossed. She stared at her husband, not moving. Esther kissed Justin's forehead before sitting on the edge of his bed.

"I'm not dead yet, Mom," he said. "I'm still here."

"This isn't a joke, son." She put her hands on the hospital table.

"If dying at twenty-five isn't a joke, I don't know what is." He let his voice sink deeper. Looking right at me, he said, "Listen, I don't care how everything else goes. I really don't. So have the normal stuff."

"I think Justin needs to rest now." Yvonne stood.

"One more thing." Justin closed his eyes. "No flowers. None. They stink. Other than that, just do whatever my parents want. The funeral's for them anyway."

"Well…" Yvonne stood in front of me in the dining room, chocolate cake crumbs speckled her beige shirt. "I guess Darrell and I will come over to the funeral home after…" She hesitated, angling her head to look around me into the other room. "…after Justin passes."

"Call any time, okay?" I handed her a card with my phone number.

"Thank you." Her eyes shifted back and forth between mine. "Oh, I wanted to ask how your mother is doing."

"She's okay." The tired spot behind my eyes tightened, sending an ache through the back of my head. "I didn't realize you knew her."

"Oh, I've met her once or twice. Such a sweet woman." Open mouthed, her tongue worked to loosen something from her back teeth. "We've just been so busy with Justin, I haven't gotten a card in the mail."

"We understand."

"Darrell and I were sad to hear from Deirdre that your mother was sick."

"You heard about it from Deirdre?" Anger burned in my chest.

"I guess she called everybody in town."

I coughed, covering my mouth, hoping to force the bile back down.

"She told me she was trying to get the whole town praying for your family."

"She did?" The burning anger cooled.

"I guess she found a good use for that mouth of hers," Darrell said, standing behind me.

"Now, you stop that." Yvonne blew out a huge puff of air. "You're no better than Deirdre is."

"And you are?"

"Anyway, Evelyn, you tell your mother that she's got the prayers of the Eames family."

"I will," I said. "Thank you."

"Now, how many pieces of cake can I send home with you?"

I walked out to my car across the loose stone driveway, a plate full of cake in one hand and Justin's funeral arrangements in the other.

When I turned to look back at the house, I saw Yvonne and Darrell through the window, holding each other.

Chapter Thirty-Two

Olga

Gretchen's time in treatment took her from us, a little at a time. Each day those chemicals pumped into her made her weaker. The poison stole the sparkle from her eyes. Getting up from her chair got nearly impossible. A time or two, she didn't make it to the bathroom in time. She'd cry so hard when that happened. A few days, she slept without waking. Those were the days she regretted more than anything. She hated to waste any moment of her precious time.

That desert just about sucked the life right out of us.

But then Gretchen got a break. A vacation from chemotherapy. The sun must have known because it grew brighter in the sky. Leaves turned a special shade of orange just for her. And she stayed outside, breathing in fall for all it was worth. Looking at her, standing in the sunshine, I wouldn't have thought she was so sick.

I praised God for the oasis.

On a Wednesday morning, she'd already started on a good day. I could tell just peeking out the window at her in the garden. Wearing her big old straw hat, she kneeled on the earth, snipping at the flower heads with a pair of clippers.

I poured us a couple cups of coffee and made to join her. I'd do just about anything in my power to soak up those good days with her. It made me plain old batty to think I might miss a minute with her.

She lifted up her head when the back door clicked shut behind me.

"Good morning, Mom." The words lilted out of her.

"You want a cup of joe?" Holding up the mug, I stepped through the soft grass to get to her.

Coffee aroma mingled with the smells of autumn. Musty leaves and drying grasses. Somebody down the road burned a brush pile. I hoped heaven had fall. I'd miss the changing watercolored leaves otherwise.

"Isn't it gorgeous today?" She pointed a gloved finger at an old maple tree. "We've got a robin up there. She's been singing to me for the better part of an hour."

"Is that so?" After I handed her a cup, I turned my eyes to the tree. "I wonder why she didn't get herself south by now. She'll be awful cold in a couple weeks."

"I don't know. But I'm glad she's still here." Green eyes full of smile and tears, she watched that bird jerk and jolt with song. "She's given me a good morning."

A good morning all around, it seemed.

"I asked God to give me joy to push out the fear." She sighed and leaned her head on one shoulder, curls spilling out of the hat. "And He sent me a robin."

"And a basket full of chamomile."

She touched the woven basket next to her. "I know. I had no idea I'd still get some this late."

I counted it a sweet joy of my life to be out in the garden with my daughter. More that morning than ever before.

"I'm going to have a whole lot of tea from this." She picked up the basket, holding it on her lap. "After I'm gone, you'll be sure to give as much of this away as you can, won't you? Like my parting gift to people?"

"I don't know if it'll keep that long." The way my blood had turned ice cold raised goose pimples on my skin.

"I won't outlast it, Mom." She smiled with a peace that so far passed understanding, it seemed unreasonable. "But, even if I do, you still have to promise to give it away. I have letters to be handed out, too. There are just too many people that I won't be able to say good-bye to."

"You just let me know who." I sipped my coffee. "I'll do whatever needs done."

I'd not sink her good day with my sadness.

"Thank you, Mom. That's one less thing weighing on my mind."

"You're welcome." As much as I fought against it, a tear slipped down my face. "Somehow you turned out to be one of the best people I've ever known."

"I had pretty amazing people for parents."

The floppy brim of her hat curved just enough so it shielded her eyes from the bright morning. Even with that shadow, she glowed. I soaked it in as deep as I could.

Remember this, I thought. *Always remember this moment.*

I thought of good old Moses, his face glimmering so bright, the Israelites couldn't take it. The very glory of God reflected off Moses, making him the brightest moon. And all on account of Moses asking the Almighty God to show His glory.

That morning, with the bright joy on my daughter's face, I didn't have to ask. His glory shone on her and through her. Only by His mercy.

Better than a thousand days of sunshine.

Behind me, shoes clicked against the sidewalk leading out of the funeral home. Turning, I saw my grandson, grinning at Gretchen and me.

"Look at that." He took a step into the grass. "Two of the most beautiful women I've ever seen both in one spot."

"Well, Calvin." Almost blushing, I flipped my hand at him. "What are you getting at?"

"I wondered if I could borrow you stunning ladies for a little bit?"

"Only if you keep calling us stunning," Gretchen said. "What do you need?"

He got up to the edge of the garden, hands in pockets.

"Well, we've got a little problem." Squatting down next to his mama, he squinted from the bright sunshine. "We were supposed to start a funeral ten minutes ago. But only one person's shown up."

The empty parking lot proved it to be true.

"The decedent was young. Just his little sister came." He cringed and shook his head. "I guess it's a pretty bad family situation. She walked a couple of miles all by herself to get here."

"How awful," I said.

"According to the girl, the family had a knock-down fight over life insurance or something." Cal bit his lip. "No wonder the kid had problems."

"Are you looking for a few mourners?" Gretchen pushed herself up. "I'm in, as long as you don't mind a little dirt under my fingernails and this big, goofy hat."

"I don't think anyone will mind." Cal offered her his hand, pulling her all the way to standing. "Thanks, Mom. I'll see you ladies inside."

Gretchen and I pushed dirt and flower petals off ourselves. She grabbed her basket and put it on the bench before heading inside.

"Hold on, honey." Touching her arm, I lowered my voice. "I hate for you to spend part of your good day like this."

"Well, I'm not going to go be all by myself, enjoying my day when someone needs me." She lifted the hat a little to push her hair in place. "Life isn't about me. Even though I'm clicking away the days, I'm not the center of everything."

Inside, Gretchen touched the hat again, pulling it tighter on her head.

"Honey," I whispered. "Do you need a comb?"

"No." She exhaled, smiling. "I think I'll just leave it on for now."

"You always have looked pretty in a hat."

"Well, it's my hair." Her eyebrows softened. "It's starting to fall out."

Patting her shoulder, I knew if I opened my mouth, nothing but blubbering would come out. So I just left it at the patting and walked toward the chapel.

Evelyn carried a stack of papers through the lobby and back into the office. Funeral brochures no one would read or keep tucked in a Bible.

"Hey." She dropped the papers onto the desk. "Will's ready to start whenever."

"Will's doing the funeral?" I asked.

"I guess Old Buster's pretty much passed that duty on." She stood between Gretchen and me. "I just can't believe this family."

"Sounds like selfishness to me."

"Well, I guess there's a lot to the story." She folded her arms. "The kid put them through some tough times."

"The poor family must have a lot of emotions right now," Gretchen said.

"Death can bring out the monster in some people." Evelyn took a step toward the chapel. "We should get in there."

"Where do you want us to sit?" Gretchen followed behind her.

"In the family row," Evelyn said. "The girl doesn't want to sit alone."

"Sure thing."

Gretchen and I walked, arm in arm, to the front of the chapel. A girl, not even ten, I was sure of it, sat alone in the front row. So thin and slumped over, she hardly looked big enough for the chair. She'd got herself all dressed up, though. Black dress and black cardigan. The way she hung her feet out the back of her shoes made me wonder if she'd worn blisters into her skin on the walk over.

She sat completely still, her eyes locked on the face of the young man in the casket.

"Can we sit with you, honey?" I made my voice as gentle as I could. "I'm Olga."

She turned her face to me but kept those round, brown eyes on her brother. "Okay."

"My name's Gretchen." My daughter moved to the other side of the girl so she'd have both of us.

"I'm Harley," the girl said. "James was my big brother."

"I'm sorry, Harley." Gretchen used her voice like soothing butter. "This must be such a hard thing for you."

"Yeah. It's real bad." She swallowed. "He did drugs. Like, a lot of them."

"That must have been scary."

Harley rubbed her nose so hard, I thought it might bleed. I got a tissue out of my pocket. I learned along the way that, as an old lady, I ought always to carry plenty of tissues. It sure paid off every once in a while.

"Here you go, honey." I put it in her little hand. "Don't worry. It's clean."

"Thanks."

Will took his place behind the podium. His face had a bit of a green tint to it. Clive had told me how skittish Will got around decedents. I said a prayer for him. Poor fella. But I sure was glad he stood up there and not Old Buster with his big words and heavy pounding fists.

"Harley, do you mind if I start this with a little prayer?" Will asked.

She bowed her head, wrapping her hands around the tissue.

"God, today is really hard. Help us to make it through. Especially Harley. Let her see and feel that she is loved today. Thanks, God. Amen."

That prayer brought the tears right up into my eyes. They didn't give me any warning before taking a tumble down my cheeks. The easy words moved my heart, and I just wanted to think on them. That prayer was pure and right and lovely. I know it had delighted the very heart of my Lord.

"Harley, I never got to meet your brother. I really wish that I'd had that chance." Will stepped out from behind the podium, leaving his notes with his Bible. "But since you're here, I know that you love him a lot."

"I do." Her little voice trembled out, just a little louder than a whisper.

"I'm glad to hear that." He moved one of the folding chairs right in front of the girl. "Do you mind if I sit with you?"

"Okay."

And he did. That man sat knee to knee with little Harley. I almost sobbed out loud from the kindness of it.

"Now, I know your brother had some troubles," Will said. "We all do from time to time. You know? And sometimes life is hard. But I think you already know that."

"Our dad killed himself last year," Harley said. I rested a hand on her back, it shook so hard, like an earthquake stuck inside her. I wanted to pull her tight to me. "James took it real hard."

Will nodded but didn't say a word. He just waited on her.

"He's the one who found our dad." She used the tissue to scrub under her eyes. "Our mom thought if we moved here, we'd forget about our dad. But that didn't work."

"It breaks my heart to know you had to go through all that." Will wiped a tear from his own face. His voice broke. "It isn't fair. You shouldn't have all that hurt."

"Thanks," she said. "James tried to quit. You know. All the drugs. He tried a couple times. It was just too hard."

"I bet."

"Yeah. He was talking to a counselor." She shrugged.

Will leaned forward and rested his elbows on his thighs. "You know, I really wish that all those things wouldn't have happened to you."

"I miss my dad." She sniffled. "James did, too."

"I'm sure. And that's okay. You know that, right?"

"Sometimes my mom gets mad if I talk about him."

"That's probably because she's still really hurt. Sometimes adults act angry when they're in pain like that." Will pushed up his glasses. "Here's the thing, you need to know that it's good for you to let yourself have a good cry. I know it helps me when I'm having a really bad day."

"You do?" She crinkled her freckled nose at him.

"Well, yeah. Not in front of a lot of people, usually. I try to cry with one of my friends." He half smiled. "It's nice to not be alone when you're sad."

She half smiled back at him.

"And then, every once in a while, I try to remember this one verse from the Psalms."

"That's the poetry part, right?" she asked. "I went to Sunday school before my dad died."

"Yup. That's right." That time, he gave her a full smile. The kind a daddy would give his daughter to show her he was proud. "Well, it says that God keeps track of our tears, even collects them in a bottle."

"That's kind of cool."

"I think so, too," Will said. "And then, in Isaiah, a couple books after the Psalms, it says that God will wipe our tears away."

"That sounds like something a dad would do."

"It does." Will's eyes filled up. "And you know what both of those verses tell me? They tell me that God really cares when we're sad. Just like a dad."

Harley's sweet face squished up something awful, and she just wailed her heart out. Both Gretchen and I wrapped our mama arms around her.

"I'm so sorry." I said it so many times, I thought my voice would give out.

"No one cares that he died except me." Harley sobbed. "They didn't even send any flowers. Nobody sent flowers for him."

Before I knew it, Gretchen had gotten herself out of the chair and halfway out the chapel. I worried that the emotion was too much for her. Made her think about the cancer and dying and all that it would do to her kids when she was gone. My flesh and heart were torn. I needed to keep a hold of Harley. But I wanted to see to my own girl, too.

Good thing Clive saw her go. He rushed out after her. In just a minute, though, he walked back in, Gretchen behind him. In her hand, she carried the whole basket of chamomile she'd picked earlier.

She got back to her chair and sat by Harley, whispering in her ear. She took the young girl's hand and they walk to James in the casket. Harley took one little flower and put it in her brother's hand. Then, she picked more and more, filling the casket with the yellow and white. Soon, all that could be seen of James was his face. The rest of him was covered over with flowers.

"You can rest now, James," Gretchen said.

"I love you, Jimmy." Harley touched his cheek but pulled her hand off real quick.

God must have needed a big bottle to catch all our tears that morning.

Chapter Thirty-Three

EVELYN

Don's number came up on the screen of my phone. Sighing, I took the call, even though I'd planned to spend my whole Saturday sleeping. In my memory, my stepfather had never called me before.

"This is Don," he said over the phone after I answered. "Your stepdad."

"Yup. I know." Sitting up made me light-headed. I leaned back against the headboard. "Everything okay?"

"I don't know."

"What's going on?"

"Well, it's your mother—"

"Is she okay?" I interrupted, forgetting how tired I felt. "What happened?"

"Nothing happened, Evelyn," he snapped at me. "Would you let me get two words out before you interrupt me?"

He waited, and I didn't say a word. Looking in the mirror over my dresser, my cheeks burned red. In a year, he'd never said so much as three words to me, let alone bitten my head off.

"Sorry." He sighed. "I'm not good at this. I'm sorry."

"It's all right," I muttered. "We're all pretty stressed out right now."

"Thanks." His breathing in and out made a rushing sound in my ear. "Well, your mother had herself locked up in the bathroom this morning. She wouldn't let me in. And I couldn't get her to tell me what she was doing."

"Don, I haven't had a day off in four months." I paused for emphasis. "Four months. And you call me to tell me that my mom was in the bathroom this morning?"

"Well, yes," he answered. "I know it sounds crazy, but I'm worried. This isn't like her."

"What am I supposed to do about it?"

"Well, I'm at work. I can't check on her for another couple hours." He cleared his throat. "I was hoping you'd go over and see what's wrong. Please, Evelyn."

"Fine." I regretted that he couldn't see my eye roll. "I'll be there in a few minutes."

I hung up, hoping that all I'd find was my mom, in the bathroom, doing her makeup.

"Mom? Are you here?" I called, stepping into her house. The silence as I walked through the living room put an uneasy feeling in my gut. "Don asked me to come check on you."

Muted banging sounds came from the bathroom. Someone, my mom, I hoped, opening and closing a cabinet. After the noise stopped, I made my way down the hallway.

"Mom, I know you're probably fine," I said. "But Don's kind of freaked out."

"Hi, honey." Her voice, muffled by the bathroom door, sounded weak. "I'll be out in a minute."

"Are you okay?"

"Yeah. Just looking for something." More of the clunking. "Go ahead and help yourself to a cup of coffee. I think Don made some this morning."

"I kind of wanted to take you out to breakfast." My hand on the door, I tapped it with my fingertips. "I'm starving."

"Honey, why don't you call Will to go with you?"

"Because, I wanted to talk about him. I can't talk about him while he's there."

Usually, that would have gotten at least a small giggle from her. She would have opened the door, her huge smile blinding me, and pulled me in to sit down and spill everything.

All I got was quiet.

"What's going on in there, Mom?"

"Nothing. I'm fine, honey."

"Can I come in?" I jiggled the doorknob. "It's locked."

"No." She sighed, then gasped. "It's coming out, Ev."

"What?"

"My hair. It's falling out." She sobbed. "I didn't know it would be like this."

"Let me come in, Mom."

"It's coming out in clumps. All at once."

"Let me see."

The lock on the door clicked. I turned the little gold-toned knob, pushing the door open. My mom stood in front of the mirror, brush in hand. The hair on her head matted in some places. Other parts, her scalp, shiny in the light, peeked out.

"It's so bad." She pulled the brush through a section of hair. Strands fell away from her scalp like they'd never been attached. "I was looking for the electric clippers. I can't find them anywhere."

"Why do you want those?"

"I just want to shave it all off." Her shoulders rose and fell. "I can't keep losing it like this."

"Do you want me to see if Cal has some clippers?"

"I don't know." Her bangs still swept over her forehead. "Will you do it? I can't hold my arms up that long."

"I can't, Mom." Saliva filled my mouth. I thought for sure I'd throw up from the grief that filled my stomach.

"What am I going to do?" She lowered the brush. It spilled over with red hair.

"I have an idea. Wait here, okay?"

I left her in the bathroom, looking into the mirror. Walking down the hall, I tried to keep my eyes from the family pictures that lined the walls. But I knew the photos by heart. And in each one of them, the bright hair curled around her face. Thick and healthy. Once again, I shoved my emotion out of the way.

I dug through my purse until I found my phone.

"Hey," Cal answered his phone. "Seriously, you'd better be calling to tell me that aliens have occupied the town and eaten all the doughnuts. If not, I'm going to shun you forever."

"I know." I tried to keep my breathing under control. "Sorry."

"Why are you calling me? We have our first day off in six months and you decide to wake me up?"

"It's been four months."

"Same thing, Ev."

"Listen, Cal, I need you to get Grace over to Mom's house," I said.

"What? No."

"It's not for me."

"We're not in a place where I can just call her and tell her what to do." He paused. "We aren't even dating. Not really."

I stepped into the kitchen, looking out the window. "Mom's hair is falling out, Cal." I waited for his reaction. "She needs some help."

"Oh, man." He exhaled. "Okay."

"Thanks, Cal."

"Listen, make sure there's hot coffee waiting for me."

I slipped the phone into my pocket and started a fresh pot of coffee. I used the pull-out sprayer to fill the machine with water. Overflowing, water spilled out, puddling on the countertop. I mopped it up with a hand towel.

Cal pulled into the driveway with Grace in the passenger seat. I watched them from the kitchen window. It had only taken Cal half an hour to bring Grace to the house. I wondered how he'd convinced her. Not that it mattered, really. She'd come, and my anxiety calmed a little.

Walking in, Cal carried a tote and held the door for Grace.

"Hi." Her light eyes looked on me with gentleness. "You doing okay?"

"I'm so glad you're here." I shut the door behind the two of them, locking it. I didn't want anyone walking in right then. It would have embarrassed Mom too much. "Do you drink coffee or tea?"

"Coffee," she said. "Please."

"I'll get it for her." Cal lowered the bag to the table. "You like cream and sugar, right?"

"Yes. Thanks. Lots of both, please." She smiled at Cal before turning back to me. "How's your mom taking it?"

"She's upset."

"I would be, too." She pulled out the contents of her bag and set them on the table. A razor, shaving cream, clippers. "I brought some stuff to do her nails, too."

"That's really nice." Her kindness sent a warm ache through my chest.

"I'm excited to meet her." She pulled a few bottles of nail polish from her purse.

"You're going to love her." Cal said from the kitchen.

Grace looked over my shoulder and smiled. "Hi."

Turning, I saw my mom. She wore an old green ball cap of Don's. I'd never seen such an uneasy expression on her face.

"This is Grace," I said.

"Cal's Grace?" My mom's face lifted in a smile. "He's told me so much about you."

Cal blushed.

"Same here. I feel like I'm meeting a celebrity." Grace stepped forward and hugged my mom like it was the most natural thing in the world for her to do. After she let go, Grace touched the hat. "Do you mind if I take a look?"

My mom lifted the hat with one hand and smoothed what remained of her hair with the other. "It's terrible."

Cal turned his back to us. I thought for sure I caught him rubbing his eyes.

"It's not all that bad," Grace said. "Would you like me to shave it clean?"

My mom nodded. "I'd rather you make it all grow back."

"I wish I could." Grace hugged her again.

"Where should I sit?"

"How about we pull a chair into the kitchen? That way I can sweep it up more easily when we're done." Grace lifted a chair.

"I'll get it." Cal rushed to get the chair. He kissed our mom on the cheek before returning to the kitchen. He lowered the chair to the linoleum in front of the stove. "Is this good?"

"Perfect." Grace grabbed a cape from her bag.

Within a minute, my mom sat on the chair, covered by the black fabric. Grace touched her hair. Not with tender, pitiful hands. But with a gentle, quick, expert touch.

"This is natural color, isn't it?" she asked. "It's beautiful."

"Thank you." My mom blinked a few tears loose.

"Now, I'm going to use the clippers first, then I'll shave your scalp." Grace held the clippers in her hand. "Ready?"

My mom lifted both of her hands out from under the cape, reaching for Cal and me. We kneeled next to her.

Ice cold fingers gripped my hand. I glanced at Cal. He had pulled his top lip in and bitten down on it. His chin shook just enough that I saw it.

"Let me know if you need a break, Gretchen. Okay?" Grace rubbed my mom's shoulder.

Buzzing, the clippers moved through the hair, making red fall, sliding down the cape and to the floor. My mom kept her eyes closed. So tight, her nose scrunched at the top.

She didn't have to watch the hair coming off.

Chapter Thirty-Four

Olga

I never enjoyed spending time alone with Bev. Her grumping and groaning could get me down faster than a sad country western song. But no amount of begging off would get me out of our brunch date. Even if Rosetta was coming late.

Bev sat on the other side of the table from me at Marshall's. Arms crossed so tight, I figured one of them would get stuck like that. A few times, I was just sure she'd fallen asleep, her eyes closed for so long.

As hard as I worked my noggin, I couldn't think of a blessed thing to say to the woman. And she didn't help much with her one word answers to every question I did think up.

So, I sat, picking at my omelet and sipping my coffee, hoping that Rosetta would get there soon to rescue me.

"Rosetta's had a visitor this week," Bev said after a quarter hour of quiet between us. The way she pushed her lips together made her look just like a toad. I half expected her to flick out her tongue and catch a fly.

"I know," I answered back. "She's seeing him off now, isn't she? That's why she'll be here late."

"What I don't understand is who this person was that was visiting her." She looked from side to side. "I think she's been getting herself into trouble. She's running with a strange man."

"I don't know what you're talking about. Rosetta getting into trouble." I chuckled. "Just the thought of it's silly, Beverly."

"What would you know?" she huffed. "You ain't around that place to see what happens. How would you know trouble? You have no idea what you're talking about."

I used my napkin to cover the laugh that broke from out my mouth. Bev had a ridiculous way about her. And she hated being laughed at.

"Okay, Bev." I recovered from the little giggle. "You tell me what you're seeing at Rosetta's that's got you worried."

"Well, Rosetta's had this man coming to her apartment." She paused and lowered her voice, leaning in closer to me over her coffee. "And that man was staying for hours and hours. Then, when she'd walk him out to his car, she'd kiss him. Right smack dab on the mouth."

Laughing as loud as I did might not have been the best idea, but boy did it feel good. I hadn't let out a good gut-busting laugh in months. The kind that made me feel like I'd done a thousand sit-ups.

"What's your problem?" Bev sneered at me. "If I wanted to be laughed at, I would'a gone to breakfast with a pack of hyenas."

"I'm sorry, honey." The giggle still shook in my voice. "Oh, but I needed that laugh."

"What am I? A comedian? Do I look like Joan Rivers to you?" Bev shook her head. "I don't think it's so funny to be worried about a friend. Gosh, Olga."

"Now, Bev, don't you sit there and tell me you don't know."

"Don't know what? How can I tell you what I don't know if I don't know it?" She held her arms around herself even tighter. "I tell you what, you got me all kinds of confused."

"Honey, you know who that man is who's been visiting Rosie."

"I do not." She curled her lip. "But I do know that she's been eating lunch most days with that Sophia. That woman who goes into men's rooms to...well, you know what she does."

"And what does that have to do with anything, Bev?" I asked.

"I think Sophia's been rubbing off on Rosetta."

"Bev, that man that's been visiting is Rosetta's son," I said.

"That's not her son."

"Yes, it is." I sipped my coffee.

Bev turned her head, glaring at me out of the corner of her eye. She opened and shut her mouth just about five times before she just let it clamp fast.

"His name is Abe, and he's a lawyer. He lives in Alabama." I nodded. "And he is a very good son."

"Well." Bev inhaled real deep. So deep, it made her cough. "I guess I was wrong."

We sat for several minutes. Nothing but quiet between the two of us. Keeping one eye out the window, I hoped to see Rosetta walking up to meet us. The waitress came and refilled our coffee.

"How's that daughter of yours? Ginger? That's her name, right?" Bev let her arms loose to pick up her coffee.

"Gretchen."

"What kind of name is that? What are you, German?"

I nodded, although I doubted she saw it. She was too busy rolling her eyes at me.

"Anyway, dumb name or not, how is she?"

"She's doing okay right now," I said. "Her second round of chemotherapy starts soon."

"It made her sick, didn't it?" Bev asked.

"Yes." I poured a little packet of sugar into my coffee. "She goes in for a scan next week sometime."

"What? A scan? Now, you don't need to use your fancy doctor words with me. I don't know what a scan is." Her eyes rolled back the way they'd come a minute before. "Sounds like something a robot gets or something."

"They're going to take pictures of her insides," I answered. "They need to make sure the tumor shrunk."

"What if the tumor didn't shrink?"

I hadn't allowed myself to entertain that thought. It would have done nothing but set my anxious heart to panicking. My hands shook so that I put them under the table and onto my thighs.

"That would mean the treatment didn't work." I lifted the napkin from my lap and dabbed my lips. "And that would mean she's going to leave sooner than we're hoping for."

Bev raised one of her eyebrows at me, turning her lips into even

226

more of a frown than usual. Her dentures clicked so loud, I thought for sure they'd fall out on the table. Instead, she pushed them into place with her tongue.

"I been praying for her. When I remember, that is," she said. "I never been much for praying a whole lot. It always just makes me fall asleep to have my eyes closed that long. But I been praying for Ginger."

"Thank you."

I decided not to correct her. God could sort out the names. I just knew He could.

Chapter Thirty-Five

EVELYN

Sitting on the porch steps next to Will, I tried to figure out how he'd roped me into helping him with the youth group.

"So was it as terrifying as you expected it to be?" He bumped me with his shoulder.

"Almost." I scratched my scalp. "I'll need to take an extra long shower tonight to get all this out of my hair."

"Yeah. Youth group is all about getting messy."

A car drove by, honking at us. Will waved.

"Seriously, who ever came up with the idea of playing Frisbee with pancakes?" I worked loose a sticky mass in my hair. "And who thought to put syrup on them?"

"That wasn't my idea." He shook his head. "Cal told me it would be fun."

"You can't listen to Cal."

"Anyway, thanks. I think the kids liked hanging out with you."

"Well, I guess I had fun."

He took my hand in his, looking at it in the dim parking lot lights. "Your nails are pretty."

"Thanks. Grace did them," I said. "I wish you could have seen how great she was with my mom. She did a good job."

"I didn't see her in church this morning. I wondered if she was feeling sick."

"She's having a hard time. You know?" I wiped my nose with the back of my other hand. "I don't think she's comfortable yet. She has a scarf, but it's still difficult for her."

He lifted my hand, giving it a little kiss.

"Wow." He let his lips linger on my skin. "You smell good."

"What do you mean?"

"I mean you smell like breakfast."

I was grateful for the laugh. I needed it. He watched me, smiling. Turning a bit sideways on the step, he leaned in closer to me.

"So, Ev, I need to talk to you about something."

"Okay."

"I talked to Barton the other day. He told me that he's planning to retire at the end of the year." Will pushed the hair off his forehead. "I mean, it's about time. He's been around a lot of years."

"When's he telling the congregation?"

"This next Sunday during the morning service." Putting his hand on the back of his neck, he exhaled. "The elders want to announce me as his successor."

"You accepted the job?"

"Not yet. That's what I needed to talk to you about." He wrinkled his nose.

"Okay."

"I think we need to discuss where this is going. This thing with us."

I sighed, taking my hand from his. "I see."

"You do?"

Nodding, I turned my eyes to the ground. I didn't have it in me to pretend. His words were about to push me back to being alone. "Go ahead."

I'd watched my parents in their unhappy marriage. How messy everything got when it fell apart. I remembered the empty feeling in my chest when I found out that my dad had left.

Sitting by Will on the church steps, that emptiness returned. It felt like loneliness. Like mourning.

"I'm glad you understand." He wiped under his nose. "And, so, you get why I'm kind of nervous right now."

"Yeah. I do." I decided that, when he said that it was over, I'd just walk away, get into my car and wait to cry until I got to my apartment. I felt my pocket to make sure I had the keys handy.

"You know I've enjoyed the last few months with you." He took in a breath. "I've never dated anybody like you before."

I pulled my fleece sweater tighter around my neck and pushed my hands against the pavement, readying to stand up.

"And I hate to spring this on you right now," he said. "I mean, with your mom and everything. I know that's enough of an emotional toll on you."

I stood, my keys dropping from my hands.

"Are you okay, Ev?" He reached for my keys.

"I don't know." I stopped, trying to gather my thoughts. "What is this conversation about?"

He swallowed. "I guess I'm still trying to figure it out."

Standing, he grabbed my hand again.

My emotions teetered. A rush of excitement blended with a throb of dread.

"I'm nervous because I want to tell you something. And I've never told any girl this before." He kissed my hand again. "Man, you smell like breakfast. You're making me hungry."

"Stay on topic, Will."

"Right." He sucked in a deep breath. "Evelyn, I love you."

"Wow. Yeah. I can understand why that would make you nervous." I gave him my other hand, too. Excitement won over the dread, joined by relief. The mourning held on, though. That wouldn't so easily heal.

"Now that I've got this job offer, I need to find out where we're going." His eyes crinkled in the corners. "It's crazy because I've only known you for a few months. But I already have an idea of where I want us to end up."

"You aren't asking me to marry you. It's too soon for that," I said. "Way too soon."

"Oh, no. I know that. Barton suggested that we just get married real quick."

"He did?"

"Yeah. I told him that wasn't a good idea. I need to get to know you some more."

I exhaled for the first time since Will started talking. "I'm so glad. There's no way I can even think about that right now."

"I told Barton that, too." He cringed. "But do you mind if we stop talking about him? Just thinking about him makes my arm hurt for some reason."

"No problem."

"Good." He sighed. "But I do love you. And I want to spend more time with you."

"Well," I said. "I'm a little worried that you're going to change your mind about me."

"Why's that?"

"I doubt God. A lot. Like, pretty much every day. I mean, I believe everything about Jesus. You know?" I squeezed his hands. "I don't know if that's the best pastor's wife material."

"Okay." His smile melted me. "But could you see yourself as Will's wife material? I mean, someday later on?"

"Probably."

"Good enough for me." He reached over our hands and kissed me. Not our first kiss. But our nicest one. "So that makes us in a committed relationship?"

"Sure."

I wished I'd met him earlier. Maybe even just a few months before. As a little girl, whenever I daydreamed about my wedding, my mom was there.

I couldn't imagine that day without her. Really, though, I couldn't imagine any day when she wouldn't be around. The sweetest moments of life would have an edge of bitterness for me without her.

Chapter Thirty-Six

OLGA

Aunt Gertie never let me mourn my mother. She'd find me on my little bed with a wet face and sick from all my crying. She'd snarl at me and tell me God had no use for my tears. She'd swat at me, her hand stinging my skin, until I got up and washed my face.

Yelling at me while the tears flooded my eyes, she'd tell me that God had a reason for my mother's death. His judgment had been swift and steady. And that, if I questioned God, I'd be in peril of joining my mother in the blazing fires of hell. That my tears would sizzle in that burning place.

Aunt Gertie sure was a miserable person.

I hadn't spent a whole lot of time reading my Bible that week. Not with Gretchie feeling as good as she was. I'd hurry up and get breakfast down my throat, say a thank You prayer on the way, and get every minute I could with my girl.

Her good days weren't sure to last long. Chemotherapy started up too soon, and I wanted to collect all the smiles I could. To gather them in my heart to last me during her sick days. And, as little as I wanted to think of them, the days when she would be gone.

I splashed in the oasis, guzzling the sweet water, fully aware of the desert that gathered up around us, getting closer all the time.

Soon, the water would turn bitter and I'd cry out to God again, wondering why He'd let it happen.

Something had woke me up earlier than usual that day. A bump in the wee morning that made my heart thump so much, I couldn't get calmed back down. I figured I might as well get my weary bones out of bed.

Tying the bathrobe tight around my waist, I got into the chair at my dinette to read a little of my Bible. I'd missed it, that old friend of mine. The leather of the cover soothed the tips of my fingers as they moved over top of it. The pages opened, making a swishing sound. Such a pleasing noise.

"I'm sorry," I whispered. "I shouldn't have stayed away so long, Lord."

He'd forgiven me. I felt it like a hug.

The tears came so I couldn't read the little words on my onion-skin thin pages. My God didn't smack me. He didn't scream at me to wash the remorse and grief off my face. He gathered my tears. Held me in His arms. And He poured love all over me.

He filled me all the way up. I sure would need every drop I could get.

⸻

Feeling whole and full of God's sweet mercy, I stood at my living room window, watching an uneven V of geese practicing their departure. I always missed them when they took off for their warmer winter homes. Summer never lasted long enough for me.

Movement on the ground caught my eye. Charlotte ran along the sidewalk past the garden. Still in her sweatpants, she held herself around the middle. Bad eyes and everything, I could still see the fear on her face.

"Clive," I hollered, feeling the way my voice went shrill. "Clive, honey. We got trouble."

"What's the matter?" he called out, alert as soon as his eyes opened, I was sure of it.

"I don't know yet." I made my way to the door where my slip-on shoes sat waiting for me. "Get over to Gretchen's when you're dressed."

"Are you dressed?"

"I got my robe on."

And down the steps, out the door, and to Charlotte I went. The morning dew wet my shoes as I rushed with her, both of us without words, to the sidewalk. All I could think of to pray was for swift and nimble feet. Breathless, I got to the porch. One light, the one over the kitchen sink, gave the house a sleepy, peaceful look.

I grabbed hold of the porch railing, about to pull myself up the steps.

"Wait, Gran," Charlotte said, breathless, holding my arm.

"What is it?" I asked, keeping my hand on the wood.

"I don't know." She licked a tear off her lip. "I heard a crash. When I found her in the living room, she was passed out."

"Did you call for an ambulance?"

"Don did." Her breathing quickened, the air only making it partway into her lungs. "I didn't check to see if she was still alive."

"Oh, Lord," I prayed aloud.

"I'm scared," she whimpered.

"Me, too, honey."

"Pray that she's okay, Gran. Please," she begged me. "I know God listens to you."

I nodded, doubting that my prayers would do any more for my daughter than anyone else's.

My hips ached as I moved up the steps, feet as heavy as rocks. My soul cried out, like the Israelites. Unsure, terrified. Feeling abandoned. Afraid that I wouldn't hear His voice until it was too late.

Chapter Thirty-Seven

EVELYN

I couldn't tolerate sitting in the waiting room with the rest of my family. The doctors had my mom in some room, hooking her up to who knew what kind of machines with tubes and needles. And, all the while, my family sat in chairs or paced around the waiting room.

I'd found a bench in the hall, right outside the door. Bending at the waist, I held my face in my hands. Whatever words I found to pray surprised me. I felt too deep in a hole to put a thought together.

"Hey, Ev," Will said, coming out of the waiting room. "You want to come back in?"

"I don't know," I answered into my hands.

"Well, the doctor just came in. He's waiting for you, if you want to hear what he's got to say."

"Do you think it's bad news?" I asked. "Did he give everybody a sad look when he came in?"

"No. He seemed really relaxed, actually."

I held out my hand for him to help me up. Feeling too weak, I didn't think I could stand on my own.

"This is too hard." I leaned into him.

"I know." He wrapped his arms around me. "I love you."

I held Will's hand, listening to the doctor's calm, steady voice. He stood next to Don's chair and used his hands as he talked.

"We have Gretchen in the ICU for right now," he said. "Just to get her stable. She's pretty dehydrated. We think that's part of the trouble she's having right now."

"But we all tried to get her to drink," Charlotte said. "She couldn't keep it down."

"I know." The doctor nodded. "This isn't your fault. I know that."

"When can we see her?" Don asked, rubbing his palms together.

"In just a little bit." The doctor put his hand on Don's shoulder. "She needs to rest up first."

"How's she doing?" Gran asked. "Is she still unconscious?"

"She woke up for us, but we gave her a little something to make her sleep. And we've got lots of fluids pumping to get her hydration levels back where they should be." He looked around the room. "I've called her oncologist. She'll be able to tell us a little more about what's going on with the cancer part of the equation."

"What about it?" Granddad sat up. "Is it worse?"

"I'm not at liberty to discuss specifics about that." The doctor rubbed his chin. "We'll have to talk to Doctor Ferris about that. I wish I could tell you more."

The doctor left the room. Every one of us sank deeper into our chairs. Slumped our shoulders more.

"Well," Gran said. "She's still alive. We know that much right now. And we'll just have to trust God with the rest."

"I'm not sure I have that kind of trust to give," Don said. He went back to pacing circles around the room.

Chapter Thirty-Eight

OLGA

Gretchen had been in the hospital three days before they moved her out of the ICU. Her new room had more space for the family. Clive joked that it was our first family vacation.

My girl sat up in the hospital bed, holding a little dish of orange gelatin, eating the littlest of bites. Seemed like all she could keep down was Jell-O or pudding. Sometimes a little ice cream, too. But only after the pain medication worked its way through her body.

Cal had left a few hours earlier. He'd grown restless after day one in that place, just sitting around, doing a whole lot of waiting. That boy had to fix things. Just like his granddad. It made him half crazy knowing he couldn't do a blessed thing for his mama. But he could go piddle around the funeral home. Clive would have gone along, if it hadn't been for me needing him beside me.

"I feel awful, sitting here eating in front of all of you," Gretchen said before sliding a small bite onto her tongue.

"Don't feel bad, honey," I said. "We'll send somebody out to get supper in a little bit."

"Well, I can tell you one thing, it doesn't taste good at all," she said. "Nothing tastes good anymore. It's sad."

A knuckle rapped on the door.

"Come in," Donald called.

Pushing open the door, Gretchen's oncologist walked in. Doctor

Ferris, I recalled. The one with the big desk and dangling earrings. She carried a clipboard under her arm.

"I hope I'm not interrupting anything," she said, noticing the room full of family. "I heard you had quite the crowd in here."

"You're just in time to watch me eat this goo," Gretchen said.

"I'm glad to see you eating. That's good." Doctor Ferris stood, her back against the wall. "Now, I met your mother a few months ago."

Gretchen, always the welcoming one, pointed at each one in the room, making introductions. She exhaled at the end, out of breath.

"Great. Thank you." The doctor addressed Gretchen. "Now, do you want your family with you right now? I have the results of your scans and tests."

"Well, can my husband stay?" Gretchen asked. "And my mom? I'd like everyone else to take a little break."

"Coffee's on me," Will said.

Clive and the kids hustled out of the room without so much as a word. Will put his arm around Evelyn as they went. That young man had become a gift from God to our family.

The doctor waited for the door to close all the way after they left before she made a peep. When the small click of the latch sounded, she turned to Gretchen.

"As you know, we did quite a few scans," she began, pinning images of Gretchen's liver onto a light-up board. "The cancer has spread significantly. We found tumors in several places."

Donald's face drooped, and his shoulders fell limp. "What does that mean?" he asked.

"It means that the treatments didn't work the way we'd hoped." She pushed her glasses up on the bridge of her nose. "At this point, Gretchen, you have a few decisions to make."

"What kind of decisions?" I asked.

"Whether to keep up with the chemotherapy or not."

"What do you think I should do?" Gretchen asked.

"I usually don't tell people this." Doctor Ferris took off her glasses, letting them hang from a chain around her neck. "But, at your stage, I think it would be good to try to stay comfortable and enjoy the time you have left."

"So you'd choose to stop the treatment?"

"I would."

The doctor explained options for pain management. Medications that had names I'd never be able to pronounce.

"Can I go home?" Gretchen asked. "If being here isn't going to extend my life, I'd rather spend my time at home."

"Let's get a few things arranged and then I'll help you get discharged." She pulled a card from the pocket of her long, white jacket. "I'd like you to give hospice a call soon. They'll help you with everything you could possibly need to do this at home. This is a very good one."

Donald lowered his head, letting it rest on Gretchen's chest. She ran her fingers through his gray hair.

"I'm sorry, Don," she whispered. "I wish this wasn't happening to you."

Hearing that man cry from deep down inside made me almost crazy with grief.

"I'll go tell the kids." I forced myself out of the chair I'd occupied for hours. My knees threatened to send me crashing to the floor. Bracing myself against the wall, I pushed forward to the door.

Just get out of this room, I thought. *Don't you dare fall apart now. This isn't the time. You wait until later.*

As I opened the wide hospital room door, I heard Gretchen behind me.

"Thank you for being such a good doctor. You have done a fantastic job."

My heart was so heavy, I thought I would drop to the floor.

Chapter Thirty-Nine

EVELYN

Easy listening music flowed through the speakers at the tiny grocery store, lulling me into mindless wandering. The whiny sound of a saxophone played music from the seventies, drawing out the notes a little too long.

All I'd needed was flour and coffee creamer. Somehow, though, in my numb aimlessness, I'd managed to fill a whole cart with food. Mostly junk. All of it quick to grab and eat along the way. And one bag of apples.

I'd broken the rule about shopping hungry and had the chips and frozen cookie dough to prove it.

Right as I walked toward the one cashier on duty, I saw Deirdre coming my direction. She waved one hand while steering her cart with the other. No matter how much I wanted to, I wouldn't be able to retreat without being completely obvious.

Strategic thinking wasn't easy on less than two hours of sleep.

"Evelyn," she called, her cart full of chocolate chips speeding toward me. "How are you?"

"That's a lot of chocolate chips." I stepped toward the cashier and pretended to read the magazine covers. Some celebrity had a baby. What did I care? I stared at the cover anyway, wondering how much the movie star had been paid for the photos.

"Charlotte and I are baking cookies for the elementary school.

They've got an open house or something later this week." She cleared her throat, leering at the tube of cheap cookie dough in my cart. "Looks like you're planning on doing some baking, too."

"I have no intention of baking those."

She laughed, holding her round, jiggling stomach. "Oh, with all you're going through, you still have that sense of humor."

"Well, thanks." I pushed my cart into the checkout lane.

Leaving her pile of chocolate chips in the middle of the walkway, she followed right behind me. "You know, Evelyn, I know what you think of me."

Stacking my groceries onto the cashier's belt, I tried to ignore her.

"But I'm not just a big gossip." She cleared her throat again. "I know that's my reputation. And I earned it. I admit it. But I'm trying to be better about it."

"I'm glad."

"I care about your family. I do. And I'm sorry." Her hand on my back felt like a limp fish. "Your mom is a really good woman. I hate to see her like this."

"Yup. Thanks." I noticed that a giant can of ravioli had landed on my loaf of cinnamon swirl bread, crushing all the center pieces. "Great."

"If you ever need anything—"

"Okay," I interrupted. "I keep hearing people say that, you know? And I couldn't tell you what we need right now if I wanted to. Which, as a matter of fact, I don't want to have to do. Mom's only been home from the hospital a week. We're completely exhausted and trying to get our feet under us. It's going to be awhile before we can even start to think about what we need."

Surveying my mountain of groceries all piled up for the cashier, I realized that I had three different kinds of salsa, but no tortilla chips. Also, I'd forgotten the flour. The one thing that my mom had specifically asked for and I'd forgotten it. I sighed, letting my entire body slump. I bit my lip to keep from dissolving into a puddle.

I'd wandered around that grocery store for over an hour. How had I forgotten the flour? I must have passed it at least half a dozen times.

"What's wrong, Evelyn?" Deirdre asked, stepping even closer and rubbing her hand on my back. "What is it?"

"I forgot the flour." Then I lost it. All the emotion I'd stuffed down over the course of months spurted out in blubbering, gulping sobs. Right there next to the rack of bubblegum.

Deirdre held me until I could stand on my own again. Then, she rushed off, leaving her cart of chocolate chips. When she came back, she had the biggest bag of flour the store sold.

"I hope this is okay," she said. "It's what we use at the bakery."

"Thank you."

The cashier, some pimple-faced high school kid, scanned my items as fast as he could, trying to avoid eye contact with the crazy crying woman in his line.

Chapter Forty

OLGA

Gretchen had gotten good at hiding all the pain. She couldn't keep it from me, though. I'd been around her in all different kinds of hurt. She wore the hurt right in the spot between her eyebrows. The way the skin gathered up. And, every once in a while, she'd clench her jaw for a flash flinch.

Oh, did I ever ask the Sovereign God to put that ache on me instead of her.

Doctor Ferris had given her a prescription for pain medicine in pill form. Donald had it filled at the pharmacy. Gretchen just refused to take a one of those pills. It didn't matter how big her pain, she wouldn't be drugged. She'd had Charlotte stick them in the kitchen junk drawer.

Gretchie sat on the couch, letting the sunshine drench her scarf-covered head. Eyes closed, her face tilted as if she inhaled the warmth.

"It's colder out there than you'd think," I said. "Downright nippy."

"I bet." Not moving, she kept right on soaking. "How are things over at the funeral home? I feel completely out of the loop."

"Oh, it's busy as ever." My washcloth scrubbed against a sticky spot on the counter. "Busiest we've had in a few years, really. They had a funeral over there this morning."

"Well, I hate that everyone has to work so hard all day, then come over here and take care of me." The side of her face tensed, her jaw flexing, popping out from her too-thin face. "I feel like a burden."

"I haven't heard one complaint from anybody," I said. "Just so long as we keep the coffee brewing, everybody seems to be pretty content."

"Well, I really appreciate it."

She breathed in sharp and wore that twinge between her eyebrows. The way she moved her legs, real slow and stiff, got my heart racing. Her body shook, and she put a hand to her stomach.

"Gretchen?" I left that washcloth and got myself to her. "What is it? You need some of that medicine?"

"I'm okay." She clenched her teeth. "It's just a jolt."

"Let me get you one of your pills. Please, honey." I started back to the kitchen. "I can't take seeing you like this anymore."

"No," she panted. "The pain never lasts all that long. It's almost over now."

Relaxing, she sank into the couch cushions. Her teeth chattered so, I worried she'd break through a crown.

"Honey, the medicine would help with that. The hurt wouldn't come on so strong."

"I'm not myself when I take that stuff. I can't even keep my eyes open when I'm all drugged up." Sucking in, she got herself a breath that pushed her chest up. "When I can't go without them, I'll let you know. I promise."

I got a clean washcloth from the drawer by the sink. Soaked it with the coldest water I could get out of the tap. That freezing water made my fingers stiff.

"Here." I made my way to her, feeling the worry in every single muscle. "At least let me cool you off a bit."

Her eyes stayed set on the trees outside her window. Wiping at her forehead, I got the edge of the scarf wet, it soaked up some of the moisture.

"Would you look at the orange leaves on that maple." Her voice still quivered a bit. "Remember when Cal put that in when it was just a sapling?"

"I don't know that I do." I moved my cloth across her cheeks.

"He found it in the woods and wanted to transplant it here. Right outside his bedroom window." Her smile bumped against my hand. "He wanted to watch it grow."

"Oh, yes." Looking where she'd pointed, I refolded the washcloth. "I remember now. That was a good many years ago."

"I was so afraid I'd mow over it. Remember how I put the bricks all around it?" Head laying on the back of the couch, she kept on talking. "I love that Don put rocks around it. It's so pretty. He found the best rocks he could."

"How is Donald doing?" I asked, getting up to finish my cleaning. "He seems so tired, honey. Is he getting any sleep at all?"

"Not much. He's not eating, either," she said. "He's taking this so hard."

"I imagine." My scrubbing cloth had gone dry. I plunged it into the lukewarm dishwater. "Is he talking to you about it at all?"

"A little." Her voice sounded so far away and dreamy. "He's scared, Mom."

"I know it, honey."

"He doesn't want to lose the family after I'm gone. He'd be all alone."

Since the day I'd met Donald, I had the hardest time feeling like I'd gained a son-in-law. We tried. Maybe not hard enough, though. Part of it might have been a dose of the jealousy poison. Clive and I had filled the spot of family for so long. Gretchen had come to us when she needed help or to talk. We'd been right next to her at the kids' basketball games or choir concerts. That long without competition had spoiled us. We had to learn all over again how to share her.

The idea that he valued us as his family had completely slipped my mind. I never would have figured. And that broke my heart.

"He'll always be our family," I said. "You make sure he knows that."

"Thank you, Mom." She smiled with her eyes closed, the glow of sun on her skin. "That puts me at ease."

"He loves you, Gretchie. We can't help but love him for that." I checked the clock. Lunchtime already. The days sped away from us too quickly. "You ready for a little something to eat?"

"Not unless you want to see me get sick again," she said. "I'm even afraid to drink water."

"Oh, honey." I fished my washcloth out of the sink full of water. "Can't they give you something for that?"

"I don't know."

Just as soon as I pulled the plug to let the water out of the sink, somebody knocked on the screen door. I tried to spy out the kitchen window to see who it was. But all I saw was a bandana hanging out the seat of somebody's faded jeans.

"Now, who could that be?" I asked, more to myself than anything.

A crisp breeze snuck in past me when I opened up the wood door. Jay Bunker stood on the porch, his old, bent ball cap held in his cracked and calloused hands.

"Hi, there," I said, pushing the storm door open. "Come in, Jay."

"Ms. Eliot, I best not come in." He nodded down at his boots, blushing a little. "I'm all kinds of dirty from being in the barn this morning."

"I can see that," I said. "Is there something I can do for you?"

"Well, ma'am, the wife and me been trying to think how we could help out with Gretchen. Her being sick and all, we figured you folks might need a little help with something."

"Is that so?"

"Well, ma'am, I was driving by the other day and noticed the lawn here could use a little mowing. Maybe even some leaves picked up." Shuffling his weight, his boots scuffed on the porch. "I thought I'd give it a once over on my riding mower."

"That's awfully nice of you, Jay."

"I rode that mower here. It's over by the road there." His eyes met mine for a moment. "And, Ms. Eliot, I'm not expecting to take your money for doing it, neither. I'll do this yard and by the funeral home. It won't take me but half an hour."

"You don't have to do that, Jay," I said.

"Mom," Gretchen called from the couch. "Will you please tell Mr. Bunker that I'd love for him to do the last mow of the year? It would be an honor."

"I guess Gretchen says yes." I sighed.

"I heard her." When Jay smiled, a trickle of tobacco juice edged up his mouth.

"Thank you, Jay."

He hopped off the porch and pulled the hat back on his head, shifting it till it fit just right. Turning his head, he nodded once before climbing onto his riding mower. It started up with a grumble and a grunt. Then turned to humming as he rode it up and down the yard.

Closing the door, I turned to Gretchen. "I know what you're going to say."

"What's that?" she asked.

"I need to let people help us."

Gretchen's best twinkle gleamed up from her eyes. "It's what he can do, Mom."

"I know it, honey. I know."

"Mom, could you please make me a hot cup of tea?" she asked. "I think it would feel good to sip. Or maybe just in my hand."

"Sure thing, sweetheart."

I made up a couple mugs of chamomile tea, letting the apple smelling steam fill my nose. And I watched Jay as he rode around on his mower, a big grin on his face.

Chapter Forty-One

EVELYN

Will stood on the step behind me. I looked at him over my shoulder, making sure he still had color in his cheeks.

"Are you sure you're ready for this?" I asked.

"Yeah. I'm fine," he answered, grabbing hold of the porch railing.

"The body won't be embalmed, you know."

"Yup. You told me. I know what to expect."

"Then you have to promise if you're going to pass out, you'll make your way outside. Right?"

I knocked on the cold glass of the storm door, hoping someone inside would hear me. A light flickered on in the kitchen. A second later, Darrell Eames pulled the door open.

His eyes fixed on the railing. "Thank you for coming."

"Of course." I took a step up and into the house. "You know Pastor Will."

"Yes. I'm glad you could come." They shook hands. "Yvonne said she'd feel better if a minister was here. She wants you to say a prayer or something. Maybe a benediction. I don't know what she wants. She'll tell you."

"I'm so sorry, Darrell," Will said. "You just let me know what you need. I'll do whatever I can to help you."

"Thank you." Darrell turned around, staring at the empty entryway as if he didn't recognize it. "Did you need to bring anything in with you?"

"Not yet," I said. "I'll get everything in a few minutes."

Will closed the door behind him. I waited for Darrell, not wanting to rush him. Rubbing his forehead with shaky fingertips, he seemed at a loss. Through the kitchen, I heard quiet sounds that came, I guessed, from the living room. Yvonne's muffled voice.

"Tell them to come on in here," she called.

"Well." Darrell motioned for us to follow him through the kitchen.

A stack of dishes, three of them, sat on the countertop. A box of crackers, opened, stood next to them. A half full coffee cup beside that.

"Sorry about the mess," Darrell whispered. "We never would have left it like this. But we were in the middle of getting a little snack when he…"

"Don't worry about it," I said.

"He's right in here."

Darrell led us into the living room. The light from a table lamp warmed the space with dim light. It took a moment for my eyes to adjust.

Yvonne stood at the end of the hospital bed, a bath towel draped across her arm. She kept her eyes on the bed.

Esther sat on the edge, by Justin's hip. A small, plastic basin rested in her lap. She moved a washcloth over the skin of Justin's hands, wiping so gently, as if she didn't want to hurt or wake him.

"He had a rough time of it," Darrell said. "I didn't know it would be so bad. And fast."

Water dripped from the washcloth as Esther pulled it up, freshened by the clean water. She wrung it, extra drops splashing back into the basin. Dabbing lightly around his eyes and nose, she moved the cloth along the face that had already lost color. Next, she cleansed his neck, then his arms. Pointing with my eyes, Will and I took a step back. They needed privacy in that moment.

"We thought he was getting better," Darrell said. "He even got up and took a walk today."

Esther lifted the basin from her lap and stood, carrying it to the end of the bed. Yvonne didn't move, she just continued looking down at her son. Esther pulled the sheet off Justin's feet with one hand and held the basin with the other. As she moved, a small splash of water spilled, wetting her hands. She didn't wipe it away.

"I'll hold that," Yvonne said, taking the basin, holding it while Esther washed Justin's feet.

Esther lowered the washcloth into the water, careful to keep it from sloshing. It expanded in the water, sinking after she let it go. Pulling the bath towel off Yvonne's arm, she used it to dry Justin's skin from his head to his feet. Then she covered him with a clean sheet.

"I don't want you to cover his face," Yvonne said. "Not yet."

Esther tucked the fabric under Justin's chin.

Yvonne lowered the basin to an end table and wiped her hands on the sides of her pants, leaving wet marks on her hips. She stepped around Esther and to the side of Justin's bed. Drawing near to his face, she kissed his forehead.

"Did you want to say a quick prayer?" Darrell asked, reaching for Will. "Just a few words, if that's okay with you."

Will took a step forward, lowering his head. His hands shook as he joined them together.

Darrell and Yvonne both bowed their heads, too. Esther, though, kept her eyes open, fixed on Justin's face.

"God, we have some badly broken hearts in this home tonight. I'm not asking You to take the hurt away, because that doesn't seem right. Justin deserves to be mourned. His absence should be felt. But I do ask that, somehow, this family will feel Your love and be wrapped in peace that can only come from You. Amen."

Darrell made the sign of the cross over his heart. Yvonne didn't open her eyes for another minute or so. When she finally did, she turned to me.

"I think we're ready," she said.

I touched Will's arm. "Will you give me a hand?"

He followed me to the hearse. When I opened the back door, the light inside glowed bright against the dark night. Pulling out the gurney, the pedals clicked into place.

"What can I do?" Will asked.

"Right now, nothing." I pushed the door of the hearse so that it didn't latch all the way. "They need a few minutes. We don't need to be in there for it. It's good for them to have a minute of privacy."

Will stood at the opposite end of the gurney from me.

"By the way," I said. "That was a good prayer. Just right."

"Thanks." He let out a sigh. "I think I'm getting used to this a little. It doesn't freak me out as much anymore."

"That's good." I glanced in the window. "We should give them another minute or two."

"Ev, you're really good at this," he said. "Especially with the families."

"Thank you."

"I mean it." He crossed his arms, shivering. "It's a gift. Not everybody can do this."

I grabbed the gurney, pushing it toward the house. Will moved around to the other side, lending me a hand.

"Okay," I said. "The steps are pretty steep, so let me go up first. Then, when we're coming out, I'll need you to go down first. Got it?"

"I think so."

We made our way back into the house, through the kitchen, and into the living room. Yvonne sat on the edge of the bed where Esther had been before, her hands folded in her lap. Darrell stood on the other side, gazing into the face of his son.

"I have to call his brothers," Darrell said. "We didn't know he would go tonight. I would have called them yesterday. If I'd known, I would have gotten them here. They should have been with Justin."

"I'm glad they weren't, Darrell," Yvonne said. "It would have been too hard. This was no family reunion."

She stood, her body stiff and slow. Her hands rested on the fronts of her thighs.

"If it's okay with you, Darrell, I'm going to leave the room now." She walked around the end of the bed. "I can't watch them take him."

The click of her shoes on the kitchen floor quieted as she moved farther from the living room.

Darrell touched his son's shoulder with fingertips before following the path of his wife.

Stepping forward, Esther took the top of the sheet in her hands, pulling it up over Justin's face. Lingering there, hovering over him, her eyes closed, she breathed in through her mouth.

Standing upright, she made eye contact with me. I hadn't noticed before how beautiful her brown eyes were. I imagined how pretty they were when she smiled. For sure, Justin had teased many smiles from her. I wondered if she'd ever find a reason to laugh the same way she had when he joked with her.

Most likely, she would. Over time, her heart would heal. Humans had a way of bouncing back from loss that alarmed me.

"Okay," she said. "You can take him."

She watched, hand over her mouth, as Will and I lifted Justin's body onto the gurney. Holding the door as we wheeled him out, she thanked us for being so careful with him. She stood in the driveway, watching us, arms hugged around her body, as we pulled away.

Chapter Forty-Two

Olga

Aunt Gertie never left a blessed thing in her garden at the end of a growing season. Not even a stray stem got overlooked by her eagle eye. She'd point at it with her crooked finger and tell me to pull it. Harvesting with Aunt Gertie wore me out.

She didn't grow a single plant in that garden we couldn't eat. Only practical, edible things. Veggies to be canned and freeze dried. She'd work zucchini into just about anything. And the stewing of tomatoes. More than any human could take. It took me years before I could even think about a peeled, squishy veggie again.

I supposed I loved keeping a flower garden because it was anything but practical. As far away from useful as I could get. It seemed such a luxury to sit among the blooms, delighting as they blossomed for no other purpose than to be beautiful. The older I got, though, the more necessary that garden became.

This year, I didn't get out into the garden until late in the fall. I waited all the way until the end of October. I'd never had to put it to bed all by myself before. Even as a little thing, Gretchie had helped me in her own way. Being out in those rows all by myself made me feel lonesome something awful.

She'd offered to come out with me, but I couldn't see that. She would have just gotten all out of breath and tired. That was, if she'd even got to the path without needing to turn around for a rest. The pain in her gut came in waves more frequently than before. I'd have hated for that to happen out in the garden.

Old leather work gloves covered my hands, and Clive's canvas jacket warmed my arms. I'd had to roll the sleeves up to my wrists. That soil, hard from the cold air under my feet…I couldn't get myself to do a thing but stare. Clumps of chamomile stems slumped onto the ground, all brown and withered. I just could not bring myself to touch any of it.

"Maybe I'll just let this garden go now." My words puffed out of me. "It's been so many years of work. It served me well. It's okay for me to be done with it."

Making my way to the old bench at the edge of the plot, I sat. Cold through my slacks, it still felt nice to take a load off for at least a few minutes. Soon, I wouldn't have that lavish pleasure. The snow would fall too thick for me to even think about sitting outside.

Overlooking the garden, I realized that putting it down for the year felt too much like giving up on Gretchen. I just did not have it in me. I allowed a whole bunch of tears loose that must have come right out of my soul, the way they burned on their way out.

Earlier, I'd read about the twelve spies that snuck their way into Canaan. So many giants in that land. Too many for them to overcome. And ten of them let the fear crush their spirits. My own spirit felt pretty well stomped, too.

"It's all too much," I prayed, letting the words steam into the cold air. "Too many giants in this land, Lord."

The sound of tires crunching on pavement caught my attention. I wiped my face with a tissue I'd stowed in Clive's jacket pocket. The car pulled all the way to the edge of the parking lot. On the door, stenciled in bright pink, CLEANING CREW had been painted. The woman in the driver's seat smiled at me as she lowered her window.

"Can I help you?" I asked, pushing up from the bench.

"I'm looking for a lady named Gretchen." The woman stuck her head out the window to see me. "Are you Gretchen?"

"No. That's my daughter." I pointed through the little strip of sidewalk that cut through the woods. "Her house is right through there."

"Great. Thanks." She pushed the button to put her window up.

"Wait." I stooped to look in the car window. "Are you going over there to do work?"

"Yeah. Somebody paid for six months of cleaning," she answered. "It's a gift."

"Do you happen to know who paid for that gift?" The biting wind whipped around me as I waited.

"Looks like two women," she said, flipping through paperwork. "Rosetta and Beverly. You know them?"

"I sure do." The way my face lifted worked to heal the pain in my heart.

I watched the housecleaner pull her car around toward Gretchen's house. A cloud rolled itself over the sun. But in my heart, at least, I felt warm.

Chapter Forty-Three

EVELYN

My mom held me, her hands around the nape of my neck. Lifting her had gotten easier. Too easy. She'd lost so much weight. I tried to put the clinical part of my job out of my mind. But, really, I couldn't deny what I knew. She inched closer and closer to the end.

Charlotte pushed a pillow behind our mom's back. "There you go," she said. "Do you think that gets you up high enough?"

Relaxing back, my mom smiled. "Just right."

"If you need another one, let me know. Okay?"

"I will." My mom formed a circle with her lips and blew out. "Thanks, girls."

She'd spent most every day on the couch. At night, we'd help her to Cal's old bedroom, right next to the bathroom. The stairs had become too much for her to get to her own room. By the end of each day, she was more exhausted than the day before. It was enough to get her to take the steps down the hallway as it was.

"Have you thought about getting a hospital bed?" I asked.

She scowled at me.

"Don't give me that face, Mom." I stood over her, my arms crossed. "It might make things easier for you."

"I feel like it's giving up." She touched the newly grown hair that stuck up short on her head. "My hair's coming in gray."

"I think it looks good," Char said. "If we put some gel in it, we could get it to spike. It would be so cute."

"It's wiry. I'll never get it to look right." She rubbed her hand over it. "It's like a scrub brush."

"No it isn't," I said.

"I thought I'd be happy to have hair again. But I wish it would have come in like it was. I miss my red hair." She dropped the hand to her lap. "It's ridiculous, isn't it?"

"Not really, Mom." Charlotte touched the gray hair. "But it doesn't look as bad as you think it does."

"Thank you, sweetheart."

"I bet we could get Grace to come over again. Cal could bring her. They're together all the time anyway," I said. "I never see him anymore."

"Maybe because you're busy with Will." My mom winked at Char.

"Not as much as Cal's with Grace. I'm telling you, his hair has never looked better."

"He should marry that girl." My mom grabbed the scarf off the back of the couch and tied it around her head. "Wouldn't it be nice to have a stylist in the family?"

"She's too good for him," I said.

"And that's exactly why he should marry her." My mom rested her head on the pillow behind her. Closing her eyes, she breathed deeply. I wondered if the pain had hit her. It had gotten difficult to tell.

"Girls, I thought we'd look through my jewelry today." She lifted a finger, pointing at the simple, wood box on the coffee table.

"Mom…" Charlotte dropped into the easy chair.

"What?" My mom rolled her head and opened her eyes. "I want to see you enjoying things. So let's do this together. When I'm dead, I won't know what you took. I want to do this with you."

"I'm just sick of thinking about it."

"Charlotte, doing it now will make things a lot easier later."

My sister slumped her shoulders and leaned as far back into the chair as she could. Like she wanted the cushions to pull her into themselves.

"What if you want to wear something again?"

"Then I'll borrow it back." Mom rubbed a spot behind her ear. "But if we want to be realistic, I'm not going to leave this house again. It's not like Don's going to take me out on a hot date or anything."

"I don't want to take anything." Char crossed her arms. "I can't do it."

"Char," I whispered. "Just do it. It's what Mom wants."

"It would feel like we can't wait to get our hands on her stuff."

"Honey, I don't have anything that's really nice. You know we never had money for really expensive things. But what I do have, I want you to enjoy." My mom swallowed. "It would be nice for me to look through this old stuff and tell you stories and share parts of my life today. That's what I want to do. Do you understand?"

Char's bottom lip pushed out, wrinkling her chin. "It's just, all the time, there are these reminders that you're going. And this is another one of them," she said. "I wish I could forget for half a minute without something reminding me."

"I know, honey." She waited, eyes watching Charlotte. "Listen, let's just look through the box. If you like something, you can just borrow it for now. How's that?"

Kneeling on the floor, I lifted the top of the jewelry box. A thin layer of dust rubbed off under my fingers.

That jewelry box had been on my mom's dresser for as long as I could remember. As a little girl, I'd climb up, sitting in front of the mirror, and try on all the different necklaces and bracelets. If a tube of lipstick had been left nearby, I'd smear it across my mouth.

My mom never got mad at me for playing dress up with her jewelry. She'd just reach around me and grab a bunch of necklaces to pull over her own head. She'd let me kiss the mirror, leaving my lip marks there for weeks.

I reached into the top, letting the velvet smooth against my fingers. I pulled out a silver chain with a single pearl dangling from it. My mom angled her head, looking at the necklace. Reaching out her hand, she took it.

"Oh my goodness." She held the tiny pearl so it sunk into the hollow of her palm. "I didn't know I'd kept this. Shows you how much I looked in that old jewelry box."

"What is it?" Charlotte leaned forward to see.

"I wore this on my wedding day. When I married your father." She cringed at the memory. "I thought I'd sold this a long time ago. It probably wouldn't be worth anything anyway. Probably just glass or plastic."

Charlotte slid out of the chair and onto the couch next to our mom's side. She couldn't have been comfortable with only a tiny bit of seat under her. But then again, I didn't think she cared.

"You know, I was in the nursery over at First Church, getting into my wedding dress. I'd managed to find the laciest dress at the bridal shop. And the train trailed almost all the way to the end of the aisle." She laughed. "It was a little much, really, when I think about it."

I leaned against the coffee table, listening to her. Since my father left, she'd never talked about him or their life together. I realized, in that moment, that at one point, they'd been happy.

"When I looked in the full-length mirror, I realized that I'd forgotten to pack a necklace to wear. I was so young, I hadn't really thought things through. But I was devastated." She closed her hand over the pearl. "You remember Mrs. Allen, right? Well, she took this off her own neck and clasped it around mine. She told me to keep it. She said a bride should always have a pearl to wear on her wedding day."

Opening her fist, she reached out to hand it back to me. "It's nothing special."

"It's the most special," Char whispered. "And I think Ev should have it."

Warmth from my mom's hand lingered on the pearl.

"Are you sure?" I asked. "I mean, if you want it, take it."

"You're the oldest."

"But I want you to have it." Pushing myself up on my knees, I slipped it into her hand. "It will make me happy to see you wear it."

I hadn't talked to my father in so long. Just thinking about him left a pit in my stomach. I remembered all the fights when he called my mom nasty names. The girlfriends he kept on the side. When he walked out, a bag full of his clothes, and drove away, leaving us in that little apartment with no car.

Char, though, had been so little when he left, she'd made up fantasies of how much he loved her. How some great and evil power had kept him from coming to see her.

I figured that necklace would, somehow, become part of that mythology.

Charlotte circled the chain around her neck, clasping it at the back. The dainty pearl hanging between her collarbones looked as perfect as anything could. "Now, pick something for yourself, Ev," she said.

"There's a sapphire ring in there." Mom pushed her eyes closed harder than before, a puff of air forced out her nose. "It has little diamonds all the way around it."

I pulled open a few drawers before I found the one that held rings. The sapphire one had been placed right in the front. I pinched the white gold ring, lifting it against the light from the window.

"Don forgot our first anniversary when we were dating," she said. "I should have reminded him, I guess. But back then, I thought he shouldn't have needed me to."

"Seriously?" Char asked.

"Girls, this is my best relationship advice." She opened her eyes. "Sometimes men need a thousand reminders about something. And, when they still forget, it isn't because they don't love you. Not even close. They just have different brains."

"But the first anniversary is a big deal, right?" Charlotte touched the pearl on her neck.

"I guess so. But we were only dating." She shrugged. "I hadn't expected much, really. Maybe a nice dinner out. But he hadn't even called. Your father, as hard as it was being married to him, was always good about remembering important days. Probably to make up for other shortcomings. But I guess that made me expect the same from Don."

Charlotte moved to the floor, taking our mom's hand in her own.

"Not that I'm complaining about Don. I'm glad for all the ways he's different from your father." She smiled. "Anyway, the day after, he brought that little ring to me. He said that any chump could do something great on the anniversary. But only a special guy does it up the day after."

"Why don't you wear it?" I asked.

"It only fit my left ring finger. After he proposed, I just wore the engagement ring." The muscles along her jaw tensed. "That was the day Don told me that he loved me for the first time."

She kept her eyes on the ring, letting them narrow as she held her bottom lip between her teeth.

"He's been so good to me." Her eyes filled. "Evelyn, I know that it would mean a lot to Don if you'd wear it."

"Are you sure?" I asked, still holding the ring between my index finger and thumb.

"It will mean the world to him."

I slipped it on my finger.

"It looks so pretty on you," she said. "I think there were a few bracelets in the big part of the box."

She tried to sit up straight. Something about how she pushed herself sent a shudder through her body. Gasping, she grabbed a fold of blanket, her knuckles tensing around it. Her breathing changed. Became shallow and ragged. Her teeth grated so hard, I could hear them grinding. Her face strained against the pain.

"Please," she groaned. "Help me."

My legs tingled under my weight. I'd been kneeling so long. I stumbled, knocking my knee against a dining room chair. The pain pills were in the junk drawer. Gran had told me. Otherwise, I wouldn't have found them.

I heard Char behind me, talking to someone on the phone. She gave the address to the house. Her voice moved out of her mouth in calm, even tones.

Reaching the junk drawer, I pulled the handle so hard, it came all the way out, dumping everything on the floor. With a roll and a rattle, the bottle of pills lodged in the space between the cupboards and the floor. Charlotte reached past me, the phone to her ear, grabbing the bottle. She filled a glass with water and carried them both into the living room.

Chapter Forty-Four

Olga

All I could think to do was bake. I just didn't know what else to do with myself. I mixed flour and sugar and butter and didn't let my mind wander to what had happened earlier that day. Keeping my hands busy forced my mind to slow down.

That evening, I could only allow myself to remember that it all ended okay. And, with the cold night shut out of my kitchen window, we'd have a new day with the dawn.

Cookies covered my whole dinette tabletop, cooling on waxed paper. Who'd eat them? I didn't know. It didn't much matter, though.

I'd started on a batch of pumpkin bread. Only a week before Thanksgiving, I thought I might enjoy the scent of spice in my oven.

Looking over the tops of my glasses, I strained to read the spice jars, trying to find the ground cloves. Why whoever put the writing on those silly containers didn't use bigger type, I'd never figure out. I would have done better to take off all the lids and sniff my way to the right jar. Squinting my eyes so tight, I just knew I'd get one powerful headache, going along like that.

Glass jars clinked against one another, then clanked as I nearly jumped up out of my skin. I let out a yelp and dropped the little bottle of whatever kind of spice I had in my hand.

"Sorry, darling," Clive said, his mouth close to my ear. "I didn't mean to startle you."

"Clive Daniel Eliot, you know better than to sneak up on me like that," I scolded him. "I'm an old lady. You're liable to give me a heart attack."

His soft lips and smooth face pressed against my neck. My heart kept beating fast as he wrapped his arms around me. He didn't laugh at my expense for scaring me. But he stayed quiet and held me so gently and close. I could feel his deep breaths.

"You just come from Gretchen's house?" I asked, taking the edge off my voice. I got myself loose enough in his arms that I turned around and faced him.

"Yes, dear." His whole, wide chest rose and fell with a full sigh.

"How is she?"

"Drowsy. I left so she could get some rest," he answered. "They got the hospice nurse coming tomorrow, I guess."

"I know." I touched his cheek. "She needs help. We need a little, too."

"This is killing me, Olga." His voice shook so, I nearly lost myself to the heartbreak.

I took the towel that hung over my shoulder and wiped his tears, smearing a dusting of flour across his cheeks.

"We don't want her pain getting out of control like it did today," I said.

"I know. I know. It's just all so upsetting."

My hands itched to get into that bread dough. To stir and whisk and measure and make all my thoughts quiet, even for a little while. I wanted to escape. Because when I left my mind to wander, I just saw Gretchen's face scrunched up when the waves of pain crashed into her. A mama can't take watching such things and come away in one piece.

"She doesn't think she can make it until Christmas." Clive's voice dropped. "She told me that, Olga. Gretchen did."

"I know it, honey." I used the smallest voice I could find. "It's happening fast."

"It makes me tired." Clive closed his eyes, wrinkling up his forehead. "I need to get into bed."

"Go ahead, Clive. You could use the rest."

"I don't want to go alone." The blue of his eyes peeked out from under their lids as he opened them. "I want you to go with me. I need to feel you close to me."

Dozens of cookies on waxed paper. Half-mixed bread dough on the counter, full of eggs and butter that would go bad overnight. But all that could wait. It could all take a hop into the trash bin, for all I cared.

Reaching my hand up, I touched his cheek again, feeling the wet of sadness that fell from his eyes. His big hand covered mine, and he bent down to kiss me.

"Will you go with me?" he asked. "I can't think about being all by my lonesome right now."

I let him curl his fingers around mine and lead me to our room. He reached out and switched off the living room lights.

"I want to be with you," I said, stopping in the hallway.

All those years with Clive, and I'd learned the way to comfort him. He needed to be close as only a husband and wife could be. Only I could give him that kind of comfort. In our marriage, the intimacy had changed a number of times. Only one thing never did, though. The way we both felt stronger for that closeness. It had the power to make me fall in love with him all over again.

We both needed a good dose of togetherness that night.

Clive turned to me, a drop of grief falling down his face. Without a word, he walked with me into our bedroom. We took to our sacred bed.

There, we comforted each other.

Chapter Forty-Five

EVELYN

Early morning, I drove to my mom's house. The hospice nurse would be there, and I needed to help her. Charlotte had to open at the bakery and Don didn't think he could handle being there alone. I volunteered.

A yellow school bus kicked up dirt from the road in front of me. Not wanting to get stuck behind it at every stop, I decided to turn down a different way.

I hadn't gotten far when I realized that the road would take me right past the Bunker farm and the tree ruined by the girls' accident. I'd driven all over town, avoiding that road, since the vigil so many months before.

I slowed for the curve, seeing the make-shift memorial still resting at the base of the tree. Two wooden crosses, weathered gray by six months in the elements. Within a couple months, the snow would cover them over completely.

Mrs. Bunker squatted by the crosses. Pulling up next to her, I rolled down my window. She glanced at me but didn't stop gathering brown leaves in her hands. She tossed them into the ditch. A lit cigarette pressed between her lips, smoke puffed out one side of her mouth.

"Hi, Mrs. Bunker," I said. "I wanted to thank you for the casserole you sent over the other day."

"That's all right," she answered, her cheeks flushed. "I had extra."

She took a slow draw off the cigarette.

"How have you been?" I tilted my head toward the crosses.

"Still get me a few nightmares now and again." She flicked a long ash off and into the grass. "But I make do."

Standing, shoulders rolled forward, she put the cigarette to her lips again. Staring out over the field next to her, cleared after the harvest, she pushed out a long line of smoke. She'd finished talking to me.

"Well, thanks again," I said. "My mom really appreciated it."

Driving away, I took a quick look at her in my rearview mirror. She stood at the edge of the road, arms crossed, facing the tree again.

A blue car had parked in my mom's driveway. I pulled in next to it. A blond-haired woman sat in the driver's seat, writing in a notebook. Getting out, I walked toward her car. She saw me and rolled down her window.

"Hi," she said.

"Good morning." I bent from the waist to look into her window. "Are you the nurse?"

"Yes. I'm with hospice." She pushed the notebook into a pocket of her tote bag. "Do you live here?"

"This is my mom's house."

"Okay, good." After rolling up her window, she cut the engine and opened the door. "I just have a few things to carry in."

"Can I grab something for you?"

"That would be great." Her warm voice cut through the cold, November air. "Thank you."

She handed me a binder that had to have weighed fifteen pounds.

"My name is Evelyn, by the way," I said.

"I'm Kathi." Slinging a messenger bag over her shoulder, she took a step toward me. "Sorry. I should have introduced myself before weighing you down with stuff."

Switching the folder to my left hand, I put out my right to shake hers. "It's nice to meet you, Kathi."

"You, too." Her soft smile told me that she meant it.

"Come on in. My mom will be so happy you're here."

Kathi set up the table with a row of orange medicine bottles. She arranged paperwork next to them. It looked just like the table at the Eames house. At most every house I'd been to where hospice had been called in. Only, that time, it was for my own mom. It felt unfamiliar and uncomfortable.

The thought of that made my throat lump up.

Wrapping a stethoscope around her neck, Kathi knelt down next to the couch where my mom lay.

"How has the pain been?" she asked.

"On and off," my mom answered. "But when it's on, it is really bad."

"I bet." Kathi touched my mom's hands. "Let's keep you comfortable, okay?"

"But I don't want to be doped up."

"I'll make sure it's under control. I want you to be awake when you want to be." Kathi used a light to look into my mom's eyes. "Have you been able to eat or drink yet today?"

"Not today." My mom let her head relax on the pillow. "I just throw everything back up, anyway."

"Okay," Kathi said. "How do you do with water? Or broth?"

"I throw up everything."

"I'm sorry. That's not very fun." Kathi pulled the blanket up to look at my mom's feet. She touched her ankles. "How has it been getting to the bathroom? Are you able to do that yourself?"

"It's getting difficult. Especially at night." A rose colored blush moved up her cheeks. "My husband has to help me a lot. Sometimes I don't make it."

"I didn't know that," I said. "Why didn't you tell me?"

"It's really embarrassing."

"How about we talk a few options?" Kathi tucked the blanket back around my mom's legs. "We can make this a lot easier for you. One thing we can do is get a commode for you."

"No. I don't want to do that." My mom shook her head. "That's just one more mess that someone has to clean up."

"I wouldn't want that, either." Kathi rubbed my mom's shoulder.

"This is a tough spot for you to be in. But we all want your days to be as easy on you as possible."

"I need a hospital bed, don't I?"

"That was my next suggestion. It would make getting you up and down a whole lot easier. And I can get you a walker so you're less likely to fall when you do want to move around."

My mom wiped her face with one of her thin, brittle-looking fingers. "Do you have an option that will make me magically healed?" She smiled. "That would be my choice."

"You know, I'll have to check with my supervisor to see if I can do that one for you." Kathi put her hand on my mom's forearm and squeezed gently. "I'm sorry this is happening to you."

"Me, too." My mom looked at me. "More for them than anything."

"Don't worry about us, Mom," I said. "We're here for you."

"But worrying about you has been my job for a lot of years. It's hard to quit cold turkey."

"Kathi," I said. "Are there any foods that she can eat? We've run out of ideas."

"Honey, the thought of eating anything makes me break out in a cold sweat." My mom spun the wedding band around her finger, so loose I wondered how it didn't fall all the way off.

"Let me check with her doctor." Kathi jotted on a notepad. "Have you tried ice chips? Sometimes that's a good way to get water in."

"Oh, that actually sounds nice," my mom said.

"As far as solid food, I don't think we should push it. At this point, if you don't want to eat, Gretchen, we aren't going to force you."

"What?" I asked. "But she needs to eat."

"Well, right now she might just be more comfortable without food." Kathi pushed her lips to one side of her face. "I know that sounds counterintuitive. But it's better than having her in pain from vomiting."

"I think the ice chips will be great." My mom's eyes smiled. "It sounds refreshing."

"Gretchen, from what I can see here, it looks like your family has been taking very good care of you."

"They're great." My mom beamed up at me. "I'm proud of them."

"I can tell."

"Can we talk about the hospital bed?" Mom asked. "Can it be right here in the living room? Do you think we could make it fit?"

"We can put it just about wherever you want." Kathi sized up the room. "It won't be a problem at all to fit it in here. We'd just have to move a little furniture around."

"I'd like that." My mom's eye caught mine. "Ev, I have a few other things I'd like to talk to Kathi about. Do you mind giving us a few minutes?"

"Yeah, of course." I tried to hold my face still so she wouldn't see how her question had hurt my feelings. "That's fine."

"I'm sorry, honey. Some things are too hard to talk about in front of you."

"No. Really, Mom. I understand." I forced a smile and got up from my seat. "How about some tea or coffee?"

"I never say no to coffee," Kathi answered.

My mom sighed, closing her eyes. When she opened them again, she looked directly at me. *Thank you*, she mouthed.

Chapter Forty-Six

OLGA

"Do you need another blanket?" I stood over my daughter. She shivered so hard, I worried she'd shake herself right off the couch. I couldn't wait for that hospital bed to get delivered. At least then, she'd have more room.

Looking up, she nodded at me. "Thank you."

Charlotte had a whole stack of clean afghans and thick blankets folded up in a wicker basket. I grabbed a bright yellow one. If nothing else, Gretchen would like the perky color.

"How did you like the nurse, honey?"

"She's great. Really sweet." Gretchen pulled the blanket up closer under her chin. "You know, it feels like I made a friend today."

"That's nice, Gretchie. I'm glad you like her." I checked the clock on the wall. "It's getting close to bedtime, huh?"

"Today went by fast." She winced. "It makes me nervous when the days speed by."

Life sped. Her life did, at least. It seemed like just the day before I got my hands on her for the first time. I blinked and years had passed.

She tried to turn her head far enough to get a look at me. The pillows behind her just wouldn't allow for it. "Mom, can you sit somewhere closer so I can see you?"

I shifted the rocking chair at a better angle and nearly dropped back down into it. I took her hand. The skin felt scratchy and dry.

Good thing Charlotte had left out a tube of lotion.

"How about I rub some of this on your hands?"

"Yes, please." She blinked slowly. "Just don't make me fall asleep. This medicine does a good enough job of that."

"But does it make you feel better?" I rubbed the dot of lotion into my hands before smoothing it onto hers.

"They don't make me feel much of anything at all." Swallowing, the tendons in her neck pushed out. "Well, except sleepy."

"I suppose that's good."

"Maybe." She wiggled her fingers inside my hand. "I'm not ready yet."

"Ready for what, Gretchie?"

"To go." She swallowed again. "Not yet, at least."

I stopped moving my hands. "Well, I'm glad to hear you say that, honey."

"I always thought that when the time got close like this, I'd be ready." When she moved her head from side to side, her scarf fell back, showing her short hair. "But, right now, I'm just really scared."

"It's okay to be scared."

"Dying isn't the part that scares me. It's the part on this side of it. That's what terrifies me." Her dry tongue touched dry lips. "Can you please get me an ice chip?"

I spooned a few small pieces of ice out of a cup, slipping them onto her tongue. I thanked God for the sweet mercy of frozen water that wouldn't make my girl sick.

"Thank you." She worked it around in her mouth.

"Honey." I went back to rubbing her hands. "You said that this side scares you. What did you mean?"

The way her eyes filled up and her mouth turned down broke my heart to shards.

"I don't want to be a coward," she said, her voice thick with sorrow. "I always thought I'd be brave until the last minute. But I'm not. I'm so afraid."

"You are the bravest person I know," I said.

"I'm worried that I'll be weak at the end."

"If you are, it won't change a single thing." I held her hands. "We'll love you just the same as always."

271

Her frown reminded me of when she was little. But this time, she didn't pout because she hadn't gotten her way or stubbed her toe. Oh, how I wished it could have been something simple like that. Every part of me wanted to fix her.

"I wanted to see my kids get married. And I wanted to hold my grandkids." She gasped from the crying. "There is just so much that I've wanted to do. So much, it makes me feel greedy."

"No, honey. Wanting to live isn't greedy." I fought the lump that tried to choke me. "And you aren't dead. You're alive. And nobody's sitting here telling you when you have to go. You're with us now, Gretchen. We'll see how tomorrow goes. And the day after that."

She lay on that couch, her body still. Just the rise and fall of her chest. After a minute or two, I started to count those breaths, not wanting to waste a single one of them that she had left in her. I watched so long, I was sure she'd fallen asleep.

But she opened her mouth, eyes still closed. She moved her lips for a moment before letting the words come out.

"Wouldn't it be something if I just drifted off?" Her voice lilted, dreamy. Light and full of air. "If I just closed my eyes and went without even knowing what was happening?"

"I think that would be the best kind of death." I had to let go of her hand to wipe the tear that had dropped to my chin. "That's the kind of death I pray you'll get."

"And I would like one more spring," she said. "I'd like to get out into the garden just one last time. So add that to your prayer list, if you don't mind."

"I don't mind at all, Gretchie."

Her words slurred, and I couldn't understand a one of them. But they carried her into sleep. Her breathing deepened. I got myself up, needing to hold on tight to the arm of the rocking chair.

I wondered if spring would ever come again. The chill in my heart doubted it.

Chapter Forty-Seven

EVELYN

Will handed me a mug of strong coffee. It warmed my freezing cold hands. He stood over me, head to one side.

"You know, I've got a perfectly good couch in the living room," he said. "You don't have to sit on the kitchen floor."

"I'm too tired to move."

"You want me to sit with you?"

Nodding my head seemed like it would take too much effort. So, I just sighed.

He got down on the floor next to me, his shoulder touching mine. He wore an old sweatshirt and flannel pants. My funeral director suit still on, I wished for something a little more comfortable.

"So, Ev." He cupped my knee in his hand. "What's going on?"

"Good question." I sipped the coffee. "This is really good. It tastes expensive."

"Evelyn, you know I love you, right?" He scratched his scalp, making his already messy hair stand on end. "Can you please tell me what's wrong? Usually people don't come banging on my door at four in the morning unless they've got something to talk about."

"I had to do a removal tonight. You know, pick up a body." I pulled my knees close to my chest. "It was bad."

"What made it so bad?"

"Suicide. Those are always bad."

Will shook his head. "I'm sorry."

"Her husband found her." I took another sip from my mug. "In the next room, their kids were sleeping. They woke up to his screaming. And they saw her."

Holding my eyes closed till I saw red splotches didn't work to toss out what I'd seen that night. The horror of that bedroom. The red-faced, sobbing kids begging me not to take their mother away.

"It doesn't make sense."

"Nope. It doesn't." The rage built up in me, lifting until I thought it would erupt. "And it makes me feel crazy that I can't do anything. Not really. All I do is come after it's too late to do any good. And I take it away. That's it. I can't fix it. I can't keep it from happening. My entire life is waiting for the tragic end so I can swoop in and remove it."

He squeezed my knee.

"Nobody gets to escape it," I said. "Everybody has all this, I don't know, this terror that they'll have to face at some point."

"I don't know what to say."

"I know. I don't either."

We went quiet. The rage calmed to a low simmer in my chest, leaving me feeling near spent.

"When I was a kid, my cousin drowned." He let his head rest against the cupboard behind him. "He was just playing in the river and got pulled under. My uncle couldn't get to him in time."

I shook my head. "You never told me."

"It made my uncle crazy to think that he couldn't save him," Will said. "So a couple years later, my uncle went back to that same river and just let the current take him."

"I'm sorry, Will."

"They lived really far away. We only saw them a few times before that. But it still messed with me a lot."

I dropped my head onto his shoulder.

"This world is broken, Ev. That's one thing I know for sure."

"When is it going to be fixed?"

"I don't know." He shifted so his head could rest on mine. "I wish I could tell you."

"Well, I really wanted you to have the answer." I let my eyes close. "A good one. Not like the ones Old Buster comes up with. But a real answer."

"Maybe there isn't one."

We sat on that floor so long, my backside went numb. I didn't care. I just liked being in the quiet with Will.

"My mom's dying, Will," I whispered.

"I know." He lifted his hand to touch my cheek.

"She isn't going to be at my wedding. And that's really bothering me."

His chest rose and fell as he inhaled deeper. "Do you think we should—"

"No, Will," I interrupted.

He sat up.

"Don't ask me that right now," I said. "I don't want that to be the reason I get married."

"Okay." He kissed my forehead. "Just so you know, I'd do that for you."

"That's nice of you."

He helped me to the couch and kissed my cheek before I fell asleep.

Chapter Forty-Eight

OLGA

Standing over Gretchen's stove, I was sure I'd reentered the days of hot flashes. Stirring and stirring butter and sugar, I wondered how those grandkids of mine ever talked me into making them toffee. That job had always been Gretchen's. And she had always made her toffee just right. If she'd ever burned a batch, she never told anybody.

I'd eat that toffee until my mouth was sore and I was in need of a dentist appointment. But standing with that heat blasting in my face, it seemed like an awful lot of work to do for candy.

But as bad as Gretchen had gotten, and as hard as the kids were taking it, I wasn't inclined to deny them that one sugary treat they'd asked for. And, with Christmas only a couple days away, I'd not got myself out to find presents. I guess, for that year, the toffee would have to be enough.

Toffee and Gretchen still with us.

"How's it going in there, Mom?" Gretchen called from the hospital bed, sitting up with her feet dangling off the side.

"I don't know, honey." Beads of sweat rolled down the side of my face. I wished for just one more hand so I could wipe at the trickle. "How long does this stirring part usually take?"

"Not too long," she answered. "Let me come take a look."

Her walker made a popping sound as she pushed against it, standing up out of bed.

"You get back in that bed. Just sit down," I scolded. "I can figure this out on my own."

"Mom, Kathi told me to get up every couple of hours. Besides, by the time I get to you, it'll be boiling." Even taking two steps took her a good long time. "You stop looking at me. Get back to stirring."

"That medicine is making you sassy, I think." But the smile on my face felt good.

"It's making me feel human again." Hands on the counter, she inched over to peek around me. "It looks good, Mom. Maybe just one more minute before you'll want to turn off the heat."

If I ever needed to know what mercy looked like, it was my daughter, standing next to me in the kitchen, her hand on my shoulder. Sweet water, if I ever tasted it.

"How did those kids ever finagle me into making this for them?" I shook my head. "You know, I think we've spoiled them, Gretchie."

"They're worth it." She squeezed my shoulder. "Thanks for making this for them, Mom."

"You're welcome."

"Next year, you should plan on buying it." She started her journey back to the bed, making her walker creak as she pushed it along the carpet. "I bet you could put in an order at Deirdre's."

"Why wouldn't we just make it?" I asked.

But then I remembered. The sweetness soured again. In two days, I would have my very last Christmas with Gretchen. Not because I was dying. She was. How strange to realize such a thing. That dread pulled my heart down to my toes with its weight.

For my daughter to last for another Christmas would have meant nothing more than suffering heaped on top of misery for her.

That bitter taste in my mouth just about caused my stomach to turn. Enough to ruin Christmas.

"Lord God Almighty, You got to help me."

"What was that, Mom?" Gretchen asked, back on her bed, dangling her feet. "Is making toffee so hard, you have to ask God for help?"

"It sure is making me nervous, honey."

Cold air pushed into the house. It turned my mind from blazing hot sorrow to soothing fresh air. That gushing chill also brought with it the sunshine smile of my Charlotte. If her face was God's idea of help, then I liked how He answered my cry.

"It smells good in here," she said. "Are you making toffee, Gran?"

"I'm giving it the old college try." I turned off the burner under the pan. "How was your day?"

"So busy. Crazy." She took her time unbuttoning her coat. "I don't want to see another Christmas tree shaped sugar cookie for the rest of my life."

"Do you have to work tomorrow, Char?" Gretchen asked.

"Nope. I'm off for five days." She pulled her arms out of the sleeves. "I guess Deirdre's really slow on the days right after Christmas."

"Probably too many people in a sugar coma." Pushing the soft, boiling hot toffee out of the pot, it spread on my baking sheet.

"Are you going out tonight?" Gretchen asked. "I know a lot of your friends are home for Christmas."

"I thought I'd stay home." Charlotte hung her coat on the back of a chair before making her way to Gretchen's side. "It isn't Christmas without watching old movies with you, Mom."

I hoped nobody minded a couple salty tears falling into their toffee. It just could not be helped.

Gretchen made it through about half of *It's a Wonderful Life* before falling off into a quiet snooze. Charlotte had curled herself up on the bed, sharing a pillow with her mama. It didn't take long before Gretchen's lulling breath had got Charlotte to doze, too.

Then I sat alone, watching all the way to the end. Jimmy Stewart with tears in his eyes, holding his curly headed little girl high up in his arms. He pulled his wife as close as he could and turned his eyes skyward.

I feared my sniffling and sniveling would wake the two beauties on that hospital bed. But they didn't stir one bit.

Tears still spilling over my eyes, I grabbed a couple blankets to cover them over.

Then I put "White Christmas" on and let myself weep, hearing Bing Crosby croon about being home for Christmas.

Chapter Forty-Nine

EVELYN

Candlelight flickered in front of my mom's face. The whole sanctuary at First Church filled with rows of little flames, passed from one wick to the next. The most important one, to me at least, glowed in the face of my mother. Thin cheeked, but with the same wonder in her eyes as always.

She'd insisted on coming to the Christmas Eve service. She'd even made sure to get extra naps in throughout the day to have the energy to sit in the pew. Her last time seeing the sanctuary full of tiny fire flickers.

Heat built up in my chest, spreading into the rest of me. Gratitude mixed with sadness. I knew if I wiped the tears out of the corners of my eyes, my mom would see. I didn't want her to break that smile that lifted her whole face.

I'd made it through the rest of the service, up to that point. The guitar man, wearing furry boots pulled over the bottoms of his way-too-tight jeans. Old Buster's angel singer butchering "O Holy Night." The big man himself, preaching about seeking the Lord. Good Old Buster's last Christmas Eve service. I hated to admit that it made me a little sad. More for him than anything.

The congregation sang "Silent Night," Charlotte's voice cutting clear through all the others. My mom's rattled, whispered notes full of mourning. I couldn't get anything to come out of my throat. I doubted I'd be able to hear that song without bittersweet grief, thinking about the flame dancing atop my mom's Christmas Eve candle.

Will gave me a ride to my mom's house after the service, both so exhausted we barely said a word in the car. He just reached over and held my hand. Squeezing it from time to time.

Once we pulled into the driveway, we waited before getting out. The heat blowing on my face made me yawn.

"Ev, I haven't gotten you anything for Christmas," Will said.

"It's all right. I haven't gotten you anything, either." Turning to him, I smiled. "This isn't the best Christmas, you know?"

"I know." He nodded. "But it's still pretty good to be with you."

"When are you leaving?" I asked. He'd planned on driving all night to make it to his parents' house by morning.

"I called my mom before the service," he said. "I told her I couldn't make it."

"Why?"

"Because I can't leave you guys right now." He leaned over and kissed my cheek. "I want to be here to help if you all need me."

"Thank you."

Out of the corner of my eye, I saw someone step out onto the porch and rush down the steps. Cal made his way to my side of the car.

"I think something's wrong." I opened the door.

"Ev," Cal said, breathless.

"What's going on?" A shiver raced through my entire body.

"I've been trying to call you," he said. "Don't you have your phone?"

I checked my pocket. I'd turned it off.

"Did we get a funeral call?" I asked. "I'm sorry."

"No." His voice sounded weak. I'd never seen his eyes so watery. "It's Mom. Something's happening."

The three of us ran to the house, getting inside as fast as we could. It still didn't seem quick enough.

Will pulled me close before we stepped inside.

Chapter Fifty

OLGA

I kept my spot in a straight-backed chair right next to Gretchen's bed. Donald slept on the other side, stretched out on the couch. Everybody else had taken to thick blankets on the floor or sitting at the table, sleeping with heads resting on folded arms. Clive sat in the recliner, snoring so loud, I wondered that anybody could catch a wink for all the noise.

By the time the sun rose on Christmas morning, Gretchen rolled her head my way, eyes open. She blinked lids over glassy eyes.

"I dreamed of lilacs," she whispered. "I could even smell them."

"That's a wonderful dream, Gretchie." I leaned in close to her. "I sure wish we had a few lilacs right about now."

"Heaven smells like lilacs." Her words joined together, slow and lazy. "Don't you think so?"

"I wouldn't mind that one bit."

"And, in heaven, I got to sit in a field of chamomile. Lilac branches dangling over my head and chamomile bumping into my legs and arms. It all smelled so good." She inhaled as if she could still breathe it in. "Fairy flowers dancing all over my yard."

"What a lovely dream." As hard as I tried to hold myself still, the shaking took over anyhow.

"I think I'll ask if you can be my neighbor. We could share the yard again. Work on the garden together, maybe."

"Wouldn't that be wonderful?" Her hand lay limp in mine.

"You won't live on top of death any more, Mom." A tear hung on to her eyelashes. "It's just going to be a blink and you'll be there, too. It will be very good."

Donald stirred, moving to his other side.

"I'm not ready for you to go, Gretchen," I whispered. "I keep hoping for some kind of miracle. I want you to outlive me by twenty years or so."

"If I could choose, I'd rather not die yet." The tear broke loose and landed on her pillowcase. "But I don't get that choice, do I?"

"I don't suppose you do, honey."

"Last night was bad," she said. "I don't want to feel pain like that anymore."

I nodded. Christmas Eve had been good, until just after we got her home from church. She'd thrashed and screamed from the pain. I thought she'd break all my fingers, how hard she clamped on them. Kathi had to come with a needle full of relief.

I'd never been so scared.

"It's getting closer, Mom. Closer every minute." She lifted her hand to wipe at another tear on her face. "I think I want to go out on the porch sometime today. Maybe sip a cup of tea out there."

"It's so cold, Gretchen." I figured the morphine had stolen her reason. "Why would you want to go out there?"

"Just one more cup of tea on the porch," she said. "Then I'll come back and rest like a good girl."

Between Evelyn and me, we got Gretchen on the porch swing. All we could see of her was her face peeking out from the layers and layers of sweaters and coat and blankets.

"Do you mind giving me a few minutes?" she asked. "Just to be by myself for a little bit?"

"Of course," I said, handing her the hot cup of tea.

"I've just had everyone around me all the time for the last few weeks. I need a little quiet." She breathed in the steam of fairy tea. "Thank you."

Evelyn held the door for me. "Let's go make some pancakes or something. Okay?"

"All right." I stepped up into the house. It took all the strength I had to leave my daughter on that porch. Out of my reach.

Charlotte stood at the stove, already pushing eggs around in a pan. Will, at the other counter, measured coffee grounds. Cal changed the sheets on the hospital bed while Clive and Donald talked in low voices in one corner.

I got myself into the recliner, hoping to ease my aching body for just a few minutes. The long night of sitting up, watching my daughter sleep, had caught up with me.

It didn't take long for me to get to snoozing.

My dream didn't have lilacs. No chamomile swaying in the breeze, either. Just me in Aunt Gertie's old attic, rummaging through dusty boxes of half broken junk. Whatever it was I wanted, it wasn't in that attic.

Aunt Gertie sat on a three-legged stool in the corner, her old wooden spoon thwacking against her leg. I decided I'd steer clear of her. The last thing I wanted was a welt on my behind from that spoon.

"She died in her sleep, you know," she said in her deep down in the bottom of her throat voice. "Your mother did. In the hospital. No. Don't ask me what she died of. It don't matter. She's dead. That's what you got to know. Nothing else."

My dream brain made her shut her yapper. And, because it was my dream, I decided she couldn't be on that stool. So she disappeared. Good riddance to bad rubbish.

The woman that replaced her sat on a metal folding chair. Charlotte turned to Gretchen turned to my mother in a way only possible in dreams. My mother. Her long, red hair all pinned up at the back of her head. How I'd loved brushing that hair with an old, soft bristled brush. Counting to one hundred, not caring that she puffed on a cigarette, making my own hair smell smoky.

"Come brush my hair." She looked at me in a mirror.

"Yes, Mama," I answered.

"You done a lot with your life, Olga." Pulling the pins from her hair, she let it fall down her back. "You done good."

"I miss you, Mama." My voice sounded small. "Living at Aunt Gertie's house was bad."

"I know it." She turned to me. "I never wanted that for you."

"How did you die?" I asked, my hands smoothing over her hair.

"Olga, baby, I got to go." She kissed my forehead. Her lips felt like feathers. "You keep being a good girl."

"Don't go," I whined. "I need you. I'll be a good girl for you."

"You need to let me go. And let old Gertie go, too, while you're at it. You been holding on to us too long. Making more of us than we ever were. For good and bad." She touched my cheek with the back of her fingers. "It's time to let go of her, too."

"Who? Let go of who?"

She faded. Light from the window behind her shimmered through her. "Gretchen."

Then she went away. Just the smell of her cigarette left, lingering in the air.

Chapter Fifty-One

Evelyn

For a full three days after Christmas, my mom slept almost nonstop. Kathi had come to insert a catheter. She also brought an oxygen tank. We moved the hospital bed closer to the window so that the sun could shine on her. In her few moments of wakefulness, she liked to look out at the evergreen.

Don couldn't get enough time with her. He didn't leave her side except to use the bathroom a few times a day. Even then, he could only stand to be gone for a couple minutes.

"Don," my mom said, her voice so soft and quiet. "Babe, go take a little break, okay?"

He opened his eyes. "I'm all right. I was just resting my eyes," he answered. "I want to stay with you."

He shifted his weight on the hardwood chair and reached for her hand.

"You haven't slept in a long time, have you?" she asked. "At least go take a shower. You need to relax. Just for a little bit. For me."

Without saying a word, Don stood, leaning over her. He kissed her forehead. Moving his head back, he looked into her face.

"You're burning up," he said.

She nodded.

"Evelyn, call the nurse."

I fumbled for my phone, pulling it from my pocket. Fortunately, I'd thought to save Kathi's number. Otherwise, I wouldn't have had the mental clarity to find it on the cluttered tabletop.

"I don't want the fever treated." My mom's voice raised, but stayed thin. "I want this. It's going to make things easier for me."

"We're calling her anyway," Don said.

The family gathered in the living room. Deirdre had sent Charlotte home from the bakery with a couple dozen cookies and two raspberry jelly doughnuts for Cal. The white box sat, untouched on the kitchen counter.

Kathi took her place at the table, filling out paperwork, her pen scratches the only sound in the room for a while.

"Is Will coming?" my mom asked. "Do we want to wait for him?"

"He'll be here soon," I answered. "We can just get started, if you want."

"Okay." She looked at me. "I want to say as much as I can before I get groggy again."

"Go ahead, Mom," Cal said.

"I want you all to do whatever is easiest. So if you don't want to do a viewing, that's okay."

"We'll need to do one the night before." Cal leaned forward in his seat. "You know a lot of people will want to come."

"That's so kind of you to say, Cal." My mom's eyes squinted toward him in a smile. Just the way they had when he'd brought a frog home for Mother's Day or got a B on his report card. She treasured those offerings. "Just make sure you don't exhaust yourselves."

"We won't, Mom," I said.

"I want to wear the green dress that's in my closet," she continued, her breath shallow. "It's got a nice black belt attached."

"I know which one you mean," Char said.

"All the rest of my clothes, well, you can go through and donate whatever somebody doesn't want." She turned to Don. "I don't want you to do that right away, babe. Take your time. Okay?"

He nodded.

"Don't bury any jewelry on me." She sucked in air, trying to keep herself going. "It doesn't matter what casket you use. Whatever's left over in the showroom." Her bony fingers rubbed across the loose skin of her chest. "Can somebody put this bed flat for me? I'm having a hard time breathing."

Don leaned across her, pushing the buttons. The bed grumbled as it flattened. Kathi got up and strung the oxygen tubes across my mom's face, letting the air push through her nostrils.

"Better?" Kathi asked.

"Much. Thank you."

The flush on my mom's face deepened to a darker red as she continued talking. I didn't have to touch her skin to know that her fever had spiked again.

The movement of the front door opening and closing caught my eye. Will pushed off his shoes and winked at me. I hardly had the patience to wait for him to sit next to me. With him, I felt like I could almost make it through the rest of the funeral planning.

"Just in time, Will," my mom said, trying to make her voice sound perky. She folder her fingers over his when he touched her shoulder. "We were just about to talk about the service."

He got to me and grabbed my hand. I was sure he felt my shaking. He let go and put his arm around my shoulders.

"No long sermons, Will. Just a few words, if that's okay with you. Something comforting."

"Do you want people to share stories?" Will asked.

"Only flattering ones." She laughed and grabbed her stomach. "Oh, laughing hurts."

"Do you need more morphine?" Gran asked, looking at Kathi.

"Not yet, Mom. I want to get done with this first." When she cleared her throat, she winced. "I want you to figure out who's going to embalm me."

"I can't do it." Granddad rubbed his face with both hands. "I'm sorry, baby girl. You know I would do anything for you. But that's just too much for me."

"It's okay, Dad," she said. "Don't be upset about that, okay? It's all right."

"Should we call in someone else to do it?" I asked.

"No. I don't want that." Cal sat back and shook his head.

"We could have them use our prep room, Cal."

"I want to keep this in our family." Cal looked at our mom. "If you don't mind, I'll do it, Mom."

"Cal," I said. "That's a really hard thing."

"I know. But it would be harder for me to have somebody else doing it." Cal bit at his lip.

"It's okay with me." She didn't take her eyes off Cal. "I just don't want it to be painful for you, son."

"I can't have somebody else do it," he said. "It doesn't seem right."

She coughed, wheezing. "I'm okay." Touching her lips, she took in the slow moving air. "Thank you, Cal."

"It's what I can do."

"I'll do your makeup," I said.

"Thank you. You always do a nice job." She let her eyes close. "I think I'm ready for that morphine now."

Kathi moved toward the bed, her footsteps barely making any sound.

Every few hours, my mom would wake. Her eyes only half opened and her breathing was slow. But we counted that as awake. Even if what she said made little sense.

I sat on the edge of her bed late at night, trying to remember what day it was. Or how long ago Christmas was. I couldn't even remember if we'd celebrated the New Year yet. Sitting in that living room, watching my mom decline had me all upside-down.

Her eyes started their fluttering of waking. I touched a cold washcloth to her forehead. A heat wave raged, trapped inside her.

"That feels nice." She reached up and wiped a drip that ran down her face.

"Are you hungry?" I asked.

"I don't know."

"Gran made some vanilla pudding."

Gritting her teeth, she flinched. I took her hand, but she didn't squeeze or tense her fingers. Her hand just fell, limp, on my knee. The exhale of air from her lungs sounded different. Thicker.

"Are you okay?" I asked.

"No, honey." She closed her eyes and licked her lips. "I wanted to tell you that I like Will. I want you to know that, okay?"

"He's good to me."

"Upstairs, in my sock drawer is my diamond ring," she said. "The one your father gave me."

"Why did you keep it?" I moved closer to her face. I could hardly hear her.

"You take that ring and sell it. Try and get as much as you can. I've been saving it for you. Use that money for your wedding, all right?"

Bubbles of emotion rushed into my throat. I pinched them off with sealed lips. My jaw hurt from the clenching. As hard as I tried, my strength failed. Gagging sobs jerked out of me. Whimpering, she tried to pull herself up to me. She reached the button on her bed, lifting her head. Her hands on my shoulders, she tugged at me, pulling me down next to her. In the bend of her elbow, she held my head. With the other, she stroked my hair.

"I'm sorry I won't be there when you get married," she said. "I always imagined I'd be there."

"Who am I going to share everything with?" I sobbed. "I wanted to do all of it with you."

"Me, too."

I sat up—the fever radiating from her made me light-headed. Staying close to her face, though, I realized that she was as beautiful as ever. Even with the sunken cheeks and the hair made dull with sickness and bed rest and too few washings. Her eyes, not as bright as usual, still green and smiling, even as she cried.

"Your wedding day will be beautiful." She pointed to the button, holding her breath. "Honey, put me flat, please."

The bed lowered under her. "Do you need more medicine?"

Flat on her back, she held the palm of her hand against her bloated belly. So much rounder than earlier that day. The washcloth had long since fallen from her forehead. Messy hair around her face soaked with water or sweat or tears. Maybe even a little of each.

"I'm going to call Kathi," I said. "You're even hotter than before, Mom."

"I know."

"I'm really worried."

"No. This is good." She smiled. "I hate to leave you all. But I've had enough. I'm ready. This is how I can drift away."

Chapter Fifty-Two

OLGA

Cal brought the coffee around, refilling my cup. Oh, his eyes looked tired. So swollen and red. I didn't know if it was more from exhaustion or crying. But he gave me a cockeyed grin anyway.

"I love you, Gran."

"You look tired, Cal."

"Always." He smiled. "Do you want anything to eat?"

"No, honey. I'm fine."

He took the coffeepot to the kitchen. When he came back into the living room, he stopped at the hospital bed to check on his mama. He used such a gentle hand to touch her face.

"Where's Kathi?" he asked.

"What is it?" I rushed out of my seat and toward Gretchen.

She lay in the bed, hands resting at her sides. But she sucked in air, working so hard to draw it in. And that sound her breathing made, I'd never be able to forget it.

"Did someone call me?" Kathi asked, coming into the room.

"Her breathing is different," Cal said, stepping back, making room for Kathi.

I put my arm around Cal's waist. He pulled me close to him.

Donald sat up straight on the couch, his eyes wide.

Kathi bent over Gretchen's face, getting good and close. She checked Gretchen's hands and feet. She untucked part of the blanket and looked under.

"Mottling?" Cal asked.

Kathi nodded. "We need to get everyone up."

"Is she okay?" Donald asked.

Kathi turned her head toward him, her eyebrows curved up toward the middle of her forehead. "No, she isn't."

"What's going on?" Charlotte asked, rubbing her eyes.

"Right now, I'm going to get her some medicine so she's not in pain." Kathi went to her tote bag.

"What happens if she stops breathing?" Cal asked. Bless his heart, he held me so tight.

"We let her."

Donald stumbled up and off the couch. When he got close to Gretchen, he touched her hair. "I love you."

Gretchen opened her eyes, just a tiny bit.

"Hi, there," I said, just the way I did when she woke in the mornings as a wee child.

But she closed her eyes back up, real tight.

All together, my family stood in the living room, watching Gretchen die. The sound of her breathing made my heart stop beating.

"This is a good time to talk to her. She can still hear us," Kathi said.

I couldn't take my eyes off my girl. It should have been me, dying on that bed. Not her.

"How about you each take a few minutes to say good-bye to her." Kathi's smiling eyes filled with tears. "Let her know that it's okay for her to go. That can really free her from this struggle she's in right now."

Clive held me, and I closed my eyes. I remembered when Gretchen had sucked in her first breath. Her little body had tensed so and she screamed out. I was sure the whole hospital had heard her. And she, all red of face and body. But when the nurse put her into my arms, she just relaxed, still singing in her shrill song, letting the world know she'd arrived. Joy never did have meaning before I heard her little voice and felt her warmth against my chest.

There, on her deathbed, she sucked in air. Body all tensed up. Clive kissed the top of my head, a sob slipping out of me.

"I can't do this," I whispered.

Donald sat right beside Gretchen, holding her hand. "Babe, we're all here. And we wanted to tell you that we love you. You've done so much for us. We'll never forget you."

He kissed her on the lips, then kept his face close to hers. "I remember the first time I saw you," he whispered. "I'd never seen anyone so beautiful. But then, when I got to know you, you got more and more gorgeous. I wish I would have found you sooner."

Moving back to the couch, he covered over his eyes with his big old hands. Charlotte, the sweet soul, sat beside him, wrapping her arms around his neck.

Cal took Gretchen's hand, holding it over his own heart. "I love you." Leaning down, he whispered in her ear before kissing her cheek.

Gretchen groaned, gasping and fighting for more air. More life. Just a few more minutes of it.

Evelyn rested on the edge of the bed. She smoothed the stubbly hair on her mama's head. Struggling to get words out, she'd start, then stop again. The mumbling words staggered from her mouth. A lot of them. But I didn't try to hear them. They were for her mama and nobody else.

Clive took his turn. "Baby girl, you brought nothing but love into this world. I hope you know that our love goes with you." His voice cracked. "We'll see you soon, sweetheart. Real soon."

Next, Charlotte took her seat on the side of the bed. Her petite hands touched her mother's face.

"It's all right, Mom." She kissed Gretchen's forehead. "We're going to be okay. You can go. It's hard for us to see you like this. We want you to find some peace with Jesus. You've done a good job raising us. We know how to love each other because of you." She kissed her again. "Thank you for being my mom."

I stepped to the bed, touching my stomach. I remembered the weight of carrying her. Would remember the rest of my days. There, my baby lay, stiff as the moment she came into the world. Inches away from going out of it. I sat down, letting my behind fit right into the curve of her waist.

I saw in her face the screaming, red-faced babe. The carrot headed little girl, bobbing up and down through the garden. Remembered how she bit her lip when she sat, coloring at the dinette. Her smile when she told me she'd be giving me my first grandchild. My girl, kneeling in the soil, hovering over a row of chamomile, pushing down the dirt with her hands.

Her body stiffened again, and she sighed out the pain. I prayed to the Almighty to give me a little of His strength.

I pulled her into my arms, cradling her. Her body went limp. Relaxed.

"I love you, Gretchie. Thank you for coming to us," I spoke real soft. "You go on now. Everything's going to be okay here. We'll miss you like crazy. But it's just going to be a twinkle of an eye and we'll see you again."

Her eyelids lifted, just one last time. She closed her mouth, letting it rise into a smile of peace.

Then she left.

I held her tighter. Kissed her face.

Just like on her first day. So it was on her last one.

Chapter Fifty-Three

EVELYN

Gran sat holding my mom for a long time. At least it felt like a long time. Long enough for the numb to set in. For me to feel slow and like my feet had sunk into the floor.

Char and I met eyes, both of us expressionless. As if we had just woken up.

"Are you okay?" she asked.

Tears stung my eyes, and I looked away from my sister and back toward Gran.

Don helped her lay my mom back on the bed. She stood, Gran did, and pulled the sheet up around Mom's shoulders, covering her hands but not her face.

That was when Charlotte started to cry. Deep, loud, wailing cries. I thought she'd fall to the floor, she shook so hard. Cal pulled her to the couch and held her.

The grief hit me, nearly knocking me off my feet. I couldn't risk letting myself mourn. If I started, I'd never be able to stop.

The screen door opened without a sound and closed just as quietly behind me. It had snowed at some point. An inch or two of white powder covered everything. A mug on the railing had overflowed with snow. I blew into it, making the flakes flurry up around my face.

Half full of frozen tea. My mom's mug from Christmas day.

Holding it, I sat on the porch swing. Right on top of a layer of snow. I hadn't put on a coat or sweater. The thin sleeves of my shirt let the cold seep into my skin. Shivering, I held myself, unable to go inside. Too weak to be in the middle of the mourning.

The sun shimmered on the snow as it rose from the back side of the house. Fat flakes fell and stopped and fell again. Time sped, then slowed. It passed and I had no idea how long I had sat on that swing, my body numb.

Cal walked out, standing next to me on the porch. "Do you want a coat?" he asked.

I didn't answer, so he took off his jacket and draped it around my shoulders before walking down the steps and toward the Big House. His shoes made prints in the snow on the sidewalk.

Will's car pulled into the driveway.

"Ev?" he called when he got out of his car.

I didn't move but waited for him to come to me. When he did, he stopped and looked down at me.

"Cal just called," he said.

The swing moved me back and forth when he sat next to me.

I let him hold me while the sadness spilled over and out of me.

Chapter Fifty-Four

OLGA

Cal pulled the gurney into the living room. How many bodies had that thing born? But not a one so precious to any of us as the one it came to remove. Cal pushed it, right up next to the hospital bed.

"I don't have to do this right now," he said. "We can wait a bit."

"No," Donald said. "We should get her over there. I think it's best."

Clive took his place next to Cal and, without having to say a word, the two of them got her wrapped all over in a sheet and lifted onto the gurney. Such quick and tender movement. The two of them walked, wheeling her to the door.

"Donald," Clive said. "Do you want to carry her down?"

"I can't," Donald said. "I don't know what's wrong with me. But I can't."

He walked down the porch steps behind Clive and Cal. I followed his steps, my hand gripping the railing, afraid of the slick snow underfoot. Will came alongside me, offering his arm. Evelyn held his hand on the other side.

I watched Clive bear the daughter he carried for all her years. Cal, the mother who bore him from his beginning.

Donald got himself up next to her, putting his hand where I imagined hers to be.

Once I got my feet steady on the sidewalk, leaning on Will's arm, I heard quick footfalls from behind me. Charlotte just about knocked us over, running past.

"Granddad," she called. "Wait."

He turned his face over his shoulder and stopped for her. We all gathered around the gurney, as a family. Charlotte, working to catch her breath, a hand full of chamomile blooms, touched the sheet over her mama's body. I held on tighter to Will's arm, the tears splattering down on my shirt. They chilled in that cold air.

"Mom has a bunch of plants under the light in the basement," Charlotte said.

Cal pulled up the edge of the sheet, showing Gretchen's hand crossed over her chest. Charlotte gasped for breath in between sniffling cries as she slipped the long, green stems under Gretchen's hands. The yellow shone so pretty.

The sun glittered on the snow. Little crystals all across the yard and the garden. All untouched and shimmery. God had decorated for my girl.

I just hoped He had all His tear bottles ready. We were bound to overflow every one of them.

My bed had never felt so hard before. The pillow under my head so flat. And just knowing that below me, downstairs, my daughter lay alone on a flat, hard table… The room would be cold and dark. I just knew it.

Clive's eyes had shut as soon as he put head to bed. Being upset had never stole sleep from him. For once, I didn't hold that against him. Instead, I thanked God.

I got up, shaky from too much coffee and too little to eat for days on end. Aunt Gertie's old mirror in the corner of my room showed the reflection of a woman too old to stand all the way straight. With hair so white and mussed up, it was a shame. A face covered over by wrinkles and dried-up tears. Red-rimmed eyes and heavy bags beneath.

I took a throw blanket and covered over that darn mirror.

Out in my dinette, I touched the cover of my Bible before I opened it. Back to the Israelites and the bitter water. Their dry cracked lips. Sweltering sun pelting them. Water turned sweet.

Then the Lord God telling them to listen to Him. To do what is right. He called Himself their Healer.

"Be my Healer," I prayed. "I don't know what that means, really. But be that for me. For us."

I put my hands on the smooth pages of the Bible and closed my eyes. Sitting so still, I wanted to hear His voice like before.

"I will take your tears and put them in a jar. I collect all those bitter tears," the voice said. "And I will make those bitter tears into sweet tears of joy."

It didn't much matter to me when or how. Just the promise would be enough.

I thought of all the sweet tears my Gretchen must have been shedding when she sat in that chamomile field in heaven, smelling the lilacs.

Chapter Fifty-Five

EVELYN

Cal sat on the floor of the prep room, his back against the cabinet. The cover-all gown still on and paper shoe covers, too, he had his knees pulled up to his chest. His head rested in his shaking hands. I bumped the door with the toe of my shoe so he'd know I'd come in.

"You did that on purpose." He squinted at me.

"Are you okay?" I asked, closing the door behind me.

"No." He kicked off the shoe covers. "But I'm done."

"Are you mad?"

"A little. Yeah." Standing, he shed the paper-thin coverall and tossed it into the trash. "I think I need a little time."

"That's okay, Cal."

"I didn't get her dressed yet." He closed his eyes. "I'll do it after I get a little nap or something."

"Don't worry. I'll take care of her."

He closed the door after stepping out, leaving me alone, our mom under a sheet. The chamomile that Charlotte had picked was in a vase on the counter. Cal had even put them in water.

I got my mom into her green dress. As loose as it was, it still looked great on her. I hadn't done her makeup yet. I'd need to get her into the casket first. Granddad had picked a cherry wood one for her. He'd ordered it months ago, holding it just for her.

I picked her up, her head in the crook of one arm and the backs of her knees in my other. So light, it took little effort to lift her. Lowering her in the casket, still cradling her head, I smoothed the skirt over her thighs.

She didn't smell like herself. The cinnamon and vanilla from winter baking. Or soil and warm sun in the summer. I let her head rest on the small, silky pillow. Crossed her arms and slipped the diamond ring on her finger.

Holding on to the edge of the casket, I felt light-headed. Dizzy. Knuckles turning white, I knew if I let go, I'd collapse. Sucking in air, the grief felt like insanity. I feared I'd never feel steady again. That smell, that sterile, too-clean smell of the prep room made my stomach turn.

Without real words, I opened my heart, letting it cry out. I squatted down, hands still holding on to the cherry wood of the casket.

Big, thick hands pulled me up and into a firm hug. I breathed in the rich aftershave smell of Granddad.

"Evelyn," he said. "I'm here. This hurts so bad. I know it. But I'm here."

His embrace didn't take the pain away. But his arms felt like God's arms, holding me together.

Chapter Fifty-Six

OLGA

I'd filled both my pockets with tissues, hoping they'd be enough to get me through the funeral. Clive held my hand as we led our family to the front of the chapel. He helped me get down into one of the chairs in the front row.

The chairs in the chapel had gotten all full up. I thanked the good Lord for Old Buster, standing in the back, setting up more and more seats as neighbors and friends flooded through the doors.

Will stood behind the podium, his fingers bent around it. Head bent, it seemed he was praying. After a moment, he cleared his throat and lifted his face.

"I know Gretchen's family is grateful that you all came here today. Your love is spoken with the clear voice of your presence in this room. But, I'm sure we can all agree, Gretchen was easy to love." Will beamed. "She was a giving person. In the time I knew her, she didn't hold back anything from anyone."

Lifting his hand, he pointed to our row. "This family needs you to be giving, now. To them. Some of you have been on the receiving end of their compassion. If you've had a friend or relative buried under the care of this family, then you have been loved. And now, they need your comfort. It's their turn to be helped out. We need to be free with our love and time and gifts."

He shared more words and a few passages of Scripture. He did a fine job. Gretchen would have been pleased. Thinking of her delight in what he said made me miss her. It made me long for her.

"Come, Lord Jesus," I wanted to holler.

"Gretchen wanted you all to have the chance to say a few words about her," Will said, holding up a microphone. "So if you'd like, come on up."

Jay Bunker just about ran up the aisle and took the microphone after shaking Will's hand. Letting his eyes rest on our row, he opened his quivering lips.

"Some of you remember when the girls had their accident in front of our property. Well, my wife had a tough time after it." He wiped a hanky over his mouth. "She got a touch of depression. The pills the doctors give her didn't make it all the way better."

He shifted on his feet and swapped the microphone to his other hand.

"Gretchen'd stop over every now and again. Before she couldn't get out no more. She'd sit across the kitchen table from my wife and let her talk. She'd bring over a thermos full of tea that helped my wife sleep easier." He opened his mouth a couple times, trying to get the words out. "I never been a man of prayer. Not much, really. But I prayed that the Lord would find some comfort for my wife. And that's what Gretchen done. She done that very thing for my wife. I want to thank you all for sharing her with us."

His lips shook, pulled down in a frown. "And if you folks find that you need anything, we'll help you out."

Deirdre took the microphone from Jay.

"After my bakery got gutted by that fire about twenty years ago, Gretchen'd bring over a bag of groceries every week. And a check once a month to help me pay the rent." She laughed, tears wetting her cheeks. "She made me realize that I wasn't alone."

Voice after voice traveled from microphone to the speakers and into our hearts.

"After my brother died when we were kids, she'd come baby-sit me so my parents could go to their counseling sessions."

"When I had open heart surgery, she'd come over to the house and read to me."

"She taught me how to garden."

A line had formed all the way down the center aisle. Beautiful people with loving words about the way my daughter had touched their lives.

"I'm going to miss our talks over cups of tea."

"Every single birthday, she's send me a card. Birthdays just won't be the same now."

"After the twins were born, Gretchen came over every once in a while to clean my house."

On and on. Too much, really. I almost burst from the mercy their words poured over us. Not sprinkles or dribbles. But gushes of spilled-out comfort.

I thanked my loving Father for the drenching.

Chapter Fifty-Seven

EVELYN

Mom had been gone for a full month. And that winter had been heavy. Drab, gray sky hovered over top of us. It seemed that we wouldn't see the sun again. The raw place in my heart just knew it to be true.

Walking into my mom's house, I realized I needed to find another name for it. Calling it Don's house seemed wrong, though.

Charlotte had called, asking me to come over. Something, she said, was wrong with Don.

She met me at the door, pulling me into the kitchen. "He hasn't left his room in a week," she said.

"Char," I said. "He's mourning."

"I'm worried about him, Ev." She crossed her arms. "But he won't listen to me."

"He's not going to listen to me," I said.

"Just try, okay?"

I rolled my eyes.

"Don't look at me like that, Ev."

I took the steps as slowly as I could. I half expected to hear my mom's voice, humming from the kitchen. That month, my brain tricked me a few times, letting me forget what was missing for a split second before thrashing me with the memory. Losing her all over again.

The bedroom door stood ajar. I knocked, pushing it open. Don sat on the bed, looking at his fingers. Laundry baskets had been set out, empty, all around his feet.

"Hey," I said. "You mind if I come in for a second?"

Startled, he jumped a little before lifting his head. "Hi," he said.

"What's going on?"

"I'm having a rough day." He twisted something between his finger and thumb. "I thought I was okay when I got up. I was going to sort through some of her clothes."

"You know there's no hurry."

"Yeah." His eyes focused on the basket closest to him. "But I thought I was okay."

"What happened?" I sat on the floor, facing him.

"I found a little hair on her yellow sweater." He held it up so I could see it. "It's hers."

He went back to twisting the tiny red hair.

"Do you remember the last time she wore that sweater?" he asked. "Because I can't. I don't remember her wearing any of the clothes in that closet."

"That happens sometimes," I said. "Grief can block our memories."

"Nope. That's not the problem." He scowled. "The problem is me. It's me."

"I don't know what you're talking about."

"I don't remember because I didn't pay attention." He huffed.

"She never expected you to remember what she wore."

"But I could have been a better husband. More attentive." He calmed his voice. "I should have tried harder with you kids, too."

"It's not too late, Don."

"She's gone, though. And I'm afraid I'm just out of place. I don't want to lose this family, too." He slapped his forehead with an open hand. "I don't want to lose you kids."

"She loved you, Don," I said.

"I know. More than I ever deserved."

"You're part of this family." I pushed myself up on my knees and wrapped my arms around his neck. "We love you."

Chapter Fifty-Eight

OLGA

I wrapped up that old mirror, the one from my aunt Gertie, and had the folks at the Salvation Army tote it away. That and a few other things the kids didn't want. The rest, I either divvied up between the grandkids or had the movers load up on their truck.

Bare walls glared down on me. When I spoke, my voice echoed around the emptiness. Fifty-three years of filling up that apartment and all it took was two afternoons to clear it all out. Seemed strange to me. But spring had come. And it was as good a time as any for a change.

Clive and I had gotten a room at the retirement home. Right down the hall from Rosetta. With a dishwasher and everything. A galley kitchen would have to make due for my cooking. All my baking would be right alongside Charlotte, though, in Gretchen's kitchen. She'd got her hands on my cookbook. Just the way I'd hoped.

The change sure made me nervous. But I figured, between Clive and me, we'd be able to scrounge up some good times.

Besides, we had tickets for an airplane ride that left in just a month. The Hawaiian flowers and white beaches called our names.

I'd sent Clive out to our old Buick to wait on me. One more walkthrough. That was all I wanted. Once Evelyn moved in, she'd want to paint and probably get some new carpet. It wouldn't look like my home anymore. It would turn into Will and Evelyn's. That was all right by me.

First, my old bedroom, where I'd spent quiet, personal moments with my love. I touched the place on the wall where I'd leaned, about to faint, before telling Clive that we were having a baby. How he'd laughed himself silly that day. Just crying and laughing with the biggest grin I'd ever seen. He couldn't seem to keep his hands off my tummy. All nine months, he'd rub it and sing to it. Kiss it. All because he wanted the baby to know him. And did she ever. He got her first giggle.

The living room where we'd put out our old, aluminum Christmas tree, boxes overflowing underneath. Gretchen's thrill every year when she'd get up and see the wrapping paper and ribbons. Pure delight.

My kitchen, where she'd learned to cook. How many pancakes had burned up on that stovetop, I'd never be able to recall. But every one was worth the screeching smoke detector.

I stepped into her bedroom last, leaning against the wall, letting the tears come. Her crib had been in the far corner. I'd gazed in at her after she'd first been born. In awe that she was mine. So thankful. Just blessed.

I remembered our talks in that room. About heartbreaks and happy days. The arguments with me, standing on the other side of the closed door. Hugs of forgiveness needed from each of us, shared just over the threshold. The first night her room stood empty after she'd gone off to college. Oh, the Lord had held me together in that lonesome darkness. The joy-filled day when we'd set that crib up again to hold the napping grandbabies she'd given me.

Bitter water had come and gone. Over and again. But I'd never had a day, not since God gave me Gretchen, when I lacked a good draught of mercy.

I realized that, all along, I'd had the sweet water.

Chapter Fifty-Nine

EVELYN

I married Will on the second Saturday of July in the middle of a heat wave. Neither of us seemed to even notice until Cal passed out during the vows. Thank goodness Grace was there to help him back up.

We'd started our life together as preacher and funeral director. The strangest marriage ever to hit Middle Main, Michigan. Deirdre had said it, so it must have been true.

We made our home, Will and I, in the apartment above the funeral home. Only temporarily, of course. At least, that was what we had in the plans.

Cal and I had a lot ahead of us, running the Big House without Granddad. But he never minded us calling with questions. I think he missed the work. But not the black suits. Gran had made him give them all away. Otherwise, he might have shown up to help with the services. She knew he never would have come out of uniform.

After working a shift at the bakery, Charlotte spent her time up to her elbows in the garden, worrying over the flowers. When she wore our mom's old stray hat, it made me smile. My mom would have been pleased to see my sister out there, pulling on weeds and talking to the tea roses.

One evening, I caught a glimpse of her. The sun inched down the sky, covering Charlotte in golden warmth.

"I miss my mom," I said, my fingers on the window sill. "Char looks just like her sometimes."

"Why don't you go down there," Will said from the desk where he worked, writing a sermon. "She'd probably like the company."

"I don't know." I scratched my neck. "I kind of think she prefers the quiet."

"Then just take her a can of pop. It's really hot out there."

I grabbed a couple of cans and took off down the back stairs, my bare feet slapping against the wood steps. When I opened the door, the heat pulled all the cool air conditioning out of me.

"Hey," Char called to me. "I was just about to come up for a glass of water."

"I hope you don't mind pop instead."

When she smiled, I saw our mom in her face. "Sounds good."

Under Charlotte's care, the garden thrived. The purples and pinks and reds brightened up the brittle grass around it. We might have lacked rain that month, but my sister had been able to keep the garden alive.

"You're doing a great job, Char." I handed her a can and popped the top of mine.

"I was worried about the chamomile." She took a long drink. "It got a little brown for a while. But it's coming up pretty nicely now."

Sitting down next to her, I touched one of the white and yellow flowers.

"It's a good thing she had all those starter plants in the basement," she continued. "As soon as I got them in the soil, I knew they'd be okay."

"She was thinking ahead, wasn't she?" A breeze zipped through the garden, making the little chamomile dance, bumping up against one another.

I closed my eyes, feeling the wind against my skin. It carried a warm smell of garden and soil, grass and a bit of sweet apple. I touched the yellow heads again, the white petal crowns.

Comforted by the mercy of my mother's chamomile.

Acknowledgments

This novel was conceived while I sat, holding the hand of a dying woman. I thought, *Don't forget this. Remember all of it.* It grew as I met the funeral directors who did far more to comfort us, the family, than I could have expected. The story was born through more emotional pain than I imagined. Pain that ended up healing me in the end.

Along the way, I've had the honor of learning from two men who minister, not only to the deceased, but also to those who mourn. Thanks to John Gores of Beeler-Gores Funeral Home. Not only did John give me the grand tour of the building, he also shared stories from decades of funeral work. And abundant gratitude to Caleb Wilde of the Wilde Funeral Home. Caleb is from a long line of funeral directors. I am grateful for his sensitivity, intellect, and honesty. Caleb understands the language of grief and is generous with his comfort. He pours out that mercy regularly on his blog, *Confessions of a Funeral Director.*

Thank you again to the WhiteFire Publishing team. David and Roseanna White for your love of books that move the soul. To Dina Sleiman for editing in such a way that I come out on the other side a different and better writer. To Wendy Chorot for your eagle eye.

To the many writers that I am blessed to call my friends. The Kava Writers Collective for cheering me on and supporting me over big bottles of Coke and gooey fruit cups. To my friends at the Breathe Christian Writers Conference and The Guild for teaching me that writing is a high and holy calling. The ladies of Novel Matters for being my loving aunties. Ann Byle, for championing me and talking me up. Ann, I'm so blessed to have you as my agent and friend.

During the writing process, I encountered difficulties that caused me to nearly give up this novel. The death of a friend, discouragement, major life changes. I called on a few friends to pray for me. Their prayers and words of mercy carried me through. Thanks to Betsy Carter, Kathi Hanson, Megan Sayer, Amelia Rhodes, Michelle Reinhold, Patti Hill, Nancy Finkbeiner, Jennifer Hullah, Jessie Heninger, Jessica Wilson, Jen (Bear) Gusey, and my mom.

Much love and many hugs to each of you.

Thanks to the best neighbor in all the world, Heather Bunker. For the steaming cups of Starbucks and meals you made for my family. To Ellen Reinhold and Betsy Carter for hours spent entertaining my kids as I got away to write.

To Jeff Manion and Ada Bible Church for feeding my soul and spurring me on. I pray that the mercy spills over to those who read what I write.

The great people of Baker Book House have done more than I could have imagined to encourage me. I can't put into words how much I appreciate your support.

Thank you to all my cheerleaders. Too many to name here. But, trust me, each of your names is kept in my heart. Your love has kept me going.

Jeff, my own Clive, I love you. More than sunshine.

All glory and honor and praise to the Great Author. Without Him, none of these words would have been written. It's all to magnify Him.

CPSIA information can be obtained
at www.ICGtesting.com
Printed in the USA
LVOW10s0543240817
546205LV00001B/73/P